The Ballerina's Guide to Boxing

Abby Rosmarin

Other Books by Abby Rosmarin:

The Secret to a Happy Marriage
Venom
In the Event the Flower Girl Explodes
No One Reads Poetry: A Collection of Poems
Chick Lit & Other Formulas for Life
I'm Just Here for the Free Scrutiny

The Ballerina's Guide to Boxing

Abby Rosmarin

For all the coaches in my life who taught me how to be powerful, and for all the people I have been blessed to call (and choose as) my family.

AUTHOR'S NOTE:

The Ballerina's Guide to Boxing touches upon a few heavy subjects, including eating disorders, drunk driving, and suicide. If you or someone you know is at risk, I have provided numbers for different hotlines at the end of this book. Remember that it is always okay to ask for help.

CHAPTER ONE

She sat in the passenger seat of her mother's SUV, her back rigid, her eyes out the window. She silently made note of every lamppost, every sign, every street light.

The AC was running, its subtle fans whirring somewhere in the background. The day was warm and the sun was bright. Aside from a handful of fluffy white clouds in the distance, the skies were clear.

It didn't feel right. None of it did. There should be clouds. There should be rain. It should be cold. It should feel just like the day of Josh's funeral back in March. Cold. Dreary. Unwelcoming.

Her mother said nothing as they drove back. Her mother had just picked her up from the church – which is where her mother had dropped her off a few hours before. Her mother didn't stay for the service – unlike Josh's funeral, where the whole family went. (They *were* his neighbors, after all.)

It made sense. Mrs. McCormick didn't know Evelyn. It didn't occur to her to stay for any other reason than personally knowing the one who had died.

Mrs. McCormick's daughter continued to watch the world through the passenger side window. One lamppost, one street sign, one traffic light. Sets and sets of electrical posts. Blue skies. Bright sun. Cheery, sunny day.

"I'm quitting," Lily said, her back still rigid, her eyes still on the street.

"You're not quitting," Mrs. McCormick responded flatly, her eyes on the street as well.

"No, I'm quitting," Lily said again with a little more force.

"This is a reaction," Mrs. McCormick replied. "You're sad about your friend. But life goes on, and you're not quitting."

"I said I'm quitting," Lily said, her voice distant, as if someone else were speaking.

"You're not throwing away your dream," said Mrs. McCormick. "You can take a week off if you need, but right back to classes, right after that. You're not throwing away your life's work."

"I'm quitting," was all Lily could really say. One street sign. Another. And another.

"This is not the time to discuss this, anyway," Mrs. McCormick sighed, hanging a left into the neighborhood. "Not after a funeral. Sleep on it, and we'll discuss it with your father tomorrow."

"I said I'm quitting. Tomorrow won't change it," Lily said, blinking slowly, passing by houses she recognized. The Peterson's. The Woodard's. The Swami's.

"If the greats had quit every time they had felt like it, they would've never become the greats," Mrs. McCormick said. "Ballet is your life, and you're not quitting."

"You can't tell me what I can and cannot do," said Lily.

Mrs. McCormick turned onto their street.

"I can and I will, because I am your mother, and you live under my roof."

Lily said nothing. She just followed the edge of the road until they pulled into their driveway. Mrs. McCormick pressed the button on her visor and the garage door slowly opened. The bright, sunny world soon disappeared, replaced by the dark, cement cave of the garage. With another push of a button, the garage door closed.

"This is your dream, and you're not quitting," Mrs. McCormick said with a touch of finality, unbuckling her seatbelt as she did.

"It's not..."

Lily unbuckled her seat and opened her car door.

"...And I am quitting."

CHAPTER TWO

Two weeks before the funeral, Evelyn was alive.

That seems a bit redundant to say, but that's what Lily focused on. Two weeks beforehand, Evelyn was alive. She was alive and she was smiling and she was effortlessly starting conversations with everyone around her.

Two weeks ago, she was her usual, outgoing, confident self. Two weeks ago, she was alive and she was pinning her hair up into a bun and she was talking to Lily before class. Ballet class, at least. They didn't speak much to each other in school. Evelyn was a senior and Lily was a sophomore, and Evelyn was popular and Lily was an outcast. In the studio, they were equals and teammates and fellow ballerinas. Outside of the studio, Evelyn had her own group of friends. But she was still civil and sweet and her clique never bothered Lily, something that couldn't be said for so many other girls at the school.

Evelyn could've been a mean girl to her, and she never was. Evelyn was kind and energetic and danced like she was already part of the New York Ballet.

Two weeks before the funeral, Evelyn was practicing alongside Lily. Two weeks before the funeral, Evelyn was a high school graduate and talking about college and plans for the future. She was going to go to NYU and she was going to major in psychology. She didn't just want to be a professional dancer. She wanted to use dance as a means of therapy, of empowerment.

Two weeks before the funeral, Evelyn was alive. And now she

3

was not.

You know how sometimes, when people go into shock, they can only focus on one thought – and then repeat it, to the point of absurdity? Like a man after a major automobile accident, waiting for the paramedics to arrive, thinking nonstop about how he hadn't checked the mail yet, that the mail must be piling up? For Lily, it was about the days between when Evelyn was alive and when Evelyn wasn't.

One week and five days before the funeral, a crash had made the news. Three minors – three names not released – hit another car. The driver of the first car was drunk. Everyone in the first car was drunk. The driver would make it out alive. The passenger in the back would make it out alive. The second driver (sober) would make it out alive. The rider in the passenger side seat of the first car was pronounced DOA.

"Such a shame," said her mother. "Young life wasted, and completely preventable." She *tsked tsked* a few times, shook her head a few times, and went back to her life before the newscasters had even thrown to a commercial.

One week and four days ago, her ballet teacher made the announcement. In lieu of practice, the girls sat around and cried. Lily took a moment. It was Wednesday. It was barely two weeks into summer. If it were during the school year, she would've learned from some type of announcement at the high school. Probably from the principal. Grief counselors would've been available. People would've congregated around lockers and talk and cry and hug each other. Everyone would've walked down the halls a little slower, a little less sure, and a little more aware of their surroundings.

It was Wednesday. Lily saw Evelyn on Saturday. Evelyn was alive on Saturday. She was alive on Sunday. She was alive Monday, and Tuesday. She was alive Wednesday morning. And Wednesday afternoon. She was dead on arrival by Wednesday night.

And now it was the evening after the funeral service. Evelyn had been not-alive for two weeks. And soon enough it would be three weeks. Then four. Then September would roll around and Lily would return back to school and Evelyn would not. Evelyn would not go to NYU and would not major in psychology and would not use dance as a means to empower young girls.

And tomorrow morning, Lily would not get up with her alarm and prepare for ballet class.

Because today Lily quit.

CHAPTER THREE

Lily woke up an hour before her alarm would've gone off, had she set it. She laid in bed, curled to one side, her eyes on the wall. The sun was up and had been up for a while. She felt so heavy and so exhausted that she was convinced she'd fall into a deep sleep if she would just close her eyes.

Instead, her heavy head sunk into her pillow and she traced the lines of her room. She stared at the shadows on the walls, made by a few nondescript, impersonal paintings, the same generic framed decorations found in hotel rooms.

She couldn't remember whether or not she had actually slept. She remembered the heaviness – heavy head, heavy body, heavy eyes – and she remembered the moments when her thoughts went nonsensical, the way they always did right before she fell asleep. But whether or not she actually slept – or slept for any period of time – was lost on her.

It certainly felt like she hadn't slept.

She rolled onto her back and stared up at the popcorned ceiling; each dot creating its own shadow, each divot housing the shadows. The room felt stuffy and alien to her, as if she had woken up in a kidnapper's home. Every once in a while, she'd remember to take in a breath. A deep one, like the counselor at school (the regular kind; not a grief counselor) had advised. Good for anxiety, he had said. Deep breath through the nose. Deep breath out the mouth. Slow and steady.

Inhale. Exhale.

Downstairs, there was just enough noise to let Lily know that the rest of the house was up. The occasional clink of ceramic. The click of a cabinet door. The voice of her little sister followed by a series of hushed and rushed words from – she guessed – her mother. It was a Monday. Yesterday was Sunday. The weather was just as sunny and tender and welcoming as the day before.

Inhale. Exhale.

It took a few tries, but eventually Lily sat up and swung her legs around to the edge. She let her head hang for a moment, her hands on the sides of her bed. Would they fault her if she stayed in her room until everyone left? Lily gave a bitter smirk at the answer to that question and pushed herself off the bed.

The kitchen downstairs was subdued. Her 10-year-old sister was sitting at the table with her cereal. Her father was standing, facing the kitchen counter, sipping at his coffee with one hand as he attempted to type something on his laptop with the other. Her mother was nowhere to be found.

"Well, good morning there, pumpkin," her father said, putting down his coffee. "How'd you sleep?"

Lily shrugged her shoulders.

"All right," she said.

"You're shuffling in like a zombie, so I take it 'all right' means 'terribly'," her father responded.

Lily shrugged her shoulders again.

"Well, maybe a little coffee will put some pep into your step," her father offered. "We wouldn't want you zombified for class. Zombies would make terrible dancers."

Lily reached for a mug, poured herself a cup, and immediately sat down.

"Someone's chatty this morning, I see," said her father. After a pause, he added tenderly: "Funeral still getting you down?"

Lily shrugged.

"Oh kiddo, I know it's not easy. But you're young. You'll bounce back."

"Aren't you going to be late for ballet?" said her sister Audrey, in that non-sequitur kind of way that only kids can get away with.

"Well, if you ask Lily, there's no more ballet to be late for," said her mother, appearing out of nowhere.

"Lily is quitting ballet?!" Audrey said, a Cheshire Cat smile bursting onto her face.

"*Apparently* Lily is quitting ballet," her mother parroted.

"When did this happen?" her father asked.

"After the service." her mother said. "Just decided right then and there to quit."

Lily shrunk in her seat, her stomach doing flips. Even the coffee looked unappealing.

"Now… we can't be making rash decisions like that," said her father. "I know she was your friend and all, but… that's not a good reason to quit something you love."

Lily shrunk back further.

"This means you need to get a job. Something," her mother continued. "I'm not having you spend all summer just hanging around the house." Her mother fished through her purse as she walked across the kitchen. "You'll have to make yourself productive."

"Oooh, Lily is in trouble," Audrey sing-songed into her cereal. The knot in Lily's stomach tightened more.

"Well, I'm sure you'll find something," her father offered in his usual, noncommittal way. "Maybe a little volunteer work would do you good. Great way for kids to get a sense of community."

"You're going to have to do something," her mother tersely added. "This is not going to be a pass to be lazy."

"I think I'm going to go on a walk," was all Lily could say, her eyes zeroed in on the rim of her coffee cup. Her mother just sighed loudly in response.

"Lily is in SO much trouble," said Audrey under her breath, staring down conspiratorially at her cereal, as if she were delivering a secret to her spoon.

Lily went upstairs just long enough to change her clothes. She snuck back downstairs and out the door, closing it lightly behind her. She took a few jogging strides off the property before she started walking more casually.

The morning was still fresh and unburdened. The air was mild, but gave hint to the massive heat that would be coming in the afternoon. The sky was hazy and pink and cast a dreamlike aura over the rest of the world. And it was through that surreal haze that Lily walked down the street and away from her house. She could feel her head bob with each step, but she couldn't feel her feet touch the ground.

She was surrounded by suburbia in the midst of a work week. It was unnerving, in a way, to watch people come out of their houses with their travel mugs in hand, enter their cars, and drive off. Unnerving to know that so many people would be leaving during this dawn, devoting their entire day to somewhere else, and not returning until it was almost time for dinner.

And what about the rest of the town? There was something very lonely about it. Like being left behind.

Lily couldn't remember the last time she wasn't part of that mass departure. How many days she spent just like the adults around her, getting ready to leave just after the sun came up, going to school, going to class, being away from home until long after the sun went down.

And now she didn't. Now she was here, walking the neighborhood, watching everyone else's lives.

Part of her wanted to turn back once she hit one of the main roads, but instead she kept going. She didn't want to risk returning home while her parents were still there – while Audrey was still there – and there was something compelling her to go forward.

It was fascinating, watching the town start to wake up. It was like, with each new driver on the road, the town itself was stretching its arms out, rubbing its eyes, yawning away any remaining drowsiness. The air was getting hotter, like the heat needed to wake up as well.

The residential area quickly gave way to a smattering of businesses. Convenience stores and flower shops and the occasional restaurant. Pet stores and martial art dojos and dance studios. The dance studio that she went to as a kid was still a little way's down, right on the town's main street, but she deliberately veered right and snaked back through the neighborhoods instead.

She had no idea how much time had passed – just that, by the time she looped back towards her own neighborhood again, the town and the sun and the heat were fully up and awake. Her skin was flushed and her legs were fatigued in a way that she wasn't used to.

Looping around the way that she did meant she'd have return to her house from the opposite side of the neighborhood. And that meant walking past Josh's house.

There was really no way to avoid it. The house was three doors down from hers. She could always backtrack and loop back the other way and completely circumvent that tiny section, but she forced herself forward.

The house was heartbreakingly simple. A white Cape-style house with a chimney to the side and windows jutting from the roof. It honestly looked like something from a postcard. The house even had an old-fashioned fence in the front yard — two parallel logs connecting at intermittent posts, everything painted white. Every few years, Josh's parents would repaint the fence, and their grass would have white freckles until they next mowed the lawn.

Now the lawn had a realtor's sign staked by the front walkway. It had been up for a little while, but it appeared there was a new addition to the sign that Lily hadn't yet seen: a little wooden rectangle hanging from metal hooks underneath the main sign: Under Contract.

Lily didn't realize that she had stopped walking and started to stare and stare and stare some more at Josh's former house. Josh's parents' house. Soon-to-be Josh's parents' former house. She didn't realize that she was staring at the empty driveway, the pulled shades. She started focusing on the windows, as if she could guess what was going on — or what had gone on — in each room. As soon as she realized it, however, she kept walking, picking up her pace until she was practically speedwalking to her house. A pace she'd immediately put the brakes on as she approached the front door, her eyes scanning wildly, assuring herself that everyone was gone.

For a split second, she worried her mother might've locked the door and hidden the extra key. She could see her mom pulling a passive-aggressive move like that. Indirect punishment for leaving the house without permission, for being so deviant on so many levels. But the door opened without any effort, and Lily stepped inside.

The only thing to greet her was the air conditioning. Everyone was gone. Her parents on their way to work. One of them detouring to drop Audrey off at summer camp (probably her father). That was usually the drill: her father carted around Audrey, and her mother carted around Lily.

Audrey had significantly fewer things to be chauffeured to throughout the year. She played soccer on one of the middle school teams — one of those casual soccer leagues where the coach is a volunteer and everyone gets some type of ribbon or trophy at the end of the season. Fun and friendship. No pressure. They even had signs on the soccer fields, reminding parents that the kids were just there to have fun. Nothing was at stake.

Lily returned back to the kitchen. Her coffee mug was still on the table, the dark liquid in it room temperature by now. She picked it up from across the table and returned it to the kitchen, tempted first to dump it down the sink before she made a beeline to the refrigerator.

Instead of throwing out the coffee, Lily opened the fridge door and pulled out the cream. She set the coffee and cream on the counter and pulled the sugar bowl from its place behind the coffee maker. She scooped two, three, four spoonfuls of sugar into the mug and filled the mug to its brim with cream. Lily sipped at the edges before grabbing a spoon and carefully stirring everything in.

Lily was used to black coffee – it was the only coffee she was allowed to drink, if she *had* to be *so* persistent on drinking coffee in the morning – and what she had in her hands was so sweet that it overwhelmed her. It was almost unappetizing, but Lily kept sipping from it until her taste buds got used to it and she finished the entire mug. Without even pausing to think, Lily grabbed a bowl and one of Audrey's boxes of cereal and poured herself a heaping serving – so heaping that it spilled over when Lily tried to add in milk.

Alternating between picking the dry pieces from the table and scooping up the pieces in the bowl with her spoon, Lily gorged herself on the unnervingly sweet cereal until both the bowl and the counter were cleared.

When she was finished, she took a moment to lean against the counter, her hands on her stomach, a weirdly satisfied look on her face. Leaving the bowl and the mug where they were, she left the kitchen, walked up the stairs, returned to her room, and climbed onto her bed. She snaked herself under the covers once again, cuddled her pillow in, and fell into a deep sleep.

CHAPTER FOUR

Unlike with Evelyn, Lily didn't focus on the amount of time between when Josh was alive and when he wasn't. That wasn't how she reacted to his death earlier that year. She instead focused on the last time she saw him – three days before his death. Three days before police lights and ambulance lights and fire truck lights would fill the streets at 4:30 in the morning, when the whole neighborhood was up and shuffling closer and closer to Josh's house – a subtle dance, as if seeing just how close they could get before police officers would shoo them away.

And they would. Eventually one officer would ask residents to return to their homes, in that kind-but-stern way that makes you obey out of a deep but fearful respect.

Lily saw him three days before that. Three days. And before that, Lily hadn't seen much of Josh. He was a senior in college and Lily was a sophomore in high school. But she saw him three days before he died, on a Saturday morning, when Lily was out taking a short walk around the neighborhood after practice.

The interaction itself was innocent and fleeting. They talked exactly how neighbors talk, the way two kids do, who grew up in the same neighborhood but in completely different age brackets and were now old enough to be considered almost-adults. He talked a little bit about college and he asked how ballet was going – a brief conversation that should've eventually slipped from memory like so many pleasantries. But Lily would go back to it time, and time, and time again. Scouring it for clues. Closing her eyes and trying to recreate the scene, trying to see if there was something off about his body language. If his smile seemed fake. If his eyes seemed sad. Did he talk about future plans? Did he sound upbeat?

The rational side of her brain tried to reason with her – that there was no way she could've known, that depression takes on so many variations. But it was repeatedly drowned out by the rest of her that was convinced that she could've done something. That she could've picked up on a somber tone or drooping shoulders. That she could've stepped in and gave him a hug and maybe that extra hug would've stopped everything. She'd imagine herself waking up in the middle of the night, three nights later, and running to his house and being the one to save the day. She imagined herself being able to see into the future and therefore skipping school that day to spend time with him so it never could have happened.

Originally, her parents wouldn't tell her what had happened. They knew, but all they would say was that he had passed away. Her mother made up a story at first, saying that he died in his sleep, but she delivered it while shaking her head and waving her fingers around – her mother's telltale sign that she was lying. Lily would eventually learn at the wake, as she shook hands with his parents and stood awkwardly around and averted her eyes from the casket, wanting nothing more than to go home and away from the noxious funeral home smell. She'd find out by eavesdropping, as two people – possibly Josh's age, possibly classmates? – talked about suicide. Talking about how they didn't understand it, how happy Josh seemed, how much he had going for him.

"Did you notice that they covered up his neck?" she would later hear a neighbor say at that wake, whispering it to another neighbor, as if his death was the gossip of the town.

"Do you think they'll stay in that house? Do you think they'll move?" she heard someone else – someone she couldn't recognize – say, in hushed whispers. "I know *I* couldn't. Find your only child like that? I wouldn't spend another minute there."

By the time her family piled back into her mother's car, Lily's mind was racing. She had seen him three days before he died. Three days before the flashing lights and the stern police officer and the return back into her house. Three days before she'd be one of the neighbors out on the streets, her coat over her flimsy pajamas, bare feet shoved into boots, shuffling closer and closer to the scene, bubbling with rising bewilderment, each step causing her eyes to widen and her heart to quicken.

Three days before that, she had walked down that street in proper clothes and saw him in the front yard collecting the mail from the mailbox and paused to talk to him. Three days before his death he was the grown-up version of the boy who would shovel her parents' driveway and rake leaves and mow lawns for $15 a chore. Three days before his death he was the quintessential neighborhood kid. And now he was gone and a mortician had to hide his neck.

The morning after his funeral, Lily had walked out of her house and crossed the street. She could see Josh's house from this angle. There were no cars at Josh's house. The shades had been drawn – had they always been drawn? Lily could've sworn they never were beforehand – and everything was silent. Too silent. Far, far, far too silent. Even for so early in the morning – just at the break of dawn, right before people would be getting into their cars for their daily commutes. Before Lily would get into her mother's car and go to school and then go to the ballet studio and then go home again.

The morning after the funeral, Lily wanted to walk by his house again. She wanted to walk right up to the fence made from painted logs and place both hands on a post and redo that day, from three days before he had died. She wanted to close her eyes and travel back in time and tell him that she knows, she knows, she knows, and she's not leaving his side and he's not going to do what he did and that is that. There was nothing more she wanted than to take that step forward towards his house and into the past.

Instead, Lily crossed the street back to her house, went back inside, and got ready for her day.

CHAPTER FIVE

Lily now had a new ritual.

For countless summers, Lily would get up with her alarm. She would come downstairs and have some type of breakfast (at some point it became a cup of black coffee and an apple, always) and then her mother would drop her off at the studio. She would be there all day, back to back classes, back to back practice. Sometimes she'd hitch a ride with another dancer's parent – Evelyn's mom was one of them – and come home. She'd lie to those parents and tell them that her mother would be home any minute, and go inside to a gloriously empty house. She'd bask in the incredible solitude, before her father would come home with Audrey in tow.

This was her summertime ritual. Get up, breakfast, practice, home. The details would shift and evolve, but it was consistent at its core. She couldn't remember a summer that didn't have it.

But now she had a new one.

Now she waited in bed – sometimes she'd read, but mostly she'd just lay still and stare at the walls – while listening to the rest of the family get ready. Her mother would deliberately make extra noise: close a cabinet door too harshly, speak a little too loud to her father, think aloud in ways that were clearly meant for Lily to "accidentally" hear. Sometimes Audrey would dart up the stairs and into Lily's room and crack open the door to see if Lily was still asleep. (And Lily would deliberately draw the covers up by her ears, her eyes closed, her breathing slow.)

Inhale. Exhale.

Eventually her family would leave for their day and Lily would get out of bed. She'd then come downstairs and pour herself a gigantic bowl of cereal and then go for a walk.

Weekends were tough. Weekends meant her family was home and she'd have to suffer through whatever it was they were going to do. Some community function. Some type of colleague get-together. A shuttling around orchestrated by her mother so they could appear to be a part of the community and her mother could pat herself on the back for "creating memories".

But the functions and events paled in comparison to the lulls in their weekend schedules, when everyone was home, when the silence was almost as painful as her mother's passive-aggressive jabs.

But the weekdays were hers. The weekdays had a ritual that she had created. On her weekdays, she could walk.

She had a set path she would walk each day – identical to the one that she did the morning after Evelyn's funeral, only this route included a sharp right to retrace her steps and avoid Josh's house.

The first week, she only walked once a day, but it soon became twice a day. Once in the morning, returning home as the sun started blazing and Lily started sweating through her clothes. She'd punctuate the end of her morning walk with a large meal – usually more of Audrey's cereal, a cup of coffee with cream and sugar, and handfuls of toast – and crawl back into bed. She'd then wake up and repeat the process, before retreating back to her room until her parents and Audrey returned.

"Have you found a job yet?" her mother asked towards the end of the second week, during one of their sporadic family dinners.

Lily shrugged and looked at her plate.

"You have until mid-July, you hear me?" her mother went on. "If you can't find a job by then, you're coming to the office with me and doing work there."

"I want to come to the office!" Audrey piped in.

Mrs. McCormick turned to Audrey and gave a soft grin.

"I know you do, and maybe we'll arrange a mother-daughter day," said her mother. "But this is about work. Lily needs to earn her keep now that she's throwing her life away."

Lily looked back at her food – a spinach and goat cheese salad that was making her stomach turn – and asked to be excused.

The evenings without any family dinners were definitely the easiest. Everyone was to fend for themselves for food. And since

Lily was no longer in dance, her mother no longer prepared a plate of food for her to eat as part of her diet (an absolute blessing; Lily didn't know how much longer she could eat steamed broccoli and cauliflower). She'd spend those evenings, free of any forced family dinner, by her window, opening it all the way and letting the summer air in. She'd sit and look for the stars and the moon and she'd breathe. Simply breathe.

Inhale. Exhale.

It was on a Monday, essentially week three of her routine, when she decided to add on some more. It had been four days since her mother's ultimatum, and barely 24 hours since she'd been dragged to a community fundraiser where people kept asking her about her ballet. With her parents and Audrey gone that Monday morning, Lily got ready for her walk, snaking through the neighborhood and eventually finding herself walking towards Main Street.

For two weeks, Lily would always hang a right a few blocks from the downtown area: a quaint strip of shops and buildings, followed by a few commercial lots, before it returned back to nondescript neighborhoods. Main Street was home to her childhood dance studio, and she couldn't really pinpoint why she was avoiding it. It simply made as much sense as stepping into the shade on a hot day, or stepping out of the way when a vehicle is approaching.

But today was a day that she had no interest in returning home, and so she continued walking.

Three blocks later, Lily found herself at Main Street. It had been a while since she'd been in this area of town. But it looked almost identical. The buildings hadn't changed. The iron streetlamps still lined the sidewalk. Even the traffic had the same cadence and melody. For a few breaths, Lily felt 6 again, and it made her smile a heavy smile.

Lily started walking down the street towards her childhood studio, unsure if it were still open in the first place. She had never visited, not once, not even to see her old instructors. It had been something left to gather dust as life went on.

Lily crossed one of the intersecting streets. It was 10 in the morning on a weekday, but the area was still busy. She tried to wrap her mind around all these different lives around her. The people walking the sidewalks and driving down the street and milling about in the shops. None of them were sequestered away in an office or school or studio or anything. At least for right now, this was their life. Free on the streets.

Her dance studio was exactly where she remembered it. It was one more relic that had survived the years. The sign outside of the door was still the same, albeit faded with sun exposure. The shades to the large bay windows were up, giving Lily a direct view of one of the classes in session. Inside was a group of girls, probably the same age Lily was when she went there, doing a few warm-ups at the bar.

The instructor was someone Lily didn't recognize. She was tall, with olive skin and a beaming smile. She was clapping her hands and bouncing her feet, as if she were more entertained by her students than she was teaching them. Lily stood by the side of the windows, surreptitiously watching the girls dance. Most of them were giggling and only somewhat following directions. A few moms sat on chairs by the adjacent wall – a few on their phones, one rustling through her bag.

Lily gave herself one more moment to watch, a tightening in her chest building up, as if someone had started to put weights there, one on top of the other. She took a step back onto the sidewalk and continued onward, her eyes scanning wildly for anything else on the road – anything that wasn't her studio.

Her eyes landed at a set of three young men in mesh shorts and t-shirts, gym bags slung over their shoulders. She watched them cross the street and enter what looked like the old fire station. Lily picked up her pace, partly to find out more about them, partly because she was desperate to get as far away from her studio as possible.

A sidewalk sign stationed just outside of the fire station read "O'Reilly Boxing Gym" in red and yellow lettering. Both of the arched doors had been raised, letting the sounds of the gym spill out onto the street. Her eyes scanned the place, looking for the guys who entered. She found instead a sprawling landscape of people and equipment.

To one side was a row of heavy bags. To the other, an open mat. In the back was a boxing ring, its ropes wrapped in red fabric, with yellow padding in the corners. Two people were paired up in the boxing ring, one person wearing padded gloves, the other person hitting the pads in rapid-fire succession. On the mats were a couple people doing stretches, talking casually amongst themselves as they touched their toes.

Lily's eyes landed on a girl at one of the heavy bags, dressed in black shorts and a black tank top, punching and kicking at the bag at a steady pace. The girl was zeroed-in and focused. Her arms were toned and strong and fast. Her face seemed almost relaxed, as if she were in the middle of meditation.

She continued at her bag, throwing in a few fancy spinning kicks here and there, backing up at times to kick the bag straight on. It was hypnotic, watching her work. Everything else faded out of Lily's view. She was transfixed on the girl – how old was she? Maybe 18? Nineteen? She couldn't have been that much older than Lily. Lily was entranced by her the same way Lily would become entranced by the lead ballerina in Swan Lake, right as the black swan is revealed.

Lily couldn't tell you how long she stood at the side of that firehouse garage door, leaning against the arched column as she stared. All she knew was that time itself stopped when the girl at the bags stopped as well, took a breath, and looked behind her, as if sensing the entire time that someone had been watching. Lily immediately turned around and walked back the way she came from.

Lily returned to her neighborhood, returned straight home. Once she was inside, she went upstairs, down the hall, and into the bathroom. She peeled off her clothes – it was at that exact moment that Lily realized that she was drenched in sweat – and started the shower. She stepped in before the water fully warmed up, and the cold was enough to jolt her out of whatever reverie she had found herself in. She plunged her head into the water, soaking her hair and feeling the water drip from her nose. She took a few deep breaths – the spray from the shower collecting in her mouth – and stood back.

She wiped the water from her face and turned her back to the showerhead. The now-steaming hot water pelted her neck. She stayed there for a little while longer, remembering all the times she did exactly this to soothe sore and stiff muscles. She closed her eyes, her body gently swaying to some unheard melody, the beat of the water tapping out code as it hit her shoulders.

*

For the rest of the day, the gym in the fire station was all Lily could think about.

She thought about the sounds of the boxing ring, the chatter of the individuals, the clank of the metal as the hooks holding the heavy bag moved.

And she thought about that girl and her dance with the bag. She replayed the memory again and again, her mind churning something she couldn't quite verbalize. The gym stayed on her mind as the day wore on, as Audrey and her father eventually arrived home, as her mother eventually arrived home. It was on her mind as she heard her mother banging away in the kitchen – apparently her mother had decided that night was going to be a family dinner night – and it was on her mind as she sat down to dinner.

It was on her mind as her mother asked her something – so much on her mind that she didn't even realize her mother was talking until she said Lily's name in that sharp, crisp way mothers do to get their child's attention.

"What?" Lily asked.

"I said, did you apply to any jobs today?"

"Oh, uh…" Lily looked back down at her plate. "Not yet."

"Tomorrow, I need you to go and start applying," said her mother. "Enough is enough. Everyone else is doing something. Your father and I work, very hard. Your sister is in camp. You can't be home all day."

Lily shrugged her shoulders again, her eyes still on her plate. She could hear her mother huff and cut into her food, the knife scrapping against the ceramic plate.

"Teenagers," she muttered under her breath.

"I'm sure the grocery store is looking for some seasonal work," her father piped in, his voice decidedly more sing-songy. "I'm always seeing high schoolers working there. A summer job is a great way to teach discipline."

There was something about her father's comment that made Lily want to laugh. But instead, she smirked, her eyes still on the table.

"Yeah, you could bag everyone's groceries," Audrey added. Lily didn't even need to look up to know her sister was smiling maniacally.

"Tell me you'll look into it," her mother prodded.

Lily sighed.

"I'll look into it," Lily parroted back.

"Good. At least that's something," said her mother. "You'll be surprised to find out that the world outside of dance is very different. It's not going to be what you expect."

Lily smirked again, a nasty, venomous thought circulating in the back of her head. A thought that seemed to transcend words.

"Can I be excused?" she said instead.

CHAPTER SIX

Lily wasn't sure exactly what she was doing that morning, or why she was doing it. But she went through her wardrobe, fished out some cotton shorts, a sports bra, and a t-shirt, and laced up her shoes.

The heat was on its steady rise as Lily got closer to Main Street. She became acutely aware of the sun, the humidity encasing her, the sweat collecting on her skin.

The fire station gym was still in its spot on Main Street (did Lily think it would move? Or shut down? Or catch fire?), the sidewalk sign already out, the garage doors already raised. Even with both archways open, Lily went in through the door next to them.

The place was quieter than it was the day before. The place was empty, save for a heavy-set man hitting the pads with a younger, leaner fellow in the ring. Lily took a few cautious steps in – still aware of the heat, her sweat, the sound her sneakers made – and walked to the boxing ring.

"Alright – one! One, two!" the young fellow shouted, and the older man responded by punching at the padded mitts. "Three! Three, four! One! One! One, two!"

As the younger guy barked out numbers, the older man let out a series of punches, a loud *whack* accompanying each. She watched the guy with the mitts dance around the ring, his black, curly hair flopping around as he did. Every once in a while, he'd swing his arm at the man and the man would duck under.

"Um… excuse me?" Lily squeaked out. Both men stopped and turned to her. Her face flushed red.

"Can I help you?" the younger guy asked, slipping off his mitts and holding them by his waist.

Lily was far too aware of how warm her face felt, like she could burst into flames at any moment.

Inhale. Exhale.

"Is there… an owner, I can talk to?"

"Oh, are you interesting in taking classes?" the younger guy asked.

Lily shrugged her shoulders and looked to the ground.

"You want Jimmy then, most likely," said the guy. "He's upstairs right now. Stairs are all the way in the back. He should be out by the weights."

"Okay," Lily responded. "Thank you."

"I'm Leon, by the way," said Leon.

She looked up at Leon and grinned.

"Lily," she responded, her voice soft.

"It's nice meeting you, Lily," said Leon. "Good luck with Jimmy."

"Thanks. Again."

Leon slipped his padded mitts back on.

"You ready?" he asked, turning back to the heavyset man. "Sorry about the interruption."

"Gave me a chance to catch my breath!" he replied.

With a chuckle, Leon started calling out numbers, the rhythm and beat almost a type of music. One. One, two. Three. Three, Four. Lily snaked around the boxing ring and found the stairs. With one last glance at the two men, Lily made her way up.

The second floor hosted an array of gym equipment: a treadmill, a few weight-lifting stations, three racks filled with weights of all shapes and sizes. A wall-length mirror ran down one side of the room. In the far corner, a middle-aged man was hunched over one of the weight-lifting machines with a wrench and socket kit to the side of him, grumbling to himself as he fiddled with the bolts.

"Um – excuse me? Jimmy?"

"Yeah, yeah, yeah. What is it." Jimmy said into the machine.

"My name is Lily, and, uh…" Lily paused. "Is this a bad time?"

"It's always a bad time," Jimmy grumbled. "But I'm all ears, hon. Shoot."

"I, uh… well I was curious about…" Lily couldn't find the words to say. What did she want to say in the first place, anyway? "Your gym. Maybe joining?"

"Wow, ya got conviction, kid. Your words ooze confidence," Jimmy laughed to himself. "Ya sure you're in the right place?"

"Um, yes, yes I am…" Lily paused and took in a deep breath. "I want to start taking classes."

Jimmy put down his wrench and stood up, his hands on his hips, arching his back with a groan.

"Kid, never get old. It sucks."

Jimmy paused and looked at Lily.

"How old are you?" Jimmy said slowly.

Lily looked away and shrugged.

"16."

"Okay, well, you're old enough to start classes with everyone else, but barely," said Jimmy. "Typically kiddos come in with their parents, but I also have a waiver form your parents can fill out and sign for ya."

"Oh."

She thought about what she could do. Ask to take the form home instead? Forge the documents? Pray her handwriting looked like an adult's?

"Do I need to?" Lily asked. "I turn 17 in October."

Jimmy shook his head.

"Ya legally can't sign the waiver, and it's a liability if one ain't signed."

Lily's heart sank and face flushed again. She looked down to the ground.

"That's… that's really not an option," she said, feeling like she was 1000 miles away.

Jimmy let out an audible sigh. Lily looked up to see that his face had softened. There was even a hint of sadness in his eyes.

"Oh man, kiddo. Ya lucky I have a soft spot for the Lost Boys and the Little Orphan Annies of the world…" Jimmy trailed off. He set his jaw and sighed again.

"I get it, kid," Jimmy crossed his arms. "I do. Ya'd be surprised how many people here come from somethin' like that. This place is a home, for a lot of people. A lot of those fighters call me Pop, and they ain't doin' it to be cheeky."

Jimmy sighed again, wiping his hands against his jeans.

"Just… don't do anythin' stupid until you're actually considered an adult by the state, or... don't sue me if ya do," Jimmy added.

A small smile crept on Lily's face.

"Thank you," she said.

Jimmy sighed again.

"So, typically people pay by the month," Jimmy continued. The tone of his voice indicating clearly that he wanted distance from what he had previously said. "You can do by class, but if you're here more than once every other week, that gets wicked expensive. There are a few options, a few payment plans…"

Jimmy stopped talking as he met Lily's gaze. What was it about her expression that gave him pause? What was she giving away? The fact that she didn't have a job? The desperate way she was trying to figure out how to get the money? She never had a job before in her entire life, and she never had an allowance, and she knew her parents would never approve, and, and, and…

"I mean, it's not a requirement or nothin'. I don't turn away people," said Jimmy. "A lot of the guys here ain't got much in the money department, anyway. I don't ever want that to be a deterrent. They'll come by early and help out with the place, clean and that stuff." Jimmy stopped and cleared his throat. He pointed a finger at Lily. "But you ain't doing that. Nuh uh. It costs me nothin' to have ya as an extra person in a class or two. I don't mind a little pro bono work."

A new heat rose to Lily's face. One that made her agitated. She didn't like the idea of being a charity case. She didn't like the idea of this man just giving something to her. Did she look that helpless? That sad? She wasn't helpless. She wasn't at all.

"I want to help," Lily interrupted.

"Ah, kiddo…"

"No," said Lily. "I can pull my own weight."

"Kid, ya gotta be, like, 80 pounds soakin' wet. You ain't gotta pull any of ya weight."

"Then... I'm volunteering," said Lily. "I want to help."

Jimmy scratched his forehead.

"Geez, I've known for ya five minutes and ya just..." Jimmy shook his head. "But, fine, fine... this is probably wicked stupid of me but... ah, what can I say, ya remind me of someone. Ya look all sorts of fragile but... ya got a fire about ya. Ya seem like someone who could benefit from learnin' how to throw a decent punch."

Lily looked down and gave a slight shrug.

"Nuh uh, kiddo, none of that. No shruggin' like that," Jimmy added. "I don't know who crushed ya spirit enough to make ya think like that's an acceptable response, but it ain't. Ya got me on that?"

"Yes, sir."

"And, God, no 'sir'." Jimmy stepped back and waved the title away. "You can call me Jimmy, you can call me Coach O'Reilly. You can even call me a jackass, because I am. But none of that 'sir' stuff. None of it."

"Got it," Lily replied.

Jimmy sighed again.

"Let me clean up what I was attemptin' to do over here. Stupid pulley keeps jammin' up. But then I can show ya around the place and introduce ya. That sound good, kiddo?"

"Yeah," said Lily. "I'd like that."

"Alright, good. I'm sick of this stupid machine now, anyway." Jimmy turned from Lily and tossed a few items into the toolbox. He picked up the toolbox and carried it into the office on the opposite side of the floor. Jimmy emerged from the office, closed the door behind him, and wiped his hands on his jeans again.

"Alright, time to show ya Casa de O'Reilly, or whatever," he said, and led her down the stairs.

"We got all sorts of classes here," said Jimmy as he descended the stairs. "MMA is gettin' pretty huge, and we're try'na evolve like that. Kickboxin', Brazilian Jiu Jitsu… but really, this is a boxin' gym. That's what ya'll see the most of.

"We got classes basically every day, some type of trainin' goin' on all the time. I can give ya a schedule of what we got. And if ya ever get to the point that ya just want to come in and work out, hey, I'm cool with that as well. Just don't get ya'self killed. People love hittin' the heavy bags on their own. We get a lot of people who'll come in on their own just to do some strength and conditionin' – which is important to do. A good fighter is well-rounded."

Jimmy lead Lily back around the boxing ring, where Leon and the older fellow were taking a break.

"This is Leon, over here," Jimmy pointed. "Kid's in school for sports medicine. Wicked smart. One of my best coaches. Ya'd do ya'self a favor takin' a class with him."

"Hey," Lily sheepishly replied with a tight hand wave.

"We actually just met, when she came in," said Leon, walking closer to Jimmy and Lily. "It's good to see you joining the family.

Welcome."

Lily's face went hot again.

"Thanks."

"And that right there is Richard," said Jimmy, pointing to the older man. "True warrior at heart."

"Until my heart gives out on me," said Richard.

"Ah, that ain't happenin' anytime soon. Keep up ya trainin' and you'll be fine."

Jimmy started walking towards the front of the gym. Lily followed suit but looked behind her. She turned her attention to Jimmy only when she met Leon's gaze again.

"So this is our open area. Heavy bags to the right; mat to the left. Speed bags over in that corner. Unless there's a class goin' on, those are free to use at any time. Again, just don't get ya'self killed or hurt," said Jimmy. "Or, if ya do, say it happened somewhere else."

Lily nodded, scanning the place. She wished the girl in black was there. She wanted to know her name, or at least watch her kick and punch again, to watch her body in motion again.

"So that's about the gist of it," said Jimmy. "Any questions?"

"Um, no. No questions," Lily responded, her eyes still scanning the place.

"So I gotta run out and do a few errands," Jimmy went on. "Damn gym equipment is gonna be more work than it's worth to fix. Now, the question of the hour: when do ya feel like startin'?"

Lily kept her shoulders down, actively resisting a shrug. Instead, she looked up at Jimmy and, in a voice that was half an octave higher than her usual tone, asked:

"Tomorrow?"

*

"So, did you find a job yet?" her mother asked that evening, at another family dinner. Lily could never prove it, but she was sure her mother was upping the number of dinners just so she could hound Lily.

"Yeah, Lily, did you find a job?" Audrey piped in.

"C'mon now, Audrey," her father gently sang out. "If we wanted a parrot, I would've gotten a bird cage by now."

Audrey casually rolled her eyes and went back to her food.

Lily took a deep breath, her shoulder blades pressing into her back, her eyes locked onto her own plate. There was a flush coming to her face and a sour taste in the back of her throat.

"I did, in fact," Lily replied quickly.

"Really?" her mother said incredulously. "That quick?"

Lily shrugged and skirted her eyes to the side.

"Yeah," Lily mumbled. "They hired me on the spot."

"And what place would that be?" her mother pressed.

Lily swallowed hard and shrugged again.

"It's a... a place on Main Street," Lily stammered out. Could she dare say that she was joining the gym? She knew she couldn't. Her mother would snoop. Her mother would outright forbid it. Yes, she found work, but it wasn't the work she could admit to.

"*Any* place on Main Street?" her mother pressed.

"A coffee shop," Lily practically interrupted her mother to say. "I'm going to help out around a coffee shop. Sweep floors, clean, that kind of thing..."

"*I* don't know of any coffee shops on Main Street," Audrey stated.

"And it's new," Lily piped in. "Very new."

"What's its name?" her mother grilled.

Lily swallowed again. She knew she had passed by coffee shops on her way to O'Reilly's gym. She had to have. Why couldn't she think of any?

"Main St Café," she heard herself say. She went silent after that, almost shocked by the words coming out of her mouth.

"Huh," was all her mother said.

"Do you need a work permit?" her father asked. "Because I know when I started my first job, I needed a work permit. Child labor laws, they're there for a reason. We don't want any more youngin's sweeping chimneys."

Mrs. McCormick looked at her husband.

"No, I don't need one," said Lily. "You only need one of those if you're under *16*."

For a split second, Lily felt like she was outside of her body, watching herself talk. She had no idea if any of the things she was saying were true, but she was delivering them as if they were. She had never been a good liar, previously. Where was this coming from?

"Well, I'm glad to see you'll be making yourself productive," said her mother. "It's the first good decision you've made all summer."

Lily looked down at her lap, tilting her head to one side.

"May I be excused?"

*

That night, Lily tumbled through light, fitful sleep, filled to the brim with rapid-fire dreams. Vivid, bright dreams that slipped away the second she would start to wake up. The only one she could remember was the one where she was back at gym again, watching the girl in black kick and punch the heavy bag. Lily watched her pivot and duck and spin, every hit landing perfectly. The sound of the chains holding the bag rattled as the bag danced and shook.

Lily watched from a distance, from her spot in front of the archways, just like she had the day before, before working up the nerve to move in. As she did – as she walked into the building, closer, and closer, and closer to the bags – Lily was shocked to realize that she hadn't been watching the girl in black, but a version of herself kick and punch like a professional.

CHAPTER SEVEN

"If ya really keen on doin' stuff, there's always somethin' that needs to be done, here," Jimmy explained the next day. "It's a losin' battle with sweepin', so that's always something to do. Mats always need to be mopped. I tell the jiu jitsu guys to clean up after their practices, but do they? Nah. And then they wonder why ringworm is so common for 'em…"

Jimmy lead Lily through the basement – a sea of chaos, equipment, furniture, and cleaning supplies – pointing out where certain items were.

"But, kid, don't kill ya'self over the cleanin'," Jimmy warned again. "These classes? Again, they'd be happenin' whether or not you were here. Ya ain't gotta earn ya keep or nothin'."

"I know," Lily said as they made their way back up to the main floor.

"Ya do anythin' before comin' here? Ya got an athleticism about ya. Runnin', maybe?"

Lily cast her eyes to the wall.

"Dance."

"Dance! How about that. Y'know, a lot of people think dance ain't athletic, but I beg to differ. I see what those dancers can do. Ya gotta be an athlete to do that kind of stuff," said Jimmy. "What kind of dance, if ya don't mind me askin'? That 'modern dance' stuff everyone seems to do?"

Lily paused for a moment.

"Ballet."

Jimmy let out a sharp laugh.

"Ballet! Well, dang! Maybe I can get ya to teach some of these knuckleheads some ballet, then! Huh? It'll sure beat sweepin' floors, let me tell ya!"

Lily shrugged and looked away.

"I'd rather not."

"Hey, hey, just a suggestion," Jimmy said with his hands up. "Ya do what's good for ya, kid. Ain't nothin' mandatory."

Lily nodded, but kept her focus on the boxing ring.

"But, if ya ever change ya mind, I heard ballet is good for boxers. Get them better at floatin' like a butterfly n' all that stuff," Jimmy continued. "But I'm digressin', kid. No worries either way."

The gym was busier that morning than it had been the day before. There was a group of people stretching. Two people were at the heavy bags: one casually practicing a few punches while the other went wildly at their bag. Another guy – a redhead whose age Lily couldn't quite determine – was at the speedbag, releasing rhythmic hits to it as it tapped out a frenzied cadence between the guy's fists and the front board.

"Good work there, Freddy," Jimmy noted casually as they walked by.

"Thanks, Coach," Freddy replied, his voice disarmingly young. Without missing a hit, Freddy peered over his shoulder at Lily.

"Fresh meat?" Freddy asked.

"This is Lily," Jimmy replied, his voice a little sterner than before. "She's gonna start trainin' with us – and maybe help out a little bit around the joint."

"Ah, cool," Freddy said, glancing at Lily one more time before turning back to the speedbag, still not missing a beat.

"That's Freddy, if ya hadn't guessed yet," said Jimmy. "Good kid, underneath it all. Excellent fighter. If he can actually keep his stuff together, he could go pro."

Jimmy lead Lily back up to the second floor and to the office.

"So, if ya want, I might need help with all this office stuff," Jimmy said as he opened the door. Inside was a modest, windowless room, wood panels for walls and a matching brown carpet. "I'm always scramblin' at the first of the month. Leon wants me to start goin' digital, but I ain't got time to figure that stuff out. Besides…" Jimmy walked over to one corner and patted the top of his metal filing cabinet. "This won't crap out on me if there's a power outage."

Lily stood at the doorframe.

"Let's see... what else is there? Oh, if there's ever anythin' – or, y'know, like, anyone – that, like, bothers ya, ya tell me, okay? And if ya ain't comfortable tellin' it to me, tell it to Leon. He's a good egg."

Jimmy scanned his office, as if trying to remember where he put something.

"I think that's about it for here," said Jimmy, clapping his hands together before ushering them both out. "And, y'know, there's the gym equipment. I tell the guys to wipe the stuff down after, but they never do, so that's always somethin' to do. Mirrors always get smudged, too. But, seriously, kid. This ain't a to-do list. Just options if ya feel like it. Got it?"

"Got it."

Jimmy paused, brushed an invisible sleeve away from his watch, and looked down.

"Well how about that," Jimmy said. "It's about time for the mornin' class. Care to join?"

"Yes," Lily replied, before she realized she had even said anything.

Jimmy lead the way back downstairs. Lily watched Leon walk through one of the archways, his large black gym bag slung diagonally over his torso.

"Alright, ya guys ready?" Jimmy shouted. "We're meeting in the ring for warm ups."

Jimmy turned to Lily.

"Ready, kid?"

Lily turned to the people standing around. Freddy was already in the ring, doing a string of stretches at a breakneck pace. A few other guys were standing at the base of the ring, wrapping fabric around their hands and in between their fingers. It reminded Lily so much of taping up her feet that it made something in her start to ache.

"I don't have those," Lily pointed out in monotone.

"Ah, the handwraps?" said Jimmy. "Kid, unless ya really going to town on those bags – and I suggest ya don't on ya first day – ya ain't gonna need 'em just yet. Definitely don't need them for warmups. Just... don't do anything to snap ya wrists, all right? I can see if I got some extras layin' about later."

Lily pursed her lips together. She scanned for the girl in black – or, really, any girl. An uneasy feeling crept into her stomach when she realized that she was the only female in the room.

"Alright, everyone! Let's go!" Jimmy shouted. He turned to Lily and winked. "C'mon. Ya got this."

Lily swallowed hard and followed Jimmy up the stairs and into the ring.

"Okay, we're doin' our circles. Most of ya guys know the drill, but I'm repeatin' it for ya so it gets into ya skull." Jimmy widened his stance and bent his knees, his forearms up by his head. "I want stomachs in, I want arms up. And I want heads level – none of this prancin' stuff, ya hear me!" To emphasize, Jimmy side-galloped one way, and then the other, to the laughter of the group. "Feet under body. When I whistle, ya switch directions. Simple enough, so let's see if ya can remember!"

Jimmy fished the whistle out from under his t-shirt and blew.

"To the left!"

After a few stumbles, Lily started moving her body just like Jimmy had demonstrated: arms up by her head, her body level as she moved, her stomach pulled in. She could already hear one of her former dance teachers, criticizing Lily's poor carriage.

"Great holdin' ya core there, Lily!" Jimmy called out. "Ya see that, boys? It's her first day and she's already got it better than you's."

Lily burned red, her eyes on the floor as they continued moving in a circle around the ring. Jimmy blew his whistle and Lily nearly bumped into the guy next to her – a pale, bald fellow with an understanding smile as she muttered her apology – before side-stepping to the right.

They continued this pattern, shifting from side to side. A few of the guys started to huff. One stepped back to catch his breath. Something welled up inside of Lily. She wasn't even beginning to feel tired.

Eventually Jimmy blew a slow, long whistle, and everyone slowed to a stop.

"Okay, good attempt, good attempt," said Jimmy. "I can't stress enough, though, guys. Hands *up*. Keep ya'self level. This is about holdin' ya core, keepin' ya weight above ya feet, and movin' with *control*. If ya look like wacko galloping horses, then ya not in control!"

This garnered a few more chuckles from the group, Lily included.

"Alright, round two: this time we're addin' in a punch. Don't worry about leverage – this ain't about power. Ya gonna be punchin' in the direction you're about to go. So if we're goin' left..." Jimmy started moving in a smaller circle in the center of the ring. "And I blow my whistle, ya punch with ya right, and then go right." Jimmy stopped, shifted his weight as he threw a quick punch through the air, and changed direction. "Again, don't be worryin' about ya stance – I don't want to see anyone changin' their footwork. This is about shiftin' ya weight and gettin' it to work for ya. Questions?"

Lily held her breath.

"Okay, then, let's do this!" said Jimmy as he moved back towards the ropes and blew his whistle.

The sideways movement was as easy as before, but the punches threw her off. She could remember the choreography: press foot down, shift weight, throw punch while changing direction. And while her legs felt powerful – ready to take on those side gallops for way longer than any of the other guys in the room – her arms felt like wet noodles, awkwardly twisting through the air.

Jimmy blew his whistle to signal the end of the round.

"Last round, last round," he said. "Okay, I wantcha ta..." He paused for a moment, closing his eyes as if to recall. "So, it's the same as before, only we're addin' on: ya startin' and endin' with the same punch, and – remember, ya punchin' in the direction ya gonna go – but I wanna see one, two, one, two, one." Jimmy punched in the air, his weight shifting from side to side. "Jab, straight, jab, straight, jab. See how I'm shiftin' weight? I want to see that first. If ya got that down, that last jab can be a hook. Really push off that hook. Use that weight. If ya ain't shifting ya weight, I don't want to see ya addin' in the hook. Ya hear?"

The group mumbled in response. Lily felt the back of her neck go cold.

"Alright, then." Jimmy blew his whistle. "Go!"

Lily continued circling the boxing ring, dreading every time Jimmy blew his whistle. While she could shift her weight on cue, her arms just flopped in the air. Left, right, left, right, left. Those were not punches. Those were signs that Lily had no place being there.

Across from her, Freddy sliced through the air, punching directly out in front of him four times before adding in a hook.

"Freddy, I said no hooks unless ya can shift ya weight!" Jimmy called. At the next whistle, Freddy punctuated his four punches with yet another hook.

Lily could've sworn the last round was twice as long. Maybe even three times. By the time Jimmy blew his whistle, Lily wasn't sure if she was ready to collapse, cry, or quit.

Perhaps all three.

"Give ya'selves a water break, then it's to the bags!" Jimmy called as the boxers filed out of the ring. Lily cast her eyes to the floor and sighed.

"Hey, you did really good," someone said while Lily had her eyes on the floor.

Lily darted her head up to see Leon standing next to her.

"What?"

"You have really good form," he said. "You did great, especially if that was your first time."

"Oh," Lily replied with an unsure grin. "Well... thanks."

"So... don't be so hard on yourself," Leon continued.

Lily looked back at the ground and shrugged.

"Why would you say that?"

"Because I've been a coach for the last three years and I can spot a self-criticizing face from a mile away," said Leon.

Lily couldn't help but smile.

"Now, c'mon. Let's find you some gloves," said Leon.

"Gloves?" Lily parroted.

"Yeah, for the bags," said Leon. "Trust me on this one: you don't want to bare knuckle those bags, especially not on your first day."

Most of the other boxers were already stationed in front of a heavy bag by the time Lily exited the boxing ring. After fumbling around underneath the ring, Leon came out with a pair of dark blue gloves.

"They're a little beat up, but they're good quality," said Leon as he handed them to Lily. "Let me know how they work."

"Okay," Lily responded. She slipped one glove on and velcroed the wrist strap into place. She awkwardly put on the second glove and, after a few failed attempts to pinch at the fabric with the first glove, Lily used her forearm to move its velcro around her wrist.

"We're practicin' jabs and we're practicin' combos," said Jimmy, stationed to the side of the heavy bags. "If ya still practicin' ya jabs, ya stayin' at jabs. Every good combo gets set up with a jab, so if ya ain't got that down, I don't want to see ya gettin' fancy. Foundations first, got it?

"So – for those who forget – start in ya stance, lead arm out..." Jimmy positioned his legs and brought his arms up. He started slow, but finished with a punch so fast it seemed to whipcrack the air. "Don't fully extend ya arm, and make sure it gets back. If ya don't have that down, practice it until ya do. Lily, I wantcha practicin' this, okay?"

The whole group turned to look at Lily, who wasn't even by a heavy bag. Her whole face went red.

"Got it," she managed out.

"And I ain't singlin' Lily out – a good number o' ya could benefit with jab practice today, if ya ask me. All that fancy stuff in the world means nothin' if ya can't get the setup," said Jimmy. "Okay, for those doin' the combos today…"

Jimmy went on to show a series of moves, his feet dancing around, punching the air with such force and precision that Lily could almost see the imaginary thing he was hitting.

"Alright guys, let's see what ya got."

Lily stood by the last bag in the line. She mirrored how she saw Jimmy stand. Left foot in front. Right foot diagonally behind. Core engaged. Slightly on the balls of her feet. Arms up.

This, she could do. Her years in ballet had perfected her art of mimicking. If only she could get her arms to mimic what Jimmy did.

She extended her arm out to the bag, tapping it lightly as if to test its reaction. The bag shifted slightly and settled back into place. She remembered the details – no full extension, hand immediately back to her head – but there was something so horribly awkward about everything else. It felt wrong, no matter what she did. She felt her face go hot again, this time with tears welling up in the corners of her eyes.

"No need for that. Ya got the form, just not the technique," Jimmy said softly as he approached her bag. "I mean, holy crap, ya hold ya'self in ways that took these knuckleheads years to figure out. But, the punch ain't just ya arm, ya get it?"

Lily nodded daftly.

"Okay, watch what happens with my entire body when I punch," Jimmy said, stepping back. "Look at my foot pivot. Ya probably can't see it, but look at my torso move." Jimmy repeated the jab from before, in slow motion.

"Ya see? It's not about ya fist just goin' out. It starts at ya core. It starts at ya feet. It starts at ya legs. And ya got strong legs already," said Jimmy. He paused, then added: "And if that sounded creepy, I apologize. I don't mean nothin' by it."

"No, no, it's fine," said Lily. Before she knew it, she blurted out: "I've heard worse in ballet, anyway."

Realizing what she said, Lily locked her eyes back on the bag and attempted the jab again. She pivoted her foot, engaged her core, imagined the punch starting at her torso, her feet. With the same slow motion speed, Lily slowly brought her fist out to the bag.

"Much better, much better," said Jimmy. "And go slow. Get that muscle memory. That's way more important. Speed and power, that's great n' all. But precision? That's what makes the greats, the greats."

Lily kept her eyes on the bag.

"We'll need to work on ya core a little bit," said Jimmy. "Not in strength, but fluidity. Boxin's all about that fluidity. Gotta be able to sway. Being stiff as a board makes ya an easy target."

Lily nodded at the bag.

"I'll leave ya to it," said Jimmy. "Keep practicin', nice n' slow. Get comfortable. It's gonna be uncomfortable until it stops bein' uncomfortable. I know that sounds like crap advice, but it's not. Just remember: the punch ain't about just ya fist. It's the whole body." Jimmy paused and chuckled. "And just wait until ya learn to throw a straight."

Lily turned back and sighed. There was something primal welling up inside her, like a sleeping beast stirring and coming towards the surface. She wanted to break down and cry. She hated her inability to execute even a single punch. Hated that she couldn't do what the people next to her were doing. Hated the fact that she had been given a remedial version of the day's lesson – that she was singled out as the one person in the entire group who needed a special learning plan.

But instead, she breathed. Long, deep breaths to quiet herself down, for times when throwing herself into a fit of tears was simply not an option.

Inhale. Exhale.

After a few rounds of deep breaths – breaths that she imagined traveling downwards, blocking whatever feeling she had from rising up – she repositioned herself in front of her bag, readied her arms, and began the slow, tedious punch. Swivel hips. Swivel foot. Turn shoulders. Use core. Retract arm back.

Repeat. Repeat. Repeat.

"Okay, for most of you's, up in the ring," Jimmy called with a slight blow of the whistle. Jimmy turned to Leon and went: "Leon, can ya…"

"Got it, coach," said Leon with a knowing nod.

Lily stayed by the bags, instinctively taking a step back to let the other people pass by her on the way to the ring.

"Not bad, rookie," Freddy said with a smirk. "Not bad at all."

"Thanks," was all Lily could say, unsure if he was being sarcastic or genuine. Her face flushed, regardless.

Jimmy trailed the pack, walking up to Lily as the rest of the guys filed in.

"Leon's gonna help ya a little more with that jab," said Jimmy. Lily's eyes shot to Leon, then over to the ring, and felt her stomach tighten.

"Don't worry. I really ain't trynna to pick on ya," Jimmy continued. "If ya ever find ya'self competin', ya'll get why a perfect jab is important. Get that down, and the rest is gravy." Jimmy leaned in and said: "Some of those knuckleheads in the ring still ain't got their jab down right."

Jimmy took a step back and clapped Leon on the shoulder.

"Ya'll be in good hands with this one," said Jimmy. "I promise."

Leon responded with a warm smile, and gestured over to the mat.

"So, I just want you to practice that jab," Leon said, putting his padded gloves up as he repositioned his feet. "Just straight for my face. Got it?"

"Punch your face?" Lily blurted out with a nervous laugh.

"Yeah, I know. It's awkward if you've never done it before," said Leon. "But, yeah. Aim for my face. Technically you could aim for my torso as well, but I can block your punch better up here."

Lily nodded and attempted a slow, methodical punch. Her fist extended out a foot from Leon's face before coming back.

Leon laughed.

"Okay, so – trust me on this – you're not going to hurt me, or upset me, if you actually punch at my face. Especially at that speed," Leon reassured, taking a few steps in. It took everything in Lily not to take two steps back in response. "So, do that again – your form is really good, and I like that you're going slow – but now actually try to make contact with my face."

Lily swallowed hard and repeated her movement. Leon shifted to the side and moved one of his gloved hands into place, essentially high-fiving Lily's fist.

"Better. In a real fight, that would've made barely any contact, but that was a serious improvement," said Leon. "Fighting is all about getting into their space – intelligently into their space, I need to add. Intelligently. But, still, getting into their space, and not so much punching *at* the guy, as much as you're punching *through* them, if that makes any sense."

"It does."

"But, that's for a later time. Much, much later. Right now, it's just about getting comfortable," said Leon. "And before you think I'm just here to criticize, I really have to say your ability to repeat the moves is amazing. The fact that you'll go slow, too? Some of the fighters here, their egos are way too big for that. So they'll swing for the fences and look sloppy and not get why. You already have the foundations to be a great fighter. Seriously."

Lily's face lit up. It was refreshing to hear such genuine encouragement and support. But bewildering, too, to say the least.

Jimmy called everyone into the ring at the end of class, congratulating them on their hard work and recapping a few of the key points. As the rest of the students filed out, Jimmy came up to Lily.

"Great first class, kid," he said. "Great first class."

"Heh, thanks," Lily replied.

"So, I can't stress enough: I ain't here to run a slave ship. Ya tell me what times ya wanna come in, that type of stuff."

Lily paused and looked out at the gym. Leon was going through a set of stretches on the mat alongside another one of the boxers. Freddy was back at one of the heavy bags, delivering a few speedy combos while glancing over from time to time at Lily. A few other people had come into the gym, bags slung over their shoulders.

"I probably can't do nights and weekends," said Lily, thinking about when she'd have to be home. She started imagining Saturdays and Sundays spent at the gym – or, really, anywhere else than where she usually was on weekends.

"Well, those tend to be some of the nuttiest hours, anyway. Lots of weekend warriors n' such," said Jimmy. "If ya wanna come in a few mornings a week, stay however long…"

"Is every morning okay?" Lily blurted out, casting her eyes to the ground as she did.

"Of course, kiddo. Like I said: your schedule."

"And… it's okay to stay for longer than the morning?" Lily said to the floor.

Jimmy paused and tilted his head to the side.

"Of course. Door's always open," he replied, his voice tender and distant.

*

Lily stayed at the gym until the early afternoon. After the morning class, it was mostly just an open gym. A few of the guys would spar under Jimmy's supervision. Leon worked one-on-one with someone around lunchtime. A few people would come in to use the gym equipment or the punching bags. Freddy stuck around until noon, silently practicing by himself, alternating between punching at the bags, punching at the air, and jumping rope.

She loved the atmosphere of the gym. The calm chaos. The fact that there was always something happening, but everything felt so casual. People would talk and laugh with each other, hanging around long after they were done working out. Even the people sparring would high five each other afterwards. It was unlike anything else she had ever been a part of.

It was hard for her to leave when the time came. But she timed out how long her walk back would be and when her family would be home and she knew she had no choice.

Plus, she realized that she had gone all day without anything to eat – a realization that dawned on her as she started walking back, the afternoon sun still strong. She was only a few blocks away from Main Street when her stomach growled at her. She started picking up the pace, mentally planning out what she would eat when she got home. No one was on to the fact that Audrey's snacks were disappearing at a faster rate than before. Maybe she would have a bowl of cereal – maybe two – and a handful of potato chips before disappearing upstairs to shower and change. Her family would be home by then and, depending on the whims of her mother that night, either they'd have a nuclear family dinner or everyone would be left to their own devices.

Once home, Lily went straight to the kitchen. She gorged herself by the fridge, a careful ear out for the sound of the garage door. She really didn't know how her mother would react if she saw Lily with a bowl full of junk food, but Lily *did* know how her mother *had* reacted in the past, and it was enough to keep her on edge. After she became uncomfortably full, Lily went upstairs to shower and change her clothes before laying down on her bed and enjoying the stillness.

As her father and Audrey came home – as her mother eventually came through the door and made a show of talking loudly to her father and Audrey – Lily continued to lay in bed and replay the events of the day, remembering every detail that she could. Her muscles were exhausted, and, for the first time in a while, she was savoring the exhaustion. The only thing more satisfying than the feel of her arms limply sinking into her comforter was the realization that there would be no family dinner that night. She smirked to herself as she stayed where she was, eventually falling asleep above her covers.

CHAPTER EIGHT

Lily came in the next day and was thrown off by the change of scenery. No one was in the boxing ring and the Brazilian jiu jitsu class was well underway. The only familiar face on the first floor was Freddy, who was in the middle of grappling on the ground with another fighter.

Lily went upstairs and found the area empty. The noises from the first floor seemed to waft up through the floorboards. She could hear whenever anyone laughed or clapped or even tapped against the mat.

She started wiping down the dumbbells. There were rows and rows of weights, all neatly arranged and organized. She cleaned the handles, placing a wipe in the palm of her hand and gripping each weight as she did so.

Lily found herself pausing at a 20-pound weight. The other, smaller weights had shifted in her hands as she cleaned them. This one was the first to not move. After glancing around the room, Lily put down the wipe and picked up the weight with both hands.

She was amazed at how easy it was to lift it. She immediately shifted the weight into one hand and used her free hand to pick up the second weight. She took a step back and stared at herself in the mirror. With one big breath, Lily curled the first weight towards her shoulder and methodically lowered it back down. With another breath, she repeated the movement on the other side.

Maybe the other people in the gym could use bigger weights. Maybe she looked dopey and childish. But Lily tried not to think about that. Instead, she stood tall – feet planted, strong carriage –

and continued alternating hands. How was it possible that her spindly arms – arms that had never touched weights before – were capable of this? Had she always been capable of this? Did she always have this strength? Where was that strength when she was flailing her arms yesterday?

Lily nearly dropped the weights as she heard the stairs creak. With a jolt, she returned the weights to the rack, picked up her wipe, and continued cleaning. Two guys walked in and casually acknowledged Lily before going over to one of the machines. Lily wiped down a few more weights before abandoning the task completely and walking downstairs.

The jiu-jitsu class was finishing up, the group now stretching and chatting. Jimmy was in one of the corners of the ring, talking to a guy while the guy wrapped his hands.

There was no one on any of the punching bags. She was tempted to go over and use one to practice. But she stayed where she was, feeling so amazingly alien and out of place.

"Lily, right?" Freddy's voice registered.

Lily turned to see Freddy walking over to her.

"Yeah, Lily," she replied.

"It's Freddy, if you don't remember." Freddy wiped his hands on his towel and jutted his right hand out. "Welcome to the gym, if I haven't said that already."

Lily gave a nervous chuckle and returned the handshake.

"Thanks."

"So, what brought you in?" Freddy asked.

"What?"

"To O'Reilly's. What made you start boxing?"

Lily looked down to the ground, as if the mat below her would have the words she was looking for. Could she talk about the girl in black without sounding like a creep? How could she explain the attraction, the compulsion? How in the world could she explain something that she was still trying to figure out, herself?

Lily shrugged.

"I don't know," she replied. "Looked like fun."

"Well, it definitely is," said Freddy. "Ain't nothing like it. Do you roll?"

Lily looked up and crinkled her nose.

"What?"

"Y'know, rolling. Jiu-jitsu." Freddy motioned behind him, where the rest of the group was slowly dispersing. "Coach wants me to focus on boxing only, but I really wanna get my hands on MMA."

"Oh," Lily said, her eyes on the people behind him as they packed up their things. "No, never done it."

"Well, then you'll have to join us sometime!" Freddy exclaimed. "It's addicting. Really cool martial art. Like human chess, almost. It's a martial art where the little guy could beat up the big guy. Well, submit him, at least."

Lily nodded, mentally repeating what he had said. *Where the little guy could beat up the big guy.*

"So, what's your story?" Freddy asked.

Lily crinkled her nose for a second time.

"Your story," Freddy repeated. "Everyone's got one. What's yours?"

Lily raised her eyebrows and took in a deep breath. It was all she could do to not shrug and look down again.

Inhale. Exhale.

"Cuz you're already in, like, scary good shape. Normal girls don't look like that," said Freddy. "I mean, that's not an insult or anything. But obviously you got a background in something. Gymnastics?"

"Dance."

"Dance – nice. Perfect for martial arts, if you ask me. That whole floating like a butterfly thing, y'know?"

Lily smirked, thinking of Jimmy saying the exact same thing. "Sure."

"How old are you, by the way?" Freddy asked. "I don't mean to pry, but you got that kind of timeless look about you. You could be 14, or 40 for all I know."

Lily caught her breath.

"Eighteen," she said as she let the breath go. She wasn't used to this sudden, knee-jerk ability to lie, but she felt it was justified in this case. She thought about Jimmy and everything he had already done for her. The risk he took on.

The lies are easy because these lies are necessary, she thought to herself.

"Ah, wow, cool," said Freddy. "You in school right now or…"

"Um, yeah, I'm in school," Lily stammered, her heartbeat starting to race.

"Nice. Like, college, or…" Freddy trailed off again.

"High school," Lily said with a jolt. "Uh, senior year."

"Like, you just graduated, or summer school, or…"

"Starting. In the fall, I'll be a senior," Lily continued to stammer. When Freddy didn't immediately respond, she added: "I was kept back a year."

"Oh. Hey, nothing wrong with that," said Freddy. "You're talking to someone who dropped out. Got my GED a few years later, but that's really not the same thing. Just ask any employer."

Lily nodded, her heart lodged fully in her throat.

"But, that's cool, all of it. Former dancer, now a fighter... I dig it. You got a good story about you," said Freddy. "Speaking of employment, I have a shift at noon today, but... I'll see you around, okay?"

"Okay."

Freddy flashed a smile before picking up his bag. Lily stood there for a bit, wondering exactly what to do next. As Freddy made his way out of the gym, Lily looked up at at the ring, catching Jimmy staring at Freddy, his eyes following Freddy intently as he left the building.

*

Lily was shuttled to some Sunday afternoon soiree, that weekend. A co-worker or church member or PTA member – someone – was having some summertime mixer. Quaint, color-coordinated decorations lined the backyard, complementing the quaint, old-fashioned pitchers and plates and serving utensils. It seemed like nobody could just do a simple barbecue anymore.

Lily orbited around the property, a plate of food in her hand, an eye out for anyone who might be watching her as she ate mini sandwiches and chips & dip.

She had just sat down by a tree in the front lawn when a middle-aged lady approached her.

"Oh, Lily, there you are!" she said. "Your mother said you were here. How've you been?"

Lily put her plate of food on the ground and stood up, self-consciously brushing off her shorts and shirt.

"Um, good," Lily said. "Good."

"Oh, you probably don't remember me – I'm Mrs. Conway. My daughter – Rebecca – she took tap & jazz with you, way back in the day."

Lily nodded in pretend recognition. She was five years old, the last time that she took a tap & jazz dance class.

"How is everything going?" Mrs. Conway continued. "I heard you became quite the ballerina!"

Lily looked her feet.

"That's not really what I do, anymore," she said.

"Oh, yes, yes, your mother told me you were taking the summer off," Mrs. Conway replied. A feeling surged through Lily that she couldn't describe. "But she told me that you started working at a coffee shop!"

Lily's heartbeat quickened.

"Yeah. Just started."

"Now, that is lovely. More teenagers should take initiative like that. My girl, Rebecca, I can't even get her to start looking at college applications. Forget getting a job!" Mrs. Conway gave a polite chuckle and Lily nodded along. An uneasy silence fell between the two. The sounds from backyard became more and more noticeable.

"Well, I better get back to the rest of the party," said Mrs. Conway. "It was a pleasure seeing you. You should come by sometime, catch up with Rebecca."

"Sure," Lily said, forcing a smile. Another uneasy silence fell between them. Mrs. Conway gave a broad smile and turned back to the barbecue.

Lily walked in the opposite direction, away from the tree and towards the street. She put her hands on her hips and scanned the road. Aside from the soiree, the neighborhood felt quiet and uneventful. She thought about where she was in relation to things – where she was in relation to the highway, her house, the gym. She closed her eyes and breathed, imagining what it would be like if she just started walking back at that very moment.

CHAPTER NINE

On Monday morning, Lily detoured to the coffee shop on Main Street, the one that adorned the sidewalk with iron tables and chairs, the one that was diagonally across the street from her old dance studio.

She could do both – the gym and a job. No one said she had to pick. And she was the one who got herself into this mess. This was the only way to clean the mess up.

Lily walked into the café – called The Café on Main, which was close enough to the lie that she told her mother – the smell of coffee grounds and baking dough filling the room. Chalkboard menus covered the upper walls, colorful chalk detailing what they served. Five or six people waited in line. Lily sheepishly walked past them and made her way to the counter.

"Excuse me?" Lily said, her fingertips lightly on the counter.

Both the woman behind the register and the man in front of the line turned to Lily.

"Is there a manager, or someone, I could talk to?" Lily continued, her voice instantly a half octave higher.

The woman handed the man his credit card. The man smiled at Lily as he left the line.

"Let me get Karen," she said and turned from the register. After a moment, she returned, alongside a slender lady with short, blonde hair.

"Hi, I'm the manager on duty – is there something I could help you with?" said the lady.

"Yeah, uh – I was curious…" Lily paused and stepped to the side, distancing herself from the line of customers. "If you guys were hiring?"

The manager stepped to the side as well, giving the two of them a modicum of privacy.

"Ah, well, I really appreciate you coming in here, but right now we really don't have any openings. But, I can imagine, come fall, there might be a drop-off in employee availability. If you'd like, I could get your name and number, and we could call you if something opens up."

Lily paused, her shoulders drooping. She didn't know what she was more disheartened about: the fact that they weren't hiring or the fact that she really had no number to give. She was 16 and without a cellphone.

"No, no, that's okay," said Lily with a sigh. "I mean… I can always come in, in a couple months, or something."

Karen smiled.

"Well, good luck with your job search. I wish you the best."

"Thanks."

Karen had already turned from Lily as she said that. Lily turned from the counter, walked past the line of people, and exited the café with a beet-red face. She took a walk around the block before going into the gym.

Even in the gym, her mind was bouncing around. She tried cleaning the rest of the dumbbell weights as a way to reset her mind and found herself just jostling them around. Her mind was still a mess during the boxing class, tripping over her jump rope during warm-ups and bumping into people during practice.

"Is everything okay?" Leon eventually asked, as class was winding down.

"Yeah, yeah, of course," Lily let out, her eyes on the ground.

Leon paused and pressed his lips together.

"You know, I know this probably doesn't mean much, but there's always someone to talk to, here, if you need it," he said. "Anything at all, no judgments. We're family here."

Lily looked up at Leon and took in a slow, deep breath. For a brief moment, she felt okay.

"That's always good to know. Thanks."

But it didn't take long for Lily to be back in the headspace from earlier that morning. She periodically looked over at Leon – who, after class, was practicing alone at one of the bags – and wondered if she could actually take him up on his offer. Tell him everything that was on her mind. The reason she felt so scattered that day. The reason for a lot of things in her life. She closed her eyes for a moment, imagining a world where they'd sit by the side of the empty boxing ring, the entire gym to themselves, as she divulged and divulged and divulged – as she got out everything that she needed to get out, finally finding words to things that always felt out of reach, and hearing those words echo off the brick walls.

She opened her eyes, looked over at the row of heavy bags one more time, and went back to sweeping the floor on the opposite side of the room, her broom just moving around the dirt and dust instead of collecting it.

Only one thing snapped her out of her foggy, scattered reverie. It took one figure, casually making her way into the gym through one of the opened gateways, her green & blue gym bag slung diagonally over her torso. She was dressed in a red tank top and green compression shorts, but Lily recognized her instantly.

The girl in black.

The girl in black walked across the gym, slung her bag on top of the ring, and pulled out her hand wraps. Lily watched as she effortlessly wrapped her hands like an expert medic bandaging a wound. She finished one hand and started on the other, hypnotically covering it in blue fabric.

"Are you taking Rachel's class?" said a voice behind her. She turned to find Leon standing there.

"Come again?" Lily hugged the broomstick to her chest.

"Rachel teaches kickboxing here," Leon continued. "Have you taken her class yet?"

"No... no I haven't."

"Well, I think you'd like it," said Leon.

Lily nodded, looking over at Rachel as she did. Rachel started twisting side to side and stretching her arms up overhead. The gym had gently filled up with a few more people, each person finding a spot along the walls to place their bags, pulling out their gloves and wraps and water bottles and towels.

"I imagine you haven't met Rachel, then," said Leon.

Lily wasn't exactly sure how to respond, so she just shook her head.

"You'll like her, I think," Leon said, leading the way over to where

Rachel was. "She's been here practically as long as I have."

Lily took a few steps forward, broom still in hand, before leaning the broom against a wall. She followed Leon across the gym, deliberately keeping a few paces behind him.

"Rachel! I want you to meet someone." Leon stepped to the side and made way for Lily. Lily took a tentative step forward.

"Hi," Lily said, and her face went hot again.

"This is Lily," said Leon. "She just started at the gym."

"Oh, really? Nice," said Rachel, stepping forward and jutting out her hand. "Hi Lily, I'm Rachel. It's nice meeting you."

"Nice meeting you, too," said Lily, returning the handshake.

"She's been taking a few of Jimmy's classes," said Leon. "Already a great boxer, but I think her talent's really going to be in kickboxing."

"I've never kickboxed before, though," was all Lily could say.

"Hey, we all start somewhere," said Rachel with a flashed smile. "Class starts soon, if you want to grab some water or what have you."

Lily nodded and walked back to the mats. She started mirroring Rachel's warm-up routine: twists and side stretches, a few shrugs of the shoulders. She kept repeating that routine until Rachel called everyone over.

"All right, guys, I want us jogging counterclockwise today," said Rachel as everyone else filed in. Lily didn't recognize any of them from the morning boxing class. One of the guys looked about her age, but everyone else was easily in their 20s, if not older. "I really want you to at least try landing and springing off with the ball of your foot. But, if that's not happening right now, don't force it." Rachel clapped her hands together. "Okay, let's go!"

Lily followed the pack as they did laps around the mats. She tried to remember the last time she jogged. Walks, walks – plenty of walks, even before she quit ballet – but she never had really gone on a run. At least, not outside of P.E. class in school.

"Okay, I want everyone lined up on this side," said Rachel, slowing everyone down and pointing to the ring. "We're going to have two lanes: one going up, and one coming back. Right now, I want you working on leg swings. This is more about warming up the hamstrings than anything else, so don't go overboard."

Rachel turned to face the end of the mat.

"I just want to see: step, kick, feet together, repeat."

Rachel put her hands on her hips, stepped forward, kicked one leg straight up in the air, and snapped it back to the other foot. She stepped forward with the foot that she had just kicked with and repeated the same on the other side. Lily watched Rachel's feet point practically straight to the ceiling, extension so beautiful and precise that it made Lily ache for something that she swore she was done with.

"Kick to the end of the mat, and then kick your way back down the other lane. Any questions?"

After a moment of silence, Rachel clapped her hands together again.

"Okay, good. Let's go!"

Lily studied the other fighters as they made their way down the mat. She watched them kick to various heights – some kicks stayed fairly low, a few went to waist height, but none got as high as Rachel's – before it was Lily's turn. With a deep breath, she placed her hands on her hips and repeated Rachel's moves.

"Woah!" she heard from behind her. Lily immediately stopped and turned around. At the end of the line, Leon was staring at her, mouth agape.

"Lily, that's amazing!" shouted Rachel from the side of the mat. "And you never did this before?"

Lily shook her head.

"You gotta have a background in dance, then, or something," said Rachel.

Lily shrugged.

"Yeah," was all she could say.

"You are going to knock so many opponents out with your kicks," Rachel continued. "That is, if you start competing."

Lily's face went hot again as she continued down the mat, her legs going fully vertical with each kick.

After warm-up, Rachel directed everyone to the row of heavy bags.

"I want this to be a bit of a circuit. There are six bags, so that means six people on the bags. The remaining three will be shadow-boxing on the mat. When I blow the whistle, we'll rotate."

Rachel then explained what she wanted done at each bag and each shadow boxing station. Lily watched Rachel demonstrate, her words lost to Lily as she watched Rachel's smooth and effortless movements, as Rachel pivoted and twirled and made contact with the bag in ways that made it jolt and swing away.

"So I'll be here if you have any questions," said Rachel. "Lily, I want you to start on the first bag. Everyone else, find yourself a station."

Lily turned red again as she walked over to Rachel, her eyes on the ground. Everyone else gravitated to their spots. Lily looked up at her bag, drawing a complete blank as to what to do at this station in the circuit. It all had blended together into a beautiful, hypnotic dance.

"So I really think these kicks are going to be your wheelhouse," said Rachel. "Everything you learned in dance, it can translate easily into the kicks. Pivoting on the balls of your feet, balance, extension... all of it."

"I want you on this one first because the roundhouse kick is the closest to a pirouette in kickboxing." Rachel lifted her leg up before pivoting her body and extending her leg out, slowly slicing through the air. "Eventually we can focus on the upper body, but right now I want you to work on this."

Lily nodded, staring at the bag.

"I mean it: you've got some incredible potential. And I want you to capitalize on it," Rachel continued, her voice suddenly going serious. "I don't want you doubting yourself, because, honey, you got it."

Lily nodded again.

"And, really, any questions, I'll be here," said Rachel. "But, any questions right now?"

Lily shook her head.

"Okay, well, then, get to work!" Rachel said with a smirk.

Lily turned and faced her bag. She closed her eyes, remembering how Rachel demonstrated the kick. Lily lifted her leg up as she spun, extending her leg out just before her leg made contact with the bag. The resulting jolt against her shin and the movement of the bag nearly shocked her off balance. She brought her leg back down, watching the bag swing as a result of her kick. With a satisfied grin, Lily repeated the movement and watched the bag dance in response.

Lily felt that same experience as she made her way down the bags. She'd mirror what Rachel demonstrated for her, watch the bag respond to her kick, and feel a surge of energy. A few times, she'd close her eyes, imagining she was already to the level where Rachel was, kicking and spinning and ducking and punching.

Rachel ended the class with stretches, leading everyone through lunges and toe touches and straddle splits. Lily held back, avoiding going completely into the stretches, but even then the people around her were gawking.

"How is that even possible?" said one of the guys, wincing as he attempted to touch his toes.

"You guys need to take dance, for real," said Rachel. "A lot of the pros do it."

Lily kept her eyes on the ground, her face growing hotter. She looked over once, only to see that Leon seemed to be moving through the stretches with as much grace and dexterity as her former male dance partners.

*

"How often are you here?" Rachel asked after class.

"Here?" Lily repeated.

"Yeah. At O'Reilly's," said Rachel. "I teach on Saturday mornings, too, if you're around then."

"Oh, um…" Lily stammered. "Just weekdays, for me. Usually out by 3 or 4."

"Ah, so right before the rush hour crazies, huh?" said Rachel.

"Yeah, something like that." Lily looked towards the open archways and the street beyond them. "I'd like to come on weekends, though. Someday."

"Well, you should. I'm really not trying to recruit you or anything, but you're such a natural at those kicks. I'd love to have you in my Saturday class as well, if you're around."

"That'd be cool."

"I wish I could teach more during the week, but…" Rachel sighed. "Teaching kickboxing doesn't exactly pay the bills. And weekday classes can be such a crapshoot sometimes." Rachel shook her head again. "But, seriously, you did a great job. I mean it."

Lily grinned.

"Thanks."

As Rachel turned to talk with another student, Leon approached Lily with a knowing smile.

"Told ya you'd like it," he said.

"You were right," said Lily. Before she knew what she was saying, Lily added: "Were you a dancer once?"

"Come again?"

"Uh… a dancer," Lily tried to repeat, her mouth suddenly going dry. "I mean, your stretches were really good, so, I didn't know if you had danced or…"

"Ah, no. No dance for me," said Leon. "Just a good flexibility routine. Any athlete who doesn't want to injure himself should have one."

"Ah."

"Not to echo Rachel, but, if you can get here on weekends, that's really when this place comes alive," said Leon. "It's also when I teach my group classes. Especially once the fall semester starts up, that's where I'll be most of the time."

Lily pressed her lips together.

"Hmm."

"Hey, maybe when school starts up for you, too, you can check out more weekend stuff," said Leon.

Lily swallowed hard. She could feel her chest starting to tighten. Inhale. Exhale.

"Maybe."

*

Someone opened Lily's bedroom door, early the next morning.

Lily was already awake at that point, lying in bed, staring at the framed paintings on the wall. When she heard the door open, her eyes instinctively shut and she curled deeper into her blankets.

Her mother's audible sigh filled the room.

"How long are we doing this?" she said. Lily had her back to her mother, but she could imagine her mother with her hands on her hips, her pantsuit wrinkling ever-so-slightly as she did so.

Lily didn't respond.

"Is this how it's going to be? Is this really somehow better?" said her mother. "You'd rather make coffee than follow your dreams?"

A venom welled up in Lily, and a copper taste started to build in the back of her mouth. She kept her eyes closed.

"I know you can hear me," her mother went on. "Do you know how many girls would kill to be in your position? To get to do what you got to do? To have the opportunities you got to have? And you're going to throw all of that away? For what? Because you don't *feel* like it anymore? Because one of your dance mates made a bad life decision?"

Lily's breathing slowed. She continued her silence.

"Do you need to see a therapist?" her mother went on. "Maybe we should get you a therapist. Clearly, you're depressed, if you think this is somehow okay."

"I'm not seeing a therapist," Lily said. It felt like someone else was speaking on Lily's behalf, like Lily had taken a backseat and allowed another entity to step in.

"You *are* awake, then," said her mother. "Your instructors are understandably upset. Do you not understand how close you were, to everything? To finding a company? These are your prime years, Lily, and you're going to spend them working unskilled labor?"

Lily took a slow but shallow breath. She let it out and paused, noticing how empty her lungs felt.

"Maybe you should just quit school, then. Quit everything. Work in fast food. Find yourself a nice trailer to live in and completely destroy your life. Does that sound like fun? Because you might as well be doing that, at the rate you're going."

Lily swallowed, her lungs still empty. They were starting to burn.

Lily's mother huffed.

"Well, I can't stop you, if this is what you're going to do," she said. "But know that your actions have consequences, and someday you're going to regret this. And I'll be there to tell you, 'I told you so.'"

Lily listened to the sound of her mother's footsteps as she turned and walked out, followed quickly by a slam of the door. The slam sent a shockwave through Lily. She gritted her teeth in response. She stayed there, laying on her side, listening with fevered intensity to the noises on the first floor. When both cars had pulled out of the driveway and she knew that she was alone, Lily threw off her covers and threw on her gym clothes. She frantically gathered her hair into a ponytail and laced up her shoes, her fingers tangling up on each other.

Lily took off for the gym, her legs shaking as she ran, her head pounding, her ears filled with the overwhelming noises of passing cars and the sound of her feet and the sound of her breath.

She didn't realize that she had started crying until she turned right onto Main Street and saw the curious looks of people passing her by. She tried wiping her face, tried slowing her pace down, tried everything to calm down before she reached the gym. It wasn't until she ran directly into gym through one of the opened archways and practically headfirst into Freddy that she was able to stop herself in any way.

"Woah, woah," said Freddy, a hand rustling through his rusted red hair. "Are you okay? You look like death."

"Yeah, yeah, yeah, I'm okay," Lily said, her hands on her hips, her heart between her ears. She took a few slow, deep breaths – breaths that felt like she was breathing for the first time all morning – and closed her eyes.

Inhale. Exhale.

"Just… wanted to get a run in. Was more than I was expecting, I guess."

CHAPTER TEN

The supermarket was in the opposite direction of the gym, but still within walking distance – and they were known for hiring high schoolers. Lily figured that she could say that the coffee shop had let her go and she had found work at the grocery store instead.

As she walked towards the shopping plaza, Lily started mapping out what she could do. She imagined they'd have her working at least some of the weekend. It would be tough to work at the grocery store and go to the gym on the same day – at least without a car – but she could do it. And perhaps shifts on the weekends would help cover her tracks in case anyone from her family felt like checking up on her.

(And they would check up on her, wouldn't they? She was shocked her cover hadn't already been blown, that her mom hadn't yet detoured over to Main Street and get coffee…)

Lily took a breath and continued walking. Maybe she could start up running and use the commute between the grocery store and the gym as a chance to get a run in.

It was doable. All of it was doable.

No matter what the sinking feeling in her stomach had been telling her, Lily was not in over her head.

Deep breaths.

Inhale. Exhale.

Lily hung a right and went into the plaza. To the left of the grocery store was a greeting cards store, an athletics store, and a bank. Acres of parking spots sprawled out in front of the building.

She cut through the parking lot, the heat of the morning sun starting to beat down on her, before going through the automatic doors.

The chilled air of the supermarket hit her. Goosebumps popped up on her arms and she instinctively started rubbing them. Lily walked along the front of the store, her eyes out for anyone who might look like a manager or supervisor. Eventually, she saw a lady in a button-down shirt and khakis standing in front of the money order counter. She rubbed her arms one last time before approaching.

"Hi – excuse me?" she said, forcing herself to look at the lady and not at the floor.

"Yes, how can I help you?" said the lady with a smooth, velvety voice, turning to Lily and straightening her posture. The man behind the money order counter looked on with a plastered smile.

"I was just curious if you were hiring," Lily managed to get out.

"Of course," said the lady. "We're always looking for people. If you're okay with it, we can go to my office to discuss this further."

"Yeah that works," said Lily, repeating to herself *don't look down, don't shrug, don't look down, don't shrug.*

The woman led the way for Lily as they entered a small room near the entrance. Inside was a modest desk, a couple TV screens displaying security camera footage, and piles of binders and manila folders.

"We can always use more people. Baggers, stockers, the whole kit and caboodle." The woman sat down by the desk and pulled out one of the folders. "So I can give you the application, and you can take this home if you'd like. If you don't mind me assuming, I imagine you'll need your parent or guardian to sign off on this."

"Come again?" Lily said, her mouth going dry.

"Well, you're under 18, correct?" the lady pressed.

"Um, yes… but I'm 16," Lily admitted, her eyes now on the floor. "I turn 17 in October."

"Which is great, but since you're applying for a job *now*, I do need a guardian's signature. And you'll also need a work permit from the town."

"A work permit?" Lily repeated.

"It's incredibly simple, if you haven't done it before. Just go into the town hall with a guardian and fill out a quick form. It'll be good for a year, so that means you'll have to renew it one more time before you turn 18, even though you'll be turning 18 in a few months, by that point." The woman handed a few sheets of papers to Lily. The paper felt smooth and cold in her hands. "It can feel like a lot of red tape, but it's really for the best.

"We can discuss this more when you come back with your application, but the hours you can work will be a little different since you're under 18, and will change again once you start school, but that's a bridge we can cross when we get there."

Lily nodded.

"Do you have any questions?" the lady asked. Lily looked down at the woman's name tag for the first time. Michelle. Assistant manager.

"No, no, I'm good," said Lily. "Thanks."

"Anytime," said Michelle. "And when you're ready, just come on in with your application and work permit and we can go from there."

Lily smiled weakly as she turned to the door.

"Sure."

Lily exited the grocery store, sweat building on the back of her neck. She folded the application in thirds and cupped it in her palm. She focused on the sound of her shoes against the pavement, the cars as they drove by.

Inhale. Exhale.

What was the point? She could possibly forge her mother's signature on the application, but she couldn't fake a work permit. Could she get Jimmy to pose as her father? No, that would be insane. And she had already asked so much of him already.

It was hopeless. Absolutely hopeless. She was, in fact, over her head.

Instead of walking past her neighborhood, Lily deliberately turned into it, weaving through the streets until she got to her house. She went inside just long enough to slip the application under her mattress and head back out.

She stepped out onto the front steps and stopped. The day was heating up and the weather was muggy. She closed her eyes and attempted to feel any trace of wind. The air was still, and nothing could be felt. She opened her eyes, walked out onto the street, and turned towards Josh's house.

She passed the two houses that separated her house from his. She walked to the edge of his property and stopped in place, leaning forward as if there were an invisible barrier in front of her.

The house looked just like it always did. It was only in the details that things revealed themselves. The lawn was overdue for a mowing. There were weeds in the garden. Bushes were taking on wild and unwieldy shapes. Window shades were drawn. There were no cars in the driveway.

In the front yard, the "For Sale" sign had changed once again: the "Under Contract" addition that had been hanging from the bottom had been removed. Instead, a wooden rectangle now adorned the top, creating a crown for the sign.

SOLD.

Lily stood there for a few more moments, looking at the fence, the yard, the sign, the driveway, the windows, the roof. She started to take a few steps backward. Lily eventually turned her back to the house and started walking to the gym.

*

"There ya are!" Jimmy's voice sang as Lily approached one of the gateways. "I was wonderin' where ya were at."

"Oh, just running some errands," Lily said, her head swimming. She attempted to casually roll her eyes.

"Well, glad to see ya," said Jimmy. "Ya missed a great boxin' class, but ya always welcome to use the bags on ya own, or even stay for the evenin' class." Jimmy scratched behind his ear. "Someday we'll get a lunchtime boxin' class in. Maybe get a few of those office stiffs to come by for a bit. Y'know, there's a lot of money, teachin' to companies. If I was willin' to sell my soul like that, I'd totally be on that train."

Lily nodded, instinctively following Jimmy across the mats. She thought about Josh's house, the SOLD sign, about the blue police lights in March...

A lot of the usual gang was still there. Freddy was moving wildly about a heavy bag, giving it punches that would've broken an actual person's ribs. Leon was beside the boxing ring, talking with the older man that she had met on her first day. A few of the other guys from the boxing class were there, packing up their equipment. She watched on in a daze.

"The day's ya oyster," said Jimmy, the last word coming out more like 'oystah'. "The gym equipment's bein' hogged up by some of the boys right now, but other than that, go to town. Safely, of course, kiddo. Safely."

"Thank you," was all Lily could say. She mindlessly followed Jimmy, feeling like her feet were barely touching the mat. Lily slowed down as she approached Leon and the older man, stopping completely when Leon looked over at her.

"Hey, there," he said with a bright smile. "You were missed at class today."

"Sorry I missed it," Lily replied, her words feeling distant.

"Hey, no biggie. We all miss class. Not a problem, especially if you're not competing," Leon said. "Sam, you remember Lily?"

"Ah, I think so – you're the fresh meat, right?" Sam said with a wink.

"Uh, yeah," Lily said.

"Well, if you'd like, we can hit the pads in a little bit," Leon offered.

But Lily didn't fully hear him. Her mind was still swimming, bottlenecking with thoughts from the morning, from who knows how long ago. She could still see Josh's house in the back of her mind.

Lily suddenly blurted out: "Did you know Josh?"

Both Leon and Sam looked at Lily with confusion.

"Come again?" Leon asked.

Lily's face went hot. The world suddenly snapped back into focus.

"Josh Decker," Lily said to the ground. "I didn't know if you knew him."

Sam looked over at Leon.

"I gotta admit. I didn't grow up around these parts," said Leon. "Why do you ask?"

Lily pressed her lips together and shrugged.

"He's…" Lily paused at her use of the present tense. "He's a college guy as well. Thought maybe you knew him."

Leon shook his head.

"Sorry, the name doesn't ring any bells. Where does he go to school?"

Lily's heart started thumping between her ears.

"Ah, not here. Out of state," Lily said, her voice a thousand miles away.

"Well, he's always welcome here, if he'd like. Sure we'd get along great," Leon said with a smile. "I'd love to continue talking – *but* – Sam's due for his workout."

"You mean my workout can't be talking to this nice lady?" Sam said with a wink.

"Talking with nice ladies doesn't improve your core strength," Leon replied.

"Nonsense!" Sam stepped back, dramatically sucked in his stomach, and puffed out his chest. "See? This is how I am when I talk with the ladies! Look at that core strength!"

"You give a compelling argument, but we're still going in the ring," said Leon. As Sam started his way up the ring's stairs, Leon turned to Lily and added: "And, seriously, if you want to hit the pads after, let me know. I can even show you how to hold the mitts, too."

Lily let out an easy smile.

"Sounds great."

It was only then that Lily realized Freddy had been on the adjacent side of the ring, unwrapping his hands and looking at Lily. Freddy waited until Leon was in the ring before he approached her.

"Were you talking about Josh Decker? Like... *that* Josh Decker?" Freddy paused and cocked his head to one side.

"I think so," Lily said and felt her lungs empty themselves of air.

"He was a good guy, Josh was," said Freddy. "I went to high school with him. Never close or anything, but I knew him. Really sucks, what happened."

The world started to blur around her.

Inhale. Exhale.

"Yeah."

"You knew him?"

Lily paused, closed her eyes, and repeated herself.

"Yeah."

"Man, that sucks. I'm sorry," said Freddy. "You really never know, y'know? People could seem all fine and then the next minute..." Freddy trailed off, the words he didn't say deliberately hanging in the air.

"Yeah."

"But, hey, life goes on, right? Gotta remember that. Life goes on." Freddy scrunched his handwraps in his palm. "Listen, I was gonna head out and just kill time before my shift started, but, I heard something about holding pads. I could hold while you practice, if you'd like. Rumor has it you've got a mean roundhouse kick."

"Who told you that?" Lily said, her eyes wide with astonishment.

"Word travels fast around these parts." Freddy gave a

mischievous grin and raised his eyebrows. "Come on. This'll be fun."

Before Lily could say anything, Freddy pulled out a black, padded rectangle from under the ring.

"I don't know, I..." Lily began, looking over at Leon.

"Ah, c'mon. It's just like kicking the bag, only better," said Freddy. He walked over to the mat, turned to face Lily, staggered his feet, and placed the pad by his left hip.

"Just a few rear-leg roundhouse kicks. Hit the pad, though. Not me. You would do some real damage if you actually made contact," said Freddy.

Lily hesitated, looking at Freddy, then the pad, then back at Freddy.

"Okay, pretend I didn't say that. It's okay if you miss. Don't psych yourself out or anything," Freddy shifted his weight and shook the pad as if it were a cape and he were a matador. Lily looked around the gym before taking a few steps closer and giving a slow, gentle kick, her shin barely making contact with the pad.

"See?" said Freddy. "And I didn't die. Now, do that again, only faster."

Lily took a deep breath and repeated. This time, she could hear and feel her shin thwacking against the pad.

"There we go! Now, do that again."

Lily repeated a few more times, each time going with a little more force. There was something satisfying in the sound of the impact, in watching Freddy stagger back slightly.

"So, how did you know Josh?" Freddy said after a while.

Lily stopped mid-kick.

"What?"

"I mean, Josh, he was in the grade below me. A few mutual friends, that kind of thing. How did *you* know him?"

Lily looked at the pad and tilted her head.

"He was my neighbor."

"Oh, shit," said Freddy. "Man, I'm sorry."

Lily shrugged her shoulders.

"That stuff? You know, suicide and what have you? It's tough," Freddy continued, who was now holding the pad to his chest. "Like, people die all the time, but usually you can get angry at whatever it was that killed them. Cancer, a car crash... And, if they're old, then it was just their time, y'know? But... I mean... it's tough. It's like when someone ODs. What do you blame, then?"

Lily looked at Freddy a beat longer than she meant to.

"You know people who've overdosed?" she asked.

Now it was Freddy's turn to shrug.

"That's life these days, y'know? People get into some stuff and… I mean, it's all around us. Y'know?"

Lily pressed her lips together.

"It's why you won't catch me around the hard stuff. Not on your life." Freddy repositioned himself and shook out one of his arms. After a moment, Freddy added: "*You* don't do that stuff, do you?"

"Me?" Lily said. She was tempted to start laughing. If Freddy had any clue of all the things she hadn't done in her life, he wouldn't be asking that question. "No, no. Not at all."

"Good. Don't." Freddy paused, his eyes intense, as if he could will Lily into never doing it. Lily couldn't help but stare back, taking in whatever Freddy was giving out.

"Sorry, that went down a road, didn't it?" Freddy said after a moment, shaking his head and letting out a soft laugh. He crouched down slightly and placed the pad in front of him. "Anyway, you should try some front kicks now. And don't hold back. Knock me off my feet. Literally."

Lily took in a breath, brought her knee into her chest, and slammed the sole of her foot into the pad. Freddy staggered back.

"Damn! You seriously have a lot of power. I mean, holy crap. I'd never want to be matched against you in the cage." Freddy steadied himself. Lily kicked again. Freddy braced for it, and laughed when he still lost his footing. He took one arm out from the pad's straps and shook it out. He switched arms and shook the second one out as well.

"We should hang out sometime," said Freddy.

Lily just looked at him.

"What?"

"We should hang out sometime, outside of the gym," Freddy said. "I work a lot of evenings, but usually Saturday nights, I'm free."

Lily faltered.

"Um… I don't know."

"Hey, hey, it's cool, I get it," Freddy said, using his free arm to put a hand up. "No offense taken."

"No, no, no – I didn't mean that!" Lily took a step forward. "Just… my parents? I don't know if I can hang out on Saturday nights."

"Oh, hardasses, huh?" Freddy said with a smirk. "I know what that's like. They never get it, though. Hold a leash that tight and it's only going to backfire on them. But, if you ever need someone to help you sneak out of their little prison system, I'd be happy to be your partner in crime like that."

Lily's face flashed hot, and she wasn't sure if it was because of Freddy's offer or just the sheer idea of sneaking out.

"I'll keep that in mind," Lily said, returning the smirk.

There was a pause, a moment, a bit of eye contact, something – something that had both of them standing there, looking at each other with stupid grins on their faces, neither of them all that concerned about the silence.

"Well, that's good to know," Freddy said after a moment, before holding the pad back up. "Okay, a few more before I have to go. I want to see those high kicks. I bet they're badass."

*

There was a family dinner that night. Her mother's clangs and bangs in the kitchen announced it.

Tonight was some type of fish with rice and broccoli. Lily's plate had already been set at her placemat. The portion size made her stomach twist – a tiny piece of fish alongside a small mound of rice and a handful of broccoli crowns. She didn't even have to look at her parents' plates – or Audrey's plate – to know that her own had half the food as everyone else's. Lily wasn't sure why her mother still did this, or what she meant by it.

Lily sat down in silence, her eyes on her plate until the rest of her family came in.

"Aaaw, fish," Audrey whined. "Why do we have to have fish?"

"Because it's brain food. Goes straight to the brain," said her father, tapping his temple.

"I expect no whining at the dinner table," replied her mother. "You have a cooked meal in front of you. That's more than a lot of people get."

Audrey huffed and picked up her fork.

Lily picked up her fork as well and began eating.

"So, how was your day?" her mother said coolly.

Lily shrugged her shoulders.

"Good."

"Did you work at the coffee shop today?" her mother asked.

Lily paused. Could this be a trap?

"Not today," said Lily. "They didn't need me."

"So, what did you do with all your free time, then?" her mother asked.

Lily shrugged again.

"Stuff."

Not once did Lily look up. She could hear her mother sigh heavily and, with that, the conversation was dropped. Lily went back to her food and finished what was on her plate.

Why she did what she did next, she wasn't really sure. She was still hungry, yes – but, on any other day, she would've just excused herself from the table, gone to her room, and waited until she could sneak back down to the kitchen. But, today, she got up with her empty plate and returned to the table with seconds.

"Helping yourself, I see," her mother said, in the tone of voice that used to stop Lily in her tracks: subtle but venomous, proof that you don't have to shout to intimidate someone.

Lily locked her eyes on her placemat.

"Yes," was all she could say.

Nothing else was said. Her mother sighed again. Lily sat back down. Her mother started stabbing at the remainder of her fish with her fork.

"Broccoli's a good source of vitamin C. Did you know that?" said her father. It took Lily a moment to realize he was talking to her.

Lily shrugged.

"No, not really."

"People just think orange juice when they think vitamin C, but broccoli is good, too," her father continued on. "It's a good pair-up with the brainfood fish, if you ask me."

Lily shoveled a forkful of rice in her mouth and made a noncommittal noise.

"Well, I have a few things to get done," said her mother. "If you'll excuse me..."

Lily continued eating as her mother cleared her spot, leaving her with her father and her sister.

"What do you do at the coffee shop?" Audrey's voice piped up from across the table.

Lily shoved another forkful in her mouth, chewed, and swallowed with deliberate slowness before she said anything.

"Stuff. Mostly cleaning," she replied. "I'm not trained for anything else yet."

"Oh. Sounds boring," said Audrey.

"I think a summer job builds character," said her father. "And it'll look good on a college transcript."

"Are you being punished for quitting ballet?" Audrey said, her words coming out slow and toneless.

Lily looked down at her plate and shrugged.

"Well, I think it's a productive way to spend the summer," said her father. He added with a wink: "Plus, a little pocket cash never hurts, right?"

"Mom is so mad at you for it," said Audrey. "I think it's punishment."

Lily stared at her little sister. Audrey was considerably younger than Lily – she had just turned 10 – and, some days, Audrey looked and acted even younger. Other days, she looked and acted like an adult. Right now, Lily had no idea which version she was looking at: the kid or the grown-up. Was she being mean or just immature?

Lily's stomach clenched. The remaining food on her plate suddenly looked bland and unappealing.

"May I be excused?" she asked.

The Ballerina's Guide to Boxing

CHAPTER ELEVEN

"These can go over in that file over there," Jimmy said from his desk, pronouncing "there" like "they-yah". He pinched his eyes with his middle finger and thumb, elbows digging into the desk, back hunched over. Lily arranged the papers in her hand into a neat pile before going over to the manila folder across the room. The open office door gave view to the empty floor.

"They never tell ya this part, when ya open a business," Jimmy said. "But the paperwork will make ya want to jump outta window." He pulled the computer's keyboard closer to him, jiggled the mouse, and began typing, his index fingers pecking at the keys.

"Technology is supposed to make this faster, but all it does it give me a headache," Jimmy continued. "Leon keeps pushin' this software stuff on me, and I'm thinkin' maybe it's time to make *him* do all this sh…" Jimmy stopped and cleared his throat. "Stuff."

Lily scanned the office, which could only be described as balanced chaos. Stacks of paper on the desk, worn out boxing equipment piled in one corner, knick-knacks scattered as if they had been left there on accident. The walls had a few framed black and white photos of boxers in action.

"Thanks again, for helpin' with this," said Jimmy, tapping three keys on the keyboard before pausing to squint at the screen.

"No problem," Lily replied. She gave a slight chuckle and added: "I mean, that's what I'm here for."

Jimmy sat up and stared at Lily in mock shock.

"Woah. You're capable of laughter," he said, his hands at the edge of his desk.

Blood rushed to Lily's face. She locked her gaze onto the filing cabinet.

"Hey, I don't mean that in any mean way. Seriously, I'm just teasin', that's all. It's good to know ya can laugh." Jimmy rubbed his face before covering his mouth with his hand. "I mean, there's somethin' very serious about ya. Very... well, it's good to hear ya laugh, is all. I hope ya do it more. Life'll kill ya if ya stay too serious."

Lily nodded, looking at Jimmy just long enough to acknowledge his words.

"How do ya like it here, by the way?" Jimmy said. "And I don't want ya tellin' me 'fine' or 'good' or any baloney like that. How'zit been."

Lily shrugged.

"I don't know what to say other than, 'good'."

"Well, if it's good, then it's good, but I ain't lookin' for pleasantries. I really wanna check in." Jimmy paused and sighed. "I know ya kinda like the baby of the bunch right now. Not a lot of kids ya age – and I ain't tryin' ta talk down to ya. I just... I get it. Especially during the day, ya get a lot of college boys wantin' to get their Golden Gloves, and that's kinda it. We got a few high schoolers, but... I don't know, parents are worried their kids'll get hurt. But they'll put 'em on the football team, which is way worse if ya ask me." Jimmy waved his hand away from his face. "But I'm goin' off topic. I wantcha to feel at home. Like, everyone here is pretty good. Couple a' knuckleheads, but the hearts are good."

"Well, good."

"I mean – I know I ain't good at this stuff, so bear with me," Jimmy faltered. "What I mean is... ah, do ya know what I mean?"

"Kind of?"

"Just... I want ya to feel comfortable here. Like, it's okay to be friends with the other fighters. They're good people."

Lily nodded.

"Gotcha."

"Have ya ever considered competin'?" Jimmy asked.

Lily stared at Jimmy.

"What?"

"Now, this wouldn't be for at least two years. Ya underage and I ain't puttin' ya in any fights, and that is that." Jimmy looked at Lily with a warm sternness. "But... ya've been here, what, a couple weeks? And the way ya catch on... you're a natural athlete."

Lily swallowed and looked to the ground. The office carpet was an ugly, dark brown.

"And, hey, that's just me askin'. Just curious. Ain't gotta do nothin'."

"I'd rather not," Lily said, feeling a thousand feet away from her voice, her body. "I'd rather just..." Lily paused, the words coming from some place strange and unknown. "I just want to do this for me. Not to compete, just... this is mine."

It was Jimmy's silence that snapped Lily back. She looked up to see Jimmy looking at her with sad eyes and a warm smile.

"And that's perfectly fine, kiddo. This is 100% yours," he said slowly and softly. "Pretend I never asked."

Lily locked her jaw and made a noncommittal noise.

"Besides, I like that. Doin' it for the personal stuff, not to get ya hands raised," Jimmy continued. "Too many fellas come in here and, after their first class, are already talkin' about goin' pro. Like, sorry buddy, ya ain't ready. Even the lowest-ranked boxer is gonna be Mike Tyson compared to ya amateur ass—self. Amateur self." Jimmy cleared his throat.

Lily cracked a smile.

"Smiles are a good thing, too – trust me on this one," said Jimmy. "Really, I mean it. Ya don't have to be so serious all the time. This is a family, and families laugh. Well, families also get into fights at Thanksgiving, but we have the Thanksgiving dinner in the ring, instead."

Lily let out a snort.

"Snorts are good, too," Jimmy said, ruffling papers on his desk. "My daughter snort-laughs like that."

"Your daughter?" Lily repeated.

Jimmy cocked his head to one side.

"Yeah, little Melanie." Now it was Jimmy's turn to sound distant. "Ain't little no more, though. Will be 24 this year."

"Oh, wow."

"Yeah." Jimmy went silent, staring at the computer screen, his elbows propping him up. After a moment, he sat up, shook his head, and added: "But yeah, laughter. Keep it up. It's important to laugh. Never wanna lose that."

*

That night at home, Lily kept an ear out for any signs that there'd be a family dinner. There were a few casual conversations – Audrey talking about some project at camp, and her mother responding. She could hear the microwave starting and stopping. It was only when she heard the TV turn on – that meant her father had taken to his shows for the night – did she come down the stairs.

"Well, hey there," said her father. Lily had to loop around the living room to get to the kitchen, and now she was within a few steps of the TV set – a remarkably outdated TV on a fairly modern TV stand. Outside, the sky was a beautiful and subtle orange, a gentle reminder that the longest days of summer were already behind them.

"Hey, Dad," Lily said, her words feeling foreign.

"How was your day today?" he asked. He picked up the TV remote and turned down the volume.

"It was good."

"Did you work today?"

"Yup," said Lily. She knew her father wouldn't try to set her up. She felt simultaneously more at ease and more guilt for lying so readily.

"How was work?"

"Good."

"Well, that's always good," he said.

Lily stood there, looking at her father. In the silence, Lily could hear the TV again. In soft words, someone on the TV was explaining the wonders of a cleaning product. She could also hear her breath, steady and a little raspy. She could also hear the footsteps over her head – Audrey's room was directly above the living room.

And yet, with all these background noises, all Lily could pay attention to was the lingering silence and how it filled the room. All Lily could pay attention to was the feeling that it created, and how, slowly but surely, her breath was becoming a little less steady.

Inhale. Exhale.

"I'm going to get some dinner now," Lily eventually said.

"Well, sounds good," her father said, picking up his remote. "Have a good night, kiddo."

"You too, Dad."

Lily left the living room, her eyes on the ground in front of her. It wasn't until she was in the kitchen that she realized she had been walking on the balls of her feet. An unconscious tip-toeing.

The kitchen was mercifully empty. She turned on the lights, opened the fridge, and pushed a few items around. There were a few leftovers – last night's rice in a glass container, something in a restaurant's cardboard doggie bag – and a smattering of vegetables. Nothing looked appealing. She opened the pantry door and looked at the boxes of pasta, the macaroni & cheese, the uncooked rice. There was cereal and oatmeal and breakfast bars. Again, nothing looked appealing.

In the way back of the pantry – perhaps deliberately tucked behind everything else – was a bag of chips, already opened and partially empty. With a quick glance around the room, Lily reached in and pulled out the bag, slowly maneuvering it around the other boxes, petrified that the bag would crinkle and the noise would give her away. She looked around again, her breath shallow and short. With deliberate hands, Lily placed the bag of chips by her hip. She turned off the lights and began to tip-toe out of the kitchen.

She passed the living room with held breath, wondering if her father would stop her a second time. Instead, his eyes darted between the screen of his cellphone and the screen of the television.

It wasn't until she was in her room, with the doors closed, that Lily could actually breathe freely again. She locked her door, turned her radio on to a soft but noise-canceling level, and walked to the opposite side of the room. Feeling like she was going in for surgery or disarming a bomb, Lily gently opened the bag and pulled out a few chips.

*

It was during a community barbecue that Lily heard the news.

The barbecue was a few blocks down the street from her house. It would make two weekends in a row that Lily had been shuttled to some outdoor gathering. Most of her neighbors were there – mostly adults, but a few children under the age of 10. Some of the faces were familiar. Others were complete strangers.

"Such a pity, it all is," said one of the familiar neighbors – a blonde lady about her mother's age. She was by the refreshments table in the backyard, talking to a lady with a bob haircut and khaki shorts.

"I can't blame them. Losing a son... and losing a son like *that*... it's going to put a strain of things."

Lily had grown accustomed to listening for subtle cues. No one ever referenced people by name, or spoke of any incidents directly. There was always a dance around communication at these gatherings, as if talking about bad things would make them happen again – or talking about people by name would mean they'd have to recognize that they were spending their day gossiping.

"She had already moved out of the house, even before it sold," said the blonde lady.

"Do you know where she went?"

The blonde lady shrugged.

"Out of state. That's all I know," she answered, before adding: "And, apparently *he* already has a girlfriend."

"Wow," said the second woman, smirking. "*Someone* is moving on…"

"Do you think they're legally separated yet?"

"I don't even know if they've started the divorce proceedings…"

"Do you think his girlfriend knows?"

"About his wife? About his son?"

"About everything."

"If she's from here, she probably does."

"I wonder if he'll leave the state as well…"

Lily took in a sharp breath, scanned the yard to see if anyone was looking at her, and began retreating back. She circled around the house, cut across the front yard, and spilled onto the street. With her ears ringing, she started running to her house. She knew she'd hear it from her mother – and she knew Audrey would relish in it – but she didn't care. She was leaving the party. She ran past all the houses she knew by heart, the June sun beating down on her.

The rest of the neighborhood was quiet. Behind her, she could hear the chatter slowly fading as she ran further and further away. The road in front of her was devoid of life. No one in their front yards. Not even a lone person walking their dog.

She kept running, the sweat building underneath her tank top, making her shorts stick to her legs. She reached her house and deliberately kept going, her eyes glued to the road as she went one, two, three houses further, landing directly at Josh's home.

She stopped herself in the middle of the road, staring at the house like it would say something to her. She stared at the "For Sale" sign, the "SOLD" placard. She stared at the windows with their shades drawn, the empty driveway, the lawn that was in need of mowing.

She stared at the white fence, the round posts, the horizontal pieces, the spots where the posts went into the ground. She stared at the white paint and where there were cracks in it.

She stared at the front door, then back at the fence, then back at the realtor's sign. She pressed her lips together, feeling something surge up so violently that she thought she'd pass out. She clenched her fists and took in a deep breath and stared at the house until the sounds of an approaching vehicle brought her back.

Lily turned around to see a black car slowing down, moving to the other side of the road in order to avoid her. Lily smiled nervously and waved one hand as she retreated to the edge of the street. She kept her eyes on the ground as the car passed, looking up only when the car was already two houses away. She couldn't recognize the car's make or model or license plate and she felt a wave of relief.

After a few breaths, Lily turned around and made her way back to her house. She stopped at the front steps, staring at door with her hands on her hips – before sighing, hanging her head, and walking back to the barbecue.

The Ballerina's Guide to Boxing

CHAPTER TWELVE

"I didn't scare you away yet, huh?"

Rachel's voice was booming and jovial when Lily stepped into the gym that following Monday. It was barely past 9 and the day was already stiflingly hot. They had hit the part of the summer where there was no break in the heat – mornings were hot, afternoons were hot, evenings were hot, nights were hot. There was no dip, no respite, nothing. Lily was already covered in sweat, just from the walk over.

Lily didn't really know what to say, so she responded with: "I guess not."

Rachel was decked out in bright red compression shorts and a baggy tank top that showed off her black sports bra underneath. Lily couldn't help but wonder if that was the same sports bra from when she saw Rachel go to town on the heavy bag – back when Rachel wasn't Rachel but the elusive Girl in Black.

"If you're free, I'm getting a bit of a workout in, if you wanna join," said Rachel

"Sure thing," Lily responded.

"Are you sure?" Rachel said after a moment. "If you have other plans, don't feel like you have to."

"No, I want to join," Lily insisted.

"Well, then, awesome," said Rachel. "But don't ever feel like you have to do all the workouts. It's not like you're one of the guys about to compete, or anything."

"Guys about to compete?" Lily parroted back.

"Oh yeah, I mean, guys are competing all the time here," said Rachel. "There's actually a regional championship coming up, and we've got three guys in it. You should see this place on Saturday. The way these guys train, and the way Jimmy trains them... it's amazing. Seriously, if you ever get a free Saturday, you need to come down."

"I'm hoping to," said Lily, her voice suddenly distant. "Beats how I usually spend my Saturdays."

"Oh, and what's that?" Rachel asked.

Lily's breathing stopped short.

"Stupid family stuff," Lily said curtly, clearing her throat.

Inhale. Exhale.

"Oh, family obligations," Rachel said with a sigh. "I get it."

Lily nodded absently.

"Well – we can get a little bit of a warm-up in, if you'd like," said Rachel, gesturing over to the mat. "Then we can play around on the bags until class."

"Sure," said Lily, following Rachel over to the mat.

"We'll just get the joints moving, nothing nutty," said Rachel. "If you'd like, you can just follow my lead. But I can talk you through it, too."

"No, no, I'll be fine," Lily responded.

Rachel smiled.

"Figured as much. Not like we're doing anything advanced, but you've got high kinesthetic intelligence. Probably what made you a good dancer."

Lily shot her gaze down to the mat. She shrugged.

"Hey, I didn't mean to touch on anything sensitive. I mean it," said Rachel, with a tone that made Lily look back up. There was something nurturing about the way Rachel held herself at that very moment. A different side of Rachel was shining through. "Trust me, as a former dancer, I get it. I really do."

"You used to dance?" Lily asked.

"Yeah – and pretty seriously for a while, too. My parents weren't too thrilled about it. They were insane about my academics. I tried to do both once I hit college and... well, couldn't. So I dropped it, got my Master's in Social Work, picked up kickboxing at some point, and, well... here I am."

Rachel opened up her arms as if to demonstrate where she literally was. There was something so welcoming and so warm in how Rachel was talking that Lily could feel something inside of her jostling free.

"That's the exact opposite of my problem," said Lily.

"You don't have your Master's in Social Work?" Rachel said with a smirk.

Lily smirked back.

"Parents," she said. "Well, my mother…"

Rachel nodded knowingly.

"I mean… my dad, he's… I don't know," Lily continued. "I guess he's okay that I quit, or not… I don't know. Does that make any sense?" Lily paused and bit her lip. "I'm sorry, I'm babbling."

"You're not babbling, and it makes total sense," said Rachel.

Lily looked to the boxing ring and pressed her lips together.

"So, what do you do, then, if you don't dance?" Lily asked.

"Well, I'm putting my degree to use," Rachel responded. "I'm a social worker."

Lily turned and looked at Rachel.

"I know, right? You think social workers, and you think frumpy old ladies in unflattering dresses," said Rachel, meeting Lily's gaze. "But, to be fair, I'm just starting out. Give me a couple more years, and I'll be wearing one of those ugly purple dresses with a turtleneck underneath."

Lily snorted.

"I work with the foster system, which is exactly as light-hearted and fluffy as it sounds," said Rachel. "But… then there's this place. It keeps my head on straight."

"What do your parents think of… well, this?"

"Kickboxing?" said Rachel. "They don't know. It's never come up in conversation and, to be frank, I'm not going to give them that information freely."

Lily nodded, a rogue smile on her face.

"We can spend a lot of time trying to get our parents' approval," Rachel said with her maternal, nurturing voice. Did she use that voice with the foster kids? "At some point we realize that, while we can be thankful for what they gave us, it doesn't mean they can dictate our every move."

Rachel gestured over to the center of the mat. Lily followed, and started mirroring Rachel as she started doing toe touches, arm swings, and side bends.

It took Lily a moment, but it slowly dawned on her that Rachel was no where close to Lily's age. She wasn't the Girl in Black at all.

She was the Woman in Black.

"The dance world?" Rachel continued on, picking up a conversation Lily didn't realize was still going. "Don't get me wrong: that was my passion. But it was brutal. So I get it. I do."

Rachel started twisting, her arms to swinging side to side, her legs pivoting as she turned from right to left.

"And if you ever want to talk about it, any of it, I'm here. Whatever it is, I promise you I'll get it," Rachel added.

Lily stopped her own twisting, letting her arms drop by her sides. The only thing she could do was smile.

"Okay, well, enough of these warm ups," said Rachel, her tone changing effortlessly to the one Lily was more familiar with. "Let's play on the bags. You can borrow a set of my gloves if you'd like. Beats the smelly communal ones."

Lily continued to smile.

"Thanks."

Rachel walked over to her bag, pulled out one set of gloves, tucked them under her arm, and grabbed a second set.

"These are my sparring gloves," said Rachel, handing the second ones over. "They've got a little more padding, so they'll probably be great for someone just starting out."

"Thanks," Lily said again.

Rachel walked over to the bags as she put on her gloves. Lily placed one boxing glove on and velcroed it in place. She slipped the second one on and used her forearm to secure it at the wrist. She looked at Rachel, looked at the heavy bag, and looked back at Rachel.

"You ready?" asked Rachel.

"Sure," Lily said, sounding the exact opposite of sure.

"Like I said – just have fun. Intelligent fun, but – fun." Rachel gave a wry smile before turning to her bag.

As Rachel's first punch landed, Lily felt transported back – back when Rachel was the Woman in Black and Lily was her watching from the sidewalk. All at once Lily was reminded why she had felt so compelled to come back the next day – and the day after that, and the day after that. It took every ounce of effort to pry her eyes away from Rachel and return to her own bag.

Lily stood there, unsure what to do first. She decided on some practice drills. She practiced her jab. Practiced her straight. Worked on her pivot. Worked on her left hook. Worked on her right. Continued to focus on the pivot, the shift of her hips, the movement of her feet. She gave a few kicks – slow and methodical, one identical to the other – before going back to her practice punches. A few slow jabs. A few slow straights.

"Are you okay with me interrupting?" Lily heard Rachel's voice. Lily stopped what she was doing and turned.

"Of course, that's terrible of me to say. I'm interrupting by asking if it's okay to interrupt." Rachel wiped the sweat from her forehead with her arm. "I just wanted to say a few things: first, your form is on point. That being said, if you want to have fun – *have fun*. I mean, if you want to keep practicing like you're doing, go right ahead, but you don't have to."

Lily attempted to tuck a flyaway hair behind her ear, but found her glove clumsily grazing her temple instead.

"I mean, Jimmy would have my head if he heard me say this, but – especially if you're not competing – sometimes it's not about form. It's about allowing yourself to be in the moment. All the best fighters have that fluidity. It's not just about knowing where you put your left foot and right shoulder. It's about not being afraid to *move*. Does that make any sense?"

"Yeah, it does," Lily said, already recounting Rachel's movement at the bag. Fluid. Dance-like. Truly not afraid to move.

"Again, do what feels comfortable, but, if you're anything like me, it's going to feel good to just move how you want to move," Rachel said.

Lily turned to her bag. She started out just like before: a few jabs, a few straights. Only now she wasn't obsessing over the ball of her right foot, or the position of her elbow. Within a few punches, she threw in a front kick – drawing her knee into her chest and thrusting her heel into the bag with such force that the bag swung wildly away from her.

She looked over at Rachel, who was looking back at Lily with a beaming smile. Smiling back, Lily turned and started throwing punches. In the back of her mind, she could hear Leon's voice calling out numbers – one, one-two, one-two.

Something familiar and yet foreign took over. It was like Lily no longer had to think or process. She could feel herself getting lost in the movement, her body on a special type of autopilot. She stopped labeling the individual moves and just let everything flow. The bag started swinging more and more with each punch and kick, and Lily simply adapted, maneuvering around when it swung out towards her.

In that dance with her heavy bag, time itself seemed to take on a different form. It neither slowed down nor sped up nor stayed the same. In all her years on the dance floor, and now her time at the gym, she had never been able to describe that feeling. It was as if she entered a different dimension, one where she was suddenly in control of the laws of physics.

It wasn't until the bag swung too much, making the metal shake and clang, did she stop. Out of breath, she looked over to see Rachel just watching her. A few of the people coming in for kickboxing had been watching her, too.

"Wow," said Rachel, with a satisfied smile. "You're a natural."

Lily blushed, looked to the ground, and shrugged.

"Thanks."

CHAPTER THIRTEEN

Mornings were about being invisible.

Sometimes that meant pretending to be asleep until the house went quiet. Other times, it was about being as unassuming as possible, leaving her room only if she absolutely needed to, as everyone else got ready for their day.

And everyone else got ready for their day. Lily could tell what mood her mother was in based on what noises she made in the kitchen and in the upstairs hallway. On days she was feeling especially nasty, the floorboards transmitted the *thump* of her uncharacteristically heavy feet and the kitchen would echo clanks and bangs that Lily knew her mother never did by accident.

Occasionally, Lily's invisibility would fail her. She'd enter the hallway the same time her father was exiting the bathroom. Or she'd pass Audrey on her way back from her *own* trip to the bathroom. The situations would be met with awkward smiles and maybe a casual, "Mornin'," as if they were vague acquaintances, people you feel obligated to acknowledge after accidentally establishing eye contact.

But the moment would pass, and Lily could go back to being invisible.

That Tuesday morning, Lily scanned the upstairs area before stepping out into the hallway. She tip-toed down the hallway, eyeing the doors of her sister's and her parents' rooms. The upstairs was silent and still.

Lily placed her hand on the bathroom door, looking back at Audrey's room as she did. Her door – usually closed, just like everyone else's – was slightly ajar. Within the small column of space between the door and the doorframe, Lily could make out Audrey's bedspread: a royal blue comforter, unnervingly pragmatic and mature.

Did Lily think of herself as pragmatic and mature at 10? It was honestly hard to tell, now that she thought about it. Her instructors definitely treated her like an adult. Gone were the fun practices of her first dance studio – now she was on the fast track to professional dancing. What did her comforter look like at 10? A pattern of large, bright flowers, if she remembered correctly.

Morning light danced through the gap in the doorway. Lily was tempted to sneak across the hall and into her sister's room. She couldn't really remember the last time she was even in there.

And, with that realization, Lily felt a thousand pounds heavier, her feet sinking into the carpet, her shoulders drooping down. Was it because of the age difference? Was it because, by the time Audrey was born, Lily was already devoted to training – by the time Audrey could walk and talk, Lily was home less than her own parents?

It was a rabbit hole Lily couldn't stop falling into. *Why* was Audrey born when she was? What did that mean, to have a nearly 7-year difference between the first and the second kid? Was it planned? Was it not? The space in front of her suddenly felt unfamiliar and disorienting. There was an ache bubbling up in her chest, and she couldn't put her finger on exactly what it was for.

All it took was a distant floorboard creek for Lily to jolt back into attention, step into the bathroom, and quickly close the door behind her.

*

"So what's ya plans for Fourth a' July?"

Jimmy's voice echoed against the metal duct. Both of his arms had disappeared into the belly of it. His was neck straining, his eyes were squinting. Lily held the ladder steady.

"I don't know. Probably fireworks, or something," said Lily. It was tradition, for her family, to go to the nearby park and unroll a blanket along the hillside. A good portion of the town would be there. Nothing had been discussed within the family about it, but, then again, when did *anything* get discussed?

"Well, Fourth a' July, good time for fireworks," said Jimmy, his chin tilted at an uncomfortable angle.

Lily nodded, even though Jimmy clearly couldn't see her nod. Truth be told, she had kind of forgotten that it was almost July. But the Fourth of July *was* coming up – that Sunday, to be exact – which meant that the summer was already a third of the way over, if not more.

"I'll probably be doin' the same. Y'know, fireworks n' stuff." Jimmy paused and rattled something inside the duct. "Still gonna be busy. No rest here – got three separate boys fightin' in Gallagher, so it's crunch time."

"Gallagher?"

"Ah, haven't I told ya about that?" Jimmy said, his head now in the duct, his voice echoing off its walls. "Really awesome event. And I got some guys in it."

"I think Rachel mentioned something about that."

"Good! She ain't competin', sadly, but maybe next year. She's a real talent, too, y'know." Jimmy stepped down the ladder. "You're invited, if ya'd like to come."

"Maybe," Lily said, looking to the floor. "When is it?"

"August 6th. That's a Saturday, if ya didn't know."

Lily took a slow, deep breath. A boxing championship sounded way more enticing than anything her mother could've had planned for that weekend.

"I'll see if I'm free," Lily heard herself say – a weird, distant feeling bubbling up within her. "I'd really like to go."

"Well, we'd love to have ya." Jimmy dusted himself off. "New filter's finally in place, so let's see how long *that* lasts. Ya'd think everyone was smokin' cigars or somethin' with how often I gotta replace it. Let's get outta the basement before it dirties itself up again."

Jimmy tossed his tools into his toolbox before picking it up with a forceful yank.

On the first floor, Lily could see Leon and a client talking in the ring, as well as a small group of people on the mats doing warm ups. Included in the group was Freddy. His usual t-shirt and shorts had been replaced with snug leggings and a compression shirt.

"Well if it isn't the kickboxing legend herself," Freddy said, midstretch, as Lily came up from the basement.

Lily could feel her face burn red.

"How ya doin' there, guys?" Jimmy addressed the entire group.

Jimmy turned to Lily and added: "These are the jiu jitsu guys, if I haven't mentioned that yet. No official class, or nothin'. Just practice for those who already know what they're doin'."

"But newbies are always welcome, if you wanna join us," Freddy added.

Lily looked over at Freddy and felt an overwhelming desire to agree and join in.

She looked to the ground instead.

"Maybe," she replied.

"Actually, if I could borrow ya for a little bit upstairs, that'd be great," Jimmy said.

"Um, sure," Lily responded.

"Nothing big – just some work with the gym equipment. Then ya free to do what ya'd like," Jimmy offered.

"Sounds good to me."

"Alright, I'll leave ya guys to ya practice. Still good for boxin' tonight, right Freddy?"

"I'm actually working tonight," Freddy said, skewing his mouth to one side.

"Then bright and early Wednesday mornin'," Jimmy asserted. "Can't play around during camp."

"Of course, Coach. Wouldn't dream of missing it," Freddy responded.

"Alright, then." Jimmy nodded at Lily. "Let's get upstairs already."

Lily followed Jimmy up the stairs. They circled around two women who were stationed by the door, lifting dumbbells in front of the mirror.

"Again, if ya feel like I'm workin' ya too much, ya gotta tell me. All this is optional, okay?" Jimmy said before pointing to a leg press machine. "I just need to replace the cord on this here machine, so if ya can keep it steady for me, I'd greatly appreciate it."

"Sure thing," Lily replied.

"Now, lemme see…" Jimmy put down his toolbox. "It looks more complicated than it is, but it's actually quite simple. I just don't like this thing wobblin' on me or nothin'. So just hold it in place for me."

Lily stood by the machine, unsure how to hold it. She held onto the metallic posts, but found the machine stable and wobble-free.

"This shouldn't take too long, then ya free to do whatever ya'd like. Even that jiu jitsu practice stuff if ya want," said Jimmy. "Personally? I believe ya can get really hurt if ya haven't had formal trainin'. Too many kids watchin' stuff on the internet n' thinkin' they can just mimic it."

Lily nodded, watching Jimmy pull out a few socket wrenches and a cord.

"All those guys are good. Don't get me wrong. I mean, some of 'em only come here for the jiu jitsu stuff, so I don't know 'em that well, but... they're good." Jimmy positioned himself underneath the seat and started unscrewing a bolt. "And Freddy? He's good. He really is. He's even competin' in that championship. He's a pain to train, but the kid's got skill."

Lily made a noncommittal noise, her eyes glancing over at the two women, the edges of their muscles creating deep crevasses in their arms as they lifted and lowered their weights.

"Just... be careful with that one, okay?" Jimmy said, his voice dropping a few decibels. "I see that he's takin' a likin' to ya, and... yeah." Jimmy squinted his eyes at the cord in front of him before jostling it free. "He ain't a bad kid. Really ain't. But I don't think he really thinks things through, if that makes any sense. More balls than brains."

Jimmy paused, and took a huff.

"Sorry. That was crude." Jimmy ran the new cord up and under one of the pulleys.

"It's okay," Lily said. "I wasn't bothered."

"Well, okay, good, but, really, if it ever does, ya say it."

Jimmy went silent for a moment as he picked up another wrench. On the other end of the room, the two women were still in the middle of weight lifting. Their upper bodies were easily twice the size of Lily's: bulbous shoulders and defined arms, back muscles rippling along the edges of their tank tops. Both women's legs rivaled Lily's in definition and tone. A shimmer of sweat had formed over their skin, with little beads dancing their way towards the ground.

"Okay, that should do it. For now, at least." Jimmy stood up, placing his palm on the seat. After it shifted under his weight, Jimmy paused, grabbed the seat with both hands, and jostled it.

"And, while I'm here, I better tighten this as well," Jimmy sighed. "Always somethin'. But, I got this. Ya free to do what ya'd like. Holler if ya need anything, alright?"

"Will do," Lily said with a slight smile.

"And… just be careful, okay?"

"Will do, too," she replied. Lily turned. She went around the women and trotted down the stairs.

Back on the first floor, the jiu jitsu practice was well underway. Lily stood at the side of the boxing ring, watching Freddy and another guy grapple on the floor. It was a sight to watch, each man positioning themselves, arms strategically placed along the other's body, toes pressing into the ground. Lily looked at the match, the way the men rolled so closely together, and imagined herself doing that with Freddy. A feeling shot up Lily's spine, so intense that she drew a quick breath in response.

Lily kept watching until one of the other guys looked over at Lily. She could feel her throat closing up on her. She immediately stepped back and looked up at the ring, where Leon was in the middle of stretches and while the client – some middle-aged man Lily hadn't seen before – sat off to the side, unlacing his shoes.

"Can I hit the pads with you?" Lily croaked out, already climbing into the ring as if she were climbing to safety.

"Yeah, sure thing," Leon responded. "Perfect timing – just finished up with Eric over here." Leon picked up the padded gloves that lay by his feet. "Eric, you've met Lily before, haven't you?"

The man turned around and gave Lily a once-over.

"Can't say that I have."

"Well, Eric, this is Lily. Lily, Eric. He used to be a regular here, and now he's getting back into the swing of things."

"Eh, by some definition of the term," said the man.

"And Lily's our next kickboxing superstar," said Leon, motioning over at Lily with a smirk.

"Oh really?" Eric said, straightening his back.

Lily flushed and looked to the wall.

"I don't know about that…"

"Well, she *is* talented. I've witnessed it firsthand," said Leon. He paused for a moment, looked over at Lily, and cleared his throat: "But, still, anyway… let me get my gloves on and we can get a quick practice in. Good work as always, Eric."

"You're a terrible liar."

Leon laughed, shook his head, and slipped his hands into the pads. He gave the pads a quick *clap* and repositioned his legs.

"You remember what the numbers mean, right? One for jab, two for straight. Three for left hook, four for right. Five for left uppercut.

Six for right."

Lily nodded.

"And it's okay if you get them a little messed up. No harm, no foul. And definitely no worries." Leon clapped the pads together again. "You ready?"

"Sure," said Lily.

"Oh, wait!" said Leon smacking one of the pads against his temple. "Your gloves!"

Lily looked down at her hands, which had been trembling slightly the entire time.

"Maybe I could try... without gloves?"

"Bare knuckle? I mean... sure, I guess. Just, be careful. The impact can really do a number on your knuckles. Friction tears are no joke."

"I'll be careful."

"And go slow at first. It's a different jungle, fighting without gloves."

"Will do."

"Well, then." Leon repositioned himself. "One, two!"

Lily hesitated before a moment, before letting her left and right fists fly. The sound reminded her of the first half of a rim shot – *ba-dum, ching!* – and all that was missing was someone to play the cymbal portion.

"Good, good," said Leon. "One, two!"

Leon continued to sing out numbers, and Lily continued to respond. Leon was right – punches without any protection was a completely different beast. She could instantly feel it in her knuckles. But she continued on, feeling a little bit more powerful every time she connected with a pad and didn't wince or back away.

"I didn't mean to put you on the spot there," said Leon in between numbers.

Lily shrugged, punched the pads, and said: "Eh, it's okay."

"But, I mean it. I wasn't trying to exaggerate," Leon continued. He punctuated the sentence with a, "Three, four!" and waited for Lily to punch. "You have skill. That's something to be proud of."

Lily shrugged again, staring at the pads.

"That's what this all is, you know. Martial arts and fighting... teaching us to have pride in ourselves," Leon continued. He added a, "Four, five!" to the end of the sentence. "It's not just about getting good or competing. It's about realizing you've got what it takes inside you. That you got that power, and no one can take that away."

Lily tilted her head to one side and let out a *hmm*.

Leon let out a few more number sequences. One, two, three. Three, four. Three, Four. One, two, five, six. Five, six. Lily did her best to keep up.

"I don't mean to be preachy," said Leon after a few more hits. "I just... even if you don't want to be that kickboxing superstar, be proud of yourself. Don't shrug it off."

Lily stopped and looked up at Leon, connecting his line of vision with hers. She stood a little taller, smiled, and nodded.

"Thanks. I'll remember that."

*

That night was a family dinner night, and Lily approached it with her head held high.

"So, what did you do today?" her mother asked in her usual tone.

"Work," Lily replied, her own tone so newly defiant that her mother didn't have an immediate response. Her knuckles still bore a vibrant red from hitting the pads with Leon. "It was a good day. I really enjoyed it."

CHAPTER FOURTEEN

Audrey stood outside the bathroom door.

It gave Lily a start when she attempted to exit the bathroom. It was still early in the morning – Lily was far from fully awake, and nearly walking into her sister sent her heart racing.

"Took you long enough," Audrey scoffed.

"It's all yours now," Lily said in monotone. When Audrey wouldn't move over, Lily angled her shoulders and shuffled to the side. She walked down the hall and into her room. She turned to find Audrey now standing in her doorframe.

"What are you doing today?" Audrey asked.

Lily sighed and walked over to her bed, straightening out the sheets and the blankets. She couldn't remember the last time she made her bed – not for at least a month, at this point.

"Work," she said to her pillows.

"And then what?"

Lily fluffed one pillow, then the other.

"I don't know," Lily said. "Hang out at home, I guess."

"It's not fair that you get to do that," said Audrey. "Not fair that you get to do what you want and I'm stuck in summer camp all day."

"You like camp, though," Lily replied. She looked up to see her sister leaning against the doorframe, arms crossed.

"Still," Audrey pressed. "It's not fair."

"Maybe you'll get to do what you want when you're 16, too," Lily said, her tone so weirdly formal that it threw her off. Did other sisters interact like this?

"Well, I don't want to wait until I'm 16."

"That's not really my decision to make."

Audrey pushed herself off the doorframe.

"Still," Audrey mumbled, walking away. "Unfair."

Audrey went back down the hall and into the bathroom. As Audrey closed the bathroom door, so did Lily with her bedroom door. She waited in her room, absently tidying things up, waiting until the house went silent, before she changed her clothes and began walking to the gym.

*

"Today is about the bob n' weave," said Jimmy during the morning class. Inside the ring were the usual Wednesday morning suspects – there was Leon, there was Freddy, there were a few other guys whose faces had become familiar. A father and son duo rounded out the group.

As usual, she was the only girl in the boxing class. It was moments like this that made her wish Rachel was there. Where were the other girls during these classes? Lily had seen a handful here and there, but no one regular. Where were the women who had been lifting weights? Was it only on the evenings and weekends that the ratio became more equal?

Jimmy tied one end of the rope onto a corner of the boxing ring, walked across the ring, and tied the other end to another post, creating a diagonal line.

"Alright, one at a time, I want ya's to walk down this line, lead shoulder to the rope like this." Jimmy paused, shimmying his left elbow for emphasis. "And I want ya to – jab, straight – *bob* under." Jimmy paused again as he took a step and a low squat under the rope, shifting to the other side. "Weave, weave." Jimmy paused again to shift his torso from side to side. "And then start again. Jab, straight – *bob* – weave, weave, repeat." Jimmy repeated the movements a second time: a step forward for each punch, a bob under the rope, and two side to side weaves. "Got it?"

The group murmured in the affirmative.

"Well, then." Jimmy blew his whistle. "Let's get to it!"

Lily gravitated to the back of the line. She watched the rest of the group start to make their way down the rope. Jab, straight. Bob. Weave, weave. Freddy lead the pack, with Leon somewhere in the middle, and everyone spacing themselves out so they didn't accidentally punch the person in front of them.

"Stop bendin' at the torso! Squat down in ya bob!" Jimmy yelled out. "Ya bend like that in a fight and ya'll be bendin' right into the guy's punch!"

The line was already circling back to the beginning when Lily went. With a deep breath, she repeated what she saw. Jab, straight. Step, bob. Weave, weave.

"Exactly!" Jimmy called out. "Great bob there, Lily!"

Lily smirked, her shrug nonchalant as she repeated again. Step forward, jab. Step forward, straight. Pivot. Step. Bob. Squat under the rope. Don't bend at the waist. Weave, weave. Repeat.

Her pace started to pick up as she continued, to the point that she had to slow herself down, or else she'd punch the person in front of her. She was getting into a rhythm, and the rhythm was hypnotic.

"Damn," she heard from behind her. It was Freddy's voice, loud and clear. "Someone's been practicing."

"Yeah, that's what happens when ya practice!" Jimmy called. "Maybe I should have *her* in Gallagher!"

"Ah, c'mon. I'll be fine."

Lily finished and turned, watching Freddy repeat the drill. Jab, straight. Step, bob. Weave, weave. He looked up at her and winked. She smirked back, flushing wildly.

She was so caught up in the movements, the rhythms, the choreography of it all, that it wasn't until she got back in line that she realized that she didn't flinch at Jimmy's joke about competition. For once, the suggestion didn't make her want to shrink away – make herself small as possible, disappear until the moment had passed.

Jab, straight. Step, bob. Weave, weave. She could do this all day, if she had to. She was proud of her footwork, her rhythm, her movement. It was the most empowering dance she had ever been a part of.

Lily went through the drill a couple more times before Jimmy switched it up. Lily watched and repeated the new drill, committing to memory like so many other pieces of choreography. She could feel her legs ache, the sweat build, her lungs start to labor. She fell deeper and deeper into the rhythm, to the point that she had to remind herself to slow down, that she'd be in serious trouble if she accidentally landed a punch into the back of someone's head.

"Okay, okay, good job, guys. Good job," said Jimmy at the end of the drills. "I wantcha guys to keep at this, even at home. Get this in ya muscle memory. Ya gonna need that when ya brains tire out."

Lily took a few deep breaths, slowing down her rapid heartrate. She looked over at Freddy, who was letting out deep, loud huffs. When he caught her gaze, Freddy flashed a smile and a thumbs up. Lily shook her head, laughed, and looked back at Jimmy.

"We're partnering up, now. Keep it simple first – trap some jabs. Then we're takin' those drills and applyin' them. Got it? Get ya gloves, ya mouthpiece, and find a partner."

Lily slipped out of the boxing ring and found a pair of gym gloves in the bin underneath the ring. She didn't have any equipment – certainly no mouthpiece – but she was happy that she was doing partner work with the rest of the team. Gone were the introductory practices like her first few classes, kept to the sidelines while everyone else got to take the real class.

No, now she was part of the group. And it made her feel amazing.

"Howdy, partner!" Freddy's voice boomed from above her. Lily held a glove in each hand and looked up.

"Howdy," Lily said back.

"Feel like trapping some jabs with me?" Freddy asked with a grin.

Lily grinned back.

"Sure."

"Awesome," Freddy paused, putting in his black mouthpiece. "Just don't miss and jab me in the face. Looks like you've got some power now in those hands."

The last few sentences came out slurred, with Freddy's mouth curling around his mouthpiece. His lips jutted out, giving him a slightly apish look.

Lily walked back up into the ring, put on her gloves, and stood next to Freddy.

It was hard to concentrate on anything else. She was inches away from him. She could feel his body heat radiating. She could smell his sweat. Her face flushed again and her pulse quickened back up.

"Remember," said Jimmy, "if ya trappin' the jabs, keep ya hand away from ya face. Won't do ya no good to trap a jab and then hit yaself with ya own glove."

Pantomiming, Jimmy put his hand up in front of his face, his palm facing out, and snapped it back, hitting himself in the face with the back of his hand. The group laughed in response.

"And don't forget to move around a little. If ya wanna add in those weaves, add in the weaves. But keep it simple – just trappin' jabs right now. Perfect the basics. That's what I always say."

Jimmy blew his whistle.

"And go!"

"Alright, you wanna go first, and then we'll alternate?" Freddy asked.

"That works for me," said Lily.

Freddy assumed his stance and Lily assumed hers. She sent out her left fist, which connected with Freddy's right glove, catching the punch like it was a baseball going into a mitt.

"Not bad, not bad," said Freddy. "My turn."

Lily held her right hand out in anticipation, her elbow locked in place. She was amazed that she could catch his punch with her hand and still stand where she was.

"Alright, let's get to it," said Freddy.

They started taking turns, alternating effortlessly as one punched and the other caught. Freddy started to add in a little footwork, dancing from side to side, throwing in a weave here and there before throwing his jab. Lily followed suit, matching and mirroring his moves.

Just like in the drill exercise, Lily started slipping into a hypnotic state. Her gaze sharpened and the rest of her mind went blank. All that mattered was keeping up with the footwork, the punches, feeling like some type of awoken warrior.

Every punch got her a little deeper into that state – this wonderful, yet slightly cold and vicious state. For a moment, she even forgot who she was partnered with. Her punches shot out faster, her movements sleeker. All Lily could hear was the sound of the gloves making contact. All she could see was a potential opponent in front of her. And all she could feel was pure, clear, cold focus.

Lily threw in an extra weave to the side before throwing another jab with nasty intent. It wasn't until she watched her glove go straight into Freddy's face that Lily realized that she had missed.

"Christ!" Freddy yelped out, staggering back. And – like that – the spell was broken. Lily was back in the real world again, back in reality, and in front of her was the handsome redhead, throwing off a glove and placing his hand against the side of his face.

"What happened?" Jimmy shouted out. Everyone else stopped what they were doing and stared.

"I am so, so sorry," Lily stammered.

Freddy took off his other glove, took out his mouthpiece, shook his head, and ran his hands over his hair.

"Hey, wow, no – no worries," Freddy replied.

"Ya need ice for that?" Jimmy asked, walking closer and inspecting Freddy.

"Nah, nah, I'll be good." Freddy gently tapped around his right eye.

"Helps when ya have a thick skull, I guess," Jimmy jibed.

"Ha, guess so," said Freddy.

Jimmy turned to Lily.

"Ya got talent, but ya also gotta control that talent," Jimmy chided, his voice soft. "I've seen that look before in fighters – the one ya get when ya really into it. And that's awesome, unleashing that 'beast mode' as the kids call it or whatever. But ya still need to keep ya head on straight. Get too wrapped n' ya won't see that major hit comin'. S'all about balance, kiddo."

Lily nodded, her face burning with a new type of heat.

"And if ya'd actually focus on only boxing, ya'da've been able to weave away from that," Jimmy said, turning to Freddy. "It's those little slip-ups that'll cost ya the fight, Freddy. Ya already know that."

"Yeah, yeah, I know. Sorry, Coach." Freddy winked through his right eye. The wink turned into a semi-squint before he started touching the area around his eye again.

"Seriously, kid – ya need ice? It's why we got ice," Jimmy offered. "Ain't gonna do ya no favors to play tough guy if it means ya ain't gonna heal properly."

"I'm fine, Coach. I really am." Freddy shook his head again and then looked at Lily. "You punch good."

Lily grimaced.

"Thanks... I think?"

"Alright, well, let's get a little more practice in with those jabs," said Jimmy. He paused to wink at Lily. "And no knockin' out ya partner, guys."

The rest of the group went back to practice. Freddy took a few steps towards Lily, laughing at he did so.

"That was impressive," he said, a wicked grin creeping up on his face.

"I really am so sorry," Lily said, her face still burning. "I really didn't mean to..."

Freddy put his hand up.

"No, seriously, no apologies. That was on me." Freddy rubbed his chin. "I'm just thankful you got me where you did. That punch had enough force to break my nose."

"Oh man... really, I'm..." Lily began.

"Enough with the apologies. I'm gonna survive, I promise," said Freddy. "Like I said: it's impressive. You hit better than a lot of the guys here."

Lily snorted out a laugh.

"Sure."

"I'm not saying that just to say that. You punch, like... I don't even know how to describe it. Just, like, man – note, to self: never make you mad, like, ever."

"Wow," was all Lily could say.

"I really can't believe you don't have a background in martial arts," Freddy continued. "Like, just dance? Really?"

"Dance is very physical," Lily defended, shocking herself with her boldness. "Dancers are athletes, especially ballerinas."

"Really? Well, my world view is officially blown to pieces," said Freddy.

"I mean it," said Lily. "Those dancers? They train as much as fighters, if not more. And the ballerinas are doing it while balancing on their big toes."

"Well, touché," said Freddy. "I don't think I'll be making fun of ballerinas anytime soon."

Lily smirked in response, enjoying this new sensation. This empowerment. Like she could say whatever she wanted to say. Like she wasn't going to be bossed around and told how terrible she was. She was sure it would all change if she were actually competing but, for now, she loved it. Loved being flattered, loved feeling strong. It was something she wished she could feel all the time.

Freddy and Lily finished their practice together. They practiced their bobs and weaves together, sometimes forgetting whose turn was, resulting in both weaving at the same time as if it were some type of dance move. Lily laughed, deliberately staying away from that hypnotic state, lest she punch Freddy in the eye again. Instead, she focused on the piercing blue of Freddy's eyes, the way he'd smile around his mouthpiece, the effortless shifting of his body as he moved about the ring.

"Alright, good practice, good practice," said Jimmy. "Cool down, stretch out, rehydrate. Those who are stayin' for sparrin', I definitely want ya hydratin'. Find ya headpieces n' we'll meet back in the ring in 10."

"Good practice, indeed," Freddy said nudging Lily. She stood up a little straighter at the feel of his elbow against her arm.

"Thanks, and good practice to you, too," Lily said.

"I have to spar after this – Gallagher Regional Championship is coming up. I'm sure everyone's been yacking your ear off about it."

"A little," Lily replied. "That sounds—it sounds cool. And you're fighting in it?"

Freddy huffed.

"Yup," he said. "It'll be my third amateur fight. Hopefully after this I can get Jimmy on board for some MMA matches."

"Ah."

"You should consider competing as well," said Freddy. "I mean, you do whatever you want, but, you could probably knock some of those female fighters out with how you punch. Probably could knock some of the guys out, too."

Lily looked to the ground.

"We'll see."

"Well, either way, I'm impressed. Even if you did almost give me a black eye," said Freddy.

Lily laughed.

"Well, thanks, I think."

Lily followed Freddy out of the boxing ring. He hopped to the ground, and Lily hopped down after.

"What's on tap for you, now?" Freddy asked.

Lily scanned the gym.

"I don't know. Maybe use the weights, or something?" Lily responded. "I'm sure there's something that needs to get done, some cleaning or whatever. And then I head home."

"Never here for the evening classes, huh?"

Lily sighed.

"Yeah. It's… it's kind of a long story."

Freddy gave a knowing nod.

"Totally understand," said Freddy. "Barely here on evenings, myself. That's usually when I work. Don't get out of work until at least 10, and by then the gym is closed."

"What do you do?" Lily asked.

"Security. Really boring. Mostly just patrol halls and stuff," said

Freddy. "Someday I'll be making money as a fighter and won't need it, but, until then…"

Lily nodded. Freddy looked at her, smiled, then pressed his lips together.

"But, yeah… I gotta admit – kinda happy that you're not here in the evenings as well," Freddy continued. "Would hate if you were punching other guys in the eye, too."

Lily blushed fiercely and stayed silent. She stared at Freddy, her heart beating between her ears.

Freddy stared back for a moment, his eyes locked with Lily's, before breaking the gaze and clapping his hands.

"Alright, time to figure out where my water bottle went," said Freddy, squatting down underneath the ring.

Lily started undoing her boxing gloves, placing them in the bin that she found them in. She looked over at Freddy, who was contorting his mouth as he searched. His face looked so silly and serious at the same time, that Lily couldn't help but smile.

"Is that offer still good?" Lily found herself saying.

Freddy looked up and cocked an eyebrow.

"Offer?"

"To hang out," Lily said, holding onto the glove bin. "Outside of the gym. Is that offer still good?"

"Of course it is," said Freddy, standing up. "What are you doing this Friday?"

"Friday night?" Lily asked, swallowing down the lump in her throat.

"Yeah. I get out around 9 on Fridays, and can pick you up around that time, if that's not too late," said Freddy.

"Um, no, not too late at all," Lily said, clearing her throat, her mind now racing. "Just… is it possible to meet somewhere? Maybe you could pick me up at the gym?"

"Can't pick you up at home?"

"Yeah… um…" Lily took in a breath and looked away. "It's… it's kind of a long story as well."

Freddy gave another knowing nod.

"Say no more," he said with a warm smile. "If there's a place closer you'd rather I pick you up at, I can do that as well. Don't know how far the gym is for you."

Lily paused. It was at least a three mile walk to get there, if not more.

"Do you know the convenience store on Washington?" Lily asked after a moment.

"Yeah, of course," said Freddy.

"Maybe there, then?"

"That works for me," he said.

"Good, then…" Lily said, trailing off, pursing her lips together to suppress a smile.

"Good," said Freddy, matching her smile. "I'll see you then, if not even beforehand."

"I'll see you then… then," Lily said, punctuating her awkward sentence with a nervous laugh. Freddy followed suit and laughed along with her.

"I'll see you then, then… then," Freddy replied. "And, until then-then-then, I'll continue searching for my water bottle."

Lily smiled as Freddy disappeared around the boxing gym and into one of the bathrooms. She puttered around a little bit as the other boxers got ready to spar. She went upstairs for a moment, using one of the machines if only to get out some of her nervous energy. But she kept coming halfway down the stairs, outright sneaking down, as if she were a kid on Christmas day, scanning to see if Freddy were sparring next. When it was finally his turn – when she saw him put on his headgear and his mouthpiece and enter the ring – Lily stationed herself at the midway point of the stairs and watched.

The electronic *bing* of the timer went off and Freddy touched gloves with his opponent. She watched as they danced around the ring, trading shots with each other, sometimes backing away, sometimes going in. Freddy's punches were faster and harder than anything she had seen in practice. His posture hunched, his chin tucked down towards his shoulder. Even from the stairwell, Lily could see a fierceness, a determination in his eyes, like a different version of him had just taken over. She recognized the look – or at least recognized what her own look must've looked like.

He bobbed, he weaved, he danced. He threw out combinations that were so rapid that his arms blurred as he moved. And she watched, transfixed, unaware of anything else happening. She kept watching even as the timer dinged and the round ended. Freddy touched gloves with his opponent again before walking to the edge of the ring and sliding off his gloves. He reached behind the ropes to where his water bottle was and looked up. Directly up. Directly at

Lily.

Lily froze, staring back, unsure what to do next. Freddy smirked and gave a salute. Lily smirked and saluted back, staring at him with a newfound sense of comfort and bravery.

After a quick sip of water, Freddy put his gloves back on and shook his arms out. Within seconds, the timer *bing*ed again, and Freddy was off for round two.

*

By 9 p.m. that Friday, Audrey was in her room, her mother was in her bedroom, and her father was asleep on the couch in the living room. Lily was expecting this. A little after 9 p.m., she turned off the lights in her bedroom, tip-toed down the stairs, and snuck through the living room and into the kitchen. She slipped out the backdoor, closing it behind her so quietly she could barely hear it latch. With nothing but the half-moon to illuminate her, Lily started walking to the convenience store on Washington St.

To her surprise, Freddy was already waiting for her in the parking lot. She noticed the rolled down driver's window, Freddy's head against the backrest, and the subtle way he lit up when Lily came into view.

"Well, there you are," said Freddy with a grin. "I was worried you'd stood me up."

"Were you really?" Lily said, returning the grin.

"Nah, but it makes for good conversation." Freddy started his car and leaned out the window. "You ready, then?"

Lily's grin spread into a smile.

"Definitely."

CHAPTER FIFTEEN

Freddy rolled down the windows as he pulled out onto the street. The smell of the summer air was intoxicating. Lily took in a deep breath, the muted strobe of streetlights streaming past her.

"So, what are we doing tonight?" she said as much to the night as she did to Freddy.

"You mean you don't have an itinerary scheduled out?" Freddy asked, his old, blue sedan taking them further and further away from the heart of the town.

Lily turned and looked at Freddy.

"Why would you think I'd have that?" she asked.

Freddy gave a nonchalant shrug.

"I don't know. You kind of give off that Type A vibe." Freddy paused and turned slightly towards Lily. "To be fair, though, aside from your ability to potentially break bones with your fists, it's not like I really know that much about you."

Lily shrugged in response.

"Oh, and that," said Freddy. "That you barely respond verbally. Your shrugs are like their own language."

Lily stopped herself from shrugging again.

"I don't know. Just don't know what to say a lot of the time, I guess," said Lily. "Is it really that bad?"

"No, not at all," said Freddy, taking a left down a nondescript street. "I'm sure Jimmy would love it if I'd shut up from time to time. I guess it just makes you a bit of a mystery, then. The fighting ballerina genius. Where did she come from? How did she get here?

And why is my nose now bleeding?"

"What?"

"The last was a joke," said Freddy, shaking his head. "Like, I'm asking all these questions, and also I'm injured – and the joke is that you're the one who injured me."

Lily sat back.

"Ah."

"Don't worry – jokes get funnier when you have to explain them."

"Well, that's reassuring, I think." Lily ran a hand through her hair before letting her arm dangle outside her window. "But, really, are we going anywhere tonight?"

"Why do we have to have a set destination in place?" Freddy asked. "Don't you love to just drive around?"

Lily gave a small laugh.

"Wouldn't know," she said. "Don't have a car."

"That would explain the walking, then," said Freddy. "But – really – you don't drive?"

Lily paused. She was old enough for her driver's license, but she had never even so much as gotten her learner's permit. It certainly had never come up in conversation with her family.

"No… I guess I should, though. Get my license and all that."

"Oh yeah, definitely," said Freddy. "I mean, I can't imagine not being able to just… drive. It's therapy, y'know? The scenery is always changing, you can listen to music, you can do whatever. Your car becomes, like, your sanctuary." Freddy paused to give his dashboard a gentle pat. "This hunk of metal is more trouble than she's worth, but I'm very happy I have it."

"Would be nice to have a car," Lily said, suddenly feeling a thousand feet away from the words she was saying.

"Now, don't get me wrong – it's not like tonight will be completely off the cuff," Freddy continued. "I got a place in mind I want you to see. I'm just taking my time getting there."

"Ah."

"Aaaaah," Freddy parroted back. "Y'know, you're gonna have to teach me this language of yours. I bet it's the kind where you say something in one tone, and you're telling someone how great they are, but if you say the same word with a different tone, you're calling their mom fat, or something."

Lily burst into laughter.

"Do you think I just called your mom fat?"

"Of course not," said Freddy. "You were telling me how great I was. Obviously."

Lily shook her head, a smile plastered on her face. She leaned into the backrest, her eyes now on the night sky. She started following the half moon, watching it slowly slide through the air as the street lamps and rooftops zipped past.

"But – I will say – I do like that you're okay with silence," said Freddy after a moment. "Some people can't stand to be in their own heads for long, so they'll fill it with chatter. I like that you're not like that."

Lily paused and bit her lip.

"You know I wanted to shrug at that, just then, right?"

"I figured."

Lily smiled and closed her eyes. Freddy drove around for a little longer, weaving through streets before eventually getting onto the highway. He revved up his engine as he passed a few exits, the nearly empty highway laying out before them. He eventually took an exit and made his way to a park.

"Have you been here before?" Freddy asked as he pulled into a parking spot and shut off the engine.

Lily looked around.

"I don't know. I don't think so," she said – suddenly occurring to her with intense clarity how little she knew about the towns around her. She knew the routes to the various dance studios by heart, but she couldn't tell you about any of the neighboring towns, even their major landmarks.

"Well, I have. Quite a few times," Freddy said with a cocked eyebrow. "There's this gorgeous area, just a little way's in. Beautiful water fountain, all lit up, even at night." Freddy unbuckled his seat and opened his door. "You in?"

Lily smiled, unbuckled her seat, and opened her door.

"Of course I am."

Freddy opened one of the back passenger doors and pulled out a messenger bag. He slung the bag over his shoulder, shut the door, and lead the way.

"So, what are your hobbies?" Freddy said as they walked into the park.

"Come again?"

"Y'know, hobbies. Outside of punching people in the face, of course." Freddy veered left onto a gravel path. "Like, what else do you do."

Lily went silent, looking at the ground as she walked.

"That's... well, that's kind of it," Lily eventually said.

"Really?" Freddy responded. "Nothing else? No collecting stamps or... I don't know, hiding dead bodies?"

Lily snorted out a laugh.

"That's a joke, just FYI," Freddy cautioned.

"I figured."

"But – really? – nothing else?" Freddy pressed.

"Well, yeah," Lily said with a shrug. "I mean... I don't know. I guess I'm used to just doing one thing at a time. Dance was my entire life for so long... I don't really know how to do just, like, hobby-hobbies."

"Aaah," said Freddy with an exaggerated shrug.

"Now it's your turn, huh?" said Lily.

Freddy cocked his head with a grin and shrugged again.

"Oh, now you're just teasing," said Lily.

"N'uh-uh!" Freddy shook his head with a pout.

"Okay, I get it," Lily laughed. "I'll try to be better about actually talking."

Freddy shrugged coyly.

Lily gave Freddy a playful shove. Freddy dramatically staggered back and threw his arms up.

"Okay, okay! I'll stop!" he shouted. "I know what happens when you resort to violence!"

Lily watched him as they walked, taking him in. His shaggy, red hair. His vivid green eyes. His broad shoulders, his effortless gait. Everything about him left her in awe.

"Ah, here we are!" Freddy said as they got to the water's edge. In front of them was a small pond, the center accented with a water display. A steady stream shot directly up before cascading down in a perfect umbrella, followed by four smaller streams shooting out towards the sides. The light below it made the water glow.

"Beautiful, is it not?" Freddy said.

"It's beautiful," Lily replied.

Freddy unbuckled his messenger bag and took out a flannel blanket.

"I know it's totally cheesy, but, I figured hanging out by the water and under the stars would be fun." Freddy unfolded the blanket, whipped it in the air, and settled it down on a swatch of grass by a tree.

"I don't think it's cheesy at all," Lily said softly.

"Well, good, because I'd be really hurt if you did."

"Really?"

"Nah, but it sounds better if I say that."

Freddy placed his bag on one edge of the blanket and sat down. He patted the area next to him, motioning for Lily.

"I'm going to look so awkward on this blanket by myself," he said.

Lily smiled and sat down next to him, a solid foot or two of space between them. She reflexively pulled her knees up to her chest and looked up at the sky.

"It's so beautiful out tonight," she said, her chin on her knees.

"Tell me about it," Freddy replied.

"I just did," said Lily, looking over with a wry smile.

Freddy laughed in response. After a moment of silence, he reached over and pulled something out of his bag.

"You smoke?" Freddy asked.

"What?"

Freddy pulled out a glass pipe and wiggled it between his fingers.

"Weed?" Lily spat out.

"No, meth," said Freddy, opening a plastic container. He paused for a moment and stopped. "Yes, I mean weed. But, I mean, that's totally cool if you don't."

"No, no – I do." Lily swallowed down the lump in her throat, the sheer weight of the things that she had been missing out on crashing down on her shoulders. "I'm in."

"Well, awesome, then," Freddy replied as he prepared the pipe.

"Ladies first," he said when he was finished, reaching the pipe out. Lily gingerly took it in both hands, staring at Freddy as he reached into his bag again and pulled out a lighter. After a few clicks of the lighter, Freddy got the flame going. Lily placed the pipe to her lips, looking at Freddy as he brought the lighter closer.

"Ah, you haven't used a pipe before, haven't you?" he said after a moment.

"Yeah I have…" Lily said, pulling back slightly.

"Well, for one, you're a terrible liar," Freddy responded. "And, for two, your fingers are in the wrong spot." With his free hand, Freddy took Lily's other hand, placing the thumb on one side and the index finger on the other.

"So you just cover up the hole with your index finger," Freddy instructed. "When I say so, breathe in. That's gonna fill this part with smoke. When you're ready, let go of your index finger and keep inhaling."

Lily nodded daftly, thinking more about the feel of Freddy's hand on hers than anything else. She kept thinking about his touch as Freddy brought the flame over the pipe, as Lily watched it fill up with smoke, and as Lily removed her index finger and watched the smoke disappear.

"Hold if you can," Freddy instructed.

Lily held her breath for the count of four before slowly exhaling, a thick, gray cloud billowing out in front of her.

"Like a natural," Freddy said, gently taking the pipe into his own hands.

Lily sat back a little. Wasn't she supposed to start coughing? That's how it was in all the movies. The newcomer smokes for the first time and they hack and gag and look like an idiot. But none of that happened.

Freddy passed the pipe back to Lily as he exhaled, his smoke creating his own gentle cloud in front of him. Lily repeated what she did before. This time she deliberately kept her mouth shut as she exhaled, watching the smoke travel out of her nose like she was a dragon. For some reason, that idea was incredibly amusing.

"This stuff ain't crazy. Just gonna mellow you out," said Freddy after his second turn. He gave it to Lily one more time, holding the lighter for her as she held the pipe. "I wish people wouldn't put this in the same category as, y'know, that other stuff. Heroin and meth and... like, how in the world is this on the same level? It really isn't." Freddy paused and shook his head. "Apparently this stuff is already starting to set in. I'm starting to babble."

Lily smirked, leaned back, and propped herself up on her elbows. She didn't really know what to expect. Things were amusing, but she wasn't doubled over in laughter (like in the movies). She was acutely aware of the texture of the blanket, the sound of the water hitting the pond from the fountain, but that was basically it. He was right – this stuff wasn't crazy.

Freddy took another hit before putting everything away. Copying Lily, he leaned back and propped himself on his elbows.

"So, dancing girl – tell me what's up," he said.

"The sky is up," Lily replied.

"Oooh, you think you're clever."

"Mhmm," Lily responded, smirking.

"Fine, then. Let me reword it: tell me about yourself."

"Well…" Lily said, hanging her head back. "What do you want to know?"

"Everything, I think," Freddy said.

Lily lifted her head, looked over at Freddy, and – without her even realizing it – started to eye him up and down. Freddy looked her straight in the eyes and smiled.

"Like, family," Freddy added. "Tell me about your family. Like, tell me about your mom, or something."

Lily sighed and laid down on the blanket, her arms hugging her torso.

"What is there to say?" she said, as much to the stars as to anyone else. "She's a bitch."

Freddy let out a sudden laugh.

"Wow, girl, tell it like it is!" he said, punctuating his statement with a slightly more controlled laugh.

"Well, she is," Lily said, feeling the blanket, the edges of her shorts, where her tank top touched her skin. "She's… yeah, she's a bitch."

"Moms can be bitches."

"Someone should make a bumper sticker saying that."

"Million-dollar idea," Freddy said, tapping at his temple. "But, seriously, how is your mom a bitch?"

Lily sighed again.

"She's… I don't know. I think she hates me," Lily said, her eyes on the half moon. "Or maybe she hates herself and everything she wasn't able to do."

"That's deep," said Freddy.

"I don't know," Lily sighed again. "She's so concerned with image. She does things purely so other people can see her do it. Doesn't actually care about being a good mom or a good member of the community or anything. She just wants other people to think that she is. As a result, her family is just pawn in her scheme."

"Pawns are used in chess games. Not schemes."

"Oooh, you think *you're* clever," Lily parroted.

"Damn right, I am," Freddy said with a self-satisfied smirk. "But… damn, though. I'm sorry about your mom. Is your dad any better?"

Lily interlaced her hands behind her head and made a face.

"I guess?" Lily responded. She closed her eyes and, for a moment, she swore she was starting to float. "He's... it's not like I hate him, or anything? But... he's just a pawn, like everyone else in the family. He's either the most oblivious man in the history of mankind, or his spirit got crushed a long time ago."

"Maybe both," Freddy wagered. "That's usually what happens: some Type A, hyper-controlling individual finds some laid back, slightly passive individual and the first person just crushes the second one."

"And then there's my sister who..." Lily paused and rolled her eyes. "She's 10 and... y'know, it kind of sucks."

"She does?"

"No, no, not her..." Lily responded. "Well..."

Lily closed her eyes again and returned to the floating sensation.

"She's so much younger, and... she's kind of like a stranger," she said. "Like, I have cousins that I'm closer to – and I don't even see my cousins that much."

"Well, that's a good segue – you got aunts and uncles?"

"My dad has an older brother and an older sister," said Lily. "My mom's an only child."

"That makes so much sense," said Freddy, his voice carrying a fascinating gravity to it.

Lily paused and rubbed her eyes.

"Why are you interested in my family tree?" Lily asked.

"Because I am," said Freddy. "I mean it – you... you're fascinating. You're a mystery. You keep to yourself so much, but you obviously have so much going on. And you're, like, crazy talented, which tells me you're either a sleeper cell or you've got even *more* going on. And I want to know about it." Freddy paused and laughed again. "I'm babbling again, aren't I?"

Lily looked over at Freddy and smiled a slow, content smile.

"No, you're not," she replied.

Freddy looked at Lily and smiled back.

"Well, then," said Freddy. "That's good to know."

Lily stared at Freddy for another beat before hanging her head back, her eyes on the moon.

"What about you?" Lily asked. "Why don't *you* tell me about your mom?"

Freddy shrugged and laid fully down.

"Well, mine isn't a bitch," he replied. "Actually a pretty good person. I don't know… won't exactly be erecting statues in her name, but I also don't need to go to therapy to sort out the damage she's done."

"That's got to be nice," Lily mumbled, her left hand rubbing her right forearm.

"Eh, it's not like my house was some homemaker paradise," Freddy defended. "She raised me and my little brother by herself."

"And your dad?"

"Eh," said Freddy. "Not in the picture."

"Yikes."

"Why 'yikes' though?" asked Freddy, his eyes now on the moon as well. "I mean, yeah, I didn't have someone to teach me catch a baseball or whatever, but, hey, I turned out okay. Not everyone is going to fall to pieces just because their dad wasn't in their lives. It's such a stupid stereotype. Besides, there are so many people in this world who have their dads in their lives and probably would be better off if those dads weren't and…" Freddy paused. "I'm babbling again, aren't I?"

"It's okay," Lily said, turning back to Freddy.

"Getting high was a bad idea if I wanted to impress you," said Freddy. "I already talk too much, stone sober."

"You wanted to impress me?"

"Well, it totally blows my cover admitting that, but, yeah, I did." Freddy propped himself up on his elbows and leaned onto his side.

"That's… that's really nice," Lily said, a content smile slowly forming.

"Oof – 'really nice'?" Freddy dramatically collapsed back down, his face resting against his bicep. "You know how to make a guy feel good."

"I didn't mean it like that," said Lily, turning to her side as well. "I like that. I don't know if any guy has ever wanted to impress me before."

"I don't believe that for a second."

"Why would you say that?"

"Uh, because you're beautiful and talented and you can be wicked funny when you want to be?" Freddy said, cocking an eyebrow and contorting his face. "What, are all those boy ballerinas, like, gay or something? That's the only explanation I can think of."

"A lot of them are straight, believe it or not," said Lily. "And jerks."

"I'd be a jerk too if I had to wear a tutu all day," Freddy remarked.

Lily gently pushed Freddy's shoulder.

"You know it's not like that," she said.

Freddy nudged Lily's shoulder in response.

"I know it's not like that," he sing-songed back. "I make jokes sometimes. I don't know if you've noticed."

"I think I've noticed a time or two," Lily replied.

Freddy went silent, an open, boyish smile on his face, his eyes sparkling.

"Wow, you're pretty," he breathed out.

Lily pursed her lips and looked to the blankets.

"Thanks."

"No, I mean it. Like, wow…" Freddy paused for a slight chuckle. "If I'm not careful I'll start babbling about that as well. Because you are… wow."

Lily blushed, looking back up from the blanket, directly at Freddy. His dumbfounded grin. His wide eyes. How every line and edge about him looked so crisp and perfect in the muted moonlight.

"I think I know one way to keep me from babbling," Freddy said, leaning closer. Freddy slid his free hand around the back of Lily's neck, his thumb resting gently against her jaw. Lily instinctively leaned in, her eyes closed, the feel of pins and needles against her lips until Freddy's connected with hers. The soft press, the subtle movement in his lips, the gentle texture of his skin.

Freddy leaned back, his hand still by the side of Lily's neck, his thumb now caressing the side of her jaw.

"I really want to make out with you right now," said Freddy. "But I'm not going to. I just want to… enjoy that."

"That was… that was nice," Lily said, her voice slow and mellow.

"I'm going to take that as the compliment you meant it to be," said Freddy, his smile now sheepish and sleepy. He leaned forward, kissed Lily on the forehead, and laid back down. Instinctively, Lily snuggled in, her head on Freddy's chest, her arm around his torso, the fountain in her peripheral vision, the sound of the water hitting the pond dancing through her eardrums.

*

She spent Sunday night – the Fourth of July – at a different park. The one near her house, the one her entire neighborhood went to in order to see the fireworks. She sat on a completely different blanket, her back to her family, her eyes on the horizon. She stared at the sky and the waning moon, long before any of the fireworks started. She paid no attention to anything else – the families, the running kids, the occasional dog. The pleasantries and platitudes and meaningless conversations. All she did was stare at the moon, gently press her lips together, and smile.

CHAPTER SIXTEEN

"Excellent! I knew you'd be here."

Rachel's voice echoed through the gym as she entered. She had a bounce in her step that made her bag dance against her hip. Lily was mopping the mats, the feel of Freddy's mouth still on her lips, the sound of the water fountain still in her ears. For a split second, she mistook Rachel's voice for Freddy's, even though they sounded nothing alike.

"Hey," said Lily, righting the mop and holding it next to her.

"So I was thinking," said Rachel. "After you're done with this, we could get a run in before class today."

Lily looked to her mop handle, as if consulting it.

"Sure. Why not."

"Nothing strenuous, but it's good to keep the cardio up," said Rachel. "I'm going to get a little warm up in, in the meanwhile." Rachel paused and added: "Away from the mats, of course."

Lily smiled.

"Would be hard to, with them wet like this."

"Sure, but this is literally the only time I wouldn't have to worry about getting ringworm on them," said Rachel.

"People get ringworm on these?" Lily looked down at the mats, her mouth skewed.

"Well, it's not like dirty mats give you ringworm," Rachel explained. "But… if one guy on your team has it, and the mats don't get cleaned, then – boom – everyone does. Mats can be like a petri dish like that."

Lily let out guttural, "uhf".

"I should probably rethink working out on these ever again, then," she said.

"Ah, I wouldn't go that far," said Rachel, waving one hand to the side. "Mats just need to be cleaned regularly, is all. I'll be up there if you need me."

Rachel motioned to the empty boxing ring. The gym itself was quiet – perhaps due to the 4th of July celebrations the day before. Rachel hopped up onto the ring and slid between the ropes.

Lily kept her eyes on Rachel, so focused on Rachel that she accidentally mopped over her sneakers. Rachel started with some simple movements – leg lifts and arm circles and a little jumping in place – before shadowboxing. Rachel's fists and feet sliced through the air as she bobbed and leaned back, dancing to the side as if avoiding an invisible opponent. Each move was accented with hissed breath. Everything was fluid. There was an intensity in Rachel's eyes, as if she were ready to fight to the death. Lily realized that – possibly even more than the brilliant, beautiful, brutal choreography of Rachel's moves – it was the intense focus that captured Lily the most. Lily could only hope that this was the look that she had when she got lost in the movement, too.

Eventually Lily stopped mopping entirely, and instead leaned on its handle, her eyes locked on the ring.

She couldn't tell you how much time had passed, or how long Rachel had been shadowboxing. Rachel eventually slowed down, taking a break just long enough to look over and see Lily standing there, mop to one side.

"I take it you're done, then," said Rachel, shaking out her arms.

All Lily could do was nod.

"Good," said Rachel. "Let's go running."

*

They began to run down Main Street. Within a few blocks, the rustic downtown area gave way to the commercial district, with car lots and strip malls.

Lily kept her eyes on the streets, scanning for any familiar-looking cars. The chance of either of her parents driving down the road was small, but she was aware of how much of a sitting duck she was making herself. Surely, if either parent asked, she could say she had taken up running (with who? A coworker at the café?).

"So, how was your Fourth?" Rachel asked.

Lily turned to look at Rachel and nearly lost her step.

"Careful there!" Rachel gave a little space before returning to her usual jog. "Just making conversation. That's how you know you're not overexerting – you can still talk."

"Ah," Lily said. She focused on the road in front of her and added: "It was okay. Went to the park to watch the fireworks."

"Nice," said Rachel before motioning for them to turn right. "I did something similar, only with my parents, and they live about an hour north."

Lily hung a right, her body tilting to one side, her feet hitting the ground at an awkward angle.

"Well, cool," said Lily, already out of breath. Clearly, she was failing whatever overexertion test Rachel was doing.

"Yeah," said Rachel, whose breath was labored but steady. "They're not bad people. They just have ideas as to who I'm supposed to be, and they're not a fan of when I go against that."

Lily shook her head with such force that it threw off her balance for a moment.

"I know that feeling."

Lily could hear her heart in between her ears. She was winded. Apparently she really did need to take up running.

"I still dance, in case you were curious," Rachel added as she motioned for them to turn right again.

"Ah," was all Lily could say.

"It's actually how I come down from a hard day," Rachel continued. "Get out of my work clothes, turn on some music, and go to town. My neighbors probably hate me."

Lily let out a small laugh.

"It's all about making sure you do what you love, and on your own terms," said Rachel. "We all need something to help us get through the chaos in life, so we make sure it's something that feeds our soul."

All Lily could do was nod. Did Rachel take Lily on a run just so she could preach to her? Lily became all too aware of the age difference. She felt like a kid next to an adult, and she hated the feeling.

The two eventually looped back to the gym. Rachel slowed down her pace as she approached the building, taking in deep breaths and long strides as she walked through one of the gateways. She looked up at one of the clocks and smiled.

"And still plenty of time before class starts," she remarked. "Now, if the mats don't completely skeeve you out at this point, we can stretch over there. Plus, I have it on good authority that they were recently cleaned, and by someone who knows what they're doing."

Lily smirked as she followed Rachel to the mat. Rachel sat down and immediately touched her toes, her body folding almost perfectly in half. Lily followed suit, coming forward until her chest touched her shins and her hands wrapped behind her feet.

"Nice little parlor trick that us dancers can do," Rachel said, lifting her head up. "Probably would make for some awkward cocktail party discussions, but, still…"

Lily laughed.

"Or maybe it's a good way to get out of a conversation," Rachel continued. "Start putting your foot behind your head and suddenly people start walking away."

"Ha!" Lily shot out. In her mind, she was already imagining herself at all those barbecues and community functions – and doing a contortionist move to get out of talking to people. She could even see the horrified look on her mother's face.

Lily took in a breath and looked over at Rachel, who was now stretching her back in a sidebend.

"What got you into kickboxing?" Lily asked.

"Kickboxing?" said Rachel, easing herself back up. "I was finishing my first semester for my MSW and, well, the funny thing is, I was just looking for a way to get back into shape. I'd been out of dance for two and a half years and didn't really have anything to replace it. So I found this cardio kickboxing class. Figured – hey – it'll get me back in shape, and maybe I can get some of my stress out with punching and kicking."

Lily nodded and transitioned into her own sidebend.

"Now, don't get it twisted: cardio kickboxing is *not* kickboxing. It's like… you remember those aerobic videos, the ones that would have all the pretend punches and stuff? It was like that. And eventually I was like, 'I need to actually kickbox.' And so I found this place. Started taking classes – at the time, a Mr. Routhier was teaching them. And when Coach Routhier left, I took over. And the rest, as they say, is history."

"That's really cool," said Lily.

"It *is* cool. I never really thought I'd be here, but I'm glad I am." Rachel laid down and moved into a twist. "Hey... if you don't mind me asking – when did you leave ballet?"

Lily pursed her lips together. She closed her eyes, laid down on the mat as well, and let her knees fall to the side.

"In June," she said with her eyes closed.

"So, recently," Rachel responded. "What happened there, if you don't mind me asking?"

Lily threw an arm over her eyes, the crook of her elbow resting on the bridge of her nose.

"It's a long story."

"Hey, it's all good," said Rachel. "That type of stuff is always complicated." She paused, before adding: "Just for the record: I don't mind long stories."

Lily gave a noncommittal noise and let her knees fall to the opposite side. She stayed there in silence, taking in deep, slow breaths. She listened to the sound of her breathing, the crinkle of the mat, the thumping of her heart.

Inhale. Exhale.

"Well, hey there, stranger," Rachel's voice echoed in the background.

Lily opened her eyes. In the periphery of her vision, Leon was stepping through the door, his gym bag slung diagonally across his torso. Lily instinctively sat up.

"Good morning to you guys," said Leon as he walked through the gym. "Am I interrupting naptime?"

"Oh, ha, ha," said Rachel. "We actually just got back from a run – something you should be doing, too, might I add."

"Oh, I know, I know." Leon slung his gym bag onto the boxing ring. He leaned against the side of it, crossing his legs at the ankles.

"It's only going to get harder once school's in session," Rachel warned.

"Thanks, Mom. I appreciate the concern," said Leon. "And I will, I will."

"You're at least joining us for kickboxing, right?" Rachel asked.

"Of course I am," said Leon.

"Always good to hear."

Leon sighed and checked his watch.

"Well, I still got some time before noon. Jimmy's here, right?"

"Yeah," Lily piped in.

Leon met Lily's gaze for a beat before saying, "Good. Gotta talk with him about the Sunday schedule real quick. He's in his office, I imagine?"

"I think so," said Lily.

"Well, either way I'll check." Leon picked up his gym bag. "And then I'll be ready to kickbox."

"Oh, why start today?" Rachel jibed.

Leon grinned sheepishly.

"Like I said, anytime you want to spar..." Leon jibed back.

"...I'll be ready to wipe the floor with you," Rachel said with a smile.

"You'll be ready, you say?" Leon grinned.

"Yeah, yeah... go find Jimmy already," Rachel replied.

Leon laughed, turned, and went up the stairs. Rachel stood up and stretched her arms above her head.

"Stuff like that is why I love this gym," said Rachel. "Leon, he's like a little brother to me. I mean, Jimmy always likes to say we're family here, but... really, it's true."

Lily could only reply with a, "Hmm." She couldn't remember the last time any dance studio felt like that.

"That's something you learn, in life," said Rachel. "You don't get to choose the family you're born into. But, you do get to choose the family you belong to."

Lily turned to Rachel, repeating the last sentence in her head.

"I like that," said Lily.

She kept repeating it to herself as she went through the kickboxing class, as Rachel eventually left for work, as Leon worked with a client and Lily cleaned the windows.

You get to choose the family you belong to.

That day, more than any other day, it broke her heart to walk out of the gym. It wasn't particularly busy – in fact, it was probably the slowest Lily had ever seen it. But, still, it hurt to leave. It hurt to return back home and throw her gym clothes in her hamper. It hurt to wash away the day in the shower. She eventually went back down to the first floor and draped herself over the couch, still repeating what Rachel had said.

As usual, her father and Audrey were the first to arrive. Audrey barreled through the door, her free arm wrapped around some type of paper-machete figure. Without seeing Lily on the couch, Audrey immediately went up the stairs and into her room.

"Well, hey there, sweetheart," her father sing-songed as he walked through the door. "Fancy seeing you down here."

Lily sat up and shrugged.

"Felt like changing things up a bit."

Her father nodded, never really establishing eye contact.

"Always good, always good to change things up," said her father. After another moment, he added: "Did you have a good day?"

"It was good," said Lily. "Worked a little. Morning shift."

"Ah, not bad, not bad," her father said, again nodding to nothing in particular. He paused again and put his hands on his hips.

"Summer is just flying by, isn't it?" he remarked.

Lily grinned awkwardly.

"Sure is."

Another moment passed. Lily took in a steady breath. Her father looked at something in the distance.

"Well, your mother should be home soon," said her father. "I know I need to get out of this office wear. You know, sometimes I envy you kids, getting to wear what you want." He paused again, and then added: "Well, I'm sure you have a uniform of some nature at the coffee shop, but, still… either way, I'll be back."

"Okay," was all Lily could say. "Sounds good."

Her father turned and headed for the stairs. Lily laid back on the couch, her eyes on the ceiling, her hands behind her head. She listened to the floorboards creaking upstairs. No one came back downstairs. She closed her eyes and sighed.

Outside, a car was slowing down. Lily sat up and looked outside the window. Sure enough, it was her mother pulling into the driveway. Without thinking twice, Lily got off the couch, hurried up the stairs, and went into her room. The door to her bedroom was shut and Lily was on her bed as her mother came inside. She heard her mother patter around downstairs, opening and closing a few cabinet doors. Lily soon heard the door to her mother's office on the first floor close, meaning there would be no family dinner tonight.

She let herself lay like that for a little while longer, listening to the subtle noises of the house, before finding her headphones, turning on her music, and drowning the world out.

CHAPTER SEVENTEEN

Lily was in the basement when Freddy arrived.

She was loading the washer with towels when she heard footsteps against the wooden stairs.

"Well, there you are," he said, skipping the last step and hopping onto the floor. "You weren't upstairs anywhere, so I figured you were down here."

"Just starting the laundry before class starts," said Lily.

"Kinda like a Cinderella – if y'know, she was good at punching people," Freddy remarked, walking up to Lily. Freddy reached out and wrapped a hand around her waist. As he drew her in, he placed his other hand under her chin and his mouth cleanly over hers. Lily closed her eyes and wrapped her arms around him, doing her best to emulate his movements, to let her tongue move effortlessly alongside his.

Freddy paused, tilting his chin away and resting his forehead against hers. Lily opened her eyes slightly, letting her gaze fall softly to the floor.

"I've been wanting to do that for... for a while," said Freddy.

Lily let out a, "Hmm," in response.

Freddy kissed Lily on the forehead. He then took a step back, brought his hands to Lily's shoulders, and looked her in the eye.

"Are you okay, that I did that?" Freddy asked, his voice disarmingly neutral.

"Yeah, of course I am."

"And you had fun on Friday, right?" Freddy pressed.

Lily smiled and touched Freddy's hand.

"I had a lot of fun on Friday," she said.

"Well, good." Freddy moved his free hand as if he were dusting something off Lily's shoulder. "I was hoping you did. And, hey – speaking of Fridays – if you're free, my friend's having this thing on Friday."

"This Friday?"

"Yeah, this Friday," Freddy repeated. "You free?"

"Um, I can be… yeah," said Lily. "I mean…"

Freddy put one hand up.

"I get it," Freddy said. "I can meet you on Washington Street at, I don't know – 9ish again?"

"Nine-ish works for me," said Lily.

A sly grin crept onto Freddy's face.

"Awesome. It's a date then."

"A date?" Lily parroted.

Freddy cocked an eyebrow.

"Yeah, a date," said Freddy. "Don't tell me you're one of those 'we're just talking' type of chicks. That stuff is exhausting."

Lily shook her head.

"No, no, not at all," she said. "It's… it's a date."

"And you're taking class this morning, right?" said Freddy.

"Of course."

"Good, then I'll see you up there." Freddy paused, looking Lily up and down before stepping in again, embracing her for one last kiss. He let his lips linger for a moment, his hand playing lightly with Lily's ponytail.

Freddy turned, took a few steps, and turned back.

"By the way," he said with a smirk. "We probably won't be able to do that during class."

"I figured," Lily said with a smile.

Freddy lingered again, this time just staring at Lily and smiling, before turning back to the stairs.

It wasn't until Freddy was long gone and the laundry had been loaded and the wash had started that Lily realized that her cheeks were hurting. It wasn't until she brought a hand to her face that she realized that she had been smiling the whole time.

*

Lily stayed ringside after class finished, watching the fighters take turns sparring.

"Remember guys, this is practice. No goin' to war," Jimmy shouted as Freddy and another fighter put on their headgear. "Save that stuff for the actual fight. Train smart. Ya guys ready?"

Both guys nodded, their mouthpieces peaking underneath their upper lip.

Jimmy started the timer, the electronic "ding-*ding*" echoing. The two fighters high-fived each other before starting.

"Hands up, Ryan – hands up!" Jimmy shouted. With his eyes on the ring, Jimmy tilted his head to Lily and added: "Can't believe the fight's in less than a month." He paused, squinted his eyes, and darted his head from side to side. "I know these guys'll do great. Win or lose, they're gonna do the gym proud."

Lily let out laugh, her mouth curling up uneasily at one corner.

"What's so funny?" Jimmy asked, his eyes still following the fighters around the ring.

"Just… not used to that attitude, I guess," said Lily. "It's, uh… it's nicer. A lot nicer than I'm used to."

Jimmy gave a soft nod of his head, his eyes off the fight for a moment to look over at Lily.

"I get it. Some places – they're so competitive. What good does that do, though? Ya not always gonna be a winner. Ya can train like one, but ya never know." Jimmy took in a deep breath, ducking his head down as if he were the one avoiding the hit. "Light on ya feet, Freddy! This ain't Muay Thai. None of that flatfoot stuff!"

Lily watched alongside Jimmy. The more she learned about the moves, the more the boxing matches felt like a dance. The way the legs shifted, the way one opponent would act and the other would react. It was like watching choreography created in real time, still raw and unrefined. There was something so real about watching the moves play out – each man with his own dance, evolving in reaction to their opponent's.

And Freddy was smooth and agile. Truth to be told, Lily couldn't see the flatflootedness that Jimmy was calling out. All she saw was dodges and ducks, swift and precise punches, arm muscles rippling with each move.

With the second "ding-*ding*" of the buzzer, both guys stopped, high-fived each other again, and went to separate corners.

"Good round, guys, good round," said Jimmy. "Ryan, stop

droppin' ya hands or ya gonna get knocked out. Freddy, stay light on ya feet or ya gonna get knocked out. Get ya waters. Round two is startin' soon."

Freddy picked up his water bottle and squeezed a steady stream into his mouth. He let a little of it drip down his neck and chest. He shook his head as he placed the water bottle back behind the ropes. He looked over at Lily, grinned, and started shaking out his arms.

With the next "ding-*ding*" both men returned to the center.

"Much better, much better," said Jimmy. He took in a deep breath and leaned against his forearms. This time he turned to Lily and said: "So... how's everything over in ya neck of the woods?"

Lily had to fight to not just look at the ground and shrug.

"Um, it's okay."

"You've been gettin' along nicely here. Makin' some friends. That's always good to see."

Lily swallowed.

"Yeah."

"And ya don't feel like ya workin' too much, huh?"

"No, not at all," said Lily.

"Also good – but, again, ya tell me if that ever changes, okay?" said Jimmy, his eyes back on the ring.

"Will do."

Jimmy let out a deep huff.

"Light on ya feet there, Freddy!"

Jimmy shook his head, huffed again, and glanced over at Lily.

"I know I'm repeatin' myself, but – careful with that one," Jimmy said, his eyes on the fighters again. "I know he's had his eye out for ya since... well since ya startin' comin' here, basically. He's a good kid – he really is – but, he's, uh... he's still learnin'. Just, uh, be careful."

"I will," said Lily, acutely aware of the beat of her heart.

"And it comes from a good place, I hope ya know that. Me pesterin' ya n' whatnot," said Jimmy, skewing his mouth into a slanted line. "I get very... parental, if that makes any sense. If ya were my daughter, I wouldn't wantcha hangin' with types like him, if ya catch me."

Lily just nodded, her eyes now locked on Jimmy. He had stopped darting his head around and was now leaning against the ring with slumped shoulders.

"Your daughter's name is Melanie, right?" Lily asked after a moment.

Jimmy's skewed mouth morphed into a tired smile.

"Yeah, Mel's her name. A bit older than ya," Jimmy said, his eyes now on somewhere beyond the ring. "And I bet she's gotten involved with a few Freddy types herself. And I'm probably to blame for some of that."

Lily watched Jimmy's posture get a little more slouched. He rubbed his mouth and shook his head.

"Yeah, funny how that works, kiddo," Jimmy said. "That's one thing life will teach ya – and usually not until later in life. But ya learn one important thing: everyone's got good intentions. Everyone wants to be the good guy. No one sets out to be the villain. But life ain't about ya intentions. The wrong circumstances, the wrong anything... one mistake, one bad, impulsive move... and that's it. Ya good intentions don't mean nothing no more."

Jimmy took in a deep breath and huffed, shaking his head one more time.

"Hands up, Ryan!" Jimmy called out. "I ain't tellin' ya that every time! Keep ya guard up!"

Within seconds, the buzzer went off again, and both men stopped fighting.

CHAPTER EIGHTEEN

With her eye on Friday night, life became a frantic series of classes, cleaning, and practicing – all punctuated by Freddy's appearances, his jokes, his smile, the way he'd get Lily alone so he could kiss her. How quickly everything else faded into the background. And in the back of her mind, as she went about the gym and walked home and returned back the next day, she kept asking herself, "Is this what falling in love feels like?"

It wasn't like she had much to reference. A few crushes at school, a few at the studios. All with boys who never gave her the time of day. The closest she came to any of that was when she was 14, when one of the lead male dancers got wind that she liked him. He responded by coming up to her, grabbing her face, planting a wet, forceful kiss on her mouth, and walking away, ignoring her completely after that. It was a complicated, humiliating, heartbreaking situation – and Lily's first kiss, to boot. She had to carry that with her, through rehearsals and training, until she finally left that studio, until Freddy's lips met hers.

The rest of the week went by in a haze. She could even feel it at home – as she suffered through another family dinner, as she listened for footsteps, closing doors, the inevitable silence of the house every morning. She felt it the most on Friday afternoon, as she lay on top of her bed and looked at her ceiling, waiting for the moment to sneak out.

It was a haze that followed her as she tip-toed into the kitchen and out the door, her shoes and an entire outfit waiting for her on the other side. She had hidden a pair of jeans and a black, flowy top – something fit for a party, right? Not exactly like she would know, but it was her best guess.

She thought of nothing but Freddy's car as she changed in the dark, tucking her pajamas in the same spot that she had hidden her clothes. With one final look at her house, she tip-toed out of the backyard.

A haze. It described the feel of the night air, the street lights, the roads in front of her. Everything was a delirious, fevered fog.

Through the blur, Freddy's baby blue sedan came into view, a streetlamp casting its light directly on it. She crossed the street and cut through the parking lot. Freddy rolled down his window as she approached.

"Well... wow," he said, leaning his forearm out of the car. "This is... a different look on you."

Lily wrapped an arm around her waist. She smiled and shrugged her shoulders.

"Oh, don't do that... it's a good thing," said Freddy. "A really good thing. I... I don't think I've ever seen you with your hair down before."

Lily instinctively brought a hand to her hair, following a lock of it all the way down to its ends. With years and years of ponytails and buns, Lily sometimes forgot how long her hair had become.

For a split second, she imagined what she must look like to Freddy. She saw herself through his eyes. Her, hugging herself slightly, her wavy hair rolling over her shoulders. For a moment, Lily felt beautiful – beautiful in a way that she hadn't experienced before. This wasn't catching herself in the mirror at a good angle or realizing how well a photo came out. This was a different feeling. It was feeling the beauty that someone else saw in you. Genuinely, truly saw in you. Lily removed the hand around her waist and placed both hands on her hips.

"So, should you get into the car, or should you keep standing there, looking amazing?"

Lily smirked and tossed her hair over her shoulder.

"My legs are getting tired," she ribbed. "Let's go."

The night sky was alive with hot air, with bright, twinkling stars, with a constantly changing row of treetops. Lily rolled down her window, her elbow on the edge, her hand dancing through the wind.

"Got out of the house all right?" Freddy asked, looking over at

Lily.

"Yeah," said Lily, her eyes on the road. "No real problems. I mean, everyone kind of does their own thing at night, so it's not like anyone noticed."

"Ah. Got it."

Eventually they were on the highway, the world flying, the wind hitting her hand, whipping through her hair.

"Are you okay with a silent car ride?" Freddy asked. "I mean, I don't want it to be awkward or anything."

"I don't mind," Lily said – and she meant it. There was a serenity about everything at that moment.

"I really do like that about you," said Freddy. "Being comfortable with silence. I like that."

Lily smiled, gazing at the passing underside of a highway overpass. Something brushed up against her left hand. She looked down to see Freddy's hand snaking around hers, his fingers sliding over her palm and weaving through her fingers. She stared at their hands together, the feel of his hand on hers, and smiled. She closed her fingers around Freddy's hand before closing her eyes, a smile burning her cheeks red.

Freddy got off the highway a few exits later and made his way through residential streets. The roads gradually became quieter. The houses became more spread out. As the road curved to the right, Freddy slowed down and pulled in on the left, down a long gravel driveway to a gray house surrounded by forest.

"Well, here we are," said Freddy, letting go of Lily's hand and reaching for his door. Lily opened hers and stepped out into the night, the rushing highway wind now replaced with hot, humid, stagnant air.

The house was relatively quiet as they approached. The sounds of people talking and laughing could be heard from the driveway, but there was something so unassuming about it all. She expected loud, booming music. She almost said something to that effect, complete with *that's how it is in the movies*, before immediately keeping that thought to herself. How foolish she would've sounded. How naïve she would've looked. Instead, she kept walking, listening to the crunch of the gravel walkway, the crickets somewhere in the distance.

"Well, look who could make it!"

A man with short, black hair opened the front door. With a wide smile, Freddy embraced him emphatically, patting him on the back.

"Of course I was going to make it!" Freddy replied with similar enthusiasm. Freddy turned to Lily, adding: "Lily, this is Mario. This is his house and, subsequently, his party as well."

He then turned to Mario and said: "And, Mario, this is my friend, Lily."

Lily stood there, her breath suddenly locked up. She repeated what Freddy had said to herself. *Friend.*

"It's nice to meet you, Lily," said Mario.

"And likewise," she replied.

"So, help yourself. Everything's in the kitchen, beer pong's going strong, and uh… yeah. Enjoy yourself." Mario gave them a cheeky grin before breaking off and returning to the living room.

Freddy took a step closer to Lily, his hand gesturing out towards the kitchen.

"Shall we?"

"Sure."

Lily scanned the area as they walked down the hall to the kitchen. There was a group of six in the living room, sitting around, cups and bottles in hand. There was another group of four in the dining room, tossing ping pong balls into red cups. Up ahead, there were a couple people in the kitchen who were making their way outside. Everything felt relatively subdued. It was disappointing in some ways. This was her first party – was every party like this?

Lily followed Freddy into the kitchen. Freddy opened the fridge and pulled out two cans.

"Want one?" Freddy said, holding the beer up to Lily.

Lily zeroed in on the can, expecting to say something – anything – other than what she ended up saying. A, "yes, thanks," or even a, "no, I'm good." Maybe even a, "I don't drink," but instead, with her eyes locked on the can, she blurted out:

"My friend died."

Freddy lowered his hand.

"Oh."

Lily shook her head and cupped the back of her neck.

"I meant to say, my friend… she died in a drunk driving accident," she said. "I guess… I guess I was trying to say… I don't drink?"

"Ah." Freddy reopened the fridge and placed both cans back. "I get it. I really do. Alcohol, it's… well, honestly it's just as bad as the hard stuff, if you're not careful. Too many people ruin their lives with it." Freddy closed the door and stepped closer to Lily. "I'm really sorry about your friend."

Lily fought the urge to shrug, and found her eyes welling up with tears instead. She closed her eyes and shook her head again.

Inhale. Exhale.

"It happens," was all she could say.

Lily could hear Freddy's deep breathing. After a few breaths, Lily could feel Freddy's hands on her shoulders and his lips on her forehead. He stayed in that position, the kiss lingering on her skin, before he stepped back. She slowly opened her eyes, looking at Freddy standing in front of her.

"Feel like seeing what's going on in the other room?" he finally said.

"Sure."

Lily followed Freddy out of the kitchen, back down the hall, and into the living room.

"So, how's my favorite Rent-A-Cop?" greeted a guy in the corner.

"It's security, you jackass, and it's fine." Freddy took a few more steps into the living room. "It's a job and I can pay my bills. Can't say the same for you, so…"

A chorus of, "Oooooh," wafted through the room. The guy in the corner laughed and tipped his bottle in Freddy's direction.

"Touché, buddy. Touché."

"And on *that* note: everyone, this is Lily. Lily, this is everyone. They all have names, but they don't matter because they all suck."

"Yeah, yeah, like you're any better," said a girl on the couch. "I'm Sheila, by the way."

"It's nice meeting you," said Lily, hugging herself at her waist.

"Lily, how old are you?" the guy in the corner piped in.

"Eighteen," Lily fired out before she could look back over at him.

"Wow, Freddy, buddy… robbing the cradle a bit, are we?" the guy replied, a chorus of subtle laughs filling the room.

"You act like I'm 30 or something," Freddy replied.

"Hey, legal in all 50 states!" Mario sang out, and the group laughed again.

"Okay, guys, enough giving Freddy's date the fifth degree," Sheila sing-songed out, her voice low and deliberate. "We're not on one of those 'catching a predator' type shows."

"Hey, he started it," said the guy in the corner.

"All bets were off once you called me Rent-A-Cop," said Freddy.

"Hey, hey, hey – it's all in good fun." The guy put his hands up. "Besides, c'mon – you're totally a Rent-A-Cop."

"Rent-A-Cops are for malls, and I don't have one of those scooter things." Freddy sat down on the piano bench behind them and motioned for Lily to follow. "And – really – does this look like the body of a Rent-A-Cop? Please."

"You're the premium upgrade version. Rent-A-Cop Plus," Mario offered.

Freddy turned to Lily with a sly smile on his face.

"See? Told you everyone sucked." Freddy turned to the group and said: "But, okay, seriously, how's things been with you guys?"

Lily sat back. She found herself drifting away from the conversation, replaying moments in her mind. Freddy calling her a friend. Sheila calling her Freddy's date. The guy in the corner pointing out how young Lily was – or at least how young he *thought* Lily was. What would they think if they knew her actual age?

And how old was Freddy? It wasn't really something that she thought about until now. He had said that he was a year ahead of Josh, and Josh had been a senior in college. That made Freddy at least 22. Was that somehow better than 30?

"So, you don't talk much, do you?" said a voice, and the whole room went silent.

Lily shot her eyes over to a guy standing by the wall.

"Excuse me?"

"Not much of a talker, I take it," he continued.

"She's in a room filled with people she's never met," Sheila intercepted. "I'd be silent, too."

Lily took a deep breath.

"I guess I don't have anything to say," she said.

"Nah, I call BS on that," the guy pressed. "Silent people are always thinking." He paused to tap at his temple. "They got a lot of stuff that *could* be said, but they don't say it."

Lily looked to the ground and shrugged.

"I think it's cool," said Freddy. "I was actually just telling her that. Too many people have to fill up every second with idle chatter. I think it takes character to be okay with silence."

"So... that means what we're doing right now is idle chatter?" Mario asked.

"What we're doing is awesome banter – it's, y'know, those *other* people." Freddy smirked.

"Awesome banter like, 'Who wants to get a beruit game on?'" said another girl.

"You mean beer pong?" said Mario.

"No, I mean beruit. That's what it's called."

"I don't know a single person outside of, well, you, who calls it that," said Mario.

"Well, then everyone you know is wrong," the girl jibed back with a sardonic smile.

The conversation quickly shifted to the proper name for a drinking game, which eventually shifted to something else. Lily observed the room, watching the body language, the facial expressions, the way people slumped back or slouched forward. What was there to say, anyway? She couldn't exactly give her opinions on drinking games… or on anything that the people were talking about.

"Feel like getting some fresh air?" Freddy leaned over and whispered in her ear. The feel of his breath on her neck sent goosebumps across her skin.

"Yeah, let's do that," she whispered back.

Silently, both stood up and started walking out.

"Ooooh, there goes the lovebirds!" shouted Mario.

"We'll be back," Freddy said over his shoulder.

"Yeah, in about 7 minutes!"

Freddy shot a middle finger up as they walked out.

Once again, Lily followed Freddy through the hallway and into the kitchen.

"Well, speak of the devil – how long have you been here?"

Lily looked up to see a guy with a large, brown beard pull Freddy in for a hug.

"A little bit! Where the hell have you been?" said Freddy.

"Around, around," said the guy. "How's things?"

"Things are going well." Freddy pulled away from the guy and placed a hand on Lily's back. "And this is… Lily."

"Well, pleasure to meet you." The guy gave a bow. "Or, as they say in Spanish, *in-con-timina de cona-see-la*. Yeah, that ain't right. Sorry, I'm drunk."

"Lily, this is Greg," said Freddy.

"Yes, I'm Greg," he said, with a sudden air of nobility. "*Estoy Greg*. And, also, I'm drunk. Very drunk, and I'm sorry. *Estoy* sorry."

"Nothing to be sorry about, big guy," said Freddy. "But, if you'd excuse me, we need some fresh air."

"Ah, say no more, *moan ah-mi*." Greg gave another dramatic bow, one of his hands circling the air.

"Yeah, buddy, you're drunk," said Freddy.

"Told ya."

Freddy held the door open for Lily as they stepped out into the hot, humid night.

"Sorry for my friends," said Freddy. "They... they can be a lot, sometimes."

"I don't mind."

"Well, that's good, then, that you don't mind." Freddy took a few steps down the walkway. "They really mean well. I guess... well, I guess without booze you realize how lame parties can be, huh?"

Lily simply nodded.

"Hey, there's this really pretty tree over that way. Do you want to, well, go over that way?" Freddy asked.

"Sure."

"That seems to be the word of the night with you," Freddy noted.

"Is that a bad thing?"

"Well, no, not really."

"Well, then," Lily replied with a knowing smile. "Sure."

Freddy smiled back and cut across the lawn to where a gigantic maple tree stood, a stone's throw away from what felt like the beginning of a forest. He gestured for Lily to sit, before sitting down next to her. Lily hugged her knees to her chest and looked up through the branches.

"You sure have a thing for sitting under trees," she said.

"There are worse things," Freddy replied. "Besides, I like nature. Just, being outside. It's calming. Life can be a lot, and we need to get out, reconnect. Y'know, find a nice tree and sit by it."

"I get it," said Lily.

"I've known Mario since we were kids," Freddy continued. "I used to climb this tree all the time." Freddy took a breath. "I don't know, just something about it."

Lily just nodded.

Freddy let out a sigh, and now it was his turn to hug his knees into his chest. He crossed his arms and looked out into the distance.

"You're having fun tonight, right?" Freddy asked.

"Sure."

"Oh boy, that's not a good 'sure'. I know that much."

"No, it's not like that. It's…" Lily trailed off. "I'm happy to be hanging out. It's… I guess it's just a little different than what I was expecting. But… yeah, I'm happy to be here. I really am."

"Yeah, I get it," said Freddy. "I guess we're all a bit boring."

"No, it's not that," said Lily. "Parties might not be my thing, or something."

"No, I get it. I really do." Freddy took a moment, looking off, his eyes trailing the treetops. A silence fell between them, accented by the crickets and the muffled sounds coming from inside.

"I'm really sorry about your friend," Freddy said after a while.

Lily hugged her knees tighter. When was the last time that she had thought about Evelyn? *Really* thought about her? As her eyes welled up, a little voice bubbled up with it, silently asking her: *have you even cried about Evelyn yet?*

"Were you guys close?" Freddy asked.

Lily took in a slow breath. No tears in front of Freddy. No tears in front of anyone.

Inhale. Exhale.

"She was a fellow dancer. I had known her since… since middle school, I think."

"Oh, wow. I'm so sorry."

"And I mean… we weren't like best friends, or anything. But we trained together, and, y'know, there's a closeness there."

"You said it was a drunk driver… what happened?" Freddy asked. "And, if I'm intruding, I totally get it."

"No, it's okay, it's…" Lily looked up. She started tracing the branches, the leaves, with her eyes. "The driver of the car that she was in was drunk. Everyone in the car was drunk. She wasn't wearing a seat belt and… and she didn't make it."

"God, that's terrible," Freddy murmured.

"It is. It really is." Lily let her eyes drift to the stars, the moon. "I mean, she died right before going off to college. She had worked *that* hard and trained *that* hard and then… that's it. Gone."

Freddy said nothing, watching Lily with his chin on his forearms.

"I mean, it's a good thing she actually tried to enjoy life and not just prepare for it, because… I mean, that *was* her life. Any preparation would've meant nothing. It all got cut short. I just don't get it. I just don't understand why."

"Life is kind of cruel like that," said Freddy after a moment. "You lose people and you don't know why and, it's like… you swear if someone tries to tell you that it all happens for a reason, you're going to clobber them."

"And that's the thing. If it can all be taken away from us like that, why even bother?"

"Bother with what?"

Lily sighed and shook her head.

"I don't know. Bother with being bothered, I guess? Why work so hard for the future, when you don't even know what the future will bring. Especially if you're not happy doing it."

"Well, that, I agree with. Life is too short. You can't always be destroying yourself *today* because maybe there'll be payoff *tomorrow*." Freddy readjusted himself, stretching out his legs. "I mean, yeah, you have to put work into things that matter, but – there has to be a line. All these people – sacrificing today for what they think will be a payoff tomorrow – and all that happens is that they live for the future, and never really *live*, and waste their lives preparing for something."

"Life gets really scary, then," said Lily.

"It does, but… I don't know." Freddy paused. "Apparently I don't even need to smoke to babble." Freddy turned to Lily, his shoulder against the trunk of the tree. "It *should* be scary. We should be constantly scared that we're wasting our lives. Otherwise we'll do exactly that. We'll get stuck and be complacent and never really get *out there*. Life should scare the pants off of us."

"But you look at all the time you've wasted living someone else's life… playing by everyone else's rules… and it just… it sucks."

"But you can't do that to yourself – then you're wasting time wishing you hadn't wasted time. It's an endless cycle." Freddy stopped and sighed. "I feel like I'm preaching there. Sorry."

"Don't be," said Lily. "I like what you have to say."

"Well, good, because apparently I say a lot." Freddy shook his head. He sighed again and smirked, adding: "I take you to a party only to get philosophical about life."

"You mean you don't do this at every party?"

"Well, sometimes people *think* they're talking about deep life stuff at parties, but they're usually just being babbling drunks." Freddy interlaced his hands behind his head and looked up at the branches. "I really am sorry, though. It sucks and I'm sorry."

Lily sighed, the echoes of Evelyn's funeral, the night she saw the crash on the news, the day after when she found out it was Evelyn in that car – the noise of it all amplifying. She did what she could to push it to the back of her mind again.

"It is what it is."

"You know, I like that I can talk with you like this. Like, about life, and what have you," said Freddy. "A lot of people… they're not like that. They just do what they're told, day in, day out, and never really question it. Certainly never talk about it. I like that you're not like that."

Lily took another deep breath and rested her chin against her knees.

"Well, thanks."

"This probably makes me a complete psycho, but I've been wanting to kiss you, like, all night long, and even talking about death hasn't stopped that."

Lily's face flushed. She turned and looked at Freddy, her eyes heavy and warm. He had on his usual, devilish smirk. For a moment, she just stared at his face, comparing his sly persona with the one that slipped out from time to time. The moments when the twinkle in his eye was replaced with this gentle vulnerability. His cocksure persona was just that – a persona. A mask. But who was *she* but someone with a whole assortment of masks – masks she wore to the outside world, to her family… really, to herself, if she was being honest.

"It doesn't make you a psycho," Lily replied, instinctively leaning in. She placed a hand on his chest and he placed a hand under her chin. She felt the warmth of his mouth, his tongue, his body close hers. She felt his other hand rest on her thigh, before moving up and underneath her shirt, underneath her bra.

It was all she could do to not catch her breath. And, even then, her body tensed up.

Freddy pulled back slightly.

"Is everything okay?" he said, the big, vulnerable eyes returning.

"Sure, sure, of course. Yes," said Lily. "Just… just ticklish, is all."

Freddy's grin returned, as he looked Lily up and down.

"Ticklish? That's so cute. I love that."

Freddy pulled Lily in again, his hands exploring under her shirt but not going any further, as if enjoying this newfound test in her boundaries. He and Lily stayed there for a large chunk of the night, as the muffled indoor voices continued on, as the crickets and cicadas sang outside. They stayed there until Freddy reluctantly noted how late it was, asking what time Lily had to be back. They stayed there until Lily forced herself to agree that they had to get back — that, any later, and she'd risk walking in as the rest of the house was starting to wake up.

They returned to his baby blue sedan directly from the backyard. They drove back, hands intertwined, a gentle silence between them. They drove through her town again, her eyes on the empty, late-night streets. Streets that might've looked exactly like this the last night Evelyn was alive.

"Let me drop you off a little closer to home," said Freddy. "I know not in front but... close. So you don't have to walk so much."

Lily agreed, giving haphazard directions to her neighborhood, directing him to the house four or five spots down from hers — and about eight houses from Josh's.

Freddy parked his car, letting the engine idle.

"I had a lot of fun tonight," said Freddy. "I mean, everything considered, this was a great night."

"I thought it was a great night, too," said Lily.

"Listen, let me make up the whole party thing," Freddy began.

"You don't have to make anything up."

"Well, I want to, and also it's an excuse to invite you over to my place," Freddy said with a smirk.

"Oh," Lily replied.

"Like, next week — maybe next Friday — I can bring you to my place. Cook you dinner. I can't cook for shit, but I promise no booze. And we can... hang out. Talk about life, or what have you."

"I'd like that," said Lily, her own devilish grin creeping up on her face.

"Okay, well..." Freddy leaned in and kissed her one more time. "Get home, and stay out of trouble, okay?"

Lily smiled.

"I will."

Freddy paused before giving Lily an additional, quick kiss.

"Now get out of here, already. The neighbors might think we're doing a drug deal or something."

Lily laughed, unbuckled her seatbelt, and got out.

"And I'll see you on Wednesday, right?" Freddy said, leaning over the passenger side.

"I'll be there," said Lily.

Freddy smiled.

"Good," he said. "Now, seriously, get out of here."

"You first," Lily countered. "I live in this neighborhood. You're the visitor."

Freddy's smile widened as he returned to the driver's side.

"Touché," Freddy said. "I'll see you next week."

Freddy drove off, leaving Lily alone in her neighborhood. It was closing in on the hours before dawn. Pretty soon, the people working early shifts would be leaving for their commutes. The morning joggers would be getting ready. Those working night shifts would be coming home. And Lily would be crawling into bed.

She walked down her road, everything playing through her head. She wished she could just replay her time with Freddy, but that quickly took a back seat. The echoes of the past were getting louder, as if they finally had permission to turn up the volume. She listened to her footsteps, the sound of the wind, anything the outside world could offer, anything to drown out what her brain was starting to conjure up. She entered her backyard, changed back into her pajamas, and slowly crept into the kitchen. She tiptoed out and around the hallway, pausing to make sure no one was awake, no one could hear her puttering around.

She tiptoed up the stairs, down the hall, and into her bedroom. She closed the door, twisting the doorknob as she did so in order to keep the latch from making any noise. She walked over to her bed, crawled across it, and flipped over to her back. She looked up at the ceiling and – before she could take in another breath – she started crying.

It was as if a floodgate had opened and there was nothing to stop the onslaught. She covered her mouth with both hands and clenched her eyes shut, crying so hard her body shook and her voice whimpered. Crying so hard she didn't stop until she wore herself out, until she was too exhausted to do anything else but lay there and eventually fall into a deep, dreamless sleep.

CHAPTER NINETEEN

Two months before that party with Freddy, Lily was a dancer.

Six months before that night, four months before Evelyn died, not even a month before Josh died, Lily was on track. She was a ballerina – a gifted, hardworking ballerina, who would easily have a successful career, who was ready to finally put to use all the hard work and money that had been spent on her. That's who she was, and that was that. No questions, no rebellion, nothing.

Lily was a dancer, because the week before that, she was a dancer, and the year before that, she was a dancer, and she had been a dancer since before she had any real, concrete memories. That's who she was and that's who she was going to be.

Through it all. Through morning classes and afternoon classes and weekend classes. Through training 20, 30, 40 hours a week. Through learning alongside women with stern faces and barking voices. Through instructors who cut her down, move after move, while praising other dancers, as if to prove something.

Through it all. Through stepping on the scale every single day and never being thin enough and the instructors telling her that she was getting "fleshy". Through male dancers who pretended Lily was too heavy to lift and female dancers who were always skinnier, prettier, more talented. Through male teachers whose hands lingered longer than they needed to, whose eyes would cast derision one moment, and an immodest intensity the next. Through the diets imposed on her by teachers, coaches, her mom. Through the days when everyone weighed in on how much she weighed. When her mother portioned out her meals and yelled at her for even looking at the sweets that Audrey could have.

Through it all. Through her mother's comments and criticisms and coldness. Through the blisters that were always on her feet, sometimes blisters underneath blisters. Through watching her toes go crooked and feeling like her joints belonged to a grandmother. Through going about the day feeling disconnected, like everything about her body – not just her joints – belonged to someone else.

Through it all. Through the physical pain and the emotional torture. Through days when she'd hurt her ankle and a part of her would hope it was broken. Through the tears that seemed to be spilled every single day, always in private, always quietly. Through the loneliness of being *around* people but not *with* them, through the loneliness of being as good as wallpaper at school. Through the subtle irony of never being able to go to school dances because she had to dance – not like anyone would ever ask her to one, or like she had a group of friends in school to go with, anyway.

Through it all. Because she was a dancer. Because her mother spent $300 a month on ballet shoes that sometimes didn't even last the week. Because her mother let her know in no uncertain terms the sacrifices being made for her talent. All the times her mother had to drive her to the studio or arrange a ride. All the times other dancers' mothers would drop her off at home, the mothers with kind eyes and easy smiles but a distance about them that made Lily feel like she was in a taxi cab.

Because she was talented. Because, despite all the horrible things her teachers said, she needed to stay because she was good. Gifted. Because she had to use that gift or she'd spend the rest of her life regretting it. That's what she was told, beside the lectures on her weight and technique.

Because she was going to regret it. She would regret it, she would regret it, she would regret it. And it loomed over her. If she left, she'd regret it. Her life would've been a waste. All those hours. All those years. All for nothing. She would lose her purpose. She would never forgive herself if she turned back now.

Because she had been doing it since before she had memories. Because she giggled and ran around with her dance partners and then the giggling stopped and everything got serious. Because she got her first real blister from dance at 5 and her feet never looked the same since.

Because without dance, what was she? She was an average student with no friends and a crappy family and no direction. Because, with dance, at least she was something. Through the tears and the quiet pain and the crushed spirit, at least then she had something that made her special. She could be in the spotlight, when so many other times she was in the background.

Because, because, because. Through everything, anything, all the things.

Through the pit in her stomach during Josh's funeral. Through remembering that cold and cloudy and murky March day. Through watching what felt like the entire town at his service, wails and cries, not knowing how it could've come to this. Through remembering the last time that she saw him. Through trying to piece together what had been going on in his mind, what clues he might've been giving.

Through the black cloud that formed around her at every practice after that. Through feeling even more withdrawn and more removed and more disconnected. Through the spring months. Through the seniors talking about graduating, talking about college.

Through Evelyn – who, Lily had to be honest with herself, was not a friend, because no one really was a friend to Lily. But Evelyn was kind and Evelyn was lighthearted and Evelyn was welcoming and sweet and friendly. Evelyn reached out and talked to everyone and had no interest in cutting anyone down. And Evelyn was full of life and full of spirit. Evelyn flirted with the male dancers with a power and effortless grace – one that showed she could toy around, but she'd always be above them. Certainly never someone who'd let one of the older dancers grab her face and mash his mouth onto hers and then never speak to her again.

Through it all. Because of it all. Lily was a dancer. Lily was a ballerina.

And then she wasn't.

CHAPTER TWENTY

Lily's eyes were heavy and tired and hard to open on Saturday morning.

Was it morning? The room was filled with light, so it was certainly daytime. At some point, Lily had crawled under her covers.

She blinked slowly and deliberately. She looked over at the clock on her nightstand. It was a little past noon.

What type of Saturday would this be? Was there a community function, or neighborhood barbecue? Would this be a Saturday where she'd be willfully ignored, where she'd keep a low profile and hope for the best?

Lily closed her eyes for a moment. The house was quiet. Incredibly quiet. Too quiet. Lily rubbed her eyelids (which were swollen and tender, and she didn't realize how much until she touched them), sat up, got out of bed, and trudged into the bathroom.

Lily started the shower, disrobed, and stepped in, pelting her face with hot water. She turned away only to take a breath.

She just wanted to wash that echo in her mind away. She wanted whatever might still be bouncing around in her brain to slip down the drain and never turn.

Lily turned the water all the way to cold and submerged her face in a steady, freezing stream. It shocked her senses and gave her goosebumps, but she held her breath and stayed. After a moment, she turned off the water, patted gently at her face (still a little swollen, a little tender, but better), and grabbed a towel.

Her stomach growled as she dried off. She returned back to her room, put on a pair of shorts and a t-shirt, and made her way to the kitchen.

The house was silent – so silent, that Lily gasped when she saw her father in the kitchen, making himself a sandwich.

"Ah, so the sleeping belle has awoken," he said, putting down the knife he was using to spread mayonnaise.

"Heh, yeah," said Lily, taking a cautious step forward.

"Well, good morning, then," said her father. "Or, really, good afternoon. Either way, salutations."

"Thanks," said Lily, her voice weirdly distant and hoarse. She took a breath, looked around the house, and added: "Where's everyone else?"

"Ah, your mom and Audrey?" her father replied. "They're off to the mall. Getting some back to school clothes, or something like that." Her father paused, shook his head, and laughed. "July isn't even halfway done, and everyone's already gearing up to go back to school. You know, I guess that's just how things are these days. One holiday ends, and it's immediately to the next one. Fourth of July ends, then it's about school. School starts, and it's about Halloween. Halloween starts, and it's about Thanksgiving... and Christmas, now, too. Soon enough, Christmas decorations will be up with the back to school stuff..."

Lily just nodded along, her eyes on the refrigerator, the cabinets.

Her father twisted on the lid to the mayonnaise jar, surveying the plate.

"And how are you, kiddo?" said her father.

"I'm fine."

"Everything going well? How's work?"

"Work is good," Lily responded. Should she feel bad that she *didn't* feel bad about lying? "Everything is good."

"Well, that's good to hear." Her father opened up a bag of cold cuts. "The summer is going by so fast, isn't it?"

Lily gave an awkward smile.

"It is."

Her father put his sandwich together and picked it up with both hands before putting it back down.

"Do you need anything, for school?" her father asked. "Like, new pens or binders or, like, new clothes..."

Lily shrugged.

"I probably have enough left over from last year," said Lily. "But I could always check."

"Well, good. You check, and... uh, if you need something, let me know." Her father picked up his plate and smiled. "Alright, well... time to enjoy my lunch!"

"You do that."

With an awkward shuffle, her father walked past Lily, out of the kitchen, and into the living room. Lily stayed where she was for an extra few breaths before walking to the fridge, opening its door, and scanning its contents.

*

Sunday night was a family dinner night. After a day spent in her room reading, punctuated only by going out for a walk around the block and a quick trip to the kitchen to find something to eat (and feeling like a thief trying not to get caught), Lily found herself in the dining room, poking at what looked like an absolutely unappetizing chicken dinner.

"So, what are your plans this week?" her mother asked, holding her fork and knife delicately.

Lily took a slow, deep breath, and poked a little more at her dish. Inhale. Exhale.

"Work, probably," Lily said to her plate.

"I'm going to get new shoes," said Audrey from across the table. "For the school year. Really nice ones. Black shoes. They'll be black, probably."

"Well, good for you, then," said Lily.

"Maybe on Monday, but maybe on a later day," Audrey went on.

"We've started preparing for back to school, as you know," said her mother. "You should think of getting ready as well. Only five more weeks until school begins."

Lily let that churn in her mind. Five weeks. And she had already been at the gym for... about the same amount of time? More? It meant that, she had to figure out what she was going to do when school started – when she couldn't just go to the gym. Would she be able to continue to lie about her job? She could feel her heart beating between her ears and she realized she'd been holding her breath the entire time.

"I figure, with the money you've been making with your new job, you'll be able to cover any new supplies you need this year," her mother went on. Lily looked up and couldn't tell if her mother was sporting a smile or a snarl.

Lily shrugged.

"Okay."

Her mind was still on the summer ending. On not being at the gym in five weeks' time. On not knowing if she could figure out a way to still go there. And it filled her with a steady and suffocating panic.

CHAPTER TWENTY-ONE

Leon was already at the gym on Monday, practicing in front of one of the heavy bags.

Leon's fighting style was noticeably different from Freddy's. Freddy had these wild, long arms that he'd swing out. Leon was considerably more contained, his elbows tight towards his body, his punches fast and precise, and his arms always snapping back to his side. Everything was more reserved and calculated.

The look on his face was different as well. Lily had noticed there were two types of facial expressions fighters took when throwing their punches. Either they looked like something feral had taken over – their eyes a little wild and animalistic – or they looked like something superhuman had taken over them, their eyes laser-focused and their expressions gracefully stoic. Freddy was in the first category. Leon was in the second. Rachel was in the second category as well. Lily wasn't 100% sure what her look was.

"Good morning, there," Leon said, pausing just long enough to greet Lily. "Jimmy had to run out to get something."

"Ah."

"He should be back soon," Leon continued, taking a few casual shots at the heavy bag. "Some of the competing guys are supposed to come in and spar."

"When's that?" Lily asked.

"Probably around 9:30, but we're on boxer time, so that's just a ballpark," Leon answered. "I imagine a few guys will come in at 9:35, a few more at 9:40, and we'll probably get one guy who comes in just

155

as we're finishing up – and Jimmy grills him for being unprofessional." Leon laughed a little and went back to punching the bag.

Lily didn't know what else to say but yet another, "Ah."

She stayed there for a moment before going upstairs to the workout equipment. She didn't really know what she wanted to do. She could wipe down equipment. She could *use* the equipment. Or she could just hang out and kill time before Rachel's kickboxing class started.

Any option seemed good to her. She knew Jimmy worried about her interacting with people at the gym, but if he only knew what was going on in her mind. How content she was to just do her own thing, in an environment where she felt like she could breathe. Or how she wished she could bring this feeling with her everywhere, especially back home.

She took a moment to look at herself in the mirror. Even though the mirror took up almost the entire wall, she rarely looked at it. When she used the weights, she'd turn her back to it and look out the window. When she used the equipment, her eyes focused on the floor. She didn't want to look at herself, plain and simple. At this point in her life, she was tired of the mirror, tired of what it represented and how it made her feel.

But today, she took a few steps closer to the mirror. She rolled up her t-shirt and flexed her arms.

Her body was morphing. In such a small amount of time, she could already feel her body change. Her arms were considerably bigger. They were thicker and more muscular. Her face was a little fuller. Everything about her was a little thicker, if she thought about it. She hadn't stepped on a scale in over a month (not since the morning of Evelyn's funeral, to be precise) but she could feel the extra weight.

No, not weight. Strength. Her shoulders were broader and more defined. And she could feel it in her day-to-day tasks, how much easier it was lifting and carrying things now. She felt it in her grip as she massaged out sore muscles, as she held on to the handlebars of the weights.

She closed her eyes and remembered the women who were lifting weights up here. She remembered the way their muscles flexed, the way they had carried themselves. The power behind the curves and cuts of their physique.

Lily opened her eyes and flexed again. There were her biceps, standing out noticeably on her arm – and, for once, it was because the muscles were big and pronounced, not because there wasn't any fat on her arms to hide them.

The noise echoing from the first floor changed, from Leon's heavy bag to multiple voices talking. Lily walked down the stairs, finding Jimmy with a few shopping bags in hand.

"Well, hey there, kiddo," said Jimmy when he looked up. "How's ya mornin' goin'?"

"Pretty good."

"At some point today, I might need a second pair of hands – that stupid rowin' machine keeps breakin' n' I'm ready to throw it outta window." Jimmy set the bags down on a counter by the back wall. "But, that's for later though. How's ya weekend?"

Lily couldn't help but shrug. How in the world could she answer it, fully and honestly?

"It was good." Lily paused for a moment before remembering to add: "And how was yours?"

Now it was Jimmy's turn to shrug.

"Ya know, can't complain. This gym's a 24-hour, 7-day-a-week thing, but things are boomin' and that's what it's all about." Jimmy rustled through the bags before letting them be. "A few of the guys are comin' in to spar soon. Did Leon tell ya?"

"Yeah, he mentioned something."

"Couldn't get all of 'em on board – and I get it. Lots of 'em work and can't get the time off. One of the guys competin' – Andrew, ya haven't met him yet – he's workin' some serious hours. Good on him for still gettin' practice in, I say." Jimmy paused and scratched the back of his head. "Guess we all can't be devotin' our lives to the craft, eh?"

"Heh," Lily said in response.

"But, either way, we gotta really hit that grindstone and whatnot – August 6th is gonna be here before ya know it."

Lily looked over at the archways, to a figure walking through.

"Well, the gang's all here!" Rachel's voice echoed.

"You're in early!" Jimmy remarked.

"I've been coming in early for a few weeks now!" Rachel replied, her voice as cheerful as her smile. "Especially with work picking up, I've been trying to get in as many hours here as I can."

"And you're just in time for sparring," said Leon. "Unlike the *actual* boxers."

"Ah, I'm too much of a kickboxer to even attempt boxing, these days." Rachel walked over to the ring and dropped her bag by the edge of it. "But, if you feel like doing some kickboxing, you know I'll gladly sign up and kick your butt."

"Well, I don't know how I could ever turn such a challenge down," said Leon with a smirk. "Except for the part where I'm meeting with a client at 11, and another after your class... but, after that, I'm in."

"Well, deal, then," said Rachel, returning the smirk.

Just then, a few of the boxers made their way into the gym.

"Just in time!" Jimmy called out. "Get ya'selves ready. Ya two are goin' up."

Rachel walked over to Lily and leaned against the ring.

"Always something going on here, huh?" Rachel smiled.

"Mhmm."

"I really wish I could get in here more, especially on days like today," Rachel continued.

"I wish I could, too," Lily murmured, her eyes on the ring. The boxers started wrapping up their hands, joking with each other as they did. Leon had stopped using the heavy bag and was now going through a meticulous set of stretches. Jimmy was off to the side, surveying the ring and his fighters.

It was a quiet morning for the gym, and there was something incredibly intimate about it. Lily had seen the gym this quiet before, the natural ebb and flow of classes, students, private clients, people coming in to use the upstairs gym. But today, there was something very homey about it all.

As the boxers put on their headpieces and gloves, everyone else sat back to watch. For a moment, Lily imagined the scene playing out like a family around the TV at night, everyone watching the same show. Because that's exactly how it felt – her and Leon and Rachel gathering together with Jimmy as their guardian. And tonight's special was a boxing match – two up-and-comers going head to head.

The thought, the sentiment, echoed through her head as the buzzer rang and round one began. How quickly this all felt like home.

And how quickly it might get taken away.

They were preparing for the August 6th championship, but she returned to school August 23rd, and she was going to have to figure out something, and fast.

*

Lily and Rachel stood in the boxing ring after kickboxing class. The sparring sessions were over, the boxers who had come in for sparring long gone. Leon was upstairs with a client. Jimmy was somewhere in the basement. For a moment, the first floor was all theirs.

"Great job, as always," said Rachel.

"Thanks," said Lily, her eyes scanning the gym – the redbrick walls, the tall windows, the two archway gates that once served as garage doors for firetrucks. To her right were the punching bags. To her left was the mat. Directly in front of her was the outside world, filtering in through those archways. Summer air filled the space. For a moment, the only things she could hear were the ceiling fans.

"Was there anything you hated about dance?" Lily said, her eyes on the street, the passing cars.

"Oh, of course," Rachel answered. "Just because it was my passion, didn't mean there weren't things I hated about it. It's a tough profession – tough on the body, tough on the mind, tough on the spirit. There were always people willing to cut you down, whether it was someone at a production company, a coach, maybe even one of your fellow dancers… You'd be destroying your body, day in and day out, and it never felt like it was enough. Never good enough, agile enough…"

"Never skinny enough," Lily added.

Rachel paused, looked at Lily, and nodded.

"That was a huge problem for me, for a lot of dancers," said Rachel. "The atmosphere is a breeding ground for disorders. And, yeah, those in the industry will speak out against it but… let's be honest, as long as it kept us thin, they don't really care. I know I lucked out: I was in modern, which gives a little more leeway – but not much. Those male dancers, for all of their strength, love to get all dramatic about lifting a 'heavy' dancer."

"Tell me about it," Lily responded, her gaze still locked on the sidewalk, the street, the passing cars.

"I know it goes without saying, but I'm saying it anyway: that type of message? It sticks around, and it's hard to undo that." Rachel leaned back. "But you eventually get stronger than the message. You really do. It's always there, in the back of your mind, but you learn to rise above it."

Lily didn't say anything and instead nodded slowly, her eyes still on the road, her shoulders suddenly heavy.

"You learn to be stronger than a lot of those messages – not just from dance. Everywhere," Rachel added. "That's kind of the cool thing about getting older. You learn which things are worth listening to and which things should be ignored. And you become more resilient through it all."

"That's good to know."

Rachel took in a deep breath and sighed.

"People cut down other people. That's the brutal truth of life. As they're scrambling to the top, they think nothing of pulling others down. And the dance world is just a condensed version of that," said Rachel. She turned to Lily. "You're an incredibly strong girl. Not just physically. Don't ever forget that."

Lily turned her head to Rachel, her eyes starting to well up. Still nodding, Lily gave a small, reassuring smile. Rachel smiled back.

The sound of footsteps coming down snapped Lily out of her reverie. Both women looked behind them, at Leon coming down with a middle-aged woman.

"So, if you have any questions, please let me know," said Leon. "Would you like to schedule a session for next week?"

"Ah, I'll see how I feel tomorrow. Maybe then," the woman said, walking ahead of Leon.

"Whenever you would like. No pressure at all," Leon responded. "You have a good rest of the day."

"You too."

After the woman left the gym, Leon turned to Lily and Rachel.

"Never hearing from her again, huh?" Rachel said with a knowing grin.

Leon shrugged.

"Most likely. But that's the nature of the beast. Especially at a place like this." Leon sighed. "She was nice enough, though. Never did a personal training session in her life, so at least she got to experience what one was like."

"Well, that's the spirit," said Rachel. "I wish I could borrow some of your optimism."

"Yeah, but then the roles would be reversed and I'd be a cynical

Cindy like you," Leon jibed.

"Ouch," Rachel said with a laugh. "And who says 'cynical Cindy'?"

"I do," said Leon. "Is that something you want to take up with me?"

"Yeah, actually," Rachel replied. "I believe you owe me a sparring session."

"A promise is a promise," Leon responded. "You have time now?"

"I have time now."

"Well, then," said Leon. "Let me grab Jimmy and we'll get to it."

Rachel gave Lily a wink as she went through her gym bag, pulling out her gloves and her shin guards and mouthpiece. Before long, Leon and Rachel were in the ring, with Jimmy supervising the two and Lily off to the side, watching the entire fight.

The match only lasted three rounds, but what happened during those rounds was nothing short of magic. Leon and Rachel both transformed. Each fighter sensed what the other was doing and countered accordingly. One would swing and the other would kick. They maneuvered in swirls around the ring, Rachel's long legs creating beautiful arcs as Leon would zig-zag in for a punch.

It was less like watching a match and more like watching two stars in orbit with each other, feeding off of each other, celestial and otherworldly and bigger than either fighter alone. Lily was so caught up in the movements, the power, the precision, that, at the end of the third round, she couldn't help but clap.

"I'm glad they put on a good show for ya!" Jimmy laughed out. "Got some good fighters here. Wouldn't trade these kiddos in for the world."

CHAPTER TWENTY-TWO

"I'm gonna get you to try grappling, one of these days."

Lily and Freddy and the rest of the Wednesday morning boxing group were on the mats, jumping rope at the beginning of class.

Lily smiled and gave as much as of a shake to her head as she could without getting caught up in her jump rope.

"I mean it! With your flexibility, you'd be insanely good," Freddy continued, his breath a little short and winded. "Like, seriously — have you considered MMA?"

"I don't compete," Lily responded, her voice lighthearted and her breath steady.

"But, like, you don't *have* to compete in MMA. You can just practice in it."

"If ya can talk durin' ropes, ya ain't workin' hard enough!" Jimmy called out. Lily couldn't help but laugh. It was the opposite advice Rachel gave when they went running.

Freddy quieted down, a sly look on his face as he went back to his warm-up. He deliberately picked up the pace, the rope creating a frenzied beat as it hit the ground.

"Alright — last 30 seconds! I wanna see high knees and doubles!"

Lily took in a deep breath and gave a large jump with both feet, the jump rope passing under her twice before her feet touched down again. Some of the boxers were doing the same. Others started jogging in place, lifting their knees towards their chests.

"Alright — and we're done! Get some water and then we're in the ring!"

Lily gathered her jump rope in one hand and joined the line of boxers returning their ropes to the hook on the wall.

"But, seriously, MMA. You'd be killer at it," Freddy pressed.

"I'm just here to have fun."

"Then have fun with things you can't do in boxing," Freddy said, pulling her to the side. "Like spinning backfists."

"What?"

"It's totally an illegal move in regular boxing, but – man, if done right, you can knock someone out. You're used to spinning around and stuff, so you could totally pull it off." Freddy positioned Lily a few feet away and assumed his boxing stance. "See, you step forward with your back leg, pivot on that foot and..." Freddy stepped forward and spun around, swinging his fist out as he did.

"You do that, and get a clear shot? Your opponent is down," said Freddy. "You try it."

"Fine, fine..." Lily said, laughing, assuming her own boxing stance. "Step forward, pivot, and..."

Lily mirrored what Freddy had done, her eyes already on where her fist would go before she fully swung around. Spotting, like in dance, was also a necessary skill in kickboxing. Something Freddy didn't demonstrate, himself – his head spun around slightly after his hand – but Lily figured it was a needed move.

"Well, there we go. I rest my case," said Freddy. "Although you don't need to lift your left knee up like that. It's not, like, an actual dance move."

Lily looked down. Without meaning to, she must've done a pique turn, at least with her legs.

"What's the holdup!" Jimmy voice bellowed. Lily looked up to see Jimmy in the ring, leaning over the top rope. Behind him, the rest of the boxers were making their way into the ring.

"Just showing Lily a spinning backfist!" Freddy responded back, his voice almost as loud as Jimmy's.

"Well, this is boxin', so save that for another time!" Jimmy said. "Ya guys coming into the ring or what?"

"Of course, of course..." said Freddy.

"I mean it when I say it – knock it off on the other trainin's until *after* Gallagher! Ya gonna get ya'self knocked out, or worse: disqualified."

"Got it, Coach..." Freddy took a few steps towards the ring before turning to face Lily again, walking backwards as he did so. "I mean it though. Grappling. Tomorrow."

"Okay!" Lily laughed out.

"And Friday is still good, right?" Freddy continued.

Lily closed her eyes and smiled.

"Friday is still good.".

"Awesome." Freddy flashed a large smile before turning back around and jogging to the ring. Lily followed suit, her eyes on the floor, her face flushed.

"Alright, I want everyone pairin' up – we're practicin' our jabs, and dodgin' jabs," Jimmy said as Lily got into the ring. "And I want to vary it up. Short guys with tall... so Ryan, I want you with Mark. Freddy, with Andrew. Lily, I want you working with Jason."

Jimmy looked over at Lily, and the expression on his face threw Lily off. She was expecting a look of annoyance, frustration – but what she found was an uneasy face, where the edges bled with worry.

*

During the tense, awkward, yet accepted, silence of the family dinner that night, Lily lifted her chin and said:

"I think I'm going to keep working at the café once school starts."

Her mother pointed her fork and knife up, forearms resting against the edge of the table.

"Really, now."

"What a nice idea," said her father. "I worked through high school as well. It builds character."

"Are you worried you'll be poor?" Audrey asked from the opposite end of the table.

"No," Lily responded back, perhaps a bit too quickly.

"And the name of this coffee shop, again?" was her mother's reply.

Lily prayed that she didn't pause for as long as she felt she did. She had been in the coffee shop before, to ask for an application. What was the name again? She could picture its sign... what did it say?

"The Café on Main," Lily replied, the storefront sliding into her memory.

"Ah," said her mother. She began cutting the chicken on her plate. "Well, *I* certainly won't stop you from continuing your employment there. It *certainly* is your life and you can do what you want."

The way her mother said those words made Lily shrink back, made the food on her plate look colorless and unappetizing, made her look down and press her lips together and take deep, deep breaths. This was supposed to be a way to keep herself at the gym once school started. But there was something about her mother's words that gave her a dreadful, sinking feeling in her stomach.

CHAPTER TWENTY-THREE

"I told you I'm getting you grappling today!"

Lily was in the middle of sweeping the floors when Freddy pulled her over to the jiu jitsu group.

There were five of them that day, all of them dressed in leggings and compression shirts.

"So, in case you didn't know – that's Rick, that's Evan, that's Franky, and that's Damien," said Freddy. "And, in case *you* guys don't know – this is Lily."

The group gave their hellos. A few of them waved.

"Hey there," Lily replied, giving a small, subtle wave in response.

"So I'm going to let these guys do what they do – and poorly, I might add." Freddy paused and flashed the guys a smile. "And I'm going to teach you a few of the basics."

"So that's what they're calling it these days," one of the guys retorted.

Ignoring them, Freddy brought Lily to the other end of the mat and knelt down, motioning for Lily to kneel down as well.

"So Brazilian jiu jitsu is really unlike any other martial art," Freddy started. "Especially competitive jiu jitsu. It's not about being stronger than the other guy. It's about being *smarter*, more technical. It's really the only martial art where the little guy can beat up the big guy."

Freddy had said that before, and Lily still loved it. She smiled at the idea of beating Freddy. Freddy was easily 6', and Lily was 5'4" on her tallest days. He probably doubled her in weight, too.

"I mean, you kind of beat me up in the ring, anyway," Freddy added, a lopsided grin peeking out. "But, still. You could watch a guy who's, like, a buck fifty, submit an outright heavyweight. Fights like that are actually how this got popular in America, but… ah, that's for another time.

"Okay, so, jiu jitsu is a lot like chess. You try to think a few moves ahead – and not just for you, but for the other guy, too. And, in a pure jiu jitsu match, you win by submitting the other guy, getting him to tap out, usually. And, while I could totally bore you with teaching all the base stuff and positions and what have you, I think it would be more fun to learn a few of those submissions." Freddy paused, and then said: "And you're cool with that, right?"

"Yeah, totally," Lily responded. She thought about how the guys in the class grappled – how it felt to watch Freddy grapple – and felt her face flush. Just kneeling next to him was an intoxicating experience, the air between them saturated and frantic.

"Okay, so, this one is really effective, but you've got to be careful with it, because, like, people can die from this. Have you ever heard of a rear naked choke?"

Lily suppressed a smile.

"No, and… who in the world thought of that name?" she said.

"I know right?" Freddy said, his face lighting up. "To this day, I hear a commentator talking about a rear naked and it's like… are we still fighting here?"

"That's one way to get someone to tap out," Lily quipped.

Freddy laughed and shook his head.

"But – okay – seriously," he said. "I want you to stay where you are. I won't do anything tight, but tap my arm if it gets uncomfortable, okay?"

Lily blushed, searching for another witty comeback, but found herself coming up with nothing.

"Okay, so, with this one, you're behind your opponent, and…" Freddy scooched across the mat until his was at Lily's back. She could feel his body heat against her. "So, with one arm, you hook underneath the chin, like this…" Freddy's right arm snaked around Lily's neck, the crook of his elbow resting at the center of her throat. He moved in a little closer, his chest now at her back. "Then I'm going to bend the other arm, hook this hand onto my bicep, then take this hand and place it on the back of your head."

Freddy's right hand latched onto his left arm, and his left hand behind her head. While he was gentle – the skin of his arm just lightly touching the skin of her neck – she felt all the air go out of her.

Freddy let go of Lily and scooched himself over to the side.

"Now *that* can be dangerous. Ten seconds, and you're out cold. Thirty seconds, and you could get brain damage," he said. "And it's 'cause it's not just, like, a choke-choke. You don't just lose air. You lose blood to the brain. Now you try it on me." Freddy turned his back to Lily. "Don't worry. I'll walk you through it."

Lily closed the distance between her and Freddy. She extended out her arm and wrapped it around Freddy's neck.

"There you go. Let me just readjust…" Freddy placed his hands on Lily's arm – one on her forearm, one on her upper arm – and fed her arm a little closer around his neck, causing her to get even closer to Freddy. Now it was her chest against Freddy's back. Every inhale, she could feel herself press into him.

"Now the big thing is to not just hook that right hand against your left bicep, but to put your left hand in the back of my head. That seals it in place. Otherwise, I could break free."

Lily bent her left arm, hooked her right hand against it, and placed her left hand behind his head, the soft tickle of his hair against her palms. It was all she could do to not run her fingers gently through it.

"And there you go. Rear naked choke. Add in a body triangle and your opponent is toast."

"Ah."

It took a gentle tap against her forearm before Lily even thought to let go. When she did, she reflexively took a few shuffles back.

"So, speaking of body triangles, that's the next thing I want to show you. It's, like, such a killer lock, and the best part is that you can do it on your back." Freddy immediately rolled onto his back and motioned Lily closer. "And, again, that's what makes this sport so much fun. You win while on your back. What other martial art does *that?*"

"Wouldn't be able to tell you."

"Exactly. Now, get in closer already so I can show you."

Lily scooched her knees a little closer, her legs by his feet.

"Okay, well, closer than that," said Freddy. "I need you in my guard."

"In your guard?"

"Grappling term. Here…" Freddy moved his body closer until

169

Lily was between his legs. "Now, tilt over a bit. I need you closer to execute this move right."

Lily leaned over slightly, awkwardly holding up her torso in a diagonal line.

"Ah, c'mon, closer than that. Get your hands on either side of my waist," said Freddy. "By now, I'd sure hope you're not afraid of getting close to me."

Lily desperately wanted to give some type of clever reply. Instead, she leaned over until her hands were on the floor on either side of him, her torso practically on top of him, her heart thumping wildly.

"Now, this is totally a move for you, because it requires a lot of hip flexibility," said Freddy. "And it's kind of like the rear naked choke, only with your legs. See, I'm going to take this leg, and hook it over..." Freddy's right leg lifted up, his calf muscle now on Lily's back. "And then bring this knee up and hook into it with my right foot..." With that, Lily was locked into close contact with Freddy, his legs making an upside down triangle around her torso. Her hands started gripping the mat and she tried her best to look at anything but Freddy's eyes.

"So, if you had just one arm through, I could submit you with an arm triangle. If you had your back to me, I could keep you in place and get that rear naked choke. It's a great lock." Freddy held on for a beat longer, another sly grin creeping onto his face. "You want to try?"

"Sure," was all Lily could say.

Freddy unhooked his legs and swung back to a sitting position.

"Alright, well, I gotta get in your guard first," said Freddy, getting closer. "So, like, you gotta lie down."

A sudden wave of heat flashed through Lily as she brought herself down onto her back. Freddy got in a little closer.

"Okay, so, I know how this sounds, but – I need you to spread your legs."

Lily's whole face went red as she moved her knees further out, and Freddy got in even closer. He leaned over and planted his hands on either side of her, his torso now directly over hers.

"Okay, so, take that leg and bring it up and over my back," Freddy instructed. Lily lifted one leg and did exactly as so, focusing on the angle, the positioning, all the technical details.

"Alright, now, take that leg and basically bend the knee over your right foot. Hook your right foot in behind the knee."

Lily lifted her other leg, thinking about the mechanics involved to hook her right foot under her left knee, the position of the joints, the flexing of her feet.

"Hey, there you go. Here, let me just..." Freddy leaned to one side and propped himself up on his forearm, using his other arm to move Lily's hooked leg forward, bringing her legs higher up on Freddy. Instead of propping himself up on both hands again when he positioned himself back, he stayed on his forearms. Now their chests were touching, his face directly over hers.

Freddy paused and looked Lily directly in the eyes. There was something incredibly tender in those green eyes. Gone was his usual grin. Instead his entire face had softened. Lily stared back, feeling her own face soften, her own eyes mirroring that tenderness.

"I think you'd really like jiu jitsu," Freddy said at a whisper.

"Damn, get a room!" shouted one of the guys.

Freddy got back up on his hands and Lily instinctively unhooked her legs.

"Just showing the triangle lock," Freddy said, kneeling. "Y'know, something you keep getting caught in?"

Lily stayed on the mat for an extra beat, feeling amazingly vulnerable as Freddy knelt in front of her. She eventually pushed herself up.

"Well, if my opponents looked like *her*, I wouldn't mind so much," the same guy said, to the laughter of the rest of the group. Another wave of heat flashed through Lily, but this time it made her skin crawl. To be talked about like that, like she wasn't even in the room, and to be talked about in such a manner... it was deeply unsettling.

"Aaaah, don't mind them," said Freddy. "I'm sure they're just jealous of your flexibility."

Lily nodded, looking at the other people in the group who were still grappling – moving and turning bodies, positions that looked so incredibly intimate.

"But, yeah, I really think you'd like jiu jitsu. And you'd be so good at it. Your strength, your flexibility... like, a lot of these guys would kill for that. There are probably a lot of moves you could pull off that they never could even dream of."

Lily nodded again, watching one of the guys flip his opponent over, the first guy now straddling his opponent's hips.

"Meet up is every Thursday, even though I usually have to leave early for work. These guys also meet on Sundays. I work on Sundays, but, y'know, you could always come in, then," Freddy offered. "Or, y'know, I could always teach you some moves, one on one."

Lily looked at Freddy and smiled.

"I'd like that."

Freddy returned her look with a soft grin.

"And, of course, we could continue this lesson tomorrow tonight," Freddy offered. "After I make you dinner, of course." Freddy ran a hand over his hair, and added: "We're still good for tomorrow, right? Same time, same place?"

"That works for me," Lily replied.

"Good," Freddy said, his smile broadening. "Then that works for me, too."

"Seriously, Freddy, are you actually going to roll today, or are you too busy playing Romeo?" another one from the group interjected.

"Why? Jealous you're not my Juliet?"

"Let me get you in an armbar, and we'll see who's the Juliet here."

"Well, looks like I've been challenged," Freddy said to Lily, his devilish grin returning. Lily watched as he made his way over to the other side of the mat, giving one of the guys a high five before getting into a semi-kneeling position.

She watched as Freddy dove in for the legs and the other guy circumvented him, getting behind Freddy's back and pulling him to the mat. Freddy's opponent hooked his feet under Freddy's knees. Freddy held onto his opponent's wrists as he straightened his legs out.

From the corner of her eye, Lily could sense Jimmy standing off to the side. She didn't dare look over and acknowledge that she knew Jimmy was watching them. There was a part of her that could sense that he had the same stern, worried expression that he had just the day before.

By the time the grappling match ended – Freddy getting submitted by the exact same choke that he had just shown Lily – Jimmy had disappeared downstairs.

*

By this point, sneaking out had become an art form. She had left the clothes she wanted to change into in a spot behind the barbecue, just like she had the week before. She quietly tip-toed out to the kitchen, barefoot and in her PJs, before sneaking out the back door and changing in the dark. By now, it seemed impossible, the idea of ever getting caught. This was now a pattern, something she could execute effortlessly. It felt like old hat now, right down to walking down the street, down to the convenience store, and meeting Freddy in his baby blue sedan.

"Your hair is down again," said Freddy, his eyes slowly tracing over Lily.

Lily ran a hand through her hair.

"It's nice having it down," she said. "Been having it up for too long, anyway."

Freddy drove them through the town, pulling a right onto Main Street and passing by the gym. He continued onto a side street, making his way through the neighborhoods, until he arrived at a redbrick apartment building.

"Welcome to my castle," Freddy quipped as he turned off his car. "It ain't much, but I have no roommates, so a worthwhile tradeoff."

Lily followed Freddy into the building. She followed him up the iron stairwell to the third floor. Freddy continued to lead the way, walking down the hall and unlocking one of the doors. Freddy opened the door, stepped back, and motioned for Lily to walk in first.

"See? An apartment fit for a king," said Freddy. "A really, really poor king."

The apartment itself wasn't much to look at. Beige carpet and off-white walls. The front of the apartment was a combination kitchen and living room, with a small hallway in the back. The furniture was sparse – a beat up sofa and some mini shelves serving as side tables. A TV hung on the wall adjacent to the front door.

"So, make yourself at home. I'm going to attempt some type of cooking... we'll see how that goes."

Lily took a few wandering steps around the apartment.

"So, what are you making tonight?" Lily asked.

"Fettuccini Alfredo," said Freddy. "Tapping into my Italian side."

"You're Italian?" Lily cocked an eyebrow, scanning Freddy's red hair, his pale skin.

"A little! From my father's side, apparently." Freddy pulled out a box a pasta, before opening up one of the cabinets and pulling out a pot. "Primarily Scottish and Irish... if, y'know, *this* wasn't an indication." Freddy gestured towards his hair. "How about you?

What's your heritage like?"

"Irish? I mean, my last name is McCormick, so..." Lily scratched the back of her neck. "I think German as well? My mother's maiden name was Bechdel, and that sounds pretty German." Lily shrugged. "I don't know, really. It's not something that ever really got talked about."

"Eh, it is what it is," said Freddy. "And my last name's MacAuslin, by the way. And I think this is the first time we've learned each other's full names."

"Oh," Lily replied. "I guess that's kind of weird, huh."

Freddy gave a halfhearted shrug as he pulled out a bag of frozen broccoli.

"Eh. There's a bunch of the boxing guys whose last names I don't know. That's just how it is," he said. "But, now I can stalk you online and stuff."

Lily froze for a moment. What *was* there about her online? Not much. And not like she'd know: there was exactly one computer in the house, and it was her mother's laptop.

"I'm kidding, by the way," Freddy added. "I won't actually stalk you."

"Well, that's a relief," Lily tried to play off. "And, if it's anything, I promise not to stalk you as well."

"Good. Then you won't find out about my other girlfriend," Freddy quipped. "That's a joke as well, by the way. I don't have another girlfriend."

Lily held her breath as Freddy casually opened up the fridge and moved things around. Had Freddy said what she thought he had said? Did that mean what she thought it meant?

"Ah, damn it," Freddy muttered.

"What is it?"

"I don't have any Alfredo sauce." Freddy closed the refrigerator door and opened the small pantry across from the fridge. "Yup. None. I officially win at preparing."

Freddy pinched at the crown of his nose.

"Well... I can offer you some steamed broccoli and dry pasta?" Freddy gestured at the stove. "Or we could order something?"

"It's perfectly fine," said Lily. "I'm not all that hungry, anyway."

"Yeah, it's a little late for dinner, anyway, huh," said Freddy. He sighed and clapped his hands against his thighs. "But, that does mean more time for jiu jitsu practice. We could also, like, watch a movie, too, but that's really lame."

Lily looked down at her jeans.

"I'm not really dressed for it," she said.

"Even better – in case you ever need to grapple in the real world," Freddy countered. "I'm kidding. Well, mostly. How about a compromise – one quick lesson and then, like, that totally lame movie or something, okay?"

Lily smiled, closed her eyes, and shook her head.

"Sure. Why not."

Freddy flashed a smile and motioned to the open area between the kitchen and the living room.

"I want you to get me into a triangle lock again," said Freddy. "And if you can, then, excellent, lesson over. Lame movie ahead, and everything."

"Movies aren't lame," Lily chided.

"Fine! I cave. Movies aren't lame. You still gotta show me that triangle lock." Freddy got on his knees. "C'mon, I gotta get in your guard first."

A bolt of heat surged through Lily as she laid down on the ground, knees bent. The heat only intensified as Freddy got in closer and leaned over.

"Okay, as quickly as you can, get that triangle lock in," said Freddy.

Lily immediately swung her legs, attempting to get into position. Freddy responded by going upright and back into a kneeling position.

"Hey, no fair!" said Lily.

"Surprise lesson – that's call posturing out," he replied. "Needed skill, especially if you know your opponent is about to try something... like a triangle."

"Yeah, but you knew I was going to because you *asked* me to."

"Never said lessons were fair." Freddy flashed another big smile. "But, there's a reason for that. I want to teach you how to get your hooks in, which can essentially immobilize your guy."

"You're tricking me left and right," Lily responded.

"I know – aren't I terrible?"

Lily laughed.

"Okay, so – how do I get my hooks in?" she asked.

"It's actually even easier than the triangle lock." Freddy repositioned himself. "So, think of how you hooked your bent leg over your other foot. It's like that, only now it's *my* leg, and you're hooking *both* feet to their respective legs." Freddy got on one forearm to guide one of Lily's legs, taking her shin and guiding it until her foot was over and underneath Freddy's leg. "Try it with the other."

Lily followed instructions, hooking her other foot under Freddy's leg.

"And – boom – you got your hooks in. Way more powerful at trapping your opponent, then, say, crossing your legs at the ankles behind my back." Freddy looked down at Lily, that vulnerable look making its way back onto his face. "God you're beautiful."

Lily blushed. She was at a loss for words.

"But, okay, seriously – I want you to try it on your own now." Freddy gently tapped at Lily's legs and Lily's unhooked her feet. "And see how quickly you can do that."

"Let's see," she squeaked out, and lifted her legs again to hook her feet. Instantly, Freddy straightened out his legs and spread them wide behind him, causing him to land directly on top of Lily.

"Surprise lesson there, too. That's how you defend yourself against those hooks," Freddy said, his face now inches away from Lily. Lily said nothing, looking up at Freddy. Her breathing became rapid, every inhale pressing further into Freddy.

"God, you are seriously so beautiful," Freddy whispered out, leaning to one side to run a hand over Lily's hair. Freddy cupped the hand behind Lily's neck and leaned in.

The feel of his tongue, the pressure of his body, its rhythmic motions, the way the hand behind her neck slowly slipped over her chest. She tried to keep up – her hands on his arms, tracing the back of his neck, her own tongue mirroring what his was doing – but she felt like she was playing a constant game of catch-up. A game she desperately wanted to catch up on.

She lifted her hips, complementing his movements with her own. Freddy brought his mouth to her neck before trailing down a little more, lifting her shirt up and kissing her stomach. His hands fed down and back up her thighs, one hand slipping in between, pressing over her jeans while another hand went behind her back and under her shirt. She felt herself moan as he gave an intense kiss, his hand unhooking her bra.

"Do you want to take this to the bedroom?" he whispered into her ear.

"I'm a virgin."

For a second, Lily didn't even realize that she had said that. It took a moment to recognize that those were *her* words, coming out of *her* mouth, and that they had come out as a bit of a yelp. She couldn't even pin down how she had said them, let alone why.

"Oh."

"I'm sorry, I…" Lily began.

"No, no. It's cool."

"I really didn't mean to say that…"

"But you *are* a virgin, right?" Freddy pressed.

Lily paused.

"Yes."

Freddy hoisted himself up until he was back in a kneeling position – almost exactly like when he was teaching her how to grapple – and sighed.

"Hey, it's cool. I don't want you feeling bad about being a virgin." Freddy moved himself back and offered a hand to Lily. She instinctively took it and he helped her sit up. "It's probably getting late anyway. Let's get you home."

Freddy stood up and helped Lily do the same. Freddy went for his keys as Lily reached her hands up her shirt and rehooked her bra. He gave a reassuring smile as he motioned for the door, opening it for her and letting her lead the way down the hall, down the stairs, and out the door. Freddy walked over to the passenger side of his car and opened the door for her.

They left the apartment complex in complete silence. Lily kept her eyes on the streetlamps, watching the light rhythmically pass by, the hypnotic pattern, the light and dark.

"I was 14 when I lost mine," Freddy said, his eyes still on the road. "Way too young. I respect when people wait a little longer. You do that stuff when you're ready. *Actually* ready."

Lily gave a noncommittal noise. She watched Main Street come into view. She watched the roads twist and turn, driving past the convenience store and into her neighborhood.

"I can't remember exactly where you want me to drop you off, so just let me know."

"Here is good," said Lily, her lips pressed together. "Thanks."

"Hey, it's the least I can do," said Freddy. "You get home okay, and get some sleep."

Lily sighed out a small grin.

"Will do."

"And I'll see you on Wednesday." Which sounded less like a pleasantry, less like a cog in the conversation machine, and more like a firm, stern statement. This is what *will* happen. This will *not* be changing.

Lily's grin went a little wider.

"I'll see you then," she stated back.

"And – hey – I *am* at O'Reilly's on Saturdays. Usually in the afternoon. If tomorrow is free, you should be there."

With that, the grin turned into a smile.

"I'd really like that," she said. "I don't know if I can, but I would like to."

"Hey, no worries," he replied. "Just wanted to throw that out there."

Both sat in silence for a moment. Lily kept her eyes on the dashboard. She was desperate to lean over, to kiss him good night, to run her hands over his thighs and in between them.

"Well, either way, I'll see you soon," said Freddy.

Lily nodded, her eyes now on her lap.

"I'll see you soon," she parroted back, looking up, wondering if Freddy would do what she wanted him to do. When he didn't, Lily unbuckled her seatbelt and opened the door.

"Good night," she said as she was stepping out.

It was only once she was out of the car did Freddy lean over to the passenger side.

"Good night."

Lily watched Freddy's car pull away before walking back to her house. She replayed what he had said in the car over and over in her mind – *lost his virginity at 14, wait until you're ready* – as she slipped into her backyard, slipped out of her clothes (unhooking that bra again, letting the sensation send shivers up her spine, lifting up her shirt to take it off, feeling the shivers be replaced with heat), slipped back into her PJs, and slipped back into the kitchen.

She replayed what he had said as she surveyed the scene, the kitchen, the living room, the stairwell, and as she tip-toed back up to her room. She replayed it as she crawled into bed, under her covers, and let her own hand slide over where Freddy's had been. His words echoed as she lay there in bed, mixing with the echoes of the reply that she wished that she had given:

I am ready.

CHAPTER TWENTY-FOUR

Lily spent that weekend thinking about what that night would've been if she hadn't said anything. How things would've gone. If she had replied with, "Yes," instead. She imagined how his bedroom must've looked like. How his bed would've felt. How *everything* would've felt. How all she wanted was to be there, like *that*, with Freddy. How she wanted her Friday night to go any way but the way that it did.

Saturday afternoon was the worst. As her father went off to golf and her mother was off on errands and her sister played in her room, she burned in a way that put the world in a haze, that softened the lines around objects and blurred the colors. She took a walk around the block, wondering feverishly if she could just walk right down to Main Street – wondering feverishly how long her mother would be gone running errands. Wondering if she could lie and say the coffee shop had just called her in.

The sensations of the present moment felt like they were happening a mile away. She could barely hear her feet against the floor. She could barely acknowledge any sounds or changes in scenery. She wondered what Freddy was doing at that moment, who he was talking with, what he might be thinking. The outside world felt fake as a result.

Her mind was filled to the brim with the things she wanted to say to Freddy, the things she wanted to do. She was abuzz in her own ecosystem, one that muffled out the actual world around her.

*

Rachel rushed into the gym on Monday, just minutes before her class was supposed to start.

"Made it by the skin of my teeth," she said, dropping her gym bag on the ground. She sported a knee-length dress, one that hugged her neck and covered her shoulders. "Emergency meeting for one of my kids this morning. This job, sometimes…"

Rachel sighed, rubbed at her face, and opened up her bag.

"Let me change and we can get class started."

There were a handful of people waiting for class to start. A few had been at the bags, others were just casually talking with each other. Lily had been vacuuming the carpet upstairs, pausing in between to lift a few weights.

She knew she needed to take Jimmy's advice and socialize more. But she was never one to mingle. She had Rachel, she had Leon, and – especially – she had Freddy. That was enough. She was already doing way better than she ever did during her time as a ballerina.

"Okay, we're warming up with a few practice kicks, starting at one end of the mat and working our way to the other. Give each other enough space. No points for knocking anyone out."

This drew a few chuckles from the group. After Rachel demonstrated the first kick, everyone lined up by the boxing ring, positioning themselves so Lily was the first to go. Or maybe it just felt like that, and Lily was, in reality, unconsciously putting herself at the beginning of the line.

Either people made way for her or she naturally moved to the front – and she wasn't sure which explanation she liked more.

Lily started kicking, her mind effortlessly shifting into something warrior-like. It was one of the things she loved most about the class. The laser-pointed focus. The sublime concentration. Everything else would slip away, including thoughts of Freddy, and what she wanted to say when she finally saw him. It all slipped away as she kicked down the mat.

"So, we're going to finish up class with a little conditioning," Rachel said towards the end, gathering everyone into the ring. "This is a little dancer's trick, and it can help you be quicker and more efficient with your kicks. We're going to work on lifting our knees *without* contracting your quad muscles."

Lily smirked. She knew this trick. It was a way to get some deeper and subtler leg muscles to engage.

"It might seem impossible at first – and it's going to feel that way, I promise you that – but I want you guys to at least get the idea in your head."

She lined everyone up by the ropes and lead them through a set of leg lifts. Some complained that they couldn't do it. Lily kept herself from smiling. It was Rachel instead who smiled as she watched Lily lift up her knees.

Rachel was out of the gym almost as quickly as she came in – another meeting, another issue as the school year was getting ready to start – leaving them no time to talk or practice or do anything together. But that afternoon, as a few of the competing boxers came in to spar, Lily practiced at one of the heavy bags, thinking of that dancer's trick, letting her leg float into the air as it struck the bag, the noise almost as prominent as the electronic buzzer and Jimmy's voice calling out to the boxers.

*

Lily was only half-heartedly practicing on the bags that Wednesday morning. She wanted to stay on the first floor before class started, wanted to see Freddy the second he stepped in.

She watched the usual suspects come in: some of the competing guys, Leon, the father-son duo. But Freddy was nowhere to be found. As the time for class approached, Lily's eyes stayed glued to the door. Every person who walked past the gym caught her eye, snagged her attention. None of them were the red haired, green-eyed guy with the cocksure smile.

She was stuck on looking outside, on practically waiting by the door. So stuck she almost didn't hear Jimmy blow his whistle, telling everyone to get into the ring.

Even as class went on, Lily's eyes stayed stuck on the opened arches, the outside world.

"Hey, is everything okay?" she heard Leon say.

She looked over at Leon, who had been holding mitts for her. Without even realizing it, she had stopped her practice punches to look outside.

"Yeah, sure, I'm fine," Lily responded. "Just… distracted, is all."

"Happens to the best of us," said Leon. "But that's something you gotta work on. Distractions like that can cost you a fight. Stop focusing for even a moment and you can get an unwelcomed surprise."

"Yeah, you're right," said Lily. "I'm sorry."

"Nothing to be sorry about. Now, where were we…"

When it was her turn to wear the mitts, Lily couldn't help but look over at the door one more time, for the tall, thin figure who wasn't there. As she looked up, she caught Jimmy's eye, who was standing between her and the outside world. She couldn't pinpoint what his expression meant, but the intensity of it was enough to snap her attention back to Leon, on holding her arms steady as Leon had his turn.

*

Time slipped back into that burning, surreal haze, where she spent the rest of the day and into the evening with barely a toe in reality. She burned through her walk back home, burned brightly in her room as the rest of the evening went on, mercifully without any family dinner.

The burning haze continued as she got up the next day, waiting for everyone else in the house to leave, waiting to walk back to the downtown area. Something was off, something was wrong. She could feel it in her bones.

The gym was as hot and as stuffy as Lily felt. The large metallic fans were running on high, filling the gym with whirring, static noise. Leon was already at the bags and Jimmy was already supervising a sparring match. She kept her head down, mumbling brief, "Hello"s until she made her way upstairs.

The weightlifting area was empty. Lily laid down on the carpet. She couldn't stop the feeling of dread, like she was just around the corner from something truly horrible. She focused on the carpet, its fibers, the texture. She tried to tell herself that she was overreacting. That nothing was wrong. That she was weaving together an unnecessary story.

Inhale. Exhale.

It did nothing to help her.

She wished she had Freddy's number. She knew what little good it would actually do, not having a phone of her own, knowing that she would be forced to use her house's landline… She thought of what would happen if Freddy ever called while one of her parents were home. If one of her parents picked up. And still, even then, even knowing all the risks, she desperately wished that she had his number. That she could call him.

That she could call her supposed boyfriend, someone she hadn't spoken to since Friday.

Through the whirl of the fans, Lily could hear the sounds of new people arriving. Lily stood up and went back downstairs, doing her best not to let her feet stomp.

The gang was all there, coming in wearing their compression shorts and shirts. Freddy was in the group, talking intently as he walked across the mat.

Lily made her way around the boxing ring, avoiding eye contact with Jimmy and walking over to the mats.

"Hey," she squeaked out at Freddy.

"Hey," Freddy said, barely registering that she was even there, before turning his back to her.

"Um... how's your week been?" she asked, jutting her head to one side.

"It was fine," he said in monotone, his eyes on his gym bag as he put it onto the floor. "Evan, you good for practicing side control?"

"You know it."

"Side control sounds interesting," Lily pressed, desperately pushing down the lump in her throat.

"Class is a bit full today," said Freddy, his back still to her. "Sorry."

"Oh, no, that's cool. That's... I've got work to do anyway. Some stuff in the basement I need to tend to. It's... it's cool."

Freddy didn't respond, and instead knelt by his gym bag and unzipped it. Lily looked briefly at the guy who must've been Evan. Before she could even register what the look on his face meant, she cast her eyes back down to the ground, and immediately left the area.

Her ears rung as she walked past the bags and down the basement stairs. Her face burned bright, even as the cold air and the chilled cement floors greeted her. She walked to the opposite end of the basement, where the washer and dryer were. She sat down in the corner and tucked her knees into her chest, the world now blocked off by the side of the dryer. She collapsed her head against her arms, closed her eyes, and cried.

CHAPTER TWENTY-FIVE

She didn't know how long she stayed that way. All she knew is that eventually she didn't have the energy to cry anymore. She didn't have the energy to think, to speculate, to recap, to replay. The only thing she had on her mind was escape.

As quietly as she could, Lily crept back up the stairs, peeking around to see what was going on. The jiu jitsu guys were in the middle of grappling. Leon was now in the ring, instructing some fortysomething on how to throw a punch. Someone was at the speed bag, the rhythmic *thwack* of the bag gently echoing off the walls. Jimmy was nowhere to be found. With a deep breath, Lily snaked around one of the archway's columns and left the building.

She walked down Main Street, back in the direction of her house, the noontime sun waging war against her eyes, her forehead, her entire face. She listened to the sounds of her sneakers against the pavement, the cars as they passed by.

She wasn't exactly sure where she was going. She certainly didn't feel like going home. But she didn't feel like staying at the gym. So she walked. She walked past her neighborhood and around town, wondering what she was doing – or what she was going to do.

She wracked her mind, trying to figure out exactly what went wrong, how things went so off course. And all she could do was come back to her virgin comment.

Virginity! What if she didn't care about rose pedals or candles or whatever it was that people were supposed to want for their first time? What if she just wanted to be with Freddy, in that way – *that* way – and what if the details didn't matter?

Why did she even say it in the first place? Was she scared? And why was he freaking out so much about it now, when he seemed so understanding on Friday night? What was going on? Why did he change his mind?

Lily walked until her legs were ready to give out. She walked through neighborhoods, past strip malls, eventually looping back around. She still didn't want to go home, but she didn't know what else to do, or where else to go.

There was a part of her that wanted to return back to the gym. She wanted to hang out and watch the fighters train. She wanted to help out and she wanted to lift weights and she wanted to lose herself while practicing on the heavy bag. She wanted to waste time in a place that felt more welcoming than her own house ever did.

But, at least for today, the idea of going back to the gym made her stomach flip.

Maybe the next day. Maybe Friday. But not today.

Lily looped around her neighborhood, deliberately taking the route that would bring her to Josh's house. She forced herself to walk up to it and she forced herself to stop in front of it.

The lines of the house felt sharp. The green of the lawn and the white of the fence felt severe. The "For Sale" sign was gone. No cars were in the driveway. Everything about the property felt isolated and intense, like the house itself was giving off a repelling energy, forcing away anything positive or warm.

Lily walked onto the property. She walked up to the fence where she last saw Josh and placed a hand on one of the posts. She looked around, trying to see if any of her neighbors were out, if any cars were passing by. Her feet led the way, taking one step in front of the other until she was at the front door.

She didn't know why, but she decided to knock. Perhaps to confirm that no one was home. Perhaps because she wanted to talk to someone in that house. Anyone. When no one answered, she walked over to one of the windows, cupped her hands around her eyes, and looked in.

The shades were up, but the curtains had been drawn. The fabric was sheer enough to see through. Though muddled, Lily could make out the lines of the room. The room itself was empty, devoid of any furniture or light fixtures or picture frames. Nothing but the walls and the floor and the corners where they met and the door on the opposite side.

If she had wanted to, she could've found out what room they had found Josh in. Or, at least, she could've paid attention to the gossip surrounding what room people *thought* it was. But she was glad she didn't know. As she circled the house, looking through each window, she wanted to pretend each room was innocent, that nothing terrible had ever happened there.

Eventually, she found herself in the backyard. It was similar to her own – simple and modest, a fence separating the backyard from those who lived behind it.

She paused there, thinking about what this backyard had once been. Josh had been a kid, once, in this backyard. Probably playing with trucks or digging up the lawn or running circles, pretending he was a superhero or an airplane. It was a side of Josh that Lily never knew. She hadn't been born yet, or was too young. By the time she was old enough, Josh was already too old for toy trucks and running in circles.

He was a good soul, if there ever was one. And it hurt Lily deeply that she never got the chance to really know him – that he had been only a kind face in a sea of obligations and busyness. Her heart sank, thinking of a world where she truly got a chance to know and befriend him. None of the superficial, sweet pleasantries that the rest of the neighborhood engaged in. But a chance to talk with him – really talk.

Maybe it would've done nothing to stop things. She was smart enough to understand that depression was far more complicated than that.

And yet, all she wanted was a scenario where she could've done something. Where she could've saved the day. Where she wasn't staring at an empty backyard in an empty house where a parent's worst nightmare had once unfolded in the night.

She stayed there for a little while longer, feeling the unrelenting heat of the sun, the saturated air, the feel of sweat covering her skin. Lily gave the house a once over before hanging her head. She sighed, closed her eyes, and placed one hand on the side of the house.

"I'm sorry," she whispered, before walking away and back to her home.

*

She was going to the gym that morning.

That's what she decided as soon as she woke up. After a night of deep, dreamless, weighted sleep, her first thought the next morning was *I'm going to O'Reilly's*. No avoiding the gym, no matter what.

The route from her house to the gym felt as familiar as the gym itself. She knew all the bends in the roads, even how long the traffic lights held their red and green lights. That day, she focused on each of the houses, the cars that passed her by. The heat was already strong and the air already thick. The day was going to be a scorcher, the type of summer's day that begs for a thunderstorm to break the intensity.

Jimmy was sweeping around the heavy bags as she walked in, even though she hadn't seen him do that chore once since she started.

"Ah, there she is!" Jimmy exclaimed with an uncharacteristically enthusiastic smile on his face. "Are ya free to help me upstairs?"

"Uh, sure," Lily responded, her face slightly contorted with confusion. She followed Jimmy to the second floor, where Jimmy sat on the seat of a weight-lifting machine.

"So... how are ya, kiddo?" Jimmy asked, leaning forward, his forearms on his knees.

"Fine."

"Hey, I..." Jimmy paused and weaved his head from side to side. "I ain't good at this stuff, okay? Never was. If ya'd been goofin' off at practice, or gettin' into fights or somethin', I'd know what to say. But this... all this. I ain't good at it, kiddo, I really ain't."

Lily looked to the ground and shrugged.

"Listen, whatever's goin' on, or whatever happened, that's somethin' ya never have to share if ya don't wanna. But... man, I wish I was able to think of what to say..." Jimmy covered his mouth with one hand. "But I never want ya to feel unwelcome or like ya can't be here, or anythin', okay? And, really, I'm here if there's anythin' ya wanna talk about. I'll be crap at givin' good responses, but I've always been good at listenin'. And I ain't gonna judge."

Lily tried to smile, but her lips made a skewed line instead.

"Thanks."

"You... you were missed yesterday. Ya took off as soon as ya got here."

Lily shrugged at the ground again.

"And, hey... I get it," Jimmy continued. "I ain't tryin'a press ya or anythin'. But I know everythin' that's happenin' under this roof. And if I don't know it at first, I know real soon." Jimmy sighed and pressed both hands into his face, letting them slide past his ears and towards his neck. "And I really want ya to... socialize. Get to know the other fighters. It might make certain... well, certain things easier. Ya know?"

Lily said nothing, her eyes gazing at the window without really looking at it.

"Ah, kiddo... I wish I knew what to say..." Jimmy shook his head and cupped his mouth with his hand. "I don't blame ya... ya know? And-and Freddy... he really is a good kid. He really is... but he's the impulsive type, ya know? Doesn't always think things through, dives into too quickly and jumps out too fast."

Lily closed her eyes. Just hearing his name produced a series of emotions that she had no interest in showing.

"I'm talkin' too much, I know I am... listen, how about this: I can arrange some training sessions with Leon. Help ya perfect some techniques." Jimmy snapped his fingers and pointed upwards, as if an idea just struck him. "And I'll make sure ya get a free ticket to the fights. How about that? Some real good fighters that night, and not just my guys. It's a good night, kiddo, and I'll throw in free transportation. How 'bout that?"

Lily smiled and closed her eyes for a moment before looking back at Jimmy.

"Sure, that sounds great," she replied, her heart full and hurting at the same time. "But... didn't you need help with something up here?"

"I ain't never met a kid so eager to do work!" Jimmy exclaimed, his whole face lighting up. "What, ya ain't gettin' enough chores at home or somethin'?"

Lily cocked her head to one side.

"Well, I mean... my mother..." Lily began.

"Ah, ya don't hafta tell me nothin' if ya don't wanna," Jimmy softly responded.

"No, it's okay... she's – she does that thing where she refuses to let you do anything, but then complains that she has to do everything. This has been a nice change." Lily paused and chuckled. "See, I wanted to tell."

Jimmy's eyes glistened as he looked at Lily.

"I'm happy you can say that," Jimmy replied. "Happy you can

share that stuff. Does that make any sense, kiddo?"

"It does," said Lily.

"And hey, I officially ain't stoppin' ya if ya wanna clean some windows. I hate that stuff."

For some reason, that made Lily burst out into laughter.

"Ah, kiddo, I hope you find a reason to use that laugh every chance ya get." Jimmy went silent, nodding to nothing in particular, before clapping his hands against his knees and standing up. "But, man, I bet it's already time for class to start." Jimmy stretched his arms overhead and leaned back. "And today's gonna be a good class. Got some awesome combos I want ya guys to try out. And some good principle moves to practice. I know I ain't gotta tell ya, but ya wanna get real freakin' good at that quote-unquote 'easy' stuff. Then the boxin' world's ya oyster, I swear it…"

*

Lily wanted to focus on class, but the familiar ache greeted her the second she stepped into the ring. She could feel Freddy there as they did their warm-ups, as if he were directly across from her, mirroring her, move for move. She felt him next to her as she practiced, to the point that it disoriented her to pair up and find herself practicing with someone other than Freddy.

She felt weighed down, even as class ended and everyone talked with one another as they undid their wraps, untied their sneakers, did whatever it was they were doing.

It was a wariness, a heaviness that stayed with her as a few people trickled in during lunchtime, as the pre-evening lull hit. And she felt it as she got ready to leave, as she walked back home, as she repeated the path she knew by heart until she was back and upstairs and in the shower.

But nothing compared to what it felt like when she got out of the shower and laid down on her bed, her towel wrapped around her, her eyes on the ceiling. It all feel so heavy, so suffocating. She imagined what it would be like if Freddy figured out where she lived, if he knocked on her front door or threw rocks at her windows like in all those old romantic movies.

That's all she wanted: for Freddy to find her, to approach her, to say that he was overreacting or that he made a mistake or that it was all a misunderstanding. If she couldn't go back in time and take back whatever it was that changed Freddy's mind so quickly, then she wanted at least that.

The feeling was so encompassing that, for once, when her mother made the clatters and bangs for dinner, she didn't move. She didn't go downstairs, even as the noises went up in volume.

She didn't move, even as she heard her mother come up the stairs and stand outside her closed door.

"Are you coming down for dinner or what?" her mother said through the door.

"Not tonight," Lily said from the other side. "Not feeling well."

"I can't guarantee there'll be anything left over to eat if you don't join us," her mother warned.

"That's okay."

"You're going to be hungry," her mother pressed.

"I'll be fine," she replied, before adding flatly: "Thanks for the concern, though."

Her mother said nothing. She huffed audibly, before descending the stairs in loud, stomping footsteps.

Lily wanted to feel relieved that, for the first time ever, she got out of one of those horrible family dinners. But all she felt was the ache.

Is this what a broken heart feels like? Lily asked herself. But she already knew the answer. She didn't need any old teen movies to tell her what it meant to hurt like this.

CHAPTER TWENTY-SIX

Lily couldn't say for certain if her disappearance from the dinner table caused it, but, that Sunday, for the first time since Evelyn's death, she found herself at church.

"You are *not* getting out of this," her mother warned, her high heels hitting the ground with extra force as she walked. "We are attending church and that is that."

Lily couldn't say for certain if church was any better or worse than the functions and barbecues and community events. But this was the same church that held Josh's funeral. And being inside those four walls, knowing what once lay at the front of that church, adorned with flowers and pictures, made the heaviness in Lily grow.

But she sat there in silence. Her back straight and rigid – her "strong carriage" on full display. She sat there in a blue, short sleeve dress, next to her father, who was next to Audrey, who was next to her mother. All four, sitting, watching, listening.

Lily looked at her family. Three individuals, who looked so completely disconnected from each other. Like a collage made of people sitting alone – like three pictures cut out of three different magazines and pasted together haphazardly.

The pastor was preaching about service, community, sacrifice... Lily wasn't fully following. The church was half empty. A few elderly people, a few families, a few couples. Whatever image her mother was hoping to craft that day, it wasn't going to have much effect.

Or, perhaps it had nothing to do with image. Perhaps this was just her mother's way of showing that she still had control. That she could still make Lily do things purely because she said so.

The drive home was a quiet one. Lily leaned her head against the window, her eyes on the outside world. A lamppost, a street sign, a traffic light. Columns and columns of electrical posts. Blue skies. Bright sun. Cheery, sunny day. The hum of the AC droning on in the background.

The family unloaded from the SUV and made their way inside, with barely a word spoken. Her father murmured something about so-many-Sundays until football season as he went upstairs. Audrey was already unzipping the side of her dress as she marched to her room.

There was a part of Lily that wanted to follow suit. Go upstairs, change out of formal wear, stay in her room for the rest of the day. But her mother stayed on the first floor and went straight into her office. And – for some reason – Lily felt compelled to follow.

"Do you need something?" her mother asked, in a tone fit more for a boss or a manager. She sat down at her desk, opened her laptop, and began typing away.

"Why did we go to church today?" Lily asked, the words forming before she even had a chance to think about them.

"Because going to church is an important thing to do," said her mother, her eyes still on her laptop screen.

"But why this Sunday, when we haven't been to church in months?" Lily continued.

"Because it was a good Sunday to go to church," said her mother. "That's why." She continued typing. "Hopefully you can learn a thing or two through church."

Lily looked at her mother, particularly at how her brows furrowed, how her mouth tightened, how she looked more like a cyborg banging away at keys than she did an actual person. As she stared, Lily could feel every muscle in her body relax.

"Are you happy?" she heard herself saying.

This time her mother looked up from her laptop.

"What?"

Lily couldn't quite describe how she felt at that moment. In some ways, she felt as cold and calculated as a cyborg, too. In other ways, she felt more herself than ever before.

"Are you happy?" she repeated, her tone neutral.

"Of course I am," her mother said. "Why wouldn't I be?"

"Are you?"

"Now why on Earth are you asking me that?" Her mother closed her laptop, staring at her daughter with her hands clasped tightly. "I told you I was happy."

"Okay, then," was all Lily said, the words echoing through her skull as if someone else were saying them. She turned and walked away from the office and went upstairs. In the distance, she heard the return of her mother's typing.

*

"So I heard you're coming to Gallagher!" said Leon on Monday morning.

"Come again?"

"Gallagher – y'know, the championship. I heard you're coming."

It took Lily a moment to remember Jimmy's offer. How quickly it had been buried underneath everything else.

"Yeah. It sounds like a lot of fun," she said. "And, I mean, you can't beat free."

"The best entertainment is free entertainment," said Leon. "It'll be my first time ringside, too. Officially, at least. So that'll be interesting."

"Sounds like fun."

"Oh, it is, and it's cool because, y'know, I'm certified now," said Leon.

"Are you thinking of becoming a coach?" Lily asked.

"Eh... maybe." Leon paused and scratched his head. "I love working with people in this field. I really do. I think I prefer the more personal training end but... y'know, I got some time. I don't graduate for another year, anyway. Plenty of time to get that sorted out."

"Are you here during the school year?" Lily asked, a sudden worry rising in the back of her mind.

"Yeah. I mean, typically more on weekends. Hard to juggle both, y'know?" Leon sighed. "Hard to believe classes start soon. What year are you?"

"Senior," Lily spat out. It didn't feel *too* much like a lie. She was only off by a year.

"I'm assuming high school, then," Leon said with a smile.

"Oh, yeah... high school," Lily said, shrinking back slightly.

"Nothing wrong with that," said Leon. "I mean, you couldn't pay me to go back. College is way better. But, still, gotta pay your dues, I guess."

"I guess," Lily replied. "And I guess that makes you... a senior, in college?"

"Yup. My last year," Leon replied. "Started looking at grad school – but, we'll see."

Lily let out a, "Hmm," before adding: "So, do you have, like, a client this morning?"

"Ah, no. Today I'm just in early," Leon replied. "But, would you like to join me on a run?"

"Sure," said Lily, scanning the gym. Another quiet Monday morning. Something she had grown to enjoy as part of her weekly routine.

"I'm ready whenever you are, then," said Leon.

"And I guess I'm ready now," Lily said with a laugh.

"Well, before the sun gets too hot – shall we?"

"We shall."

Lily joined Leon as they walked out the main door and down the street. She ran slightly behind Leon, keeping up pace as he periodically looked back to check on her. Unlike the last time she ran, Lily didn't care if someone saw her. There was a sense of belonging – just jogging along with a fellow fighter – that trumped any sense of dread over her mother driving by at just the wrong time.

They got back to the gym as Rachel was coming in. She stopped and waited for them by the archways, her gym bag slung by her side.

"Going for runs without me now, huh?" she called out, a big, beaming smile on her face.

"Hey, I didn't know when you were going to show up," Leon replied in puffing breaths.

"Phone lines are always open," said Rachel. "You could text."

"My bad, my bad." Leon smiled. "Next time we'll text."

"No worries," said Rachel, walking through one of the archways. "Hope you didn't tire yourselves out too much."

"Of course I didn't," said Leon, continuing to catch his breath.

"Your wheezing begs to differ," said Rachel, before turning to Lily. "And how about you? How are you doing?"

"I'm okay," Lily said, deliberately keeping her eyes off the floor, deliberately keeping herself from shrugging. "I'm, uh, going to the championship next week."

"Ah, you're going to love it!" Rachel exclaimed. "I can't go this year, but it really is a lot of fun. A lot of great, local fighters."

"And one of those fighters should be you," said Leon.

"I've told you – I don't box. I kickbox. I'd get disqualified within the first round."

"You're missing out..." Leon trailed off.

"Well, what about kickboxing championships?" Lily asked.

"Eh, y'know... it's just not for me, right now," said Rachel. "Worrying about winning just sucks all the fun out of it."

"So you don't compete?" Lily asked.

"Nope," Rachel responded. "Jimmy used to bug me about it, but – that's the beauty of doing things for you, and not for other people. If it doesn't feel right, you get to actually say no."

"Where was this when I was a dancer," Lily replied with a smirk.

"Ah, it takes a while, learning that you're in control of your own life," said Rachel, her tone shifting again. "And it's something you have to remind yourself of, every step of the way. But, it certainly beats the alternative."

Lily said nothing and simply nodded.

"But – hey – I gotta chat with Jimmy about the fall schedule before class starts. I'll see you in a few, alright?"

"Sure thing," said Lily.

"We should probably stretch before we've fully cooled down," said Leon, motioning towards the mats. "Even the super flexible need to stretch a little bit."

She went and stretched with Leon until some of the other kickboxing students came in. Throughout class, and even afterwards – as some of the students lingered, casually chatting as they packed up their bags – Lily forced herself to be social, to interact with the people around her. It felt against her nature, but she wasn't going to retreat upstairs again. Jimmy was right; she needed to expand out more. She couldn't simply latch onto three people at the gym, especially now that one of those three wasn't speaking to her.

There would be plenty of time for being alone at the gym. And those moments of solitude came effortlessly, as the rest of the class and Rachel and eventually even Leon left – as a few fighters came in to spar and a few others came in to lift weights or practice on the bags. There was plenty of time to observe in silence.

Besides, in that silence, there was too much room to think. And, even though she tried her best to focus on anything else, eventually she'd think about Freddy. She was desperate to see him, desperate to ask him what happened. There was an ache in her chest every time she looked out at the gym and imagined him there. Her head swirled, imagining a world where he'd still sneak a kiss, a world where he'd babble and then apologize for babbling and stare at her with his big, green, vulnerable eyes.

She'd try to fight that feeling with lifting weights, watching the sparring matches, helping Jimmy around the gym. But it still snuck in, sometimes when it was quiet, and sometimes when she swore she had her mind locked on something else.

This is what it feels like to have your heart broken, she thought to herself – and just letting that thought come up seemed to break her heart even more.

CHAPTER TWENTY-SEVEN

Tuesdays were always slow days at the gym. There were no scheduled classes for the morning or early afternoon. A handful of people would come in to lift weights or to practice or to spar. Sometimes Leon would be working with a client. Sometimes the jiu jitsu guys would show up to practice (although never with Freddy). But that was it, at least while Lily was there.

Usually Lily would spend her time cleaning, practicing on her own, using the weights – all while keeping to herself, a phantom in the room, quiet and unassuming.

Today, the jiu jitsu people were on the mats. One of the boxers was at the speed bag. Jimmy was tinkering with one of the metal fans. Leon was with a client. No one was upstairs. And Lily kept herself downstairs, idly sweeping, deliberately keeping the boxing ring between her and the jiu jitsu team.

Lily surreptitiously watched them. She couldn't imagine what they were thinking, or if they had any opinions of her. Some of them had seen what had happened that past Thursday. It was a humiliating feeling, one that made her skin crawl and made her want to hide again in the basement.

But she wasn't going to hide. She was going to fight that feeling and stay where she was.

A relatively quiet Tuesday. Everyone doing their own thing. Meanwhile Lily was fighting something so loud that it drowned out the sounds of the fan, the speedbag, people talking, anything else going on in that room.

*

Freddy wasn't at Wednesday morning practice. Again.

This time, she was expecting it. But that did nothing to stop the ache, the hurt, the anxiousness cluttering in her mind as they went through warm-ups, as they practiced drills, as they paired off to work on offensive and defensive moves.

It didn't stop her thoughts from racing. When was she going to see him again? What he was going to say – *if* he would say anything? She got so caught up in her thoughts that an innocent dodging drill resulted in a sudden jab to the face, just strong enough to toss her head back.

"Oh, shoot, I'm sorry – are you all right?" her partner asked.

"Yeah, no, I'm fine," Lily responded, shaking her head.

"Everything okay, here?" Jimmy asked, walking over.

"Yeah, no – I lost concentration… I'm good though, really, I am."

Jimmy stepped in a little closer and gave Lily a once-over.

"Well, doesn't look like anything's broken, so I believe ya," said Jimmy, stepping back. "And – hey – it's all part of learnin'. Besides, the next step after learnin' how to punch is to learn how to *take* a punch. Even the best fighter's crumble if he – or, she, sorry – can't learn that. Learn to take that punch and keep on goin'. It's a good skill to have."

*

Lily didn't sleep much Wednesday night. Thursday morning rolled in with a mix of dread and anticipation and anxiety. She felt like she was floating – floating around her bedroom, floating down the stairs after her family left, floating through the kitchen as she tried to eat something, drink something.

At some point, she floated out of her house and down the street, through the town and into the gym.

The feeling of floating only intensified as she looked across the gym and saw the jiu jitsu team in the middle of practice, with Freddy in the middle of grappling. She held onto that floating, surreal feeling, as she moved herself across the floor, over the mats, and towards the group.

"Are you free to talk?" she said, her words echoing off in the distance.

"Kind of busy," said Freddy, as he continued his work, pinning down the arms of the opponent underneath him.

Lily stood there for a moment more.

"We need to talk."

When Freddy said nothing, Lily floated away from the group and around the ring, her head swirling, a hot, vile feeling forming in the back of her throat.

"Hey, if ya lookin' for somethin' to do, I'll probably need, like, a tester to see if how the rowin' machine's workin'," Jimmy's voice rang off in the distance. "Finally got that dang thing fixed, if ya wanna try it out."

"Yeah, I can try that soon," Lily heard herself say. She absently tidied up the counter, moving forgotten water bottles to one end and gathering scattered pens.

The rest of the gym became a fog around her. Through that fog, Lily watched and waited.

Freddy was the first to pack up his things as practice wound down. Without glancing back, Freddy slung his gym bag over his shoulder and walked out. Lily followed suit, floating around the boxing ring and across the floor and out the archways. An, "Oh boy!" could be heard through the fog.

She walked out of the gym and onto the sidewalk, her eyes darting around. When she found Freddy walking down the street, she took a sharp left.

"What is going on?" she called out to the back of Freddy's head.

He remained silent. She quickened her pace.

"Is this it? Just, like that?" she continued. "You're not going to talk to me?"

The world around her continued to blur, until there was nothing but the back of Freddy's body, his gym bag, his gait.

"At what point were you going to tell me you were done?" Lily pressed.

Freddy stopped, spun around, and walked towards Lily.

"At what point were you going to tell me you were 16?" Freddy countered.

Lily froze, and the floating feeling crashed down.

"Like, do you have any idea what you were doing?" Freddy took another step forward, his fingers pressed against his temples. "I could've gone to *jail* – do you understand that?"

Lily said nothing and just stood there.

"So, yeah, we're done. And just... leave me alone." Freddy looked Lily up and down, shook his head, and turned back around.

Lily watched Freddy walk away, watched Freddy approach his baby blue sedan, watched Freddy throw in his bag into the trunk and walk over to the driver's side and get in. As he pulled away, Lily continued to stare, until his car disappeared down the road and countless other cars took his place, driving up and down Main Street.

A deep ringing filled Lily's ears, filling her head with a static that she couldn't describe. The ringing stayed as she stared down the road, at a car that she could no longer see. The ringing stayed as she stood on the sidewalk, not moving nor wanting to move. The ringing stayed as a pedestrian passed her by, effectively snapping her from her reverie. With one last look back, she turned to the gym.

She walked into the gym and felt a heaviness fill her lungs and press down on her head and make the ringing even louder. It gave the world around her a disjointed, disconnected feeling, as if she were only partially in the world.

The heaviness and ringing stayed, even as she gave a smile to Jimmy and tried out the rowing machine. It stayed as she gave a few half-hearted tries at the weights and it stayed as people sporadically came in.

It followed her home, as she walked down the streets and back to her house and up the stairs and directly into the shower. It stayed as the shower water pelted her skin and the heat of the water became unbearable.

The ringing and the heaviness started to evolve as the rest of the family came home, as the silence let Lily know that there would be no family dinner. It evolved into nausea, one that made her sick to be in her own skin. One that made her want to crawl immediately into bed – and one that made it impossible to fall asleep.

That night, all she could do was focus on her breath, focus on the feel of the sheets and the hum of the air conditioning pumping air through her vents. All she could do was pray that, by the morning, she wouldn't feel so wretched.

CHAPTER TWENTY-EIGHT

There was a nagging voice in the back of her head as she set off for the gym the next morning, one that kept telling her that she messed up, that this was all on her, that she should be ashamed. She tried to focus on the cars passing her by, the gentle breeze, the sweat collecting on the back of her neck.

She focused on the beauty of Main Street, on the hardware store and the boutiques and the café that she was supposedly working at. She focused on the repurposed fire station that housed the O'Reilly Gym. She focused on the red bricks and on the archways that the firetrucks once entered and exited from.

This was her gym now, and, despite messing up, she was included. If anything, her flub was because she was protecting the gym. She had said she was 18 for that reason, and that reason only (right?). Could anyone really blame her?

She stayed on the first floor that morning, staying in close proximity to the boxers coming in for class. They joked about upcoming fights, and about up-and-coming fighters. They effortlessly wove in stories from the rich history of boxing, talking about which fighter could've beaten whom in another time. They did this as they ruffled through their bags, as they wrapped up their hands, as they lounged around like they were at a friend's place.

Leon was amongst the group, his face lighting up as he discussed legendary fighters and legendary fights. Every once in a while, he'd turn to Lily and give her an explanation to what they were talking about. It was her only line to the conversation, but Lily was okay with that.

"Alright, guys," Jimmy called as he descended the stairs. "In the ring!"

Lily entered the ring and they did their signature warm-up: the sideways shuffle around the ring, punctuating every change in direction with a punch. It was a hypnotic exercise, going in circles with her back to the ropes. It was easy to get lost in the feeling.

"Alright, we're addin' in an overhand this time around," Jimmy said, getting into position. "I wanna see two things: I wanna see a pivot with the same foot ya punchin', and I wanna see ya eyes still facin' forward. None of that closin' ya eyes and hopin' for the best, okay? Keep that chin tucked and don't be punchin' the dude next to ya."

The group laughed and Jimmy blew his whistle. Lily followed suit, pivoting the right foot, forcing her eyes forward. She could feel the temptation to turn away and close her eyes. Chin tucked, pivot foot, core engaged...

Inhale. Exhale.

"Today, it's all about reaction to that overhand," Jimmy told the group after warm-ups. "It's one of the most telegraphed punches ya'll ever see, but that works to ya disadvantage if ya don't know how to react. If ya see it comin' and flinch, or decide to just take that hit, ya ain't helpin' yaself. I want ya guys to practice this. Leon?"

Leon stepped forward, and assumed his stance.

"Say Leon comes at me with an overhand right, and I..." Leon came forward with a slow punch. Jimmy brought his arms up, shielding his head. "Now, look what I did. I opened myself to all sorts'a punches to the body. Ain't good. Instead, I want ya's to..."

As Leon repeated the move, Jimmy stepped forward, swiveled to the left, and landed a pretend punch against Leon's ribs.

"Step *into* that punch! Don't be scared of it. Counter it with a hook to the ribs." Jimmy stood back up and they repeated the move again. "We're teachin' ourselves to go forward, even when we feel like flinchin' back or just takin' the punishment. Good lesson to learn, guys! Now pair up."

Lily found just how right Jimmy was as she paired up to practice. The first few times, she immediately flinched. Even when she told herself to step forward, her instinct was to protect herself and avoid. It took a few more tries, but eventually she got the hang of it. Eventually she started stepping forward, pivoting, and landing a soft hook against her partner's ribs.

After a few more drills, Jimmy rounded out practice with time at the bags. He brought the guys down – some taking the stairs, some just sliding through the ropes and hopping to the ground – and set them up, one at each bag.

"Alright, so this is gonna be total freestyle," said Jimmy. "Pretend this here is ya opponent. Think about how they'd counter, how they'd punch. And do what ya gotta do. Jabs and straights and hooks and overhands and uppercuts…" Jimmy demonstrated each of the punches as he said them, rolling them out with the same ease as he was saying them. There was power in Jimmy's punches, even though he was clearly doing them with little effort. She could only imagine how strong those punches were when Jimmy put force behind them.

"Alright, ya guys get it? Any questions?" Jimmy walked over to the timer and turned it on. The electronic *ding-ding-ding* filled the gym. "And, go!"

Lily closed her eyes, took a deep breath, and dove in. The bag in front of her was no longer a bag, but her opponent – someone who could come at her and punch her and knock her out. She kept her hands up, ducking and weaving, throwing punches with precision and force.

She had learned to really love these moments in front of the bag – and not just because of that first time seeing Rachel at them, before Lily had even joined the gym. Lily could slip into this weird, fluid reality, where all that mattered was the next punch, the next strike. Time became meaningless. Everything else melted away.

She dipped in and out of this feeling, coming up for air as the bell dinged and diving back down when it dinged again. Something from deep within her had been dredged up, and she was using it as her fuel source. Something deep and primal. Something that forced her mind even blanker than before. Something that made her feel closer to an animal in the jungle than a person in a gym. By the third round, she had exhausted herself and the world around her had started to blur.

"Alright, that's good, that's good," said Jimmy. "I want ya guys to get ya'self a bit of a cooldown now, okay? Ya know what to do. Stretch and walk and stuff – we're startin' sparrin' after class. Kyle, Mark, Ryan – that means you guys. This ain't voluntary for ya. In fact, Kyle, Mark, ya guys get ya headpieces on. Everyone else, I wanna see some stretches and stuff!"

Lily walked over to the mat, her body radiating heat. She sat down and could feel her sweat-drenched legs slipping over the rubber of the mat as she straightened her legs out. She leaned forward and touched her toes.

"Sheesh, I'm starting to believe you don't have any bones," David, her drill partner, remarked.

Lily shrugged.

"I used to dance," she replied.

"I figured as much," said David. "Still, though. That's intense."

Lily shrugged again, this time smirking. She turned her attention to the ring, as the electric bell dinged and the first two fighters tapped gloves.

She watched as the men circled each other, both coming at the other with quick, explosive punches, before backing away. They weaved and zig-zagged, staring each other down, finding openings and taking advantage of them. All the while Jimmy stood off to the side, shouting advice as he watched.

The sparring match ended after 5 rounds. By then, most of the class had already dispersed. The next set of fighters went into the ring and began their match. Lily stayed where she was, watching the new fighters.

Lily got up at the end of the fourth round and walked over to Jimmy. She leaned against the ring, propping her elbows against the edge in the exact same way Jimmy was doing.

"Good job guys, good job," Jimmy shouted out. "Ryan, what did I say about keepin' those hands up?"

The electronic bell dinged again. The fighters made their way back to the center of the ring. Lily's eyes locked in on the way they traded punches, the way they pivoted their hips and feet, the way no single punch was just about the arm or the fist.

"I want to spar."

Jimmy pushed back from the ring and stared at Lily.

"Say what?" he said.

Lily turned to Jimmy. She wasn't exactly sure where those words came from, but now that she had said them, she knew she meant them. So she repeated them.

"I want to spar."

Jimmy cleared his throat, his eyes back on the fight.

"You've been here long enough to do a little practice sparrin' – Larry, tuck that chin in! – but yeah… maybe some tap sparrin'. Tap.

It's like regular sparrin', but ya ain't gonna be killin' anyone anytime soon."

"Can I do that today?"

Jimmy smiled and shook his head.

"Sure thing, kiddo. We can see."

Lily continued watching the fight, imagining what it would look like if she were the one up there. She watched how they danced about the ring and imagined herself there, moving her feet, ducking and weaving.

The bell for the last round dinged and both fighters touched gloves again.

"Again, good job, good job…" Jimmy called out as they took off their headpieces. "All the usual stuff, guys. Now take it easy for the rest of the day – especially you, Ryan, okay? No overtrainin' right before the fights. Good fighters get themselves injured doin' stupid stuff like that. Now, Lily, ya hold on a second there…"

Jimmy walked away from the ring and up the stairs.

"Ya free there, Leon?" Lily heard Jimmy call out.

After a muffled response, both men came down.

"Alright there, kiddo, Leon's gonna go a round with ya," said Jimmy. "Good way to get introduced. Remember, this is tap: Leon ain't gonna be throwin' hard punches at ya, and ya ain't gonna throw hard punches at him."

"Let me show you where the headpieces are," said Leon, guiding Lily over to the bin under the ring. "Any of these should fit…" Leon pulled out a headpiece, which looked like an old school football helmet, and handed it to her. Lily slipped it over her head and buckled it into place. "Do you have a mouthpiece?"

Lily shook her head.

"Hmm… well, Jimmy might have my head for saying this, but we can spar without it for today. Especially if we're going light. We have some in the office. We can get you one afterwards."

"Why not now?" Lily asked.

"Because it won't fit," said Leon. "You need to set it so it can actually fit your teeth."

"Ah."

"But, really, we should be fine. Just don't tell Jimmy," Leon said with a wink before handing her a set of gloves. "Alright, I think we're set. Do you have any questions before we get started?"

It was at that moment that Lily realized what she was doing, and a panic set in. She took in a deep breath, cleared her mind, and shook her head.

"Well, then, let's get in the ring," said Leon.

"Ya guys good?" Jimmy asked.

"Yup," said Leon.

Lily nodded.

"Alright, we're doin' one 3-minute round. Remember: we're goin' easy here," said Jimmy. "And don't worry. Ya in good hands with Leon."

Lily looked at Leon one more time. He looked back and gave a reassuring nod. She walked up into the ring, sliding in between the ropes as she did so.

"Ya guys ready?" Jimmy asked.

"I'm ready," said Leon. "Are you ready?"

"Ready," Lily responded.

The bell dinged somewhere in the distant background. Leon reached out, presenting his glove for Lily to tap. Lily responded in kind, extending her arm out and gently bumping Leon's glove. Leon stepped back and assumed his stance. Lily stepped back and did the same.

Lily couldn't tell you exactly what happened during those three minutes. In some ways, she dove into that side of herself – that primal, primitive side, the one she found in front of the bags. But it was so much more than that. Now she had a moving target, moving in unexpected and unpredictable ways. She focused in on every move Leon took and the rest of the world blurred away. She watched his arms shift and his hips pivot. She dipped and ducked when she needed to.

It was then that she understood why Jimmy had them do those drills over, and over, and over again. There was no room to really think things out. All she had was muscle memory and instinct. It was a moment that existed outside of time and space and logical thought.

Off in the distance, the bell rang again. It took every ounce of energy to make herself stop, to snap out of that side of herself. She took a deep breath and tapped gloves with Leon.

"Good job. Wow," Leon said, taking off one glove and removing his mouthpiece.

"Really?" said Lily, removing her gloves.

"Seriously. And that was your first time doing something like this?"

"First time," she replied.

"Wow."

"I second that, kiddo," said Jimmy. "A natural. Ya really are."

Lily blushed. She looked up to see Leon outright beaming at her, the brightest glint in his big, brown eyes. Lily couldn't help but smile at it.

"Now I *really* need to make sure you get that mouth guard," said Leon.

"Wait, wait, wait – Lily, ya ain't got a mouthpiece?"

Lily shook her head.

"Leon! And ya let this happen? Good thing this was just tap sparrin', or else, man… well, like Leon said. Let's get ya one."

Lily let the gloves drop to the ring as she undid her head guard. She couldn't put her finger on exactly what had changed, but something had shifted. And she liked the feeling. She liked it a lot.

*

The McCormick family filed back into the house Saturday evening, after a community fundraiser for the high school football team. No one in the family had any connection to the sport, and yet, they went anyway. Lily's mother had gone around, talking to everyone, holding herself like she had been the one who had spearheaded the event. Lily had spent the entire night making herself as small as possible.

The McCormick family silently went in through the front door of the house and up the stairs and into their rooms. Lily slipped off her shoes, leaving them by the edge of her bed, before walking back out into the hallway.

Lily stood outside the door of her parents' bedroom, opening it slightly. Her father was untying his shoes while her mother was taking off her earrings. The room felt cold and unwelcoming.

Lily opened the door a little more and stepped in.

"Yes?" her mother said, glancing over.

"I just wanted to let you know that, starting next Saturday, I'm going to start working weekends at the coffee shop," Lily said.

Her mother paused.

"Oh."

"Yeah, it's… it's a thing," said Lily. "Since I'm going to start school soon and all. They're going to shift my schedule."

"Ah. I see."

"I just wanted to let you know," said Lily. "Since it starts next Saturday, and all. This was my last free Saturday."

"Well, then," her mother said, turning away from Lily and to the closet. "Thank you for letting me know."

After a moment of silence, her father said, "I like that you're going to work during the school year. That builds character."

Lily looked to the ground and shrugged.

"Thanks," she said.

Something started to make Lily's skin start to crawl.

"Well, have a good night," she said, backing out of the room.

"You too, kiddo," said her father.

Lily froze, holding her breath. She looked at her father in shock. Her mother opened the closet door and started fishing around inside.

"Thanks," she said and nearly raced out into the hallway. She went into her room, closed the door, and flopped on her bed. She didn't realize until just that moment that both her father and Jimmy called her "kiddo". Her head spun, flooding with contradictory emotions, making her wish for things that she never had really wished for before, making her grieve for things she didn't realize she was capable of grieving for.

CHAPTER TWENTY-NINE

"I sparred!"

Those were the first words out of Lily's mouth when Rachel came in on Monday.

"You did? Nice!" said Rachel. "How'd it go?"

"It was fun – a lot fun!" said Lily. "I sparred with Leon."

"Perfect first partner, if you ask me," said Rachel. "When you're just starting out, you need someone like Leon. Too many fighters with egos who'll go all out even if you're brand new." Rachel placed her bag on the ground. "I have to hightail it out of here after class, but – next week, if you're interested, we can do a little kickbox sparring."

A surge of adrenaline shot through Lily.

"That would be great," she said.

"Awesome!" Rachel unzipped her bag and pulled out a few items. "Sparring is a lot of fun. You get to take all that technique and finally apply it. Takes the practice to a whole new level."

Lily gazed at the empty boxing ring, imagining how she must've looked in it.

"Speaking of sparring, a lot of the guys competing this Saturday will probably be coming in," said Rachel. "So we might end up having to do a lot of today's class on the mats. Those last days before weigh-ins and the fight... they're nuts. I have no clue what the schedule is, but we'll play it by ear."

"Sounds good to me," Lily said.

"But, seriously, sparring... it's like, I don't know, freestyle dance.

Every fighter has their own beat, their own choreography. And once you pick up on that... oh, it's just..." Rachel started beaming. "Yeah, it's a lot of fun."

Lily couldn't help but smile.

"You did modern, right?" Lily asked.

"When I danced?" Rachel asked. "Yeah, modern, contemporary... I mean, I started out like every other little girl in dance – ballet and tap, and eventually just ballet, but that quickly morphed into jazz and eventually modern. Have you ever done it?"

Lily shook her head.

"Only ballet. Didn't even do tap, to be honest."

"Well, that makes sense. Ballet, it's... it's got pretty rigid rules. Makes it hard to experiment with different styles," said Rachel. "But you do know what modern is, right?"

"Of course," Lily said, lowering her eyebrows.

"I know – that was a pretty condescending thing to say. I apologize for that." Rachel ran a hand over her head, touching her ponytail and letting it flip through her fingers. "But, modern... it's kind of the opposite of ballet, if that makes any sense. The body becomes this... this morphing, evolving shape. And you get to be a little ugly sometimes, if that's what the piece calls for. Flexing feet and rounding backs... and I think that's why I loved it, why it resonated with me. There was a freedom in moving the body in these creative ways. To feel strong and graceful, but also shapeless."

"It sounds pretty cool."

"And, y'know, absolutely no pressure or anything, but if you ever want to play around with that style, we can always just dabble a bit before kickboxing," Rachel offered. "I'm happy to share my wisdom."

Lily smiled, but quickly looked at the ground.

"Maybe. I don't know."

"Hey, no worries either way," said Rachel. "So, what are your thoughts on warm-ups? Should I make everyone suffer through jump rope or give them a break and just run laps instead?"

Lily's smile turned into a smirk. She knew exactly what Rachel was doing – changing the subject, getting Lily engaged in the mechanics of the class. A little social worker trick, she imagined. And she was okay with that.

The morning itself had blended perfectly into the afternoon, as the class ended and the kickboxers trickled out, as Leon came in to help with the sparring matches and Rachel left for work. The first floor was buzzing with its competitive fighters. Leon held pads for one fighter while Jimmy watched the sparring matches. It was electric and energetic, but still Lily made her way up the stairs.

She knew eventually some of the boxers would come up to lift weights (or use the scale, which was tucked away in a corner. Each fighter trying to get to an exact weight, but not wanting to go lower. A specific cut-off. There was actually such thing as too skinny in the world of fighting) – but, for now, she was alone. The entire floor was hers.

She stood in front of the mirror, looking directly at herself. Her arms were noticeably bigger. Her shoulders were broader. There was a part of her that wondered what weight class she would be in. Over the last few weeks, she was learning more about what weight meant for boxers. She watched Jimmy hound his fighters about getting where they needed to be in healthy ways – that extreme changes and last minute fixes would spell trouble for them in the ring. She listened to it all with something growing in the back of her heart – a pit, a ping, an echo of something darker.

There was a part of her that wondered what the ballet world would've been like if such an attitude existed there: don't be skinnier than you need to be, don't lose weight in ways that will affect your health.

Lily closed her eyes and let her hands run over her arms. She started to sway a little. She imagined herself strong and empowered and graceful, but shapeless as well, able to morph into whatever she wanted.

Her torso started to move. Her muscles protested, attempting to keep her carriage strong like she had been trained to do. But eventually they relaxed, eventually they found a rhythm, and eventually her hips started moving as well.

Lily let go of her arms and did a gentle spin. The fibers of the carpet swirled underneath her feet. She paused, balancing on one leg while the other went into the sky. She looked at her perfectly pointed foot and immediately flexed it.

She closed her eyes and she let her body move. She thought about modern dancers and how *they* moved. The dramatic back bends and the outstretched arms. The wide-legged squats and rolling on the floor. Lily indulged herself in all of it, her body morphing from shape to shape, everything spilling out like the container had finally broken open. She morphed into the moves that she had seen and moves that she made up on the spot. She took a step back from trying to think so much about the mechanics of it all and just allowed herself to feel the dance, feel the imaginary music, feel the moment.

A creaking bottom step jostled the moment and Lily snapped to standing still. Two of the boxers came up the stairs, casually talking to each other. Lily wiped the sweat away from her forehead and looked at herself in the mirror.

Her reflection showcased sweaty skin, a slightly flushed face. It revealed how hard and fast her breathing was. But there was something else in the mirror: there was a softness in her face that she hadn't really seen before. Her eyebrows were relaxed and her jaw looked less tense. And, most importantly, the corners of her mouth had naturally turned up, creating an effortless smile.

*

The entire gym continued to buzz in the days that followed. Almost every fighter came in every day, to work with Jimmy or Leon, to spar or lift weights or even just be around their fellow fighters. There was an energy and comradery that filled every nook, every crevasse, every corner.

Almost every fighter. Freddy was absent again for the Wednesday class – and his absence struck Lily in a peculiar way. She simultaneously wished to see Freddy walk through those archways and dreaded it with her entire being. When he didn't show up, the overwhelming relief let her know she had dreaded it far more than she had wished for it.

"Is Freddy done with the Wednesday class?" Lily asked Jimmy, letting the question come up as Jimmy poured over paperwork at his desk.

"Freddy? Ah, he's... he's focusin' more on nights. He's... well, he's still competin', but I think he's got a bit more stuff to fight than just his opponent, if that's makin' any sense," said Jimmy. "But... kiddo, how are ya? I... well, I can't imagine Freddy's, uh, change in stuff is, uh, well... how are ya, kiddo? Are ya holdin' up?"

"I'm holding up," said Lily with a sigh. "I'm... yeah. I'm holding up."

"It ain't easy, kiddo. It ain't easy. Ya can't pay me to be a teenager again. Ya just can't. But you're a strong one. Ya hold ya own really well. I got faith that, y'know – all this? – it'll all be behind ya soon enough. Does that make any sense?"

"It does," said Lily. "It does."

"Ya got this, kiddo. Ya really do." Jimmy shuffled a few papers together. "Y'know, if I'da known ownin' a gym would involve this much paperwork, man... I'd've, I dunno. Make someone else own the gym, or somethin'."

*

Freddy was there on Thursday, first with his jiu jitsu team and then on his own, practicing on the bags.

It felt like a standoff. Lily kept her distance, sticking to the second floor or the area behind the ring. She wouldn't dare go anywhere else until Freddy was gone.

But Freddy stayed. His presence made the building heavy and stuffy. It made her want to bolt outside and down the street as far as she could go.

Lily eventually just stayed upstairs, cleaning the wall mirror, wiping down the equipment. She eventually went into Jimmy's office, closed the door, and sat in his chair behind his desk.

With the door shut, the noises of the gym were muffled and inaudible. She closed her eyes and swung her head back, forcing long, deep breaths into her lungs.

Inhale. Exhale.

With her eyes closed, she started thinking of the night under the full moon, of the party, of the look in his eyes whenever he looked at her. She thought of the way he kissed her, the way his hand slid behind her neck. She thought about how it felt in his apartment that night, how desperate she was to finish what they were doing.

Then she thought about the time when he asked how old she was.

"I could've gone to jail!" his voice echoed in her head.

Her eyes shot open. Gone were all the memories before, replaced only now with a rolling and nauseating dread.

She wasn't sure how long she stayed in the office. All she knew is that, when she came out, the air around her felt like static. There were a few people using the gym equipment, paying no attention to her. She tip-toed down the stairs, petrified of what she was walking down into.

Her breath caught again as she saw two fighters in the ring. When

215

she realized neither of them were Freddy – when she realized that he was nowhere to be found – Lily walked over to the bin under the ring, pulled out a set of gloves, and went to town punching one of the heavy bags.

*

The gym was eerily quiet on Friday morning.

So much so that Lily stepped in, only to take a step back. There was not a single person on the first floor. She had never seen it so still. There was something haunting about it. Nothing moving. Nothing going on.

She walked in and across the first floor, scanning the empty mats, the motionless punching bags. She made her way upstairs.

"Hello?" asked a familiar voice, smooth and reassuring.

"It's me, Leon," Lily said as she continued to climb the stairs. "It's Lily."

"Ah, of course," he replied. "I should've known."

Lily came up to find Leon by the weights, two 40 pound dumbbells by his feet, a sheen of sweat over his arms and forehead.

"Where is everyone?" Lily asked.

"Ah – weigh-ins!" Leon said, slightly out of breath. "I'm holding down the fort in case anyone comes in… which they haven't, as you can see."

"Pretty quiet down there," Lily replied.

"Yeah, I figured that would be the case. But, that works for me. Gives me a chance to get a proper workout in." Leon picked up his weights. "And the fights are tomorrow, so that's exciting."

A jolt of adrenaline surged through Lily.

"It is."

"Speaking of – looks like I'm going to be the one giving you a ride. Do you want me to pick you up at home, or do you want to meet here?"

"Meet here," Lily spat out, perhaps a bit too quickly. "Yeah, uh, meet here, if that's okay."

"Perfectly fine," said Leon. "Get here by around 3 tomorrow, and we'll be set."

Lily started running the numbers in her head. What time did the café close?

"Three works great," said Lily.

"Awesome," said Leon as he began curling the weights, slightly grunting as he did each rep. "You know, you're more than welcome to do whatever you'd like. Whole gym is, well, quite literally all yours."

"Thanks," said Lily. "I'll have to take advantage of that."

Leon put down the weights and let out a huff.

"I'm technically running the morning class today, but if no one shows up, we can always hit the pads, if you'd like."

Lily's eyes went to his glistening arms, the beads of sweat traveling along the muscles' lines, before looking back at his face.

"That would be fun," said Lily. "I'd like that."

"Awesome," Leon responded. "I'm almost done with this. I'll see you downstairs?"

"Yeah, I'll see you downstairs."

Lily traveled back to the first floor, back to the vast and empty and quiet gym. It was the first time she noticed how high the ceilings were. It was the first time she noticed the way a passing car could cast brief, slanting shadows onto the floor. Even when empty, there was something welcoming about it. Even without anything going on, Lily felt content. Even alone on the first floor, Lily felt like she was home.

Leon walked down the stairs, wiping his face with his towel.

"No one here, still?" said Leon.

"No one here," Lily replied.

"Ready for the pads, then?"

"Sure thing."

"Do you want to go, or me?" Leon asked.

"I can do either."

"Well, I'll hold the pads first, then," Leon replied. "Then we'll switch."

Lily couldn't tell you how much time passed, how long they danced around the ring. But she could tell you how quickly she responded to the numbers Leon called out. She could tell you the laser-focus she felt. And she could tell you how easily she switched roles, wearing the padded gloves and barking out numbers. She could tell you how effortlessly they took turns, how the rest of the world dissolved away, how there was nothing but that ring and those gloves and the sequence of punches.

She could tell you how they stopped only when Lily's arms started fatiguing and the gloves shook as she held them up. She could tell you how, even then, there was a part of her that didn't want to stop, that wanted to keep going.

She could tell you about the rush she got, even after the gloves came off and she tried to catch her breath. And she could truly, definitely, tell you about the look of pure joy Leon had, like a little boy on Christmas day, something amazing and innocent and cheerful, beaming over something like practicing punches.

CHAPTER THIRTY

Lily decided to tell her father that she was leaving, that Saturday afternoon.

She considered sneaking out, but thought better of it. Who knew what would happen if someone in the house asked where she was and no one could give an immediate answer.

She wanted to briefly tell her father before bolting out the door – ideally, while her mother was out of earshot. She knew her father wouldn't ask too many questions, wouldn't give her any icy stares, wouldn't throw passive-aggressive shots her way. If she was lucky, her father would be so engrossed in whatever he was doing (most likely watching TV) that he would barely respond. That was her hope, at least.

Lily walked down the stairs to find her father doing exactly what she expected: watching TV. Some type of baseball game was on. Her father was slumped against the armchair, eyes locked on the TV. Her mother was nowhere around.

"I'm off to work now," Lily said in a low voice, barely louder than the TV itself.

"Okay, kiddo," her father replied, taking his eyes off the TV. "You have a good shift, okay?"

"Okay," Lily responded and started walking to the front door.

"Do you need a ride?" her father asked.

Lily stopped and turned around.

"A ride?"

"The downtown area is a bit of a hike," said her father. "I can give you a ride, if you'd like."

"No, no. That's okay. I'm good." Lily took another step towards the door. "Thank you, though."

"Anytime, kiddo. Have a good one."

With one last look at her dad and the TV, Lily opened the front door and jogged away from her house. She walked to Main Street with her ears ringing and her head buzzing. She was halfway there before she realized she was caked in sweat.

*

Lily had never seen the gym so alive. So many people, so many sounds, so much going on.

She recognized a few faces, but, for the most part, everyone was a stranger. She scanned the gym, trying to find Jimmy, or Leon, or any of the competing fighters. Instead she found people practicing on every punching bag. She found people milling about and talking and laughing. Music pumped from a stereo system. She snaked around the groups of people and made her way upstairs.

Everyone she was looking for was on the second floor. Jimmy and Leon and all of the competing fighters – including Freddy. Freddy and Lily locked eyes for a moment and Lily went pale. Both of them quickly looked away.

"Ah, there ya are," said Jimmy to Lily. "We're just gettin' the final details. It's gonna be one helluva night."

Lily said nothing and just nodded.

Jimmy turned back to the group.

"But this is our night, guys, right?"

The guys responded with a motley of "yeah"s.

"Ah, that ain't the spirit – we're carryin' the O'Reilly Gym name! We're doin' this place proud! We're gonna let those people know what we're all about. Now – again! – this is our night, right?"

This time the whole group erupted in unison: "Right!!"

"Alright, then, let's do this." Jimmy lead everyone back down the stairs. Lily kept her head down as Freddy passed, her eyes locked on his sneakers. Soon the only people in the room were Leon and Lily.

"He's about to give a riveting speech to the people downstairs," said Leon with a laugh. As if on cue, a swelling of clapping and cheering filled the first floor. "We probably don't want to miss that."

Leon reached behind Lily to turn off the overhead lights.

"I don't know if there is any gym that will have this big of a following in the audience," Leon continued, leading the way back down. "I mean, that's what makes this place so special. Most of those people downstairs are going tonight. We're a family, through and through."

"I really like that," she said.

"Me too," Leon said with a warm smile.

Downstairs, the noise was hitting a crescendo. It filled Lily's ears and lungs and heart and head. Through the cheers, she could hear Jimmy's voice – passionate and loud and commanding attention – rallying his people together, proving they were one big family.

*

The building still felt electric, even after everyone had filed out. It was eerie to be in the gym as the garage doors closed. They were always open when Lily came in, the brownstone archways greeting her morning after morning, day after day. But now she watched the metal doors descend on their metal tracks, sealing the inside world off from the streets.

Leon scanned the place one last time before locking the main door. Lily waited outside, looking up. The building looked so majestic, the blue skies behind it, the sun reflecting off the windows, as if the sun existed only to shine on the windows, as if the building were the center of the universe.

"My truck's over there," Leon said, motioning to the right. A stone's throw from the building sat a black pickup truck. Lily walked over to the vehicle, and Leon opened the passenger door.

"Thanks," she said.

"No problem."

Lily hoisted herself inside and buckled herself in. The cabin smelled of heat and new leather. It was intoxicating and Lily closed her eyes to it.

"Sorry about how hot it is in here," said Leon as he got into the driver's side. "I should've started this earlier, or something."

"It's okay," Lily said with her eyes still closed. "I don't mind."

"Ah, I guess practicing in a gym with no AC will get you used to the heat, huh?"

Lily opened her eyes and chuckled.

"I guess so."

Leon started his truck and pulled out into the street. They drove away from the gym, past the road that lead to Freddy's apartment, and further down the road.

"Are you excited for tonight's fights?" Leon asked.

"Yeah," said Lily.

Leon chuckled.

"Your tone begs to differ."

"No, no, I am," said Lily. "It's just the first time doing something like this, so, I don't know."

"First time watching fights?" Leon asked.

Lily hesitated.

"Yeah."

"Ah, well, they're a lot like the sparring matches here, only more rounds, and there's judges and ring girls. But it's still a fairly low key affair. We're not professional fighters in Las Vegas, or anything. Just a bunch of local guys going head to head." Leon paused for a moment to merge onto the highway. "But, these fights can be more fun than the professional bouts, sometimes. Some career fighters can be really conservative, and it can make the fight boring. These guys? They'll go all out."

Lily smiled and looked out the window. The afternoon was in full swing, cars passing left and right. The world was awake in the summer heat.

"How long has the gym been open?" Lily asked, her eyes on the road.

"Oh, hmm... longer than I've been there, definitely," said Leon. "I think around ten or so years? Maybe more?"

"Ah," Lily said, pausing, then adding: "I used to take dance just down the street from it."

"Really?" said Leon. "When was that?"

"When I was a kid. About ten or so years ago, actually." Lily shifted in her seat. Even indirectly referencing her age made her feel uncomfortable. "I was curious if the gym was there when I was there."

"It might've been... I mean, this isn't my hometown, so I can't tell you exactly when that stopped being a fire station, but... man, now I'm curious. I'll have to ask Jimmy."

"Hmm."

Leon changed lanes, passing a car before returning back to the right-hand lane.

"I knew you had a background in dance, but I didn't realize you've been doing it your whole life."

Lily closed her eyes.

"I was dancing since before I could remember," she said. "I think I started when I was three." Lily let out a sigh. "That's when it was fun, when I was a kid. Then it became my whole life and... it stopped being fun. And then I, y'know, stopped doing it."

Leon let out a soft, "Ah."

Lily pressed her lips together and looked out at the highway ahead. Trees lined both sides of the road, creating a hypnotic effect as they drove.

"That's tough. That really is," Leon said after a moment. "And changes like that, they're not easy. But the important thing is that you're living true to yourself."

Lily let out a small, cynical laugh.

"Tell that to my mother," she said before she realized she had said it.

Leon gave a slow, sad smile.

"Mothers can be like that," he replied.

Lily looked over at Leon, watching him drive, his hands on 10 and 2 on the steering wheel, his eyes on the road.

"Sorry about that," she said. "That was... unnecessary."

"No, don't worry about it," said Leon. "I get it."

Lily sat back in her seat and took in the smell of leather again. The cabin had cooled with the air conditioning and the smell took on a new, crisp texture. Leon pulled off the highway and into a town Lily vaguely knew, maneuvering around the neighborhoods until they came to a high school.

Leon parked his truck, reached into the back of the cabin, and pulled out a backpack.

"Before I forget, let me give you your ticket," said Leon. "Once we get inside, I can help you find everyone else. Then I have to get back with the fighters."

"Sure thing."

"I think you've met some of the guys. They're all really good people. Probably will give you insights on how each fighter could be better, regardless as to whether or not you want their advice – or if the advice is even valid."

This gave Lily a chuckle. Leon fished out the ticket and handed it over. Lily gingerly took it from its bottom edge, the heat of Leon's fingers radiating against hers. She paused for a moment, reveling in the feeling, before fully taking the ticket.

Lily exited the truck and followed Leon into the school.

She wasn't sure what she had been expecting, but a high school gymnasium was not it. A part of her had imagined some type of arena, or maybe even a high end function hall. She felt like she was going to a fundraising event, complete with people sitting behind white plastic tables in front of the gymnasium entrance.

A boxing ring stood in the center of the gym, surrounded by metal chairs. The bleachers had been expanded out from the wall. There was already a good number of people there, sitting or milling about, casual chatter filling the air.

"There they are," said Leon, directing Lily to a group of people sitting down on the opposite side of the room.

"Guys, if you haven't met Lily already, this is, well – this is Lily," Leon said as they approached.

The group gave a few "hello"s and "hey"s. Lily gave a slight wave.

"Lily's one of our newest fighters," Leon continued. "So no monkey business with her. She's got a mean roundhouse kick."

Lily's face flushed. She forced a deep breath into her lungs.

Inhale. Exhale.

"We'll be good, we promise," said one guy, a complete stranger to Lily.

"Alright, enjoy the fights, guys, and I'll see you afterwards," said Leon.

"And we'll see ya in the ring!" said another guy, his accent similar to Jimmy's.

Leon tilted his head to one side and shrugged.

"Close enough. I'll be in the corner."

"Is ya mother sendin' ya there?" said the second guy.

"Ha ha, very funny," Leon responded. "Seriously, have a good time."

Leon turned to Lily.

"You all set?"

Lily looked at Leon, her face still red and hot.

"All set."

"Then, I'll see you after the fights," he said with a smile.

Lily smiled back.

"Sounds good."

Leon made his way out of the gym and Lily made her way to one of the seats.

"So, Lily… how long have you been at the gym?" the guy next to her asked.

"Oh, since… since the start of the summer, basically."

"Ah, very nice," he said. "How come I haven't see you around?"

Lily looked at the boxing ring.

"I don't know. I'm there on weekdays, from the morning until around 3."

"Ah, that's why," he replied. "You're there during the quiet hours. Me, I'm an evenings person. This sport tends to attract the night owls."

Lily nodded in response.

"But the guys who compete, they're there all the time. Bet you know at least some of them."

Lily sucked in her breath, her face flushing one more time.

"Yeah, yeah, I do," she said, taking a hard swallow.

"Ah, that's good," he said. "Lets you know who to root for, then. I'm Curtis, by the way."

He shifted to one side and stuck out his hand. Lily met his with hers.

"Nice to meet you."

"Nice to meet you, too."

One of the guys in front turned around to face her.

"You're the kickboxing girl, right?" he said.

An uneasy smile crept up on Lily's face.

"I guess?"

"Well, I mean, the one who kicks really high. I only took class with you once, but, like, yeah, I remember *that*." The guy turned more in his seat. "You really should take the Saturday kickboxing class. It's a lot of fun."

"I think I'm going to do that," Lily said.

"Ya wonder if Jimmy's gonna start a kickboxin' team?" the guy with Jimmy's accent asked.

"I really don't know. He should, especially since it's on the rise," said the guy in front of her.

"Not as popular as MMA," said Curtis. "Really, if he wants to expand, he needs to be a bit friendlier to mixed martial arts. Get a coach on board who's trained in it."

Lily sat back as the conversation shifted. There were a few guys a couple seats down that she recognized, but, for the most part, she was in a sea of strangers. But she sat back and listened, observing them, content to just watch.

Yes, she didn't know them, but soon she would. Soon she'd be coming to the gym on weekends – maybe even evenings after school, all under the guise of her new job schedule – and she'd get to know them.

And she *would* get to know them. She'd continue to interact and mingle and be part of the group. She was going to spend time talking with these guys – and learn more about the fighting world and contribute to the conversation.

Suddenly the lights started to dim and the gym filled with cheers.

"Ladies and gentlemen, we'd like to welcome you to the 5th annual Gallagher Regional Championship..."

"Showtime," said the guy next to her.

Lily watched the first set of fighters make their way to the ring. Each walked in with a handful of people behind them, music blaring and a spotlight leading the way.

Both boxers were unknown to her, but that didn't take away from the fight itself. In some ways, it was like watching a different dance troupe perform choreography that she knew by heart. It was thrilling to watch the ways they moved.

The first fight went all the way to a judge's decision ("They went the distance!" one of the guys next to her said). A man with a microphone came into the ring as the ref held each boxer's arm. The crowd cheered as the MC announced the winner and the ref raised that boxer's hand.

There was barely a minute or two break before the music came back. This time, the spotlight landed on some familiar faces.

Lily bit her lip as she watched Freddy walk down one of the aisles, his face stone cold. His usual t-shirt and gym shorts were replaced with a shiny blue robe and equally spectacular boxing shorts. His mouthpiece was already in, making his lips protrude out. Behind him walked Jimmy and Leon, their faces equally stoic.

She held her breath as he took off his robe, revealing his high-waisted boxing shorts and bare chest. She continued to hold her breath as the referee gave him a once-over and checked his gloves. Freddy entered the ring, shuffled side-step around its perimeter, and then paused in one corner.

She focused on Freddy, even as the second guy came in, as the group around her started talking about Freddy's odds, Jimmy's game plan, the gym itself. Freddy stood in his corner, looking straight ahead. Behind him was Jimmy, talking in one ear, his hands jutting around in a slightly muted fashion. Even from where she was seated, she could see Freddy's chest moving with his breath. Slow, deep, methodical breaths. His chest rising. His chest falling.

Her eyes never left Freddy as he walked to the center of the ring, as Freddy touched gloves with his opponent and took a few steps back. The ring of the bell (a real bell – not the electric buzzer, but a real, brass bell) gave Lily a jolt.

Freddy danced around the ring like he usually did, coming in for wild throws before backing out. This clearly did not sit right with Jimmy. Jimmy was shouting something from his spot at the bottom of the ring, his face slightly contorted.

After one of the wild throws, Freddy's opponent came in with a punch that sent Freddy back. The ref paused the fight and assessed Freddy before resuming. Jimmy's arm gestures had become as wild as Freddy's punches.

Freddy continued to dance around the ring, swinging his legs out and behind him as he moved. His opponent went in with an overhand punch and Freddy reacted by rushing in. Instead of punching back, he grabbed his opponent around the waist before immediately backing off. The ref paused the fight again. Jimmy's shouting intensified.

The round finished soon after, the bell ringing again and the guys returning to their corners.

"See, George? *This* is why Jimmy doesn't expand out in that MMA stuff," said the guy with the accent. "Too much goin' on. If ya wanna be a boxer, ya gotta only box. Too many fighters out there tryin' to be Jack of all Trades and such."

The bell rang again and Freddy came out to the center. In some ways, the round played out just like the one before, only this time one of the punches knocked Freddy back, causing him to fall and land on his butt. The audience started going wild. The ref came over, made an assortment of gestures at Freddy, and then continued the fight. Within minutes, another hit threw Freddy back, and the ref started waving his hands in the air.

"What!" George stood up. "Early call! Bullshit!"

"Nah, I get it, I do – this ain't the big leagues. Ain't nothin' to be won by givin' a kid a concussion there," said the guy with the accent.

The referee brought both guys together and the MC came back

into the ring.

"And the winner, by TKO in the second round..."

"Well, hopefully this isn't an indicator of how the other fighters are gonna go," one of the guys in front said.

Lily's eyes went back to Freddy, watching him come out of the ring, watching Jimmy put both hands on Freddy's shoulders and give him a gentle shake. Freddy walked out of the gymnasium, his head down, his eyes directed towards something in the corner. No spotlights or music followed him out this time. With Jimmy and Leon directly behind him, he exited through the double doors and disappeared from the room.

The day continued on. New fighters entered the ring. Lily got to watch Jimmy come out every three or four fights with a new fighter ("I think Jimmy's got the most number of guys here," Curtis said). The second of Jimmy's guys lost, but the third and fourth both won their fights, which resulted in her side of the room erupting in loud, boisterous cheers.

Day quickly turned into night. The sun set and the world outside of the gym bathed in dark. What time did the coffee shop close? Would her parents know? It seemed like all the national chains were open until late. She hoped her parents would continue on with their Saturday, paying so much attention to their own lives that they wouldn't notice Lily not coming home.

Lily tried her best to enjoy the rest of the night, but the thought started to nag at her. She didn't consider how late the event would go. And now she was relying on her parents being negligent, on coffee shops being open until late. It didn't matter how many breaths she took, or how much she focused on the fights. Her mind was stuck on what could happen.

Nothing will happen, she kept telling herself. *You'll go home and slip into bed and continue on with life.*

Inhale. Exhale.

Dammit.

As the last fight finished and the crowd started to file out, Lily turned to Curtis.

"What time is it?" she asked.

"Ah, lemme see, it's..." Curtis pushed back an imaginary sleeve on his wrist before looking down at his watch. "Just a bit after ten."

"Ain't past a curfew now, is it?" the guy with the accent asked.

"No, no, I just.. just curious."

Lily joined the crowd of people making their way out. The crowd quickly separated her from the rest of the group. She stepped into the lobby and moved to the side.

She scanned the area as the hordes of people passed. She had no clue where Leon or Jimmy were, or where she was supposed to meet Leon. Off to her right was a hallway leading into the heart of the school. She started walking in that direction.

"Oh, sorry, there," said a voice.

Lily turned around to see a middle-aged lady.

"That area is restricted for now," she continued.

"Oh, I..." Lily looked down the hall. "I'm... I'm with some of the fighters..."

"Well, that's nice, but we can't have anyone wandering the halls of the school right now," the lady replied. "Perhaps the fighters can meet you in the parking lot?"

Lily looked around one last time and sighed.

"Yeah, I guess so."

Lily went back into the crowd and left the school. She walked through the parking lot. Off in one corner, Lily could see the shiny black bed of the pickup truck. Snaking through the people and cars, Lily returned to the truck and waited.

And she waited. She waited as the crowds dispersed to their cars and she waited as the the parking lot became a traffic jam of people trying to get out. She waited as the jam turned into a trickle, until the packed parking lot turned into a handful of cars.

"There you are!" a voice echoed.

Lily pushed herself away from where she was leaning against the truck and looked across the lot. Leon jogged over.

"I was looking for you after the fights," he said.

"They wouldn't let me go back to where you guys were," said Lily. "So I waited here."

"When I couldn't find you, I figured as much," said Leon. "I'm really sorry about that. Did you have to wait long?"

Lily looked around the parking lot, the streetlights creating spotlights on the empty spaces.

"Not too long."

"I really am sorry about that," said Leon, gripping one of his backpack straps. "Did you have a good time tonight, at least?"

"Yeah," Lily said. "I did."

"Well, that's good," said Leon. "Here, let's get inside. You've spent enough time out here this evening."

Leon walked over and opened Lily's door for her.

"Thanks," she said with a sheepish grin, climbing into the pickup truck's cabin.

"The least I can do," said Leon, closing the door behind her.

"Where's everyone else?" Lily asked when Leon opened the driver's side door.

"The guys, they're going out to celebrate now," Leon said as he hoisted himself in. "Meaning they're going to find a bar somewhere."

"Oh," Lily said, looking at the dashboard. "Shouldn't you be with them? Y'know, celebrating?"

"And leave you stranded here? C'mon now." Leon paused to start his truck. "Besides, that's not my thing, anyway."

"You don't drink?" Lily asked.

Leon started to pull out of his parking space.

"No, not really. Never been my thing," said Leon. "Maybe I'm too straight-edge or whatever, but... yeah, I just don't see the purpose in it. Besides, I don't really feel like being around those guys when *they* drink, either. They're a rowdy bunch sometimes."

Lily watched the high school disappear from view.

"I'm not trying to pass judgment," Leon continued. "I mean, if that's your thing, that's totally fine. Within reason, of course."

The corner of Lily's mouth twitched.

"I don't drink," said Lily. "Never have and... I don't know, maybe I never will?"

"It's not a prerequisite for life. Some people never drink and live great lives. Some people do and also live great lives."

"And some people ruin their lives over it."

"That's true, too."

Lily let out a sigh and kept her eyes focused on the world outside the passenger window.

"Did you ever know Evelyn Manning?" she asked.

"I can't say that I have," said Leon. "Why?"

"She... she was a few grades ahead of me," Lily said, her eyes still focusing on the passenger side window. "A dancer, too. She died in a drunk driving crash a few months ago."

"Oh, man. I'd heard about the crash, on the news," said Leon. "I'm so sorry."

Lily shrugged.

"I mean, that's life. People get into drunk driving accidents and die. All the time. And that's just life. Now she's gone."

"I'm really sorry," said Leon.

Lily looked over at Leon, who had been stealing glances as he drove.

"No, I'm sorry," said Lily with a sigh, looking down at the leather seat. "That was... that was just a complete blurt-out."

"Hey, it's okay," said Leon. "Something like that, it'll stay with you. And it's tough. It's really tough."

Lily sighed again.

"I guess I'm still not over it."

"You don't have to be," said Leon. "Really, losing someone isn't something you 'get over'. It's something you learn to deal with, in time."

Lily said nothing, her eyes on the road in front of her.

"And if you ever want to talk about it, or anything, I'm here," Leon continued. "That's how we learn to deal. We talk to the people who care about us. We remind ourselves of the people who are still around. You can't adapt by pretending it never happened."

Lily turned and watched Leon driving, his hands still at ten and two, his upper arms flexing slightly as he manned the steering wheel, his eyes – deep and rich and filled with concern – focused on the road.

"Thank you," she said, her voice feeling like it belonged to someone else. "I really appreciate that."

"Hey, anything I can do," Leon said, glancing over, his eyes locking with hers for the briefest of moments. And during that briefest of moments, her breath caught, her heart paused, and the world itself hung in suspension.

Leon said something else, something muffled and indecipherable.

"What was that?" she asked, shaking her head slightly.

"I said – what's your address?"

"My address?"

"To drop you off?" Leon said with a laugh. "I mean, it's way too late to be dropping you off at the gym."

"Oh," Lily said with a nervous laugh, and proceeded to give him the address of the house a street over from hers.

Lily kept her eyes on Leon throughout the ride back. She just wanted to observe him. To watch the subtle ways his arms moved. To watch his right knee bend as he gently applied the brakes. To see him periodically check his rear view mirror. To see his black hair bounce as he moved his head. She was so content to just watch. It felt like she could see his soul, the very essence of who he was, shine through in those simple actions. There was something so beautiful and so fulfilling about it.

Leon made his way off the highway, through the downtown area, and eventually into her neighborhood.

"I didn't realize you lived this far out," said Leon.

"It's only a few miles."

"Still, though," said Leon. "Does someone drop you off?"

"At the gym?" Lily asked. "No. I just walk."

"Well, hey, if you ever need a ride, let me know," said Leon. "Especially once winter hits."

Lily could feel herself beaming.

"Thanks," she said. "I really appreciate that."

Leon pulled over in front of the house of a neighbor that Lily had met only a few times before. A virtual stranger, in some ways.

"Well, here you go," said Leon.

Lily unbuckled her seatbelt.

"Thanks. Thanks a lot," she said.

Leon turned and faced Lily.

"No problem. I'm glad you had a good time," said Leon. "And I meant it, about being here if you need someone to talk to. I'm here, truly."

Lily locked eyes with Leon – his big, brown eyes, eyes that always seemed to speak the truth. Eyes that didn't need sporadic moments of vulnerability to show what lay underneath. There were never any pretenses.

With one sweeping act, Lily leaned forward, held one side of Leon's face, and kissed him. She closed her eyes and felt his gentle, full lips against hers, the heat from his body warming her own.

Leon pulled back, nearly hitting his head against the driver's side window as he did.

"Woah, woah... Lily... I...." Leon took a hard swallow and looked way. "I'm sorry if I gave you the wrong idea but... that... that's not what I meant."

Lily shrunk back in her seat.

"I'm sorry..." she said, her skin suddenly cold.

"You're such a great girl, but, you're... you're like my little sister..."

"Sister?" Lily parroted.

"I didn't mean it like that... I... I'm sorry if I lead you on, or..."

"I'm sorry, I... *I'm* sorry..." Lily mumbled. Before Leon could say anything else, Lily opened the passenger door and spilled out. She slammed the door behind her and started running. She ran until she looped around a side street and disappeared from Leon's pick-up truck. She ran until she was finally home, finally back to her house. And she didn't stop running until she was in her backyard, catching her breath, staring at the lights inside.

Even with her mind spinning, she narrowed in on the lights. The kitchen lights and the hallway lights and the second floor lights were still on. No one was ever awake this late, not even on a Saturday.

She slowly opened the kitchen door, tip-toeing inside. She scanned the kitchen and found it mercifully empty.

"So, how was work."

Lily snapped to the right to see her mother walking into the kitchen, followed behind by her father. After a moment, Audrey followed suit.

Lily looked to the ground.

"It was fine."

"Home late," said her mother.

Lily shrugged.

"They needed me 'til close."

"Really? At the Downtown Grind?"

Lily shrugged again.

"Sure."

"See, it's funny, because I just made that name up," said her mother.

A sudden, sharp ringing started in Lily's ears. She stared at her feet, which felt a thousand miles away from her.

"When I *did* go down to the *actual* coffee shop that's on Main Street – y'know, the Café on Main? – yeah, I was pleasantly surprised to learn that they had no clue who you were," her mother continued. "It's really, really funny, because they have no employees whatsoever named Lily."

Lily's skin went cold and clammy. Her feet drifted further and further away from her.

"So why don't you tell me where you *really* were?" her mother pressed.

Lily said nothing.

"Or, how about, you tell me where you've been this entire

summer? Clearly, you haven't been working."

"You've been lying," Lily heard Audrey say in the distance.

"Audrey, enough…" her father said in an infuriatingly gentle, paternal voice.

"No, Audrey's right. Lily *has* been lying. She's been lying this whole time," said her mother.

Lily closed her head and felt the room spin.

"I can't believe this. First, you throw away your dream. Then, you lie to your family. You're not to be trusted, plain and simple." Her mother paused and huffed. "Now, tell me where you were."

Through the spinning and the coldness and the clamminess, Lily remained silent.

"Okay, I see how it is. Your life is all about deceit now, isn't it?" Her mother's voice went up in volume. "Well, fine, then. You're a delinquent now. Are you happy?"

Lily still said nothing, but could feel her hands balling up into fists.

"I'm *so* furious right now, I can't even think of a proper punishment for you," said her mother. But Lily knew that was a lie. Even in that moment, Lily knew that was a lie. She knew that her mother had been plotting. Coldly and maliciously plotting, formulating the perfect responses, the perfect punishment. Because that's how she operated. That's how she always operated.

"So you're going to go to your room and you're only going to come out when I've figured out the best course of action," her mother continued.

Lily snickered. Deliberately withhold information under the guise of "thinking". Holing Lily up in her room. She could write the playbook on her mother's tactics.

"Oh, I'm glad *you* think this is funny, because *I* sure as hell don't," her mother snapped. "Now, get to your room, right now, and don't come out until I say so."

With gritted teeth and cold skin and her feet miles and miles away from her, she left the kitchen. She avoided looking at her mother, but looked up at her father. He let out a quiet, "Sorry, kiddo," before looking away.

"Lily's in trouble, Lily's in trouble…" Audrey started sing-songing.

Lily kept walking, refusing to acknowledge her sister.

"Audrey…" she could hear her father say again.

"No, Lily *is* in trouble," said her mother. "And it's nobody's fault but her own."

Lily continued up the stairs and into her room and shut the door. She kicked off her shoes and plopped on her bed.

All at once, the events from the last few minutes descended upon her. She thought about Leon's truck and her mother's tone and her sister's mocking and her father's passivity. She thought about the kiss and she thought about getting caught. She thought about the gym and the fighters and the upcoming school year. She thought about how it felt to walk into that gym, and she thought about what it would feel like to never walk in there again. And suddenly she was walloped with a flood of emotion. The reality of what it all meant hit her like a blow to the back of the head. She grabbed one of her pillows, buried her face into it, and started crying.

CHAPTER THIRTY-ONE

Her mother didn't come into Lily's room at all on Sunday. Her mother made a spectacle of coming up and down the stairs, making as much noise as she could, but never once did she come to Lily's room.

Not that Lily even wanted her there in the first place. She could only imagine what her mother would say, walking into her room like an invader to a foreign country and announcing what the "punishment" would be. Just the thought of it made Lily's skin crawl.

Lily's mind was focused on other matters, anyway. She was focused on the night before, on Leon's truck, on the kiss that should never have happened. She focused on how the gym felt like home, on how Jimmy went out of his way to look after her.

She closed her eyes and imagined herself in the gym. She could see the first floor vividly, the boxing ring stationed towards the back, the assortment of punching bags off to the left, the mats to the right. She imagined herself walking up the stairs to the second floor, to the weights and the gym equipment. She imagined the door to Jimmy's office, and the cluttered mess inside. She even traveled to the basement in her mind, looking at all the storage containers and the washer & dryer and the pipes hanging from the ceiling.

She thought about the people who went there. She tried to reimagine their faces, the ways they moved as they talked, as they practiced. She thought about the smiles and laughter and jokes and comradery. She thought about how stepping through the archways always made Lily feel a little bit lighter.

And then she thought about never stepping through the archways again.

A sharp and overwhelming panic swept through her, making her want to bolt out her room, down the stairs, and back to the gym. It made her want to run and run away and beg Jimmy to take her in and never let her return home.

The panic eventually ebbed, replaced by a sinking, paralyzing feeling, one that weighed heavy on Lily and made it far too easy to just lay in bed, her eyes on the ceiling, the rest of Sunday passing her by.

*

"Get up. You're coming to work with me."

Lily groaned and rolled to her side. Mrs. McCormick was standing in the middle of Lily's room early that Monday morning. It was barely 6:30, and yet her mother was dressed, her hair and makeup done.

"What?" Lily slowly sat up.

"You heard me. Get up. Get dressed. Wear something respectable. You clearly can't be left home alone and it's too late to put you in any program. So you're coming to work with me, so you can do some *actual* work."

Lily said nothing and looked at her knees.

"I expect you downstairs and ready by 7. At the latest."

Lily continued to say nothing, continued to not look her mother in the eye. After another moment of silence, Mrs. McCormick left the room, slamming the bedroom door behind her. With a sigh, Lily got up from bed, trudged over to her closet, and pulled out a blouse and slacks.

*

The car ride to her mother's office was silent and cold and tense. Lily sat in the passenger seat of her mother's SUV, her back rigid, her eyes out the window. She silently made note of every lamppost, every sign, every street light.

The AC was running, its subtle fans whirring in the background. The early morning sun was bright and sharp. Aside from a handful of fluffy clouds in the distance, the skies were clear.

238

"You are to behave yourself in my office, do you understand?" her mother said after a while.

Lily continued to watch the world through the passenger side window. A lamppost, a street sign, a traffic light. Sets and sets of electrical posts. Blue skies. Bright sun. Cheery, sunny day.

Inhale. Exhale.

Mrs. McCormick pulled into an industrial park, snaking her way down one of the roads before taking a left into a parking lot.

"You are here because you can't be trusted at home," her mother said as she unbuckled her seatbelt − said as if they were in mid-conversation, as if they hadn't just spent the last 10 minutes in complete silence.

Lily followed her mother into the building, onto an elevator, and eventually through one of the hallway doors.

The building atmosphere was suffocating. Everything was beige and illuminated with fluorescent lights. The energy was negative and tense. Lily continued to follow her mother past a cubicle farm and into an office.

Her mother closed the door behind her, walked to the chair behind her desk, and motioned towards a seat on the other end of the room.

"You do as I say and nothing else, do you hear me? When I have work for you to do, you're going to do it. No questions, no complaints. And when I don't have work for you, you're going to sit there and think about what you're doing with your life. Do you understand?"

Lily said nothing, walked over to the seat, and sat down. She closed her eyes and crossed her arms and hung her head back.

The day moved tediously. Her mother worked in silence. Whenever her phone rang, Mrs. McCormick would pause, pick up the receiver and, after a few quiet words, reply with, "Is this something we can discuss via email?" Each time she hung up the phone, she'd look over at Lily, a viciously cold look in her eyes, as if Lily were the reason she hung up in the first place. People would knock on her office door, and Mrs. McCormick would get up and step outside of her office to talk with them, the door kept mostly closed but slightly ajar, her voice low.

She attempted to give Lily work to do. Papers to file, to copy, to sort. Each time, Lily asked questions about the work assigned − where was the copier, where should something go in the filing cabinet. Each time, Mrs. McCormick took the work back and said she'd do it herself.

Lily tried her best not to think about the gym. She knew it would drive her mad. But she couldn't help herself when noontime came around. Had things gone differently, she would be in Rachel's kickboxing class. She probably would've been discussing the fights, or talking about dance. She closed her eyes and imagined how that class would go. Within seconds, she opened her eyes and focused on one of the lamps and tried like hell to keep from crying.

Inhale. Exhale.

She spent her entire day in this drudgery. The hours ticked by in a slow, brutal manner. Lily focused on the lines of the walls, the carpet, the window to the outside (which gave nothing more than a view of another building). If there had been a lunch break, her mother definitely didn't use it. At some point, Lily fell asleep, stirred awake only by the sound of the phone ringing again.

The car ride back home that evening was just like the car ride to the office. Cold and silent and tense, with Lily's eyes focused on the outside world. She placed one hand on the leather seat and briefly thought about the leather from Leon's truck. Even after everything that had happened, she'd kill to be in his truck over her mother's SUV. Perhaps, next to Leon, she could properly apologize, better explain herself. At least there, she'd feel heard, she'd feel forgiven, she'd feel better. Here, all she could do was count the telephone poles until they reached their garage.

*

It went like that for the entire week. Each day, dressed up in something formal, bored senseless. Wasting time in that stupid chair in her mother's office. Her mind vacillating between a thousand thoughts a minute and absolutely nothing at all.

Each day, her mother became more restless, more irritated, more anxious. Phone calls started getting ignored by Thursday. People stopped knocking on the door. Her mother's office became more and more inhospitable. The air got thicker, the room got smaller. And still Lily sat in her chair, waiting, waiting, waiting – the only thing keeping her head on straight was the fact that school started in another week. She knew that would bring a whole new set of problems to the table, but at least she wouldn't be spending the days in the office with her mother.

Friday evening, as she was pulling out of her parking spot, Mrs. McCormick let out a huff.

"You're spending next week with your father," she said, her head turned to the back window, as if she were telling someone over her shoulder.

"Oh."

"Hopefully he'll know what to do with you." Mrs. McCormick turned back to face the front and put her SUV in drive. "Because I certainly don't."

Lily said nothing.

"You throw away the only thing you had going for you, you start lying and sneaking out... you've become a complete delinquent," she continued on.

Lily continued to say nothing.

"Really, I don't know what I did wrong to deserve such disobedience. I don't know where I went wrong."

There was something Lily wanted to say in response. A lot of somethings. An outright eruption of "somethings" that could've sprang out from Lily's lungs until her throat went sore. Her mind filled to the brim with every angry and frustrated and sad statement, bottlenecking and becoming incomprehensive, indistinguishable from each other.

And there was nothing she could do but sit there, ears burning, face flushing, heart pounding. She didn't even dare cry, because if she started crying, she might then start screaming.

CHAPTER THIRTY-TWO

Lily heard a gentle knock on her door on Monday morning.

"Kiddo?" her father asked, his voice muffled through the door. "Are you awake?"

"Yes." Lily had been awake for a while. Or, to be more precise, Lily had never really fallen asleep.

Her father slowly opened the door and looked in.

"So, I think your mother already told you, but, I'm bringing you with me to work this week," he said, already dressed in his button-down shirt and khaki pants.

"Ah."

"Your mother's going to take Audrey to day camp," her father continued. "And, well, yeah, I'm going to take you to work."

Lily looked to the adjacent wall.

"Okay."

"It'll be fun," he continued on. "It'll be, like, take your daughter to work day. Or, week, I guess."

Lily gave a small smile and nodded.

"Sure."

"So, um, when you're ready, we can go?"

Lily took a deep breath and sighed.

"Sounds good."

Her father stood in her doorway for a moment longer, looking away from Lily and at one of the corners in her room.

"Well, I'll be downstairs, then," he said finally. "Come down when you're ready?"

Lily looked at her father, his posture, his face. His slightly slumped shoulders, the creases in his forehead. His hands buried deep in his pockets. His averted gaze. There was something about it that made her heart both full and hurt at the exact same time.

"Sure thing."

*

"So, are you excited about school?"
Her father looked over briefly from his spot at the driver's side.
Lily let her head slide back against the headrest.
"I guess?"
"Oh, well, that wasn't very optimistic."
Lily shrugged.
"It's school."
"Yeah, but it's your junior year. Now you get to think about colleges and all that stuff. That's fun."
Lily didn't know what else to say aside from another, "I guess?"
"Well, yeah, I guess applying for college isn't exactly the funnest thing in the world," her father replied. A gentle silence fell between the two of them. After a heavy sigh, her father added: "You know, if you need anything for school – any supplies, or anything like that – we can always pick some up after work. Or, if you'd like, you could raid our supply closet and I'll look the other way. You'll have all the manila folders and printer paper a girl could ever ask for."
Lily couldn't help but chuckle. She smiled and closed her eyes and shook her head.
"I didn't realize stealing was part of 'Take Your Daughter to Work' day," she quipped.
"Of course it is! It's right there in the brochure. Show your daughter around, introduce her to your boss, raid the office supply closet... oh, and then you break for lunch."
Lily let out a sharp, loud laugh.
"Ah, good to know the old man's still got it," said her father.
Lily watched the world through the windshield. The steady movement of the cars on the highway. The occasional overpass. An entire community up and commuting to work.

*

In many ways, her father's office building was no different than her mother's. Another industrial park, another set of bland, gray buildings. Beige cubicles and gray carpets and fluorescent lighting. It made her skin crawl, just thinking about how people came here, day after day, all day long, for weeks, months, years... it made Lily ache for the gym all the more.

Instead of going straight to her father's office – which was actually set of desks in one corner of the building, cordoned off with a few cubicle walls and shared with another person – Mr. McCormick showed Lily around, introducing her to coworkers and pointing out meeting rooms and machinery.

"And that over there is the kitchen," said her father. "We've got a vending machine if you're hungry. Free coffee and tea, which is always a plus."

He eventually showed Lily to his workspace. It was bigger than the cubicles in the center of the floor; more spacious, with a circular table in between his side and his coworker's side. Both desks were filled with files and folders.

"So, what I do, usually, is kind of boring," said her father. "A lot of answering emails and filling out spreadsheets, that kind of thing. I don't have much in the way of entertainment, but... hmm... do you know origami?"

"Not really."

"Ah, well... I was going to say, I could give you some paper to fold but... paper airplanes?" Her father paused and picked up a sheet of printer paper. "So long as you promise to not fly them?"

Lily smiled and closed her eyes.

"I'm good," she said. "But thanks."

Even with all of the introductions and friendly greetings, the first half of the day trudged along. Her father tried to keep her engaged – showing her how the copy machine works, narrating what he was doing, asking if she was doing okay – but Lily spent most her time sitting at the table, idly folding a piece of paper.

"And – sent!" her father said around noontime, before swiveling around in his office chair. "So, kiddo. What do you want to do for lunch?"

"Lunch?"

"Yeah, lunch," her father responded. "There isn't too much around here, but there's a restaurant down the street we could go to."

Something about the offer made Lily's heart heavy.

"That works for me," she said.

"Well, excellent, then." Her father got up from his chair before turning to his cubemate. "Randall, I'll see you in a bit."

"Have fun at lunch," said the cubemate, his back still turned to Lily, still typing methodically away.

Lily and her father snaked their way out of the cubicle farm, into the elevator lobby, and out of the building. Lily stepped into the sunlight, pausing and closing her eyes and feeling the sun against her forehead.

"Are you okay?" her father asked, pausing, watching her, his keys in his hand.

Lily opened her eyes.

"Yeah, sure, I'm okay," she said, and walked with her dad to his car.

The restaurant was a modest, national chain, but Lily was hard-pressed to think of the last time she had been out at *any* restaurant. It made the clichéd, cookie cutter décor feel welcoming and homey.

"So, what are you thinking of getting?" her father asked as they sat down.

Lily picked up the menu.

"I'm not sure."

"Well, pick whatever you want. My treat."

Lily looked up from the menu and into her father's eyes. The heavy feeling returned to her heart. When was the last time she spoke more than a few lines to her father? When was the last time they had spent *any* amount of time together?

"Thanks," said Lily, "...Dad."

Lily scanned the menu, unsure of what she wanted and yet wanting to order everything. She paused to look up at the waitress, who came to get their drink order, and then went right back to the meal options.

A burger. A big, juicy burger. With bacon. And fries.

"So… how do you like my work?" her father asked after a while.

Lily looked up.

"Your work?"

"Yeah, what did you think of it?" said her father. "I know, it's probably not that exciting. The adult world is a bit of a drag like that."

Lily shrugged and looked at her menu, zeroing in again on the picture of the burger.

"It's okay," she said to the menu. "I mean, it's nicer than, well... Mom's."

She paused and licked her lips and took a hard swallow. She said that word – "mom" – so rarely that it sounded foreign. She felt like a fraud for even using it.

Her father gave a half-hearted laugh.

"Well, every office will be different."

"Hmm," was all Lily could say in response.

Another silence fell between the two. Lily kept her eyes on the menu, this time scanning the appetizers and the desserts. She could get whatever she wanted.

"Listen, kiddo..." her father began, his words slow and strained. "I know... I know things have been tough. And I know it hasn't been an easy year for you. And if there's anything you want to talk about, I'm here to listen."

Lily skewed her mouth to one side and closed her menu, still staring downwards.

"Thanks," she said.

"I mean, I get it. Who wants to talk to their dad? I didn't, when I was your age," he continued. "But I get it. And I get wanting to do your own thing. When I was your age, I was going off to parties all the time, sneaking out..."

"I wasn't at a party," Lily blurted out. She looked away. It was closing in on 12:30 now. Rachel's kickboxing class was probably in full swing.

"Well, I believe you, that you weren't at a party," her father said, and then fell silent.

Lily didn't know what else to say. She scanned the restaurant; the people in the booths across from her, the decorations hanging from the wall, the flat screen TVs that all had on baseball.

"Is it okay if I ask where you *actually* were, then, on Saturday?" her father asked, his voice suddenly soft.

Lily looked at her father.

"It would stay between you and me. Pure confidentiality. I wouldn't tell your mother, or Audrey, or anyone." Her father put up three fingers in the air. "Scout's honor."

Lily smirked and gave a slight roll of the eyes.

"Because, really, if you weren't at a party, where were you?" her father pressed. "Is there a boy?"

Lily looked back down at the table, at her menu. She thought about Freddy, and she thought about Leon. She thought about everything that happened with Freddy. She thought about what happened with Leon.

Lily shook her head slightly.

"No boys," was all she could say.

"Well, okay. No boys," her father replied. "Although you're at an age where that *is* okay. Normal, even. You're sixteen. You want to go to the mall and hang out with your friends..."

"I don't want to go to the mall," Lily interrupted.

"Okay, you don't want to go to the mall," said her father. "And, hey, if you don't want to tell me, that's okay, too. I totally understand..."

"I was at a boxing event," Lily said, slowly and deliberately, with her eyes closed. For a brief second, it felt like she was back at the event, back watching the fights with other gym members around her.

"Oh... a boxing event?" said her father. "How did you end up at a boxing event?"

The waitress stepped in at that moment. They ordered their food and Lily watched as their waitress walked away, checking in at other tables as she made her way back to the kitchen area.

"It's a long story," she said to the kitchen door.

"Well, if it's anything, I like long stories."

Lily looked around the restaurant again. Diagonally across from her was a mother with her two-year-old son. Her whole face lit up as she patted his hands and sang some type of song. Her son giggled and wiggled and hit at his mother's hands with all his might.

"I never worked at a coffee shop," she said, her eyes on the mother.

"I gathered as much."

"I started going to a boxing gym, instead."

"Oh, wow... a boxing gym," her father responded. "I didn't realize those were still around."

Lily looked at her father. She didn't know what response she was expecting from him, but somehow that wasn't it.

"Well, they're around," was all she could say.

"And... and the boxing event? Were you... were you fighting in it?"

"No, just there to watch," said Lily. "Some of the people from the gym fought in it, though."

"Oh, well, that's good…" her father said, trailing off.

"Yeah…" said Lily, trailing off as well.

There was a pause as their food came out. Two plates slid in front of them: a grilled sandwich for her father and a cheeseburger for Lily. Lily looked down at her plate, picking at the fries.

"Did you like it?"

"Like what?"

"Boxing," her father said. "Did you like it?"

Lily pressed her lips together and sat up a little straighter.

"I did. I really did," she said, her words distant and disembodied. "It made me feel strong."

"Strong, like, feeling like you could lift heavy things?"

Lily gave a weak laugh.

"Like I was actually capable," Lily said, her voice becoming more and more foreign. "Like I could just be me and not apologize for it."

"Wow, Lily… kiddo…" her father said, his voice bordering on a coo. "And dancing never made you feel like that?"

"I hated dancing," Lily said with a slight bit of venom. "I hated how it made me feel."

"Kiddo… if I had known…"

"I would've stayed in it anyway," Lily said. The more she talked, the more it felt like she was slowly separating from her body. "That's what… Mom… would've wanted."

"Oh, kiddo, I'm so sorry…"

Lily looked at her food. The edges of her vision were starting to blur, but the burger and fries came in crisp and sharp.

"Do you love my mother?"

"What?"

She looked up and zeroed in on her father.

"Do you love my mother?" she repeated.

"Of course I do," her father said. "I love her. I love all you guys."

"But… loving your family… that's different," Lily pressed. "What I mean is… love. Do you love her?"

Her father took in a deep breath.

"Your mother gave me two beautiful, intelligent little girls," he stated, his words slow and measured. "Two daughters who mean the world to me. And we have built a wonderful life together. It's all I could've asked for."

Lily caught her breath. She could feel her entire face flush. All she wanted at that moment was to get up from her spot, walk around the table, and hug her dad.

Lily bit her lip and picked up one of her French fries instead.

"Please don't tell Mom about the boxing gym," she said, taking a tiny bite.

"I wouldn't dream of it."

*

"Imagine this hypothetical scenario."

Lily and her dad were at the restaurant again for lunch the next day. Different table, different waitress, different food, but still the same atmosphere, still the same surreal feeling.

"Okay," he said.

"Tomorrow, you wake up, and you're not married to Mo—you're not married to Nina anymore. There's still me and Audrey and the house… and, like, finances are not a problem, and all that stuff. But now you're in a universe where the marriage has been wiped from the records. Nina is still out there, but you now live in a world where she isn't married to you anymore. Would you track her down and marry her again?"

Her dad gave a slight, nervous chuckle.

"Why the sudden interest in our marriage, Lily?"

Lily tilted to her head to one side. Was there a clean answer to the question? Was it not something she had been wondering about, for years, and only now was there reason to talk about it?

"I'm curious."

"Well, of course I would," said her dad. "She's my wife."

"But she's not. Not in that universe," Lily went on. "And she'd still be her. And she'd still be passive-aggressive and snippy and…" Lily sighed and rested her head in her hands. "Our family is so messed up."

"Lily…"

"No." Lily lifted her head. "It's true. Nothing that happens in that house is normal. At the very least, it isn't healthy. And maybe I just want to know why."

Her dad sighed and rested his forearms on the table.

"We're doing the best we can, with what we have," he said after a moment.

Lily bit her lip. Around her was the idle chatter of a restaurant. Lighthearted and fun and easy.

"I'm sorry," she said after a moment. "I shouldn't have said any of that."

"It's okay, kiddo." Her dad's voice was gentle and soft, yet strong and affirming at the same time. "You were speaking from the heart. That's a good place to speak from."

Lily gave out a small, forceful exhale.

"And I'm sorry," he continued. "I'm sorry for any time it felt like I contributed to that... that 'messed up' feeling."

Lily placed one hand behind her neck and squeezed at muscles. Inhale. Exhale.

"It's okay," she said. "Like you said. We're all doing the best we can, with what we have."

*

The rest of the week went by lightheartedly. They still spent every lunch at the restaurant, but the conversations never went back to heavy topics. And the topic of her mother – of his wife – was never brought up again.

The topic of the O'Reilly Gym was never brought up again, either. Perhaps it was because it was now a secret between the two, something that would never be shared with the rest of the family. Something delicate and sacred.

But Lily wanted to bring it up. She wanted to bring it up again and again and again. She wanted to talk about the gym and she wanted to talk about Jimmy and she wanted to keep talking until she found a way to get back there again. Lily had been wondering feverishly what she could do to return. Sneaking over there seemed highly unlikely, not with her mother cracking down.

But now that her dad knew, now that her dad understood – perhaps, maybe, there was a chance.

But now the conversations were willfully superficial. It was as if both of them had teetered too close to the edge of something and were now acting as cautiously as possible, avoiding the cliffs by all means necessary.

Before Lily knew it, the week was over. That following Monday, instead of going with her dad to his job, she would be returning to high school.

It would be her first year as a non-ballerina. It would be her first year without Evelyn walking the halls. But it would be yet another year of mean girls and tedious assignments and a feeling of complete isolation.

*

The weekend before school started was spent like so many other weekends before: Lily, for the most part, staying in her room. Holed up and partitioned off. The rest of the world went on. Even her father went back to his usual routine.

She thought about getting a job. An actual job. And getting a job near the gym. She'd work her shifts without ever sneaking over to the gym for the first few months, in case her mother came by to snoop. But then, maybe, she could get to the gym before and after work. And her father already knew of the gym, so it wouldn't be like she was being completely dishonest, right?

It was a terrible plan, but it was the only plan she had. She had to get back. She just had to.

*

Sunday afternoon, Lily crossed paths with Audrey, as Lily was heading to the bathroom and Audrey was heading downstairs.

Lily gave an awkward smile. Her own little sister, and yet their relationship was like two mild acquaintances. It reminded Lily that family was not about blood. Similar DNA does not create connection, and it doesn't guarantee a bond. Perhaps, someday, when Audrey was older (and Lily had moved out), they would bond. But maybe not.

"School is tomorrow," she heard from behind her.

Lily turned.

"Yeah. First day," she responded. She forced another awkward smile.

Audrey looked at the stairs.

"Where were you, on Saturday night?" Audrey asked.

"I'm not telling you," Lily spat back. Her response felt odd against Audrey's dispassionate demeanor.

"Why?" Audrey asked, with the same level of detachment.

"Because you'd tell Mom."

Audrey paused again.

"You didn't get in trouble for sneaking out."

"Yeah, I did," said Lily.

Audrey continued to look at the stairs.

"It wasn't really a punishment," she replied. "You snuck out and lied."

Lily sighed and tilted her head back.

"I'm sorry if you didn't think I got punished enough."

Audrey was silent.

"It's not fair," she stated.

Lily didn't know what to say, or how to respond. She looked at her sister, who looked simultaneously 10 and 100 years old, her eyes fixated on the stairwell, her gaze a thousand miles away.

"I'm sorry," was all Lily could say.

Audrey shrugged her shoulders and started walking down the stairs. Lily watched her turn the corner, disappearing onto first floor. A heaviness in her heart resurfaced, but it didn't make her want to give her sister a hug – not like the feeling had with her dad. It made her want to stand there and continue staring and feel the hefty thump of her heart against her chest.

CHAPTER THIRTY-THREE

The high school looked exactly the same. Same redbrick building, same scattered shrubs and trees, same narrow windows. The sameness of everything made it hard for Lily to think she was starting a new year. It made Lily feel like she was repeating her sophomore year all over again, like she had stepped into a time machine and was given a chance to redo the year with everything that she knew now.

Her mother stopped her SUV in front of the building, the car silent except for the AC blasting.

"I can pick you up this week, but we'll have to do something about the ride situation after that," she said, her voice cool and calm and deliberate. "You're not going to the studio after school anymore, so there's no reason for me to be taking time out of my day to act as shuttle service. I think there's a bus stop nearby. You can start taking the bus."

Lily looked at her backpack and shrugged.

"Okay."

Lily unbuckled her seatbelt and opened the door.

"And no 'good-bye'? No 'thanks for the ride, Mom'?" her mother said.

Lily pressed her tongue to the roof of her mouth and took a deep breath.

Inhale. Exhale.

"Thanks for the ride, Mom," she parroted back.

"Have a good first day at school, then."

Lily exited the SUV and shut the door. She turned to the building and made her way in.

The world around her was both busy and isolating. Groups of kids hung out in small circles around lockers, talking and laughing loudly. Others snaked around the groups, either alone or in pairs, filling the hallways even further. The noises echoed around Lily. She gripped both straps of her backpack and maneuvered her way around, her head slightly ducked down.

"Welcome back, Thumbelina," a voice called out from beside her.

Lily looked over to see Bella, one of the girls from the grade above her, and her clique of friends. Bella smiled wickedly and Lily quickly looked away, walking just a little bit faster to her homeroom.

Lily sat in silence as the morning began, finding a spot in the back and moving only when the homeroom teacher started assigning seats. The chaotic world around her felt muffled and distant. The morning announcements from the speakers sounded like they were coming from a mile away.

Her junior year. Lily had to remind herself that that meant only two years' worth of mean girls – and, soon enough, there would be only one, and then she'd be gone. She reminded herself that she had already survived two years of high school and that she could survive two more.

And then she could go to college and move away and maybe, finally, feel like she could breathe.

The same way she felt like she could breathe while she was at the gym.

She knew her mother's game. She knew exactly what her mother was doing, telling Lily to take the bus. But she was okay with it. It could be a great avenue to sneak back to the gym. Take the wrong bus, go to the downtown area. She could only be there for an hour or two, but it would be at least something. And, if her mother ever came home early, she could always say she had taken up running. She could stash her gym clothes in her backpack. She could make it work.

Devising this plan was the only thing that kept Lily going, as she moved from one class to the next, listening to teachers introduce themselves and talk about the year ahead. It kept her going as she moved through the sea of people in between classes, a mass of people so large Lily couldn't fathom how all of them fit into one building. It kept her going as lunchtime hit and Lily realized that, for once, she didn't go to school with baggies of chopped carrots and celery, and she didn't have any money for a cafeteria meal – and, furthermore, she didn't have any interest in going into the cafeteria, of rehashing that painful and familiar isolation.

Her plans kept her going as she spent lunchtime in the bathroom, hiding one of the stalls with her head hung back.

In some ways, it was the only thing that got her through the entire week. A week filled with monotony and noise. A week where someone (she wasn't sure who) went, "Where's your tutu?" while walking past her locker. A week where she went from class to class, counting the hours, counting the minutes, until she was able to leave the building and suffer through a car ride with her mother and get back home and retreat to her room.

She needed it. She needed to think about ways to get back to the gym. She realized her complete immersion in ballet was what originally got her through school. Without anything to buffer it, the mean comments stung worse, her classes grew more tedious, and the sheer loneliness of it all became palpable.

She didn't really have any high school friends to speak of. She didn't even have people to speak casually with before homeroom started. Whatever few friendships she had made in school had fallen by the wayside long before high school hit.

But the times she felt most alone was when her mother pulled her SUV into the garage instead of the parking lot of the dance studio. It happened when Lily walked up to her room instead of down the hall to change into her leotard.

It happened as she spent her time in her room, listening to her mother conduct business directly below her, listening to her father and Audrey's casual voices, listening for the clanking and banging of pots and pans that never happened (it had been almost a month without any type of family dinner, Lily realized).

That was when she felt it the most. That was when something heavy and cold and persistent made its home in her chest. That was when she felt like there was no true ground underneath her, that part of her was floating away. It made her long for the dance studio, if only to have that sense of groundedness, that sense of belonging – to remove that pain in her heart, that ache in her soul.

She had to get back to the gym. By any means necessary. She just had to.

*

Lily waited to see what event or function her mother would be dragging them to that weekend. But yet, there was nothing. There hadn't been an event in weeks. Maybe a month. About as long as they had gone without a family dinner.

Lily wondered what her mother's angle was, with such a dramatic pullback. Because there was an angle. There *always* was. There was no way this was a coincidence. There had to be a reason. There just had to.

Sunday morning came. No declarations of going to church, no community luncheon, nothing. Just the rising sun and the air of late summer and the heralds of the upcoming Monday. Her father wished her a good morning. There was a little pitter-pattering happening downstairs. But that was it.

That was, until Audrey showed up at Lily's bedroom door.

She didn't say anything at first. She just stood there.

"Can I help you?" Lily asked, clearing her throat.

Audrey skewed her mouth slightly and looked towards the bed. She had this slightly disconnected look about her, something she got from time to time, as if her brain was too busy processing to stay in the real world.

"Mom says you're taking the bus from now on," she stated.

Lily let out a slow breath.

"Yeah, I'm taking the bus," she said.

"I'm not taking the bus."

"You're right. You're not," Lily responded, her voice matching Audrey's flat tone. "Dad will still drop you off, like he always does."

Audrey paused again.

"Where were you, that Saturday night."

"I'm not telling you," said Lily. "Like I said before: you'd just tell Mom. Why would I tell you anything?"

Audrey tilted her head.

"You know they like *you* better." Her words were still without any melody, but now there was a sadness, a wariness, about them.

"'They'?"

"Mom and Dad," Audrey continued. "They like you better than me. You know they do."

"No they don't."

"You got to do ballet. You got ballet shoes and ballet classes and... you got everything. They like you more."

"You could've done ballet, too, if you wanted."

Audrey shrugged.

"No," she said. "Not the way you got to. You were the star. They like you better."

"Dad drives you everywhere. You spend all that time together," Lily said. "And I don't think Mom likes *anyone*."

That got a slight smile out of Audrey.

"Ballet, all the training – all of it – I never asked for it," Lily continued. "You know that, right?"

Audrey said nothing.

"It's not something to be jealous about. It really isn't."

Audrey shrugged again.

"And you still won't tell me where you were on Saturday?" Audrey asked.

"I'm not going to."

Audrey turned away, but didn't leave. Audrey's behavior, these little ticks, things that Lily could never fully understand. And maybe she never would.

"I hope you had a good first week of school," said Lily, forcing her words to sound warm and welcoming.

"Thanks. You too," Audrey said in monotone, before walking down the hall and into her room, closing the door behind her.

CHAPTER THIRTY-FOUR

"Did Thumbelina gain weight?"

Bella and her group were stationed outside the main entrance that Monday morning.

"Yeah, I think she has," her friend – Cora – chimed in.

Lily kept her head down and took a wide circle around the group.

"I can't believe it. Miss Prima Ballerina ate a meal or two."

"Better not make it a habit," Cora added. "Nobody likes a fat ballerina."

A chorus of laughter erupted from the group. Lily could still hear their voices, even after she went inside, long after the door closed behind her. Words that made her ears sting and bones shake. She reflexively touched her arms. She swore she could feel the muscle that she had built up already disappearing.

She had to get back to the gym. She just had to.

*

The bus ride back to her neighborhood that afternoon was a flurry of background noise. Just like the ride to school, Lily spent it with her eyes out the window, counting the telephone poles as they swept by, tracing the phone lines with her eyes.

Lily got off at her stop and snaked through the neighborhood, deliberately taking a right when she should've taken a left, going down a route she knew that she had to take.

She rounded the corner of her street, her eyes on the white house just ahead of her. There were cars in the driveway now, and grass sprouting from the spot where the "For Sale" sign had been. The shades were up and the curtains pulled back, revealing their inner world to the street. The TV was on in the living room, situated next to a few opened cardboard boxes.

Lily walked up to the white post fence, her hands on her hips, her eyes on the windows. Did the new owners know what had happened there? Would they have purchased the house if they knew? Did they believe in ghosts?

Lily kept staring until a figure walked into the living room, temporarily blocking the image on the TV. Lily immediately turned and kept walking. The house was filled with life again, and Lily couldn't tell if she was happy or heartbroken about it.

*

Her own house was empty when she entered. She had at least an hour or two until her father would return with Audrey, back from afterschool care. Three hours is plenty of time for a visit. Lily was going to figure out if a school bus went near Main Street and if she'd be able to sneak on. She already thought about the things she'd tell Jimmy, what she'd try to say to Leon, if he were still there.

Her mother's newest angle was apparently neglect, and Lily was going to use that to her advantage. If she said she had joined a club or two, how would her mother know differently? Would her mother leave work and spy? Maybe she would've a month ago, but it looked like she was playing a different game now.

Lily went to her room and threw her backpack on the bed and closed the door. She was coming home from school around the same time that she had once been coming home from the gym. She closed her eyes and imagined what the gym would be like right now. She imagined the people strolling in. She imagined Jimmy's boxing class, and the students jumping ropes or stretching or going at the bags. She imagined the fighters practicing drills and partnering up. She could hear Jimmy's voice, hollering about technique and the importance of *keepin' ya hands up*.

Lily stood in her fighting stance and brought her arms to her head. She opened her eyes, but they weren't looking at her room. They were looking at the open space on the second floor at the gym, with nothing but the gym equipment and the mirror near her.

She started throwing punches into the air. Quick jabs and straights, her arms snapping back to guard her head. She let out a few of the punch combos that she knew by heart, bobbing and weaving in between. She swung her legs out for a few kicks, letting them sail high into the air.

Her breath started to match up with her movements. Quick, forceful exhales on her punches, making the sound of released steam. She continued to shadowbox, her body pivoting and weaving and moving seamlessly. Jab, straight, hook. Front kick. Side kick. Spinning hook kick. Jab, straight, jab. Her breath played out a staccato beat and her body moved to the rhythm of her own music.

Time became as irrelevant as the scenery around her. She stopped only when she thought she heard the garage door open. She looked out her window to see who might have pulled in, only to find a large truck passing by. Her driveway stayed empty. The garage door stayed closed.

Lily took a step back from her window and turned to face her room. Everything was still in its place. Furniture and decorations that had been there, in those exact spots, since she was a kid. But everything felt foreign. Everything felt different. It felt like Lily had been transported to a new universe, one that was just slightly off from the one she originally belonged to. The only things that felt real was her pounding heart and the dull, gentle ache in her muscles.

*

Tuesday morning rolled around. Lily was getting into the routine of getting ready for school in ways that made her invisible – never really in the same room as anyone else, out the door for the bus before anyone could say anything.

She waited for the bus alongside a handful of other kids – mostly freshmen, with one sophomore. Lily was the only junior. No one in their senior year was there. She watched the bus come around the bend and she gave a sheepish grin to the driver when she boarded. She found a spot near the front and slid to the end of the bench, her eyes already out the window. The bus was barely half-full but already bursting with noise. But the racket didn't bother Lily. Unlike her mother's SUV, Lily didn't feel guarded there. There was nothing that she had to say. She could disappear in her seat and watch the world pass her by.

She got through her morning, going from class to class, walking through the sea of people, pausing occasionally at her locker to drop off books. The monotonous pattern of it all lulled Lily into a hypnotic state.

The hypnotized feeling continued on into the afternoon. She walked through the hallway after lunch, a chaotic and chattering world around her. People walking in every which direction, a few off to the side, a few cutting through. A highway of students.

Lily was only able to recount what happened next long after it happened. Perhaps that was due to the hypnotic nature of it all. Perhaps the hypnosis was the reason it happened in the first place.

In some ways, it was something Lily had gotten used to. Every once in a while, one of the mean girls would push her as she walked past – not enough to cause a scene, but enough to get her off-balance, to move Lily just enough to get a good laugh.

And there Lily was, walking down the hall, when a set of hands came rushing towards her. Hands meant to shove Lily to the side, to get a good laugh. Lily didn't even see who the hands belonged to. She didn't even think about the hands, or the act of getting shoved, or anything of that nature.

She just reacted.

Lily dropped her books, weaved to one side, and countered the would-be shove with a hook to the right.

She didn't plan such a countermove. She didn't plan any of it. If she had, she might not have done it. She might have allowed herself to get shoved and she would've kept walking and she would've heard the maniacal laughs of the girls behind her.

But pure muscle memory had kick in. Pure instinct. So pure that Lily zoned out in those few seconds, aware only when Bella hit the ground in a semi-stunned state and everyone around them stopped walking and a teacher came rushing out, yelling:

"What the hell is going on?!"

Lily looked down at her books, at Bella, at the people around her, at the teacher coming towards her. Only then did she realize what had happened.

Bella had tried to push her. And Lily had just punched out Bella.

CHAPTER THIRTY-FIVE

"This is unbelievable!"

Her mother stood in the principal's office, her arms crossed tightly over her chest.

"She was pushed..." her father began from his spot in a chair.

"I don't care! We're lucky that the parents don't want to press charges!"

Lily sat in the other chair, arms crossed protectively over her torso, her eyes on her lap.

"It was self-defense—" her father began again.

"It was a fight!"

"Mrs. McCormick, I understand your frustration. We are taking this matter very seriously."

Lily's principal – a tall lady with short hair and a perfectly pressed suit – sat behind her desk, her hands gingerly clasped, and looked at her mother with sincere, caring eyes.

"Well, this is a very serious matter!" her mother scoffed back.

"Nina, isn't this a bit much?" her father asked.

"No, it's not a bit much," her mother responded. "Clearly our daughter is out of control. Quitting ballet, sneaking out, lying to her family, and now *this*? Now she's getting into *fights*?"

"It wasn't a fight," said her father.

"She punched another girl in the face!" Her mother took a step closer to Lily. "Who taught you do to that, huh? To hit people like that?"

Lily met her father's gaze. Her father closed his eyes in response.

"Now, if I am hearing you correctly, Lilian," Principal Cuddy said, turning to Lily. "Isabella would push you, pretty routinely. Am I correct?"

Lily shrugged.

"Yes, ma'am."

"Bullying of any nature is never permitted here," Principal Cuddy continued. "However, responding to bullying with violence isn't permitted, either." Principal Cuddy sighed and unclasped her hands. "Now, as per the rules of the school, both girls will be receiving three-day suspensions."

Mrs. McCormick threw her hands in the air.

"Great! Just in time for college applications," she sneered. "That is, if Lily would even be *going* to college anymore. At this rate, I won't be surprised if she drops out of school entirely!"

"Nina, that's enough…"

"No, no, it's not enough," she retorted. "I'm dealing with a delinquent! A delinquent who just got suspended! For three days! Three!"

"Nina…"

"And I'm not staying home for those three days," Mrs. McCormick went on. "I refuse to have to work from home so I can babysit a criminal."

Blood rushed to Lily's face so quickly and so fiercely that it felt like her whole body would catch fire.

"Then don't."

All three turned to Lily, whose eyes were still on her lap.

"What was that?" Mrs. McCormick barked.

"Then don't," Lily repeated, this time looking up.

"I can stay home. It's okay," her father offered, his voice gentle and reassuring.

"Seriously, if I'm such a criminal, why even bother putting in all this time and energy?" Lily continued.

"Lilian…"

"You have to control every little thing I do," Lily continued, facing her mother head-on. "And when I don't do exactly what you want, then I'm the bad guy. How dare I not do everything you say, how dare I not live out your dreams? How dare I even do anything that didn't first get your stamp of approval? Honestly, are you *that* unhappy with your choices in life that the only way you can handle it is making all of mine?"

For the first time in nearly a half hour, the office was quiet. No one said anything. No one moved. Not even Lily, who refused to break eye contact with her mother.

"She's all yours, Brad," Mrs. McCormick broke the silence with. "You deal with your daughter." She turned to Principal Cuddy and added: "Am I set to go?"

"If you would like," Principal Cuddy said slowly.

Without another word, Mrs. McCormick left the office, slamming the door behind her. The rest of the office sat in silence.

"Mr. McCormick, I don't mean to pry, but, if you would like, I know the names of some great family counselors."

Lily's father sighed and rubbed his eyes.

"No, no. That's alright," he said. "That's… alright."

"Well, then." Principal Cuddy responded with a sigh. "I think that is all, for now. Lily will be welcome to return back to school on Monday. And – Lily?"

Lily turned to face Principal Cuddy.

"You let me know when people are being mean to you," Principal Cuddy continued. "I have no tolerance for bullying. None. But, please, let me handle it. Don't take matters into your own hands."

Lily looked back down at her lap.

"Okay," she gave, her tone noncommittal.

Her dad sighed again, and got up.

"C'mon, then, kiddo. Let's get you home."

*

After a long car ride – punctuated by a few shallow words from her father as he made note of the traffic, on hitting every red light – Lily disappeared into her room. And she stayed there that night, her ears fixed on what was happening in the rest of the house. She listened to her father as he left a second time, this time to pick up Audrey. She listened as her mother eventually came home (late, very late. Way later than she ever had before).

And then everything became quiet. There was a part of her that had been waiting for some type of blow-up. Maybe something from Audrey. Anything, really.

But nothing. Silence.

(Did her sister even know that she had been suspended? There was a chance that she didn't.)

Nothing but chilled and eerie silence. For hours. Later that night, the sound from the TV made its way through the floorboards. Some type of sporting event, most likely her father watching.

And, for some weird, strange reason, the sound of her father's TV lulled Lily into a deep, dreamless sleep – the most sound sleep she had had in ages.

*

Lily woke to the sound of the garage door. She got up and looked out the window and watched her mother's SUV pull out of the driveway. As her mother turned onto the road, Lily could make out Audrey in the passenger seat.

(If Audrey didn't know about the suspension yet, she probably knew now.)

Lily trudged over to her bed and threw her covers over the mattress, making her bed in a haphazard manner. She tugged lightly at the corners, rubbed her eyes, and looked back at the window.

Day one of her suspension.

There was a gentle knock at her door. Lily turned around and opened it. At the doorframe stood her father, dressed in his usual business wear.

"So, ah, today is the first day, of, uh, well, you know," her father stammered out. "I can work from home… or, or we can go to the office, if you would like."

Lily tilted her head to one side.

"I'd rather stay home," she said.

Her father tilted his head to the opposite side.

"Yeah, I figured," he said, his eyes on the ground. "That whole 'take your daughter to work' thing was kind of your mother's idea, anyway. I can easily work from home."

Lily simply nodded in response.

Her father took a few steps away from the door and then turned around.

"And – if you need anything. Anything at all. I'm here," he said. "Okay?"

Lily gave a slight smile.

"Okay."

"Okay, then." Her father walked away, trotting down the stairs and disappearing onto the first floor.

Lily walked over to her bed and plopped herself on it, her eyes on the ceiling. It was Wednesday. If the schedule were still the same, there would be a boxing class in a few hours. She wondered who would be there, and who wouldn't. Were any of them also in school? College?

Lily thought about Leon. She thought about Jimmy. She thought about Rachel. Man, if she could only tell them what she had done at school! Jimmy would be so proud of her. Rachel would be concerned, but secretly happy that Lily stood up for herself. And how would Leon react? Possibly with a smile and a nod. Nothing fancy. But she could go into that building and talk about punching out a mean girl and it would be the talk of the day.

And there would be class. The lessons, the drills, the technique. The sweat and the good ache and the feeling of fatigue that gave hint to how strong you were becoming.

She could hear Jimmy's voice as clear as if he were right next to her. She could hear the noises of the gym – the clanks of the metal loops holding up the heavy bags, the sound of the speedbag as it *thwapped* against its frame. She could hear the ding of the bell. She could hear the sound of gloves hitting mitts and she could hear Leon's voice shouting, "One! One, two! One, one, two!"

She could even smell the concrete walls, the hot, humid air, the musk of sweat. She could feel and see and hear and smell so much of the gym that, for a brief moment, she forgot she was in her room. She forgot that she was surrounded by pastel colors and enveloped in chilled air pumped out from the vents. She remembered only when she heard a noise from the first floor and opened her eyes and took in the room around her.

With a sigh, Lily got off her bed and went downstairs and into the kitchen. The coffee pot had been turned off, but the carafe was still half full. Lily pulled out a mug, poured herself a cup of coffee, and leaned against the counter.

What was she going to do that day? What was she going to do Thursday, or Friday? What were people saying at school? What would they say when she got back? Would this mean she'd be left alone, or did she open the floodgates to people who wanted to fight her? None of those questions, she felt like answering.

She sipped her coffee – lukewarm and bitter – and hung her head back. Maybe her mother was right. Maybe she had been throwing her life away, piece by piece. And now she was suspended from school. Really, what *was* next?

Lily finished her coffee, placed the cup in the sink, and looked at the cupboards. She knew she could have any food she wanted. She knew her father wouldn't mind. But her stomach was in knots. Nothing looked appealing.

Lily trudged back up to her room and threw herself back onto her bed. She had no interest in staying cooped up inside her house for hours, upon hours, upon hours on end. She had been doing that for too long, and the idea of doing it one more time was unacceptable. She looked out the window again, pushed herself off her bed, and changed out of her pajamas. She grabbed her sneakers, threw her hair into a ponytail, and walked downstairs to the office.

"I'm going for a walk," she said to her father.

Her father turned from his computer and smiled.

"Oh, okay, kiddo," he responded. "Have fun."

Lily pressed her lips together.

"Will do."

Lily stood for a moment longer, challenging the awkward silence. Challenging either of them to say something more. When nothing else happened, Lily walked out of the house.

Lily turned right at the end of the walkway and towards what was once Josh's house. She was ready to stop in front of it, ready to say some type of prayer, pay some type of reverence – something. But as the house came into view, so did two little kids darting from the front door to the car in the driveway.

A woman came out of the front door as well, following the kids. She looked over at Lily and waved. Lily waved back. The woman immediately returned her attention to her kids, cutting across the front lawn to the driveway.

Lily looked at the car, the kids, the mom, the white post fence. She smiled, looked to the ground, and kept walking.

She snaked through her neighborhood, letting her mind wander. She passed by the place where Leon had dropped her off, the place where Freddy had dropped her off. She thought about their cars, their words, their interactions with her.

The air felt so similar to how it was when she first did these type of walks, back in June. She remembered those days vividly – feeling unmoored, unanchored. Walking the streets as if on autopilot. Unsure what to do next. And how it was only luck that she stumbled upon O'Reilly's Boxing Gym. Jimmy's gym.

And was she doing now? Walking around, unanchored, unmoored. The closest thing she felt to feeling grounded again was devising plans to return to the gym. And all of them were set in the hypothetical future. All of them were slightly fantastical. All of them were unsustainable and designed to fail.

And all of them involved her being sneaky, of hiding herself. They all involved constantly looking over her shoulder and hoping she wouldn't get caught, wouldn't be found out. They all involved her denying herself any chance of living her life the way she truly wanted to.

And what exactly was stopping her? What was keeping her locked up in her room and waiting away the hours and wondering how she could move about in the shadows? Why was she living like a prisoner in her own home – in her own life?

How was this any different than forcing herself to ballet practice, or eating what her mother told her to eat, or living the way she was told to live?

She was the girl who punched out Bella Sampson. She was the girl who could get the attention of an entire gym with her kicks and punches. She was the girl who said, "No," to ballet and never returned again. And she had only grown stronger since that day.

So – truly – what was stopping her?

What was stopping her from doing anything?

Lily immediately turned around and took the most direct route home. Her mind zeroed in on exactly what she was going to do next, what the first words out of her mouth would be.

She started jogging back to her street, back to her house, and in through the front door. She walked down the hall, stood in the office doorway, and stated with a voice she had never heard herself use before:

"I'm going back to the gym."

CHAPTER THIRTY-SIX

"The gym?" her father repeated.

"Yes," Lily said, attempting to catch her breath. "The gym. I'm going back."

"The boxing gym?"

"Yes."

Her father pushed his chair away from the desk and closed his eyes.

"Okay."

"Today."

Her father gave a slow nod.

"Okay."

"And I don't care if I get in trouble with Mom, and I don't even care if you tell her that I'm going," Lily continued, her face getting hot. "I'm going back, and then I'm going to *keep* going back."

"Okay," her father said. Another awkward, suffocating silence filled the space between them, making Lily more than ready to leave the room, leave the house, and just go.

Her father sighed, rubbed at his mouth, and stood up.

"Do you need a ride?"

"What?" Lily reflexively shot back.

"A ride," said her father. "I can drive you there, if you'd like."

Lily's heart caught in her throat.

"That would be nice," she said.

*

"You walked this, every day?"

Lily watched Main Street come into view from the passenger side, her dad's car making a right down the road Lily knew by heart.

"Every weekday," Lily corrected.

"I wish I had known," he responded. "I could've dropped you off in the morning."

"No, you couldn't," said Lily. "You would've gotten in trouble with Mom."

"There's more to life than trying to avoid getting in trouble," her dad said as he found an empty spot by the old firehouse.

Lily said nothing as he parked, and simply stared at the building with her lips pressed together.

"Now this is a cool place to have a gym," said her dad.

"It really is."

She took in a deep breath and reached for the door handle.

"Thanks for the ride," she said.

"Anytime, kiddo," said her dad. "And, if you can borrow someone's phone, you can always call when you need a ride back."

"That sounds good."

Lily unbuckled her seatbelt and opened the door.

"And, uh, y'know… you could always join the gym, too, if you'd like," Lily offered.

Her dad smiled.

"Maybe," he said. "I think that would be fun."

*

Lily took a few steps into the gym. The boxing class had just finished, and a scattering of guys were hanging out by the boxing ring. Freddy was off to the side, practicing on the speedbag.

"Lily? Lily! Kiddo!"

Jimmy walked over, arms extended, and wrapped Lily in an emphatic hug. She could feel herself slowly relax into the hug, her tense shoulders dissolving, her head resting against his shoulder.

"Geez, kiddo!" Jimmy exclaimed, holding Lily by the arms as he took a step back. "Where've ya been? Isn't school back in session? What're ya doin' here?" Jimmy looked around before saying, "Actually, come upstairs, kiddo. Let's chat upstairs."

"Sure," was all Lily could say. She started following Jimmy across the gym to the stairs in the back. She walked by the speed bag, holding her breath and staring straight ahead as she passed by Freddy. Freddy kept his eyes on the bag, acknowledging neither Jimmy nor Lily.

Lily walked up the stairs and into Jimmy's office. Jimmy sat down at his desk and let out a sigh.

"Ah, kiddo, ya had me worried," he said, planting his elbows on his desk. "Ya just disappeared. Couldn't call ya, couldn't do nothin'..."

"I'm sorry," Lily replied.

"Listen, kiddo, Leon told me... well, when ya weren't showin' up anymore, he said it might be because of... of that night, ya get what I mean? When he dropped ya off?" Jimmy cleared his throat. "Hey, kiddo, really, it's okay. If I had a dime for every time I did that when I was young..."

"That wasn't why..." Lily began, trailed off, cleared her throat, and started up again: "I got caught, and... I couldn't come anymore."

"You got caught?" Jimmy repeated.

"My parents, they thought I was working. But then they realized I wasn't. And then I wasn't allowed out of my parents' sight until school started."

"Ah, geez, kiddo... listen, I don't want ya gettin' in trouble..."

"No, no... it's okay..." Lily paused. "I mean, I was lying because I was scared. I was scared of what my mother would do, but... I'm done being controlled by my family."

Jimmy said nothing and simply nodded.

"They never knew about the gym. Even when they caught me in my lie, I didn't tell them about it," Lily went on. "Well, I eventually told my dad. But, he's all right. I even invited him to join, if he wanted."

"Ah, Lily..." Jimmy chuckled.

"But, this..." Lily pressed her tongue to the roof of her mouth. No tears now. "This is my home. And I'm not losing that."

"Ah, kiddo..." Jimmy got up from his desk, walked over, and took Lily in for another big hug.

No tears. No tears. No tears now.

Inhale. Exhale.

"The door will always be open for ya here. Always," Jimmy stated.

"But, I gotta ask – what are ya doin' here, on a school day?"

Lily sighed and looked to the ground.

"I got suspended."

"Suspended? Kiddo! What happened?"

Lily cocked her head to one side.

"I punched out a girl who tried to push me."

A bright, conspiratorial smile spread across Jimmy's face.

"That's my girl," he said, his eyes gleaming, and gave her another hug.

"I mean, I don't want ya startin' fights, ya hear?" Jimmy added. "But, y'know, if someone is bullyin' ya – ya let 'em have it. Don't let nobody push ya around. But, ya didn't hear that from me, okay?"

Lily laughed and nodded.

"I hear ya," she replied.

"And – ya know, ya dad? He's welcome any time. He really is. I mean, he's gotta pay. This ain't a *total* charity, ya know? I still got a business to run, but, yeah, kiddo, invite ya dad. He can finally sign that waiver for ya," Jimmy gave out a short exhale. "And, kiddo, I really hope he joins. I mean, father-daughter relationships, they can be complicated, but, never too late to try to fix things, right?"

"Right," said Lily, a new weight suddenly placed on her heart. She rested a hand over it and added: "Do you think that'll be the case, with you and your daughter?"

"Melanie?" Jimmy gave a slight chuckle before covering his mouth. "Ah, kiddo, I hope so. We'll see. Maybe, someday. I think ya'd like her. I think you two have a lot in common. You're very similar. Very."

Lily stood there, imagining what Melanie must look like, how she held herself, how she talked.

"What happened, with your family?" Lily heard herself saying. She cleared her throat. "If you don't mind me asking."

Jimmy sighed and looked out his office door, to the gym equipment, the mirror.

"Ah, kiddo. That's a long story... and I hope someday I can figure out the right words to tell it. But... kiddo, just know, people are complicated. They really are. And that don't change once they become a parent. People are complex beasts. But they mean well. Every single one of them. No one wants to play the bad guy."

Jimmy paused, rubbed his eyes, and gave another sigh.

"But, y'know, I really gotta get out there, back to work..." he said. "But ya welcome to do whatever ya'd like. The place is yours, as always."

Lily smiled and fought the urge to give Jimmy one more hug.

"Thank you," she said.

"Ah, kiddo – don't mention it," Jimmy replied, waving one hand in the air. "I'm just happy ya back."

Lily scanned the second floor. The weights, the machines, the mirrors, the windows.

"Me too."

*

Lily walked down the stairs to see Freddy taking off his gloves. Lily set her jaw and walked over to him.

"Can we talk?" she asked.

Freddy kept his eyes down, undoing the black linen wraps on his hands.

"There's nothing to talk about," he said sternly.

Lily looked around her, her skin cold, her heartbeat thumping wildly between her ears.

"I'm sorry," she said, pressing her feet into the floor. "I lied to you about my age and that was stupid and I'm sorry."

Freddy gave a slight roll of his eyes.

"The courts don't care if you lied. You know that, right?" said Freddy.

"There's nothing I can do to change the past," said Lily. "And you have every right to be mad at me."

Freddy started unwrapping his other hand.

"Damn right I do."

"I don't want things to be weird."

"It's a little too late for that."

"I get it. I messed up, but… we go to the same gym. Our paths are going to keep crossing."

Freddy sighed and began rolling the handwraps into a ball.

"I've been leaving you alone. You're the one talking to me."

"If you need to be left alone, then I will leave you alone. But I wanted you to at least know that I'm sorry."

Freddy stayed silent for a moment, zipping up his bag and throwing it over his shoulder.

"You're a really cool girl," Freddy spoke quietly. "And you're stupidly talented. But you're 16. I'm seven years older than you. That's — to be honest, I don't even like to think about it for too long."

"I don't want to get back with you. I just wanted to apologize."

Freddy hung his head and readjusted his strap.

"Well, apology accepted then," he said after a moment. "This gym is home to both of us. You have a point about not letting it be weird."

Lily wracked her brain, trying to figure out what to say next.

"I really am sorry," was all she could think of.

Freddy just nodded in response.

"I'll see you around, okay?"

"Okay."

Freddy turned and started to head out of the gym. Lily watched him go, watched him walk out of the archways and down the sidewalk and out of sight. She thought about his words, his voice, his stature. She thought about sitting next to him under his friend's tree and lying next to him under the moon. She thought about his smile, his green eyes, his smirk. And she thought about the look of pure betrayal he had when he told her that he knew that she had lied to him.

And as she thought these things, she ached. She ached in her heart and she ached in her spirit. She ached in a way that let her know that she still had a long way to go to fully process how she felt for Freddy, what she did to him, and what it all meant for her, going forward.

*

She was tempted to stay at the gym — stay into the evening, let her mother know the truth by her absence.

But she decided against it. She wanted to be home. She wanted to look her mother in the eye. She was done feeling so unmoored and yet so controlled.

It wasn't enough that she told her dad. She couldn't *let* that be enough. She had to confront every area where she felt like she had to scuttle around or it would all be for nothing.

"I'm going to tell Mom," she told her dad that afternoon, when he came to pick her up.

"I support you, in whatever decision you make," he replied.

The sound of the garage door that evening brought Lily to the living room. She watched the front door open, and she watched Audrey pour through. Audrey glanced at Lily briefly before making her way upstairs. Her mother walked in and closed the door behind her.

"Well," she said when she saw Lily. "How was your first day of suspension."

Lily stood a little taller and looked her mother in the eyes.

"It was good," she said. "I realized a lot of things."

"'A lot of things'?" her mother repeated. She started walking to the kitchen, shrugging off her purse as she did. "Okay, then. Like what?"

"For one, I'm done feeling like I can't be me."

"Huh," was all her mother said, continuing to walk into the kitchen.

"I was at a boxing event, that Saturday night," said Lily.

This made her mother turn around.

"Now why in the world were you at a boxing event?"

"I was invited, by my boxing coach," said Lily. "By my boxing *gym*, which I'd been going to all summer – and I'm going back to it."

"A *boxing* gym!" her mother laughed out. As if on cue, her sister came downstairs. "It all makes sense now! So *that's* where you learned to hit people."

"No," Lily asserted. "That's where I learned to be myself. That's where I was today, and that's where I'll be tomorrow – and Friday. And where I'm going to be after school, and on weekends."

Her mother huffed.

"No, you're not."

"Yes, I am." Lily took a step towards her mother. "You don't get to decide my every move like that. Not anymore."

Her mother looked over at Lily's dad.

"Can you believe this?" she said, pointing at Lily.

"I can," said her dad. "And I'm proud of her."

"What?"

"She found something she loves. She's devoted to it. And it makes her happy," he said. "I support it, 100%."

Her mother threw her hands up.

"So you support her becoming a delinquent?"

"This does not make her a delinquent," said Lily's dad. "Truly, Nina, she's not joining a gang. She's part of a gym."

"Well, I'm not paying for it," she retorted.

"Then don't," Lily replied. "I didn't need your help before. I won't need it now."

Her mother said nothing and crossed her arms. The silence filled the room.

And – like that – Lily felt something drain out of her. Lily was suddenly exhausted. She was exhausted in her body and in her mind and in her soul. But still, she stood tall.

"Now, if there's nothing more to say, I'm going to my room," she forced out, crossing her own arms. "You know where to find me."

She stood there for a moment longer, staring her mother directly in the eye, before heading for the stairs. She passed by Audrey, who refused to meet Lily's gaze as she walked past. Lily continued up the stairs, down the hall, and into her room.

The first floor erupted before Lily even closed the door.

"I cannot *believe* you're okay with this!" her mother shouted to Lily's dad. "What has gotten into you?"

"What has gotten into *you*? It's a gym!"

"She's getting into fights at school – and you think this is a good influence?!"

"She punched a bully! That's not the same thing!"

"She lied all summer long, and you're going to *reward* that?"

"Maybe she would've told us about it if you hadn't shut her out the second she quit ballet!"

"She was throwing her *dream* away—"

"No, she was throwing *your* dream away."

Lily closed her door and draped herself across her bed. The voices downstairs were now muffled, but the tone and the volume were still crystal clear.

She stared at the ceiling, tracing the textured lines from one corner to the other. She couldn't remember the last time her parents fought. She had plenty of memories of terse words and silence, but she had no memories of them arguing. Ever.

She felt bad for being the cause of it – but, at the same time, she wasn't. She wondered if her dad always had that in him – this ability to shout and be upset. It was refreshing to hear him raise his voice.

She thought about what he had said at lunch a few weeks back. She thought about the deflection he gave when she asked him if he loved his wife – really loved her, the way a husband is supposed to love a wife.

She thought about what she had told her mother in the principal's office, about life choices. Could the same be said about her dad? Did he regret his choices in life, and instead of dealing with it by micromanaging his children, he became someone who just went about life with his head down?

Your mother gave me two beautiful, intelligent little girls. That's all I could ask for.

As the fight went on, Lily crawled under the covers, the exhaustion sinking into her bones. Her mother's shrill voice rose up through the floor boards. Lily could hear it as clear as day:

"I can't *believe* you!"

Did her mother regret her choices in life? It had been on Lily's mind for a while. Maybe there'd be a day in the future when she could sit down with her mother. Maybe sometime after she graduated high school and wasn't living at home anymore. A time when she could look at her mother and ask her – not as her daughter, but as a fellow adult – about those choices. Why did her mother marry her dad? Did she want to have kids? Did she want to have only one?

Audrey was six years younger than Lily, after all. Would that explain why she harped so intensely on Lily, but essentially left Audrey alone?

Did she want to be a dancer? There were no pictures of her as a dancer, no evidence of a background in dance. What happened to that dream? What happened to her as a kid?

These were all questions she hoped to ask someday. Not today (*certainly* not today), and not tomorrow. Not for a while, most likely. And she might ask those questions and not get a genuine response. But it was something to think about, something to consider, especially as the yelling match wore on downstairs, as she listened to her dad's voice, a surprisingly deep and strong force, as the heat of the argument temporarily melted the icy feeling of the house.

CHAPTER THIRTY-SEVEN

"You're back!"

The gym that Saturday morning was alive with energy. There was jiu jitsu off to the side, and people working out upstairs. And there was a good number of people milling about, preparing for Rachel's class.

"Geez, we missed you!" Rachel outright beamed at Lily. "Where were you?"

Lily sighed.

"It's a long story."

"Well, I'm glad you can start coming on weekends now," said Rachel. "Leon's class is right after mine, if you feel like doubling up."

"That works for me."

While Leon hadn't yet shown up that morning, Lily had a chance to see him on Friday night. He had walked in that afternoon, coming in with his big sport bag and usual grin on his face.

"Well, hey there," he had said when he had spotted Lily. "Long time no see."

"Yeah, long time no see," Lily had parroted back.

"I'm really glad you're back," he had replied. After a pause, he added: "I really am sorry about that night—"

"No. I'm the only one who needs to be sorry," Lily interrupted. "I shouldn't have done that. It was inappropriate of me."

"Hey, it's water under the bridge, then, okay?"

"Yeah, water on the bridge."

Water under the bridge. Lily found herself repeating those words to herself that Saturday morning, as Rachel brought up Leon's name. She felt a peculiar and yet familiar ache, a confusing sense of heaviness, a reminder that it might be a while before she'd sort out everything that was going on in her mind.

"And – correct me if I'm wrong – but word on the street is that you knocked out a bully," Rachel continued.

Lily blushed.

"She didn't get knocked out. Just... fell. She was trying to push me."

"Wow... I mean, for the record, I can't advocate that," said Rachel. "If you were one of my clients, I'd be letting you have it right now. But, as your friend, I say right on. That'll teach 'em to mess with you."

Lily smiled.

"Thanks."

"I'm seriously glad you started coming to the Saturday classes now," said Rachel. "I mean, I'm assuming you're coming on Saturdays, right?"

"Right," said Lily. "That's my plan."

"Good," Rachel responded. "Because I need your help with some of these guys. They plant their feet during all the spinning kicks, and my knees hurt just looking at it. If I could use you to show how to actually pivot on the balls of your feet, that would be incredible."

"Sure thing," said Lily.

"Like, for real. These guys? They just don't get it. It's like their feet are cemented to the ground."

Lily laughed and shook her head. The people around her were gathered in small groups, talking and laughing, doing stretches.

"Maybe there should be, like, a dance class here," said Lily. "Teach them the basics, like how to actually spin without twisting your ankle."

"There should be," Rachel agreed. "And I think you should teach it."

Lily cocked an eyebrow.

"Not, like, hardcore classical ballet or anything," Rachel explained. "But I think you'd be really good, teaching dance to fighters. I mean, you're already both, so you'd know what would work and what wouldn't."

Lily paused for a moment. She was still technically at the gym for free. And she did feel guilty for all the charity Jimmy had given her.

Perhaps this could be a way to settle her debts, even though Jimmy insisted there weren't any.

She could do it. She could teach. And it would be lighthearted and fun, just like her first ballet classes used to be, back when she was a kid. It would be about laughter and movement, not about perfection.

She could do it. She definitely could do it.

"Maybe," she said, and then smiled wickedly.

Lily fell into the rhythm of Rachel's Saturday morning class, playing the role of model as she showed the rest of the group how to pivot in a turn. Time slipped away from her as she continued her practice, as she became hypnotized by the sound of the kicks against the heavy bags, the feel of the air whipping around her, the intoxicating energy of the group.

The boxing people were coming in as the kickboxing class wound down.

"Missed my class again, I see!" Rachel called out to Leon.

"Hey – some of us like to sleep in a little on Saturdays," Leon cheekily replied, setting his bag down.

"Ah, you just can't handle the fact that I'm a better kickboxer than you."

"Let's answer that question in the ring, shall we?" Leon raised an eyebrow.

"Deal – after class, you and me. Let's do it."

Leon laughed and unzipped his bag.

"And how are you doing, Lily?"

"I'm doing pretty good," Lily answered, her heart heavy, her breathing shallow.

Inhale. Exhale.

"Well, always good to hear," said Leon. "Hopefully Rachel didn't tire you out too much. My class can be pretty killer."

"Oh, you big softie. No it isn't," Rachel countered.

Off by the garage door archways stood a tall guy with red hair. Lily's breath caught. Freddy looked over to where Lily was, locking eyes with her. She set her jaw and gave a slow, knowing nod. She watched Freddy do the same, before walking over to a group of people by the mats.

Lily walked to the boxing ring and sat on its edge. Between the kickboxing people lingering around and the boxing people coming in and the jiu jitsu guys off to the side, the gym was electric and loud and busy. She didn't know the majority of the people, but she was looking forward to getting to know them. She was looking forward to coming to the gym after school, and on weekends. She played with the idea of coming there straight after school and doing her homework at the gym, perhaps squirreling herself away in Jimmy's office.

And she was looking forward to getting her dad in for a class or two. She really was. She was looking forward to teaching the fighters how to dance (if Jimmy would be okay with such an idea – and she got the feeling that he would. Wasn't he the one to first make the suggestion, anyway?). She was looking forward to perfecting her jab and learning how to spar and getting just a little bit stronger, every single day.

Jimmy was right about this place. It wasn't just a gym. This was family, only better. This was a family not by chance, but by choice. This was a bond that stretched beyond similar DNA. This was a home for those who didn't feel like they had one.

"Alright – those who are here for boxing, I wanna see you in the ring!" Leon's voice shouted.

"That's us," Rachel said to Lily, giving her a slight nudge with her elbow. "By the way, the offer still stands about sparring together someday."

"I'm down for that."

"Excellent," Rachel said. "We could even go after I'm done sparring with Leon. And, when you totally kick my butt, I can say it's because I was tired."

Rachel gave a wink before getting into the ring. Lily stood up and placed one hand on the ropes. Off in the corner, Lily could see Jimmy coming up from the basement, carrying a large, overstuffed cardboard box.

"Do you need help with that?" Lily called out to Jimmy.

"Ah, I'm good, kiddo! I'm good!" he hollered back. "You enjoy ya class! Show those amateurs how it's done!"

Lily laughed and went up into the ring. She stood next to Rachel, helping to create a circle of people. A circle that felt right, that felt like Lily belonged in. This was where she was supposed to be. She could feel it in her bones. She couldn't think of any other place she'd rather be at that moment.

Yes. This was home. And it was good to be back.

"Alright, guys! Time for warm-ups!"

The Ballerina's Guide to Boxing

National Suicide Prevention Hotline:
1-800-273-8255

National Eating Disorder Hotline:
1-847-831-3438

SAMHSA (Substance Abuse Mental Health Services Administration) Hotline:
1-800-662-HELP (4357)

ABOUT THE AUTHOR

Abby Rosmarin is the author of several books, including *The Secret to a Happy Marriage, Venom, In The Event the Flower Girl Explodes,* and others. Her work has been featured on *The Huffington Post, Bustle, Storgy Magazine, Chaleur Magazine, the Bangalore Review, the Esthetic Apostle, Literally Darling, xoJane,* and others. A former model and current yoga teacher, Abby currently resides in New Hampshire.